the **retail**

the **retail**

a novel

JOSHUA
DANKER-DAKE

Cover by Mary Anna Simon

This is a work of fiction. All names, characters, places, and
events are the work of the author's imagination.
Any resemblance to real persons, places, or events is
coincidental.

www.joshuadankerdake.com

To Carrie F.

Day 1 – Tuesday, November 11

And so it came to pass that in the fall of 2003, I, Penn Reynard, entered the employ of the House Station, America's third-largest home improvement chain. They hired me on the spot.

"The store doesn't open until January?" I asked.

"But you can start this week if you take the drug test today," they said. "Can you do that?"

"Sure," I said. Pee in a cup? I had nothing else going on.

Day 65 – Wednesday, January 14

"You have a lot of women in this store who look like men," said the guy with the paint can.

"Okay," I replied, not wishing to pursue this line of conversation.

"I need to return this paint. It's white. It's supposed to be eggshell. Look at the sample card."

"Maybe they forgot to put the color in this can," I said. "Did you get more than one can? Sometimes they miss one when they add the tint."

"'Miss one'? I just got this off the shelf."

"You didn't have anyone put color in it?"

"It says eggshell on the label. See?"

"Sir, eggshell is the *sheen*."

1

"It is?" The man forced laughter. "How about that?"

"If you want to take that back to the Paint Desk, they can tint it any color you want," I said.

When the man had gone, Angry Pete wandered over from the Service Desk, tugging at the straps of his apron. "Idiots," he said. "Blood and fire and idiots."

Pete was shrill-voiced and thin, with bad skin, a long nose, and unkempt hair. He was a couple years younger than I was—twenty, maybe—and he was one of those people that took a lot of energy to talk to. His mom worked at the House Station across town.

"'Better Living Through Home Improvement,'" I said, quoting the House Station's Big Brotherish slogan, which was emblazoned across his and every other canary-yellow apron in the store. "'The House Station—Your Place For Excellent Customer Service.'" That was the new secondary slogan.

Pete shrugged. "Better living for *customers*. Nobody ever said anything about better living for us. Life sucks, you paint your house, and then you die."

"That's the spirit."

"Life's a bitch and then you marry one, and then you buy a new washer and dryer. Tell me this, Penn: is it wrong to take pleasure in the self-inflicted misfortunes of stupid people?"

"It's called schadenfreude," I said.

"Well, it's what gets me out of bed in the morning." Angry Pete glanced around. "Man, it's completely dead in here."

As Pete strolled back to the Service Desk, I looked out from my yellow Returns counter past several yellow signs and down a yellow-shelved aisle. I didn't see a single customer. Not what you'd expect from the nation's third-largest big-box home improvement chain, but it was something we'd become familiar with in the two weeks the store had been open for business.

"It's still better than before we opened," I called over to Pete.

2

"No way. How is this better than training? I sat on the computer for half the day."

"I didn't get all that Service Desk training, remember? I put cardboard in the baler for eight hours. Did you ever get a cardboard cut?"

"How long are you going to cry about that?" Pete sat in the Service Desk's rolling chair and put his headset back on. "Just because Returns is the bastard child of the Service Desk and you didn't have anything to do?"

This was, in fact, true. Pete and I were in different departments, although we spent most days twelve feet apart. Returns was under Cashiers, and we were that department's orphan stepchild.

"Excuse me?"

I turned. A girl about my age with short brown hair was leaning over the four-foot-high chain-link fence that enclosed three sides of my fifteen-by-fifteen Returns area. She was wearing a House Station apron, but I'd never seen her before.

She was subtly attractive: I thought she was cute, but it took me a minute, like when you cut yourself, look down at the blood beginning to stream from your finger, and say, "Oh."

CHLOE was written on her apron in large, neat handwriting.

"Hm?" I said.

"Hi, I'm Chloe. Do I have any Returns?"

"I'm Penn," I said, coming over to the fence.

"Nice to meet you," she said. "So . . . do I have any Returns?"

"Heh. Sorry. What department?"

"Paint."

I looked in the appropriate bin. "One roller. Amazingly still in the plastic."

I fumbled the roller as I handed it across the fence, and we both lunged for it. Our foreheads smacked together loudly,

3

and I staggered back, clutching my head. I felt like I'd been hit with a brick.

"Oh my God!" Chloe exclaimed. "Are you okay?"

I peered between my fingers. She didn't look hurt in the slightest. I tried my best to shake it off, but I could see stars.

"I'm okay," I said. "Are you okay?"

"Oh, good. Yeah, I'm fine. I'm so sorry!"

"Don't mention it." The paint roller had fallen on my side of the fence, and I retrieved it for her.

"Thanks," Chloe said, and went back to Paint.

But she lingered in my mind along with the headache she'd given me. I went across to the Service Desk, where Pete was doing some work on the computer, or pretending to. "Should be some Tylenol in the first aid kit," he said.

"Who's that girl?" I said.

"The one who just knocked your weak ass out? Chloe something, I think. What did her apron say?"

"I *know* her name's Chloe," I said. "Get the phone list and look it up."

He did. "Chloe van Caneghem. She started Monday."

"Hm."

Pete looked up at me. "She's fat, Penn."

"No, she's not. What are you talking about?"

"She's got a cute face, but she's got kind of fat arms. And a fat ass."

"It's not fat!"

"It's too big for the rest of her. She could lose a good fifteen pounds."

"That's your opinion only. They're childbearing hips. I bet Kord thinks she looks good, too."

"You can't be after the same women as your boss. It doesn't bother you that you share the same taste as lesbians?"

I shrugged.

Pete persisted. "Plus, she comes up a little short in the chest department. Speaking kindly."

I said nothing. Facts were facts.

4

Pete glanced at his watch. "It's quarter to five. Shouldn't you be going home?"

"Yeah. I see Landfill coming."

His lip curled. "That guy again? Man, I thought he was part-time."

"He is. But nobody else wanted all those closing shifts. That's the only reason they made him a head cashier."

Pete snorted. "He goes to that televangelist school, right?"

"Take it easy," I said. "I went there too."

He shrugged. "Lot of good it did you."

Bradford Landfield was a pudgy twenty-something they'd hired the week before we opened. He thought he was friends with everyone and had no idea that nobody liked him.

Landfill arrived with my usual replacement, Johnisha. "Pete and Penn, the Returns men!" he said.

I was already counting down my till.

"Land*fill*," said Angry Pete in greeting.

"I told you not to call me that," Landfill said. "I'll be back for you at nine." He had already turned back toward the other end of the store, where the sales registers were.

"Come back!" I called. "Unlock my tube!"

"Man!" Landfill said, like it was my fault he'd forgotten.

I put the contents of my register into a small yellow bag, which I stuffed into a cylindrical canister, which I placed in the pneumatic tube next to my counter, which conveyed it to the vault at the press of a button. I removed my apron, stuck it under the counter, grabbed my coat, logged into the service menu on my register, and clocked out.

Landfill protested. "Hey, you're supposed to clock out in the break room!"

The break room was at the other end of the store.

"Next time," I said. I walked briskly toward the door and out into the cold. I was off the clock, and I wasn't about to have a conversation with him for free.

* * * * *

5

Leetown is nestled obscurely in southeast Missouri. Ostensibly, it's a college town, although the college really isn't that big, and neither is Leetown; "Wal-Mart town" might be a better term.

Kerry Lee University, founded by and named for the popular televangelist, has been here since the late sixties. It's the reason I came to Leetown—to study English. It's also the reason I hadn't left.

KLU emphasizes the development of each student's mind, spirit, and body. "Mind" means the usual academics, "spirit" means the chapel services they made us go to, and "body" means the one-credit gym class everybody had to take each semester.

Everything was well and good until the spring semester of my senior year. I took badminton because it was easy and because the name of the teacher caught my eye. Colonel Goodenough was never in the military; that was his real name. But he turned out to be more anal about attendance than any teacher I'd ever had, gym or otherwise.

It being my last semester, I focused on my real classes and generally took it easy otherwise. Two months before graduation, I calculated I had five absences in badminton. If you got six, you automatically failed. Then Goodenough, who usually spent our classes playing basketball with other teachers, pulled me aside and told me I already had six.

"Reynard, you'll have to take it again next semester," he said.

"But this is my last semester. I'm graduating."

"Oh, don't do this to me!" he lamented, clearly in the throes of a moral crisis.

"Can I make it up?" I asked.

"Well . . . don't miss another class. And do the Fun Run. Then we'll see."

I didn't miss another class. And I did the Fun Run.

Every semester, we had to run a timed three miles. The Fun Run (nothing remotely fun about it) was an opportunity to pay twenty dollars in return for a cheap T-shirt and a letter-grade extra credit boost. I saw it as contradictory to the principles the university stood for; the PE Department, which was struggling to justify its existence financially, saw it as a chance to make a few bucks.

I got an average time. It was the best I could do—I'd gained a few pounds in college and I hadn't played sports since high school, and I was never that fast to begin with. I'm six feet tall, but I have short legs or something.

Two days before commencement, they were supposed to tell you if there was any problem and you weren't eligible to graduate. Nobody said a word to me. I went to graduation, walked across the platform, then went home to Saint Louis.

A month and a half later, I got my report card in the mail. I had an F in badminton, and I wasn't going to get my diploma until I made up the class.

I called St. Louis Community College. They had PE classes, but the monkeys that ran KLU wouldn't tell me if the credit would transfer until after I'd enrolled there. By that point, it was too late: I'd missed summer school admissions deadlines; I'd have to make up the class in the fall semester. My diploma wouldn't be awarded until the following May, a year late.

I was furious beyond words about every aspect of the situation. None of this had a thing to do with an English degree.

But in the end, what choice did I have? I gritted my teeth, came back to Leetown, got an apartment near the school, and enrolled in a fall swimming class.

The class only took up two hours a week, and I had to get a job. I did some part-time stuff for a while until I found Leetown's brand-new House Station (Leetown already had one House Station and a Home Depot; Lowe's was apparently unaware of the town's existence).

Conveniently, my apartment was only a five-minute drive from the new store, which allowed me to go home, eat a sandwich, and take a nap on my lunch hour. That was typically the highlight of my workday.

Day 67 – Friday, January 16

My roommate Jeff was cleaning our second-floor apartment. That he was home this early *and* cleaning could only mean one thing.

"Milla's coming over," he said over the roar of our terminally ill garbage disposal. "Sorry I didn't tell you earlier."

I nodded, then went into my room and closed the door.

Adele, my fat, fluffy calico, was asleep in my ancient sling chair, which was precisely where she'd been on my lunch break. She opened one eye and grunted.

"Watch yourself," I said. "Promilla's coming."

Jeff and Promilla had a lot in common: they'd met at KLU and they'd both been home schooled. That was practically their whole lives, right there.

Jeff, unequivocally the most good-natured and gullible person I'd ever met, was attending KLU part-time, with two years to go on his degree. He ran the KLU Athletics Center, which meant he opened the building at five in the morning and came home at three in the afternoon. Promilla had already graduated and, like so many of us, worked at a job that had nothing to do with her degree.

I changed out of my work clothes, which smelled of dust, and ventured into the kitchen. Jeff was loading the dishwasher in a most inefficient manner. I said nothing; at least he was trying for once.

"How's it going, bro?" he asked.

"Good. What's happening?"

"Not a lot. Making dinner for Milla."

I dug through the refrigerator. "So don't make a mess, is that what you're telling me? When's she coming?"

"Six. We're going to watch a movie. You're welcome to join us."

"I'll pass, but thanks," I said. "I need to work on my book."

"That romance novel?"

"It's not a romance. It's a love story."

"What's the difference?"

I found some leftover chicken and put it in the microwave. "Everything. Romance novels are a dime a dozen. A love story is *deeper*. It's not just about bodices ripping and bosoms quivering. There's a *story*."

"What's it about?"

"It's about a police detective who loses his wife in tragic circumstances. Several years later, while he investigates a case, he runs into an old flame, a singer. *But,* she has a secret that could destroy their relationship," I added dramatically.

"I didn't think men usually wrote that kind of thing."

"You shouldn't be afraid to get in touch with your sensitive side." I got my chicken and sat on the couch.

Jeff leaned against the counter. "I'm sorry, bro, but would you mind keeping Adele in your room tonight?"

"Jeff, we've been over this."

"You know how Milla gets!"

"She's not allergic. I don't buy that for one minute. She hates my cat."

"I like your cat," he said, like that had anything to do with it. "She's the best cat I've ever seen. She never bites or claws or anything."

I sighed. "Fine."

"I'm sorry!"

I shook my head. "Forget it."

I finished eating, left my plate on the counter, and went into my room. I shut the door and dislodged Adele from my chair. I sat there for ten minutes trying to think about the next chapter in my book, but I couldn't focus. I was still irritated about Promilla.

Then she knocked on the door. My window was near the front door, and I could hear everything said or done out there through the uninsulated glass.

Jeff opened the door and Promilla said, "Hey, sweetie."

"Penn's here," Jeff said quickly.

I returned to my book with more diligence. Over the next hour and a half, I wrote two pages, which for me was quite productive. I was in the zone. I hadn't thought of a title yet, though.

I was interrupted by a faint crying sound. It sounded like a cat. Adele was stretched out on her back across the bed with her ears perked up.

The cry came again — from outside.

I went out into the living room. Jeff had his arm around Promilla. They were cozy, but not so cozy that I was embarrassed for them. That had only happened once.

"Penn," said Promilla icily, "could you shut your door? Your cat might get out. We wouldn't want that."

Promilla had mousy brown hair and wasn't the slightest bit attractive. Or maybe it was just that I didn't like her.

Disregarding her instructions, I stepped outside.

"It's cold!" Promilla shouted after me. "Close that door!"

A tiny gray kitten shivered on the steps, a cross-eyed Siamese. I reached out slowly and let it smell my hand. Then I picked it up. I would later come to regret these acts.

"Where are you supposed to be?" I asked. It rubbed its face against my chest.

Jeff, who had undoubtedly gotten up at Promilla's order to shut all the doors, was standing at the top of the stairs. "What is it?"

I turned and held up the kitten.

Jeff's soft heart melted. "Aw! It's so cute!"

Now Promilla was behind him. "Ugh! Get rid of that thing! Dirty wild cat!"

"He's clean," I said. "No fleas, no ear mites. See?"

She crossed her arms. "And how do you know?"

"I worked in a pet store all through high school," I said. "Besides, he's a Siamese. They don't usually wander around homeless." I started back up the steps.

"Where are you going with that?" Promilla shrieked.

"It's freezing. I can't leave him out here."

"You're not going to keep it?"

I shrugged. "I might. He's friendly enough." I looked at Jeff, challenging him to object.

"Jeff!" Promilla exclaimed. "That thing is going to shed all over! Just like the other one!"

Actually, the one who shed the most was Promilla herself. We always found long brown hairs on the couch and in Jeff's bathroom. I did *not* point this out.

I held up the cat in front of Jeff. "Look at him, he's freaking adorable. There's no extra burden on you. I'll take care of him. Tonight I'll just lock him up in my bathroom until I can take him to get shots."

"Augh! Jeff! I'm not coming over here anymore!" Promilla cried.

Better and better.

I took him into my bathroom before Adele could get wind of him. I gave him a dish of food, which he obliterated, and then I put him in a warm bath, which, to my surprise, he enjoyed.

I got him water, litter, and another bowl of food, then put a rolled towel at the base of the door, quarantining him. Jeff and Promilla were sitting in the living room when I came out, but the movie was still paused.

"Are you going to just keep whatever walks past?" Promilla asked. "He probably belongs to somebody."

"I'll put a sign up by the office. But I don't think anybody's coming for him. There are a lot of apartments around here. He was starving; wherever he's from, he's been gone awhile."

"But you're going to pay for shots for him anyway?"

I sighed. "What do you want me to do? Throw him back outside to freeze? Now then, he needs a name."

"What about Max?" said Jeff, and Promilla thumped him on the arm.

I shook my head. "He needs a *manly* name. Like . . . Drimacus. The Eviscerator."

There came a persistent rattle. Adele was running her paw up and down the Venetian blinds of the balcony door. I walked over and looked down at her, and she grunted.

"It's cold," I said.

She didn't care, and when I opened the door she ran outside like the house was on fire. Two minutes later, she was ready to come in. After readmitting her, I went to work on my book while Drimacus the Eviscerator tore at the bathroom door like a rabid badger.

Day 68 – Saturday, January 17

I was off on Saturday. Little did I realize it would be the last Saturday I'd have off for three months. Before the store opened, none of us grunts had worked on the weekends.

I left a note at the office, then took the cats to the vet for shots. With the exception of daily trips to the balcony, Adele was an indoor cat, and I couldn't remember the last time she'd been to the vet.

I stuffed Adele ingloriously into the pet carrier. Then I found a cardboard box, punched some holes in it, and went to get Drimacus.

When I opened the door, I didn't see him. He'd spilled his water dish, and as I bent down to pick it up, he sprang from the bathtub onto my head. I shook him off and he hit the side of the tub with a loud clunk. Unfazed, he dashed out of the room.

I finally corralled him and got them both in the car. Adele cried incessantly on the way there, pausing only long enough to throw up in the pet carrier.

When I got home, I was looking forward to a relaxing day. I was scheduled to work at ten on Sunday, which was early enough that I couldn't reasonably make it to church but late enough for me to enjoy a good, late Saturday evening—to loaf around the house and maybe watch a movie.

There was a message on the answering machine.

"Penn, it's Kord." Kord was the Front End Supervisor at the House Station: she was in charge of all the cashiers and registers and was my most immediate and significant boss. "You're scheduled for ten tomorrow, but don't forget about the store meeting at six. Remember to clock in when you get there. Bye."

I sighed. Drimacus took my sock and dragged it away. I never found it.

Day 69 – Sunday, January 18

I cast myself out of bed at six, threw on some sweats, and headed over to the House Station. It was pitch black, I was half-asleep, and I forgot my coat. The heat in my car didn't kick in until I pulled into the parking lot.

I staggered inside, rubbing my frigid arms, clocked in on the Returns register, and headed toward the mass of people congregating in Lumber. Folding chairs had been set up in rows down one of the wide aisles; they were all filled. I'd never seen half of these people before. Not very many of them were fully awake either; there wasn't that constant background of chit-chat you usually get from idle crowds.

There were donuts and orange drink on a table at the rear. Bypassing these, I went to a bay of ten-foot two-by-twelves and lay down across them. There was another rack just above me, so there wasn't room to sit up, but I squeezed in nicely.

Finally, Rex, the store manager, got up in front of us. Fifty, gray-haired, chubby, and flannel-shirted, Rex had been working for House Station only a couple months longer than I had. They'd brought him in from an independent plumbing company to run our store.

Rex seemed all right, although he spent a lot more time with the female employees than with the male ones. I don't think there was anything along the lines of sexual harassment going on . . . at least, nothing to the degree where there could be a lawsuit.

Rex thought he was a pretty clever guy. He dropped corny catchphrases and maxims every chance he got, gave us unwanted and inapplicable advice, and was convinced he had the correct approach to life and that everybody else was best served by shutting up and doing as he said. It was the ideal store manager personality, I guess.

Rex had most recently been quoted as saying he'd leave his wife for Stevie Nicks. This constituted one of his better attempts at humor.

The three assistant store managers, Madeleine, Rovergial, and Osric, were lined up next to him. We were all still feeling them out. There was a lot of chatter around the store about Osric because nobody knew what race he was or had worked up the nerve to ask him. He had black hair and olive skin, and he could have been anything mixed with anything, with some type of anything thrown in. Angry Pete guessed he was Filipino, but had no evidence.

Rex tapped the microphone. He was the only one wearing his yellow apron. "Hey, guys. Let me start by saying you've done a great job getting this store ready to open. But this is where the real job begins! I want every single associate in this store to focus on providing Excellent Customer Service!" You could hear the capital letters. "That's the most important thing, and I don't care if you're a cashier or if you're back in

14

Millwork, it goes for everybody! Remember, you chose this as a career!"

I would have laughed out loud if my brain hadn't been so sluggish. I'd get my diploma in a few months, and then I'd go to grad school somewhere far from here. I'd already finished making up my gym credit; I could leave *now* if I wanted.

My head jerked up, and I realized I'd dozed off. Rex was still talking.

". . . want you guys to focus on this month. Keep this thought in mind at all times: if you were accused of being a House Station associate, would there be enough evidence to convict you? Now, if you have any problems, I want you to feel free to come to me. Remember: it's my job to help you make your dreams come true."

When he was done, the assistant managers each talked. Then all the department heads talked. I dozed through most of it. At quarter to eight, the meeting ended and people dispersed to either leave or get ready for the store to open. I went home and went back to bed.

Even though I'd already been up, I followed my usual work routine for my ten o'clock shift.

I set my alarm clock to go off fifty-one minutes before my shift started. When it beeped, I hit the snooze button at four-minute intervals until my second alarm clock went off seven minutes before my shift.

It was 9:53.

"Rngh," I said.

I got up and headed to the bathroom, brushed my teeth, and threw on some clothes. My work wardrobe consisted of one pair of old jeans and five short-sleeve collared shirts on a rotation.

I sprayed on some "smells just like . . ." cologne from the dollar store to mask the Station's ubiquitous dust smell, put on my shoes and coat, and left without eating.

I was in the car by 9:58. It was a five-minute drive, but for a ten o'clock shift, the computer didn't count me as late until 10:07:30. I had it timed perfectly.

I clocked in on my register, right by the entrance. It was 10:06:37. I grabbed my water bottle from under the counter and went back to the break room, wondering if I was missing anything good at church.

I filled my bottle, went to the cashier counter behind Register Eight, and signed for my money, a five-hundred-dollar Returns till.

Paige was the head cashier. She was very short and very solid — not fat so much as *dense*.

"I'm not in the mood to be here," she told me as she handed me my money. "I'm so hungover. Ready to go? Where's your apron?"

"At my register."

We were required to have escorts whenever we carried cash around the store. She hooked her arm in mine — this she did with most of the cashiers in our age bracket.

"Oh, my God, I was out all night drinking, and then that damned meeting," she said.

I was still feeling sleepy, couldn't think of a good response, and didn't feel entirely comfortable in her grip.

Angry Pete was off; Atwater was working instead. At least when Pete was there, I had somebody to talk to. The one time I'd tried to chat with Atwater, I'd caught him working on his cross-dressing stand-up routine. He was straight, though, if the way he hit on unaccompanied middle-aged lady customers was any indication.

"Woo, woo!" said Atwater as we walked up together. He stroked his bushy mustache vigorously, dislodging his headset.

Whoever worked the Service Desk had to answer the phone. You didn't have a choice: the call went directly to your headset, where it connected automatically and didn't even give you the option to let it ring. So Atwater was leashed to

16

the desk, which was a good thing since he was prone to wandering off, usually to the snack machine.

We ignored his remark. Paige went back down to the sales end and I counted my money into my register, wondering if that cute girl in Paint was working.

I don't think most people knew our store was there, never mind open. House Station #1492 was on State Street, which was a small, two-lane deal that had more apartments than businesses. You couldn't see the store from the nearest intersection, so the House Station had put up a huge yellow sign on the corner. So far, it wasn't working.

The whole store was dead. Boredom was a problem even when the store was busy, though, because the job used just enough of your brain that you couldn't zone out or think about other things, but not anywhere near enough to keep you interested in what was going on.

A little after one, a lady came in to return a paintbrush. Dressed in her Sunday finest, it was clear she'd come straight from church.

The House Station's return policy is straightforward. With your receipt, you get your money back in the same form you paid with: cash for cash, credit for credit, eye for eye, tooth for tooth. Without a receipt, we can only give store credit, and we have to see an ID.

"Hi, I need to return this paintbrush," the lady said, disposition friendly.

It was still in the shrink wrap. "Anything wrong with it?" I have to ask that, even if the answer is obvious.

"No, we never used it. I got it at the other House Station across town before you were open."

"Do you have your receipt?" That's the other question I have to ask. It makes people nervous.

"No. It was only three dollars."

"Do you have an ID?"

Her eyebrows narrowed. "Why?"

17

"I have to have an ID for every return that doesn't have a receipt."

"You *have* to have it?"

"Yes, ma'am. Otherwise, the computer won't let me run the transaction."

"Fine." She slapped her driver's license onto the counter, still moderately cheerful.

I processed the return. "Okay. You're going to have three dollars and fifty-seven cents in store credit. I just need —"

"I don't want store credit. I want cash."

"How did you pay for it?"

"Yes, I paid for it," said the woman.

"No, *how* did you pay for it?"

"I paid cash, so I want cash."

"Ma'am," I said, sweetness and light on my face, "without a receipt, all I can give you is store credit." I indicated the ten-foot-high sign above my head that thoroughly explained the House Station's return policy. They could have taken it down and burned it for all the good it ever did.

"You can't just give me three dollars?"

"The computer won't let me."

Now she was irritated. "Just open up your drawer and give me three dollars!"

"I can't do that."

It was true. The computer didn't give me the option to do a cash refund. In the middle of the transaction, there wasn't a blessed thing I could do to make my cash drawer open.

She smiled at me. "I like the House Station. I like shopping here. You know, I probably spend about ten thousand dollars a year here. But I *need* that three dollars in *cash*, and if I don't get it, I'm never shopping here again!"

I took a deep breath. Was there somebody in the parking lot waiting to break her legs, a loan shark whose three dollars were long overdue?

I reached for my phone. "Ma'am, I'm sorry, but there's nothing I can do. I can call a manager if you want."

This was how it worked. I would call the head cashier — Paige, in this case — who would come up and say all the things I'd already said. If the customer complained further, Paige would call Kord, or one of the assistant managers. She could work her way up to Rex if she was so inclined. All he could do was put them in touch with the corporate headquarters in Austin. This lady could call the President of the United States; the three dollars were not coming out of the drawer.

"Fine, call," she snapped.

I was already dialing. There was nothing else I could say to this woman.

When I hung up the phone, the woman exclaimed, "I hope this store fails! I hope you go out of business!" Then she turned and stalked out the door.

A minute later, Paige arrived. "What's up?"

I shook my head. "She left because I couldn't work the magic. I need you to void this transaction." Canceled in-process transactions had to be cleared by a head cashier or manager.

"Sure. Here you go." Paige held up the paintbrush the woman had left behind.

Day 71 – Tuesday, January 20

Kord, who was probably my favorite person in the store, was working the afternoon head cashier shift. She came down to see me with huge yellow sheets of paper and the fattest marker ever constructed.

Kord was tall and lanky with short, gelled hair, and she always wore baggy men's jeans. Not everybody figured out she was a lesbian at first glance; some people thought she was a man.

"I need you to make some signs for me for the stuff in the entryway," she said.

19

"Like those ladders?" There was a rack of them on the opposite side of my fence. "Do you want me to be clever?"

"Not *too* clever."

"Something corny, then. 'Move up in the world with a ladder from the House Station.'"

Kord laughed. She laughed a lot, at least around me. "Perfect."

So I made that sign for the ladders and another one that said, "A day without light bulbs is like a day without sunshine." Not my best work, but it got the job done.

"What are you making?" Atwater called.

"Signs," I answered, so intent on writing legibly that I wasn't really listening.

He walked over to have a look. The headset cord grew taut as he approached, and then the phone clattered loudly on the concrete floor. "It always— Thank you for calling the House Station." He returned to his desk to take the call.

A few minutes later, a customer appeared. "Can I check out here?" he asked Atwater, as though this were some secret privilege. "It would save me a walk." They always said that.

Angry Pete and I believed in getting the customers into good habits, so we usually told them to go check out at the sales registers. Although we each had our own registers, the Service/Returns area was not designed for two-way traffic.

But Atwater, with a till of his own and no current phone calls, pointed his long, bony finger at me and said, "Sir, Penn will be happy to check you out right over there."

"Thanks, Atwater," I said.

Day 73 – Thursday, January 22

When customers brought back merchandise that was broken or too used or in any way unresalable, we marked it with a Return to Vendor (RTV) tag. Anybody who worked

Returns was supposed to take the RTVs back to Receiving at the end of the shift.

At seven in the evening, with an hour to go, I was bored and it was slow. I loaded my few RTVs into a cart. "Atwater, I'm taking these back."

His mouth was full of M&M's, so he just nodded and waved.

The route from Returns to Receiving took you right past the Paint Desk. As I passed, I saw Chloe was working. Business being what it was, we typically only had one person in Paint at a time.

I felt a pang of disappointment when I saw she had a customer. I took my time putting the RTVs away.

I pushed the cart slowly back through the deserted store. The customer had gone. Chloe was cleaning up the Paint Desk. There was a splash of dark green paint on her yellow apron.

I stopped in front of the desk. "How's it going?"

"Oh, hi . . . Penn," she said, glancing at my apron. "It's going fine. Hey, sorry again about the other day."

"Don't worry about it," I said. "No permanent damage. So . . . you like it back here?"

She nodded. "I do. I like paint."

"You got some on you."

Chloe frowned at the stain. "Yeah, a customer grabbed the can before I'd gotten the lid back on it."

"You can get another one. The aprons are in a cabinet in the break room. Throw this one away. It's no big deal."

"I will, thanks."

"Let me ask you this," I said. "Why do painters wear white? It's the worst possible color when you're spilling things that stain."

Chloe grinned, and that was it. It was over. I was smitten.

"The way I see it," she said, "each painter is his own canvas."

The conversation had taken a serious turn for the corny, but we were talking, and that was what mattered.

"So," I said, "are you from here?"

"Yeah. My parents live about forty-five minutes away. I've got an apartment in town. Bethany's my roommate. She works the night crew."

I hadn't met her. "So what are you doing at the Station?"

She shrugged. "I'm taking some classes at LCC and working here about twenty hours a week." LCC was Leetown Community College.

"What are you studying?"

"Education. I'll finish next fall."

"What do you want to do with that?"

"Teach middle-school kids."

"Any particular subject?"

She tucked a stray lock of hair behind her ear. "I like English."

I grinned in spite of myself. "I got my degree in English."

Chloe was looking at me with more interest now. "Really? What are you doing with it?"

"Working Returns," I said. "Seriously, I want to be a writer. Well, I *am* a writer. I want to be a *published* writer."

She laughed at that, and it made me glad. "That's great. Do you have anything I can read?"

"Well, I'm working on a novel right now, but it's not anywhere near finished. I could show you a couple of short stories, if you want."

"Yeah, that'd be great!"

Score.

"I'll print one out for you," I said. "The one I won third-place in a national competition for."

"All right," she said, and she was smiling at me.

"Well, I need to get back up front," I said reluctantly. Atwater would sooner page me than check a customer out himself.

"Sure," Chloe said. "Stop by any time."

22

Day 74 – Friday, January 23

"Fielding Vargas is in the store," Paige told me over the phone. "Make sure your Sensormatic logs are caught up. Check receipts. All that."

Fielding Vargas was in charge of House Station Loss Prevention regionally. He went to and fro among all the stores in the district, doing whatever it was he did besides make cashiers anxious. Sometimes he would be in our store all day and we'd never see him. All that mattered to the Front End was that we did what we were supposed to do as far as Loss Prevention was concerned so that nobody got yelled at and nobody got fired.

Colonel Goodenough came into the store with a return. The store was a mile from the school, and I'd seen professors in here before, but one never expects things like this to happen. Instantly, all manner of anger I thought I had dealt with boiled up inside me.

Let me clarify. I wasn't mad that he failed me. I'm not complaining because he didn't look the other way and do me a favor. I'm on the up and up as far as all of that goes.

I was mad because he strung me along, because I didn't find out that I'd failed until halfway through the summer, when it was too late to do anything about it. Why couldn't Goodenough have said, "No, you can't make it up, you fail," when it first came up? It would have saved me half a semester of going to that class. More importantly, I would have been able to make up the class in the summer and get my diploma with 2003 on it instead of 2004. It felt like being held back a grade.

Goodenough was a fit man in his forties (he *should* have been fit, considering all the basketball he played during class). He looked like Dennis Quaid, but I doubt that Dennis Quaid could inspire this kind of animosity in anybody, except maybe Meg Ryan or that other lady he was married to before her. But I digress.

When Goodenough got to my counter, he didn't appear to recognize me. Why should he? Like I said, he spent most of our class time playing basketball, and I'd missed six (five) classes.

Goodenough had a various and sundry mix of small items, leftovers from numerous projects. But he didn't have any receipts.

I worked as quickly as I could, trying not to look at him. I chewed my lip the entire time. When I entered his license information, the transaction suspended.

This happened when a customer made a lot of returns without receipts. It was designed to flag people who stole and then tried to return merchandise or perpetrate other kinds of shady dealings. In any event, it required managerial authorization. I dialed and got Osric, he of indeterminate ethnicity, who promised he'd be right up.

"What's the problem?" Goodenough asked.

I fixed my gaze on the screen. "The transaction suspended. I need a manager to approve it. It'll be a minute."

"Why did it do that? This is the first time I've been in this store."

"The computer keeps track of all the stores. If you returned a lot of stuff to the store across town without a receipt, it's the same."

I turned and walked away to the far edge of my little area, watching for Osric and getting Goodenough out of my personal space. Osric was coming down the main aisle.

"Here he is," I said.

But Osric walked right on past, heading for the Garden Center. I dialed him again. Most of our non-register people — managers, head cashiers, and department workers — carried portable phones.

"I'm on my way," Osric said before I had a chance to say anything. "Just give me a minute."

"Who are we waiting for?" Goodenough asked. "That Chinese guy that just walked past?"

I nodded, still not looking at him.

Finally, Osric returned. "What do you need, Penn?"

"This suspended," I said. "I need it approved."

Osric entered his password on my register and perused Goodenough's returns history. "Okay, sir, I'll go ahead and do it for you this time, but you need to start keeping your receipts."

"What's the problem?" Goodenough asked.

"Well, if you return too many items without a receipt, eventually, the computer will lock you out, and you won't be able to return any of it without a receipt." I wondered whether that was true.

"But I remodel homes," Goodenough said. "I can't keep track of all the receipts."

Osric finished on my register and backed away. "You just need to keep them."

Goodenough snorted. "If you stop letting me return stuff, I'll just start going to Home Depot instead."

"We don't want you to do that, sir," Osric said, utterly good-natured. The ability to appear perpetually cheerful is the most useful talent a manager can have.

I handed Goodenough the return slip and a pen. He could go to Home Depot with my blessing.

Goodenough dragged the pen straight across the signature line and handed the slip back.

"I need you to print your name and a phone number," I said, indicating the two lines he'd left blank.

He was annoyed. "You don't have to do that at Wal-Mart."

When Goodenough handed the slip back, I gave him his store credit card, and he went off to shop.

The experience left me riled up, and when Kord came by a few minutes later, I told her about it, including all our KLU history.

"That bastard," she said when I'd finished. "What an ass."

That was why she was my favorite.

Day 79 – Wednesday, January 28

On the House Station calendar, the week started with Monday and ended with Sunday. This week, my off days were Wednesday and Friday.

I wasn't a big fan of this for two reasons: I liked to go to church on Sunday and I liked my off days to be consecutive. When they weren't consecutive, I didn't feel like I got a good enough break from work. The worst was when I closed, had the next day off, then opened the day after that.

I spent the better part of the morning filling out applications for graduate school. I was looking for a masters in fine arts in creative writing.

I was considering schools all over the Midwest: Saint Louis, Chicago, someplace in Iowa. I wasn't about to go back to KLU, even if they had the program I wanted, which they didn't, or if I could afford any more years at a private school, which I couldn't.

When I stopped for lunch, I found Drimacus the Eviscerator conspicuous by his absence. He was probably destroying something in Jeff's room.

I'd warned Jeff to keep his door shut when he was at work, but he was an absent-minded guy. He was also a slob. When I was a kid, there was a game show on Nickelodeon called *Finders Keepers* where kids would ransack a room as they raced the clock, trying to find a specific object. At the end, the room often looked like a tornado had gone through it. Jeff's room looked like that, and I wasn't about to go hunting in there for sleeping cats.

When I stepped into the kitchen, Drimacus came tearing around the corner and jumped on my foot. I kicked him off, sending him sprawling. Then I rooted in the fridge for sandwich components.

As I was spreading mayonnaise, I thought I heard Drimacus crying, but I didn't see him. When I was washing lettuce, I heard it again, muffled.

I pulled open the refrigerator door and Drimacus sprang forth.

"You're even dumber than I give you credit for," I said.

Adele came out from my room and Drimacus pounced on her. Adele, ordinarily sociable, hissed at him and ran off. I knew cats needed time to adapt to new kittens, but Drimacus had made her downright antisocial, and I was starting to resent him for it.

Nobody ever called about claiming him, so we were stuck with each other.

Day 86 – Wednesday, February 4

The shifty-looking man in the huge coat made me nervous, and that was *before* he tried to rob me.

He leaned across the counter and indicated a bulge in his pocket. "This is a gun. Give me the money out of your drawer. Put it in a bag."

A sharp wave of terror washed over me. I went numb. It was surreal.

A guy about my age sidled up behind the robber. "A gun, eh? That's not safe. You'll shoot your eye out!" Whoever this guy was, he was an idiot.

The robber whirled on him. "You didn't want to get involved. Give me your wallet."

What could I do? Going for the phone was ill-advised. Trying to take him out from behind was even dumber.

The brave/stupid guy had pulled out his wallet. As he handed it to the robber, he fumbled and dropped it. In the movies, that kind of thing is always intentional; here, I had no idea.

The robber had seen those same movies. "Pick it up," he ordered.

"Sure thing." The guy bent down, and as he did, he grabbed the sleeves of the man's coat and yanked his arms down—the gun was now pointed at the floor.

The robber cursed at him, trying to squirm free.

"I swear, if you shoot my wallet, I'm going to be mad," the cocky guy said.

The robber was now out of his coat and scrambling away. The guy reached into the coat pocket and pulled out a screwdriver. "That's it? That's the best you can do?" he said.

The robber was now behind the counter, in my area, and I was just trying to stay out of his way. He snatched a large steel pipe bender out of Electrical's return bin and waved it at the cocky guy, who was pocketing his wallet.

"You don't want to do that," said the guy.

The robber swung the pipe bender at him and he blocked the blow with his forearm. It made an unpleasant *clunk*, and I winced. The guy didn't even flinch. He snatched the bender out of the robber's hands and put it on my counter. Then he grabbed the robber's collar and slammed him to the floor. He clucked his tongue. "I saw you steal that screwdriver."

I just stared. This guy was a younger, less hairy Chuck Norris.

The robber scrambled to his feet and made a break for the door. The choke-slam guy gave chase. "You should probably call the police or something," he called to me. "I'll take care of him, don't worry."

I let out a long breath and dialed the manager on duty.

I had to tell the story four times: once to Osric, once to Rex, once to the police, and once to everybody in the break room. I had a feeling I'd be telling it quite a few more times over the next few days.

Since there wasn't an actual gun, a remarkably small fuss was made. Before I'd known it was a screwdriver, I'd been traumatized, but Rex didn't seem to think it was a big deal. Sure, I was fine now, but that really wasn't the issue. Rex

28

clapped me on the back and said he was glad I hadn't done anything stupid.

We filled out an Incident Report. The cocky choke-slam guy never came back. Rex collected the robber's coat and gave it to the police. When all the paperwork was done, they sent me back up to Returns to finish my shift.

Day 87 – Thursday, February 5

I thought I was fine. I really did. The guy had a screwdriver and some kung fu expert came out of nowhere and handled him. No big deal, right? Happens every day.

But I woke up in a cold sweat at five in the morning on my day off.

I went into the bathroom and washed my face. When I returned to bed, I couldn't sleep. I switched on the computer, because what else was there to do? I picked Adele up from my chair and set her on the bed. She grunted and gave me an irritated look, then promptly went back to sleep.

I wasted most of the day not writing. By mid-afternoon, I had a page and a half, eight hundred words.

Eventually, I quit pretending that I was working and decided to do something deliberately entertaining. Ninety minutes of video games helped get my mind off my troubles, but the instant I stopped I was bothered again.

I worked on graduate school applications. I did all of the menial fill-in-your-name parts and none of the creative essay stuff.

I was actually settling into something resembling a groove when Angry Pete called me from the Station.

"How did you get my number?" I asked.

"I have the phone list. What are you doing tonight?"

"Nothing."

"I'm closing."

"Sorry," I said.

"You want to meet at IHOP? The one right down the block? Say, 9:45?"

"I have to be at work at eight tomorrow."

"So do I. Come on, I'm going crazy here."

I sighed. "Fine. Call me when you get off."

I got there first, and I waited in the parking lot. Five minutes later, Pete arrived. As he got out of his car, Chloe got out of the car that had pulled in just behind his.

I was shocked and aghast. Pete and Chloe? He'd said he didn't think she was cute. I made myself take a deep breath. Strike while the iron is hot, as they say, and I'd always been slow in such matters. Pete was quicker; power to him.

"Hi, Penn," Chloe said to me.

"Hey," I said, trying not to look at her.

Pete gave me a sharp elbow. "Is that your Mazda with the 'My Other Car Is Battle Cat' bumper sticker? That's classy."

We went inside and got a booth. Pete slid in, and I matched him on the opposite side. Chloe excused herself to the restroom.

"What are you doing?" I demanded. I didn't mean to say it.

Pete was examining the menu with cherubic innocence. "What do you mean?"

"Come on. Chloe? You didn't say anything about that."

Pete shrugged. "I wanted to surprise you."

I sat back and crossed my arms, chewing my lip. "You did."

He finally looked at me. "Penn, what's the matter with you?"

I shook my head. "Nothing. So . . . you and Chloe, huh?"

Pete threw his head back, cackling. "Are you serious?"

I didn't reply. My face was flushed.

"You are a gold-plated dumbass," said Pete, when he'd managed to stop laughing. "I brought her for *you*."

"You— Wait, what?"

He leaned over and winked. "Word on the street is you've been spending a lot of time at the Paint Desk."

I made a reasonably quick recovery. "I . . . yeah, okay."

Pete shook his head. "I already told you she wasn't my type."

"She knew I was coming?"

"Of course. She closed tonight, too. I ran it by her and she was game."

"Thank you."

Pete grinned. "Don't mention it. You've already made tonight worthwhile strictly from a comedy standpoint."

"Do you think she, you know . . ."

"What? Likes you? She came, didn't she? She's taking a long time in the bathroom, isn't she?"

A girl rose from a table halfway across the restaurant where she was seated with her friends. She was hideous to behold, her makeup caked on and her clothes several sizes too small. She headed for our table, and I suddenly became very interested in the menu.

Thankfully, she addressed Pete. "Hi there. What's your name?"

Pete looked up and scrutinized her. "No thanks," he said.

Her eyes widened and her face went red. After a sufficiently indignant moment, she stalked off.

"Dear God," Pete said into his hand.

"You handled that pretty well," I said, grinning.

"She smelled like cigarettes and cooking oil," Pete muttered. "I thought she was going to hit me. I would have been killed! She had man hands! Did you see?"

"There are worse things," I said.

He glared down his long nose at me. "Like what?"

"Well, like—" I broke off. Chloe was coming back and a swarm of butterflies had infested my stomach.

Pete followed my gaze. "I've got you covered." He slid to the middle of the booth so Chloe had to sit next to me.

31

She reached for a menu. "Did I miss anything exciting?"

"No," said Pete.

"Yes," I said. "Love is in the air."

Chloe gave me an odd look, and I related what had just transpired.

Chloe craned her neck to see the girl at her table. "I like her shirt."

Pete rolled his eyes. "Does it come in her size?"

"You should go ask her," I said.

He scoffed. "My ass."

"That's what she was after," I said.

Pete glared. "I hate you."

"You can antagonize him, too," I told Chloe. "It's fun."

"Is that why they call you 'Angry Pete'?" she asked.

"I wonder if they would let me write that on my apron," Pete said.

"Why would you possibly think they would?" I asked.

He shrugged. "I knew a guy that worked at the Station across town—every time he got a new apron, he wrote a different name on it. Just regular names, but a new one each time. They let him. Customers don't know the difference."

Chloe unrolled her silverware. "You didn't answer the question. Angry Pete, remember?"

"Because I'm an angry guy," Pete replied. "Don't you think I'm angry?"

Chloe shrugged. "Not really."

"You should have seen me earlier."

"Earlier when?"

He ignored this. "Take Penn here. He's a pretty friendly guy, wouldn't you say?"

"Sure."

"He's a friendly guy because you know him. But if you just walked by and saw him, he doesn't look friendly at all. 'My mouth turns down by itself.' That's what you were going to say, isn't it, Penn? It is. Have you ever seen Penn when he's mad? No? I have. Twice, in two months since we've been at the Station. When Penn's cheerful, he looks indifferent. When he's indifferent, he looks mad. When he's mad, he looks like he's about to beat you to death with a stick. And they call *me* the angry one."

"But I'm not actually angry." I felt like I had to say *something* after that. "I'm pretty laid back."

Chloe clapped a hand to her forehead in frustration. "How did you get the nickname? Because you make *other* people angry?"

"See?" said Pete. "Look at this. I'm the least angry person here. The hell is this slacker-ass waitress at?"

"Just tell her," I said.

Pete jabbed a finger at me. "You take it easy. Remember everything I've ever done for you. Anyway, I was at this furniture store for a while. Sofa King. Do you know where that is? No? Only the few assholes that shop there do. But everybody's seen their God-awful commercials. *Mister Rogers' Neighborhood* had better special effects. Speaking of which, did you hear that rumor that was going around a while back that Mister Rogers was a Marine sniper during the Vietnam War?"

"That's the stupidest thing I've ever heard," I said. "He was a Presbyterian minister."

"Exactly my point. Of *course* it isn't true. Somebody made it up. Using the damn internet irresponsibly. That show was on since the sixties, right? Where'd they film it? In the bush, in between kills? Did you ever see any Vietcongs running around the Land of Make-Believe? Because I sure as hell didn't. That's stupid-ass people for you. A lot of stupid people, many of whom I have the misfortune of personally knowing, believed this rumor and spread it around. Now, I don't really care one way or the other if he was or wasn't, but he wasn't, and therefore, people who say he was are stupid and they piss me off."

"*That* is why they call him Angry Pete," I said. "Nothing he can say could explain it better."

"What?" said Pete. "I'm not mad. But how the hell am I supposed to eat some pancakes if the waitress doesn't come?"

After the waitress finally came and we ordered, Pete went back into his dissertation. "You've seen the Sofa King commercials?"

Chloe nodded.

"Bastards. I got my ass fired from there. Have I told you about that?"

"Yes," I said.

"No," said Chloe.

"She hasn't heard it," said Pete.

"That makes her the last one in the store, doesn't it?"

Pete banged his silverware on the table. "Do you want to fight me? I will kill you with this rusty spoon! Is that rust? What *is* that? Ew!"

I rubbed my temples. "Calm down and tell your story."

He sighed as though bearing some great burden. "I did all kinds of things at Sofa King. Sales, loading, delivery. So this lady comes in one day and buys this loveseat. She says, 'Put it in my SUV.' First of all, it's not an SUV, it's a station wagon, a tiny Saturn. So of course it isn't going to fit, and I see that right away. But this lady doesn't want to pay the delivery charge. She rambles on about how she measured the loveseat and she measured the car and it has to fit. She's going, 'I measured this and I measured that,' and I'm like, 'Look, bitch, you can fart around with that tape measure until the cows come home, but—"

"You actually said that?" Chloe asked.

"Not in those words, exactly. I calmly and rationally explained that she had failed to take into account the fact that the back of the vehicle narrowed at the top, whereas the loveseat did not."

"So what was the problem?"

"Don't believe he was as polite as he claims," I said.

34

"Of course not," Pete agreed. "But I didn't do anything to get this lady *that* upset. I'm not the one who told her to try to put a big-ass loveseat into a tiny-ass Saturn."

"You told her she *couldn't*," Chloe said.

"Exactly! Shoot the messenger! Well, we tried to stuff that bastard in there, and of course, it didn't go, and then she got mad about us scuffing up the sides of the loveseat. No regard for the laws of damn physics. So she takes her tape measure sob story to the manager and blames it all on me. And I'm doing my best to stay calm, but this guy was an idiot, too, and he never liked me, and he took her side, got all accusatory, so I finally did lose it. I started yelling and screaming—scared the hell out of that lady, let me tell you—it was pretty funny. So the manager fires me. I was going to quit anyway; I was just building up to it. Trying to get my money's worth—I didn't need that kind of grief."

"Is the Station really so much better?" I asked.

"Let me tell you something: Rex isn't the greatest manager in the world, but this guy there . . . he actually came up with the slogan 'It's not just great furniture, it's Sofa King great,' and then he couldn't understand why they wouldn't let him put it in the commercial."

Chloe raised an eyebrow. "Are you—"

"You're damn right I'm serious. It sounds like a lie because that joke is as old as the hills, but it's true—this dude may never have been on the internet in his life. Anyway, the upshot of that was, we all went around saying 'Sofa King great' all the time and there wasn't a lot he could do about it, because if customers called us on it, we'd just tell them the manager came up with it, which was the God-honest truth. He got yelled at a couple times for that. As did we. But it was worth it."

"Sofa King worth it?" I said.

"Stop!" Pete slapped both hands on the table. "It's not funny! It's old! It's tired! It's not even remotely clever! We got it out in the open, now let it die, like— like—"

"Like a malignant cancer of ignorance?" I said.

Pete hoisted a finger in the air. "Exactly! That is why I keep you around."

"But why are you so proud of getting fired?" Chloe asked.

"Because the place was stupid. I'm proud not to be in any way affiliated with them. I'm proud that they and I are at opposite ends of the universe in every relevant way." He opened his palms. "Some places are just like that, and you have to act accordingly. Like, when I get fired from the House Station, I'm going on a rampage. I'm throwing my cash drawer down the aisle. I will escalate the situation."

Our food came as Pete brandished his fork and said, "Enough about me. I hear Penn got held up at gunpoint with a screwdriver yesterday."

Chloe looked at me sharply. "What?"

I sighed. "What about it?"

"Landfill said you got held up yesterday. The guy had a gun and it turned out to be a screwdriver."

Anxiety began to gnaw at my stomach. "That's right."

"Did you give him the money?" Chloe asked. "Isn't that what you're supposed to do?"

"Landfill said some Chinese kung fu master kicked the guy's ass," Pete said.

Appetite suddenly gone, I pushed my plate away. "Landfill wasn't even there. The guy was white. But yeah, he choke-slammed the guy."

"Why would he take the chance, though?" Chloe asked. "It doesn't matter how much kung fu you know if the other guy has a gun."

I shrugged. "Said he saw the guy take the screwdriver. It was our screwdriver."

Pete shoved a large wedge of pancake into his mouth, then struggled to talk around it. "So what was it like? It's not like we're going to get to see the security tape."

"It wasn't 'like' anything," I said. "It wasn't a big deal. The whole thing took two minutes."

"Oh, come on," Pete persisted. "Why don't you—"

"Stop it," Chloe said. "You would have been scared out of your mind if somebody stuck a gun in your face."

"It wasn't a gun!"

"He didn't know that." Chloe put a hand on my arm. I was acutely aware of the fact that, barring the time she'd almost knocked me out with her head, it was the first time she'd ever touched me.

I composed myself. "I'm fine. Yes, it was . . . *intense* while it happened. And it still kind of bothers me. What if it was a real gun? Then what?"

"Then you give him the money out of the register," Pete said. "That's what we're supposed to do."

I leaned back and crossed my arms. "How? We can't just open our registers whenever we please. You have to ring a cash transaction to get the drawer to open."

"You can't ring a no-sale?" Chloe inquired.

"Not without a head cashier's password."

"That'd be great," Pete said. "'Hey, man, I'll give you all the money in the drawer as soon as the head cashier gets here.' They'd blow my damn head off."

"That's exactly my point," I said. "Or, he's got a gun on you and you start scanning merchandise so you can ring it out as cash. Customers don't know what you're doing half the time as it is. It's not safe."

Pete had somehow managed to finish his meal during the few seconds he hadn't been talking. "'Excuse me, sir, would you take a gift card instead?' Try that one. The House Station's money stays in the drawer while we, the little people, get shot in the face: that's the way the world works."

Chloe moved food around her plate. "Can't you tell somebody?"

"Who?" Pete said. "Rex? He wouldn't care. Kord would, but what can she do?"

"Rex might care a little," I said. "Just because he has to. He might even forward the issue to corporate in Austin. But it wouldn't do any good."

"You could get in touch with Austin yourself," Chloe pointed out.

I shook my head. "It would involve redoing the register's program. The software. That would affect every House Station everywhere. Then they'd have to retrain all the cashiers. They wouldn't go to that expense."

"You're forgetting something," Pete said. "That system's there for a reason — so we can't go rooting through the drawer however we please."

"Except that we *can*," I replied. "It just takes a little doing."

"So you guys can steal, but robbers from outside can't," Chloe said.

"That's basically it," said Pete. "We're screwed. It'll take a cashier getting shot before they do anything. You've heard stores say 'the customer is everything.' Logically, then, the associate is *nothing*. Because there isn't anything left. That's another thing that chaps my ass. This whole 'associate' business. We're not associates. It's just a half-assed attempt at political correctness and making us feel less crappy about our jobs. Am I any happier to come to work and be an associate than I would being an employee? They should at least make a concerted full-assed effort, like 'administrative professionals' or 'sanitation engineers.'"

"This ought to be good," I said. "Well?"

Pete chewed on his fork as he thought. "What immediately springs to mind is 'little bitches trod underfoot for the benefit of The Man.' I'll work on it. Anyway, it's got to be worse for you, Penn, seeing as you've got your college degree in the bag and here you are, overqualified to provide Excellent Customer Service."

"You can always leave," Chloe said.

"Can you?" Pete mused. "And then what? Go home and live with your mom and dad? Get another job somewhere else that pays even less? Here, at least, we get eight-fifty, for whatever that's worth."

"It doesn't matter 'and then what,'" Chloe said. "At least you can go whenever you want."

"You know what I love?" Pete said. "I love the people who work at places like the Station who decide they don't want to work anymore and try to get fired."

"*Why* do you love those people?" I asked dutifully. Talking things out had helped, but I was glad for Pete's change of tack.

"Because they're too stupid to know that places like the Station, places that don't pay squat and who replace cashiers the way you replace your underwear, never pay any kind of severance."

I pulled my plate back to me. The eggs were cold. "That's because monkeys can do our jobs," I said.

"True!" exclaimed Pete. "So true. And now they're trying to turn us into commercial harlots."

"Now what are you talking about?"

"That's right, you were off today. You won't believe what they've got us doing now."

"I'm sure I'll be doing it tomorrow," I said.

"Oh, you will be. They decided we weren't selling enough firewood, given how it's cold and winter and everything. So they put bundles of firewood at each register endcap and a big stack right outside your cage. Whenever we check anybody out, we have to ask, 'Would you like some firewood with that?' like this is freaking McDonald's. It's for real. Kord told me."

"Did you do it?"

Pete looked at me like I was crazy. "Hell, no, I didn't do it. I'm not pimping any logs unless Rex is standing right next to me."

"What's the big deal?" asked Chloe, who I thought was doing an admirable job of keeping up. "It takes two seconds to ask."

"It's the *principle* of the thing! It's *firewood*. If people want to buy firewood, let them buy it. If they don't, it's no skin off my face one way or the other. I'm not going to go around whoring firewood. It's degrading. It sets a bad precedent. The customers'll be there all damn day listening to me go on about crap nobody but Rex and those bastards in Austin care about. 'Do you want to sign up for a House Station Consumer Credit Card? No? Good call. Do you need a Lot Attendant to help you carry that one bag to your car? You can handle it? Are you sure? Do you want some firewood? Why am I asking you? Hell if I know, sir, but thanks for shopping at the House Station, Better Living Through Home Improvement and all that, don't let the door hit you in the ass on your way out.'"

"Don't you think you're overreacting?" Chloe asked.

Pete waved a hand. "Irrelevant. Penn agrees with me. How many people go home and say, 'Damn, honey, I forgot the firewood! How are we going to get through the day? I might as well curse God and die right now!' 'No, dear, it's not too late! Take your ass back to the House Station and get you some logs!' 'But I was just there! There was a huge-ass stack right in front of the door, but that bastard cashier at the Service Desk didn't say they were for sale! The humanity!' These Station assholes think eight-fifty buys them the world. They think they own me until I get home. For *eight-fifty*."

"Speaking of getting home," Chloe said, digging in her purse, "I need to do that, as enlightening as this has been. I have class tomorrow morning."

"And I've got to be at the Station at eight," I added.

Pete winked at me. "Just leave the money with me and I'll take care of the check."

"Thanks," I said, tossing some cash on the table.

"All I have is a ten," Chloe said.

"No problem," said Pete, holding up a fan of bills. "Here're some ones. Help yourself."

Chloe took two, handed him the ten, and stood. "Goodnight, guys. Thanks for inviting me, Pete. It was fun."

40

Pete nodded. "Night."

I started to say good night, but Pete kicked me under the table.

"Hey, I'll walk you to your car," I said instead.

Chloe smiled a tiny smile. "Okay."

When I glanced back, Pete was muttering to himself, a smug expression on his face.

Day 88 – Friday, February 6

The man returning the boxes of tile looked like James Earl Jones with a perm. His tiles were some of the bigger ones we carried, each a foot square, in containers of ten. The packaging consisted of cardboard frames banding each set together: big square holes on the top and bottom of the box saved on packaging and let the customer examine the tile.

James Earl Jones with a Perm handed me his receipt.

"Any problem with the tile?" I asked.

"It was the wrong color."

"No problem." I lifted the box out of the cart and broken pieces cascaded to the floor.

"It's broken," I said.

"Yeah," said James Earl Jones with a Perm. "But it's the wrong color."

I ran the return and negotiated the box of tile to the RTV box, trying my best not to spill the rest. It didn't matter that it was broken; this was the House Station—with a receipt, we'd take anything back (we usually took anything back *without* a receipt).

When Kord was at the House Station across town, she'd had a man come in with a flatbed of dug-up trees. He was getting divorced and his wife was getting the house, so he'd dug up every single tree on the property, fifteen- and twenty-foot trees that had been in his yard for years. But each tree of a

41

species we carried was exchanged for store credit. The rest he threw away. I don't know what happened to the ones the Station took back; maybe they became firewood.

The huge Returns sign that hung over my head like the sword of Damocles expressly stated that the House Station reserved the right to refuse any return at any time for any reason, but refusal never, ever happened. The sign should have had only one sentence on it: "Yes, we will take your crap back, especially if you complain a lot and tell us it was broken when you bought it."

Who was I to argue? It wasn't my tile.

But I *was* trying to figure out Mr. Jones with a Perm's rationale: if the tile was the wrong color, we'd take it back, but if the tile was broken, we might *not* take it back. So if it was the wrong color *and* broken, then we'd still take it back. However, none of this did me any good since I was the one who had to sweep it up.

As I searched for the broom, James Earl Jones with a Perm called to me. "Can I get out this door?" He was standing in front of the entrance, but not close enough to activate the sensor. I watched with some amusement as he inched his way up to the automatic doors, which finally opened.

While I was sweeping up, Kord stopped by to examine my mess. "What'd you do, Penn?" she asked good-naturedly.

"A customer got broken tile everywhere," I replied.

"What a jerk. I need you to make me a sign when you have a minute."

"Yeah, great. But I need to go the bathroom first."

"You always need to go to the bathroom. What's the matter with you?"

"Have you never heard," said I, "the cautionary tale of Tycho Brahe?"

"Who?"

I leaned on my broom. "Tycho Brahe was a famous astronomer. In his day, it was considered extremely bad manners to leave a banquet in the middle, even to use the restroom. So, as tradition goes, he held it and held it until his bladder ruptured. He died several days later from the resulting infection."

Kord grimaced. "Take your ass to the bathroom."

I did so, then stopped by the break room to refill my water bottle. Pete was there. He had taken down a sign HR had posted and was grading it for punctuation and spelling.

"Helen won't appreciate that," I said.

Helen was in charge of HR and scheduling. At most House Station stores, these were two separate jobs, but we were doing things on the cheap on account of business not being up to expectations. I never thought you needed one person who just did schedules, but ours were never the same twice. It was ridiculous.

Pete capped his red pen and looked up. "Atwater asked me to work his shift."

"Okay, but why are you in the break room?"

"He told me his shift started at 12:30, but it actually starts at one, and Helen won't let me clock in yet and I don't have time to go home. What time is it now?"

I glanced at the big clock on the wall next to him. "Quarter to."

Pete was shaking his head. "That bastard Atwater. You know why he's not here? His car broke down."

"That happens to everybody."

"It happens *all the time* to Atwater. This is the third time since we've been open. I've worked his shift each time. Have you seen Atwater's car? It's a 1979 Ford Fairmont with two hundred thousand miles on it. It's got rust holes in the door. The foam padding is coming out of the seats and the upholstery is disgusting. Smells like French fries. Care to guess why he won't trade it in?"

"Can't afford a new one?" I said. "He does work here, after all."

"A worthy guess, but wrong. He'll keep it forever. You haven't seen him roll up in it wearing that awful pedophile

43

denim trenchcoat he always wears?" Pete tapped his pen on the table. "You wouldn't believe me if I told you."

"Try me."

"He won it on *The Price Is Right* in 1979."

"He told you that?"

"I didn't believe it either, but he's got the episode on tape—he loaned it to me. He had that same ridiculous mustache when he was eighteen. He also won a microwave. He got out on the part where you spin that big wheel."

"Does he still have the microwave?" I asked.

"Probably. On the show you can see it's one of those wood grain ones with dials. Looks like it weighs fifty pounds. Probably gives you cancer to stand next to it. You going to lunch now?"

"No, I go at two."

"Just wasting time, then? Good idea. Who's at the Service Desk right now?"

"Brook."

Brook was a muscular Asian woman who didn't like me very much, which wasn't that big of a deal because she didn't like anybody very much.

Atwater and Pete were the two full-timers on the Service Desk. There were a couple others who were part-time, plus Tekla, overseer of the Service Desk. Brook technically wasn't in that department; she was the Delivery Coordinator, but since she was usually in the phone room next to the desk, she got called out to cover shifts occasionally.

"Brook'll put me on the phone," Pete predicted. "It's just as well. It's going to be dead tonight. There's that big Leetown High basketball game. Who's replacing you today?"

"I haven't looked. It's usually Johnisha."

"She won't keep me entertained. She always does her nursing homework when the store's dead. Penn, you're bleeding."

There was a ribbon of dried blood on my right forearm. I couldn't for the life of me remember how I'd cut it.

44

"There's a first-aid kit behind the Service Desk," Pete said.

"It and I are well acquainted," I replied. "There's one under the sink in here, too. This has got to be the tenth time I've cut myself since I've been here."

I was scheduled to get off at five. That was before Paige came alongside and put my arm in an affectionate death grip.

"Johnisha called in. She said she had a big exam tomorrow and had to study."

"Tomorrow's Saturday."

"That's what I told her. She stuck with the story." Paige shrugged. "Nothing we can do about it."

I sighed. "So what are you asking me?"

"Can you stay late? Otherwise it'll just be Pete up here closing the Service Desk and Returns."

I raised an eyebrow. "How late?"

"As late as you can. Until seven, at least. Preferably eight. Maybe sooner if we're slow. Please?"

That meant 8:30.

"It's Friday night," I said.

"I know. I'm sorry. Do you have plans?"

"I . . . no."

Now I was stuck.

"I'll get overtime," I said, my last try. The House Station believed in nobody getting overtime ever for any reason.

"You can go home early tomorrow instead."

As far as I was concerned, trading a busy Saturday afternoon for a dead Friday night was a great deal. "Okay."

"Thanks!" she threw her arms around me, her ample bosom constricting my lungs. After a moment, I patted her on the shoulder and pulled away.

"It could be worse," she said. "You could be closing with Landfill instead of me."

* * * * *

45

Brook went home when Pete came back from lunch, so it was just the two of us for the rest of the night. As Pete predicted, it was dead.

Pete seated himself in the Service Desk's rolling chair, which was about twenty feet away from my counter. We could talk to each other at this distance, but it required the slight raising of voices, which was frowned upon by managerial types. So I went over to the Service Desk and leaned on the counter.

"If the payphone rings, let me get it," Pete said, referring to the one just inside the front door. "People keep calling that number thinking it's Blockbuster Video."

"It's all yours."

Pete rolled around in his chair. "So, last night. I helped you out, right?"

"Yeah. You did. Thanks."

"Too bad Chloe's not the one throwing her arms around you."

"Paige does that to everybody," I said.

"She doesn't do it to me."

"And why is that?"

"I'm the only one that doesn't flirt with her," said Pete.

"I've never flirted with her."

"Penn, listen to me. I know you have no serious interest in her, and that's perfectly natural. But you encourage her."

"What am I supposed to do? Act like a jackass around her?"

Pete shrugged. "Hasn't failed me yet. Seriously, you encourage her. You let her walk arm-in-arm with you. I know you'd never do anything with her, but she seems like the type who gets around. Based on what I've heard, anyway."

"Heard? From who?"

"From Merlin," Pete said.

"Merlin van Gorp?"

Pete gave me a condescending look. "How many Merlins work here, Penn? And who the hell names their kid that?"

46

Merlin was a cashier, another kid making his way through community college. His days revolved around drinking and getting laid. Or at least *discussing* getting laid — he was the sort that made you instinctively disbelieve anything he said on the topic.

"Merlin and Paige, huh?" I said.

"I'm not saying that, although it's well within the realm of possibility. Merlin's standards are pretty low . . . although he's already shot down Chastity Loman."

"He told you this?"

"I *saw* it. Jesus, why wouldn't he? She's got a kid and a restraining order against the kid's dad, and she's on *probation*, for God's sake. Word on the street is she's pushing weight to help pay the rent. But seriously, I'd put the kibosh on that thing with Paige if you're serious about Chloe. Hell, I'd put the kibosh on it either way."

"There is no 'thing with Paige'! Look, I *like* Chloe. But I'm still getting to know her. And you know I'm not like Merlin."

"You're a good little church boy, I know," said Pete. "Savin' it for marriage."

"That's right," I said guardedly.

Pete held up his hands. "Take it easy, Penn. I'm on your side here."

The phone at my register rang and I went to get it. It was Paige.

"Do you see the Lot Attendant down there anywhere?"

"I haven't seen anybody," I replied. "Who am I looking for?"

"Booker."

"No. He's not down here."

"Thanks. I'll page him."

"Who were they looking for?" Pete asked.

"Paige was looking for Booker," I said.

Booker Shoeboot, a big burly guy with some kind of mental disability, was the most beloved of the House Station

47

Lot Attendants. He was on the slow side, but he was by far the most friendly and the most helpful of the bunch.

"Hey, have you met that new Lot Associate?" said Pete. "Started yesterday? He's Indian. Like Pakistani Indian."

"Name?"

Pete picked up the phone list and scanned it. "Hell if I know."

"It's not there?"

"Oh, it's *on* here. I just have no idea how to say it."

I took the phone list from him. The kid's name was Bhagwandas Sivasupiramaniam.

"We've got to come up with something else," Pete said. "I can't go paging that over the intercom. People will think I'm possessed."

"Just ask him how to say it," I said.

"Superman," said Pete. "I have decided his name is Superman."

"Random," I said.

"Not at all. Look at his last name. There's kind of a Superman in there somewhere."

"If you say so."

The nickname stuck.

Day 89 – Saturday, February 7

I woke up anticipating going home early. I'd stayed three hours late last night, which entitled me to get off at two today. I wondered if they'd let me skip lunch and go home at one.

Saturdays were busy when it wasn't college football season. KLU didn't have a football team, but people would drive up to Columbia to see Mizzou.

On Saturdays, we sometimes had two Returns cashiers simultaneously. I came in at eight, and then Edna, a charming but decrepit geriatric, came in at 12:30. She worked two jobs—

48

the other was at a button factory — with the end result that she worked sixty hours a week with no overtime.

From time to time, we had to page a Lot Associate on the overhead. You had to enunciate when you talked and it came out garbled no matter what.

Rex didn't let us page and say, "Lot Attendant, please come to aisle four for customer assistance." Instead, we had to tell the Lot Attendant to call our register. Then we'd tell them, "Please go to aisle four for customer assistance," because Rex thought telling them directly was Bad Customer Service because the customers would think we were short-staffed. Which we constantly were. So we kept them in the dark with our clever subterfuge.

We *could* page the Lot Associates and tell them to come to specific registers. The problem was that Edna *shrieked* into the phone. She'd say, "I need a Lot Attendant to come to Returns," and it would come over the speakers as "INEEDALOTTA-HEEEEEEENAKOMMAAAAARETURNS!" It was so shrill it made people's fillings ache. I'd seen people literally jump in the air when she did it. Others looked around like we were having an air raid. It sounded like somebody was dialing up to the internet with a 56k modem.

Edna arrived while I was helping a friendly old man trade out a toilet tank that he claimed had been damaged when he bought it. She deposited her coat and travel mug on her side of the counter and headed back to clock in.

"Do you need any help loading this?" I asked the man. "I can get a Lot Associate up here for you."

The old man waved a hand. "No, but if you see me lying down in the parking lot, send someone out."

Rex, who perpetually emanated an apprehension-causing cloud, stopped by, but only to point out that my originally sunshine-yellow apron had become mustardy-gray. He sent me to the break room to get a new one.

A hardware store is a dusty place, and the yellow aprons really showed the dirt. There were murmurings on the TV in

49

the break room (it was permanently set to the House Station Channel, which fed us a constant stream of House Station propaganda and the occasional national weather forecast) that corporate was considering a switch to black aprons with yellow print so that we would replace our aprons less frequently, thus saving the company untold millions.

We weren't allowed to take our aprons home at any time for any reason. Even putting one in your car in the parking lot was a fireable offense. The old aprons had to be cut up and thrown away in the store.

There was actually a pretty good reason for this: let's say somehow you got hold of a House Station apron and put it on with some jeans and a polo shirt. Poof! You're a Lot Attendant. What do Lot Attendants do? Yeah, they bring the yellow shopping carts back into the store, but they also load merchandise into cars for people. Now, the House Station is a big place, and nobody knows *all* the associates — and nobody would say a word when you loaded that washing machine into the back of your pickup.

I understand this has happened more times than you might expect.

Like most men, I thoroughly enjoy destroying something every now and then, and I took great relish in shredding my apron with the little yellow safety knife every single associate in the store carried. Anybody who dug my apron out of the trash would have a worthy challenge awaiting them.

Kord brought Edna back up at quarter to one. "Count down," she told me.

"Already?" I asked. "I was scheduled until two."

"We're cutting hours," Kord replied. "Unless you want to stay."

"You twisted my arm," I said.

Chloe wasn't there, or I would have dropped by on my way out. I hadn't had much of an opportunity to see her this week; our schedules conflicted perfectly. So I just went home.

Day 91 – Monday, February 9

The TV was blaring an infomercial and Jeff was snoring on the couch. Channel-surfing was his hobby.

The kitchen was a disaster. In spite of my constant complaining and Jeff's equally constant apologizing, if Promilla wasn't coming, he never washed any dishes.

Here was our cycle: first, I'd load the dishwasher and run it. If I wasn't around to empty it, instead of putting the dishes away, Jeff would take what he needed each time he ate and leave the rest. He would then stack these dishes in the sink and all over our severely limited counter space. To then use the sink or counter, one had to empty the now half-full dishwasher and load it again, at which point it would be completely filled just from the dishes on the counters and sink. You should never have to make a stack of dirty dishes on the floor just to get the kitchen clean.

After eight hours at the Station, I usually didn't have the energy to deal with the kitchen, so off days were cleaning days. I did it now, and it took me forty-five minutes.

Halfway through, Drimacus wandered in, tipped over the trash can, and seized a banana peel, which he dragged into Jeff's room.

When I was about finished, Jeff stumbled over, bleary-eyed. I'd made quite a bit of noise, but that didn't matter; Jeff slept through everything, including his three alarm clocks.

"Oh, hey, bro, I'm sorry, I didn't want you to do all that yourself."

I found this apology irritating. Four out of five times, I was the one who cleaned the kitchen. The fifth usually had something to do with Promilla.

"Forget it," I said.

"I'm sorry, bro," he said again.

I spent much of the day going over my applications for graduate school. I'd ended up picking the University of Iowa,

Ball State, and the University of Missouri–Saint Louis — nothing too terribly far away. UMSL was my safety pick since going there almost certainly entailed moving back in with my parents.

I was confident that I'd have my pick of schools. I'd had a 3.6 GPA at KLU and I'd gotten a pretty decent score on the GRE. Not great (I hadn't prepared much), but above average.

I wrote the requisite essays and set them aside. I'd revise them tomorrow and get them in the mail by the weekend.

When that was done, I felt better about life, so I went to see if Jeff wanted to hang out.

Jeff wasn't a bad guy; far from it. Some people are passive-aggressive; Jeff was passive-passive. But he was honest, he was friendly, and we usually got along pretty well — a man can't live with just anybody. On the whole, our living arrangement was pretty good. I just didn't like his girlfriend or his kitchen-cleaning habits or his constant apologizing.

He was in his room, slogging his way through *The Silmarillion*. He agreed to rent a movie and pick up some snacks. It was a good day.

Day 97 – Sunday, February 15

I was typically glad to see Angry Pete. Having a friend at work, somebody to talk to, made the day go by faster. But when he was reigning from the battlements of his tower of high dudgeon, he just made me tired.

"'Have a good weekend,'" Pete was saying. "People told me twelve times yesterday to have a good weekend. I counted. Have a good weekend, my ass. Open your eyes, people! I'm not having a good weekend! I'm at work! I worked Friday night, Saturday, and Sunday! How does that constitute a good weekend?"

"Take a deep breath," I said.

"I don't even *have* a weekend! My off days this week are Monday and Wednesday. That's not a weekend by any stretch of the imagination!"

"They're just trying to be polite," I said. "They don't think about that stuff."

Pete twisted the headset cord around his finger. "They don't think about us at all. We're not real people to them. It could be me or you or Charles Manson or Martin Luther King and people would say the exact same thing. You know who I hate the most? The ones who don't make eye contact, who put their crap on the counter and stare at it for the whole transaction." He slapped the counter. "Look me in the eye! I'm a man, God damn it! That really frosts my balls."

"You may want to keep your voice down," I said. "Just a thought."

"It pisses me off," Pete said, not lowering his voice. "People do whatever the hell they — Thank you for calling the House Station."

I laughed out loud. Those calls clicked in automatically. If the person on the phone had heard what he'd been saying, he'd be in trouble. And Rex liked to call the store when he wasn't there and pretend to be a customer.

I do have this to say for managers: they work some bad shifts, often eleven hours, and they almost never ended up leaving when they were supposed to. We had a 4 a.m. to 3 p.m. shift — working that in the winter meant you had only a passing acquaintance with the sun.

While Pete was on the phone, I got an irritated customer with two five-gallon paint buckets. "These are the wrong thing," he said.

Usually paint was "the wrong color" or "the wrong sheen." Did "the wrong thing" mean he'd meant to buy a hammer and nails instead?

I pried open both buckets. Tricky people liked to fill the cans with water, add sand to get the weight right, and then try to return them. We had to check every can of paint that came in.

Although, I think if somebody did bring in a can of water and sand with a receipt, we'd take it back. At the very least, we'd give them more paint. We were good like that.

He handed over his receipt. "This is going to refund to the credit card you bought it with," I said.

He was muttering to himself, not paying attention to me. He signed the Returns slip but didn't print his name or write a phone number, then snatched the receipt I handed him and stalked off toward Paint. I put the cans away, then filled in the blanks he'd left on the slip with indecipherable scribbles.

Two minutes later, he was back with two more five-gallon buckets.

This was a trend: even when I did a straight refund (rather than an exchange) and gave the customer his money back, he typically came back to check out at Returns.

Technically, it was impossible to do an exchange on a House Station register unless you wanted to trade a broken something for a working exact same something. If you bought a 5/16-inch screwdriver and you brought it back to get a 3/8 instead, that's not an exchange as far as the computer is concerned, even if they're the same price. You're returning one and buying the other in two different transactions. I was Jesse Owens on the register, though, so most customers never realized. Maybe monkeys could do my job, but I took pride in being the fastest cashier in the store.

I rang up the new paint. "One hundred and twenty-eight dollars and thirty-nine cents," I said. Same as the paint he'd returned.

He waved a hand distractedly, looking out the storefront window. "I just want to exchange them for the ones I brought back."

"Sir, I already refunded those to you. I need you to pay for these."

"What? I don't have money for that."

"It refunded to the credit card you bought them with."

Now he was looking right at me. "I don't have that card. It isn't my card!"

"Excuse me?"

His teeth were clenched. "I'm a contractor! The card is the guy's whose house I'm painting!"

This was getting ugly fast. I held up a hand. "One second, sir." I dialed the head cashier and got Kord. "Can you come up here for a second *right now*?"

"What's up?" she asked.

"I'll tell you when you get here," I said in an undertone.

Kord sighed. "One of those."

Thirty seconds later, I was explaining the situation to her. She tugged on her ring of badges as she thought.

Kord looked at me, and I shrugged. That this guy was returning stuff bought with someone else's credit card wasn't necessarily shady, but I knew she was thinking about it.

"I'm sorry, sir," she said finally. "Refunding it to that card was all the computer will let us do."

At the House Station, the computer is often the scapegoat, and rightly so.

The man shook his head, confused and enraged. "I don't want a refund! I just want to exchange that paint for this paint! Wal-Mart does it!"

"I'm sorry," Kord repeated. "The computer won't let us do that." She was frowning, looking sorry and sympathetic, on the customer's side against the evil register. She was good at it, but it wasn't working this time.

"Then I can't buy this paint! I need this paint to do the job! It's a thirty-minute drive from here! I can't make an extra trip!"

"I'm sorry, sir, I really am," Kord said. "The system won't let us."

"Let me talk to the manager."

"I am the manager," Kord said.

Kord wasn't technically a manager, but she was the Front End Supervisor and the buck stopped with her as far as any register issue went.

"So I'm screwed, is that what you're saying?" the man was screaming now. "I'm screwed! *Screwed!*"

We just watched.

The man's face was crimson. "HORSE'S *ASS!*" he bellowed, drawing the attention of a half-dozen customers. "I'm never coming here again! I'm going to Home Depot!" He turned and stalked out the door, muttering obscenities.

I let out a long breath. "Well."

Kord gave me a reassuring pat on the back. "Not your fault. He was an ass. Don't let it get to you."

"You mean a *horse's* ass. Ha." I snapped my fingers. "Hey, I just thought of a way we could have done that transaction."

"How?"

"You could have post-voided the return. Then we could have run it again as a no-receipt and given him store credit, then checked him out with that."

Every completed return had a ten-minute window in which a manager could void it. But post voids were rarely needed and rarely thought of.

Kord considered this. "You're right. But he was a jerk, so don't worry about it."

Day 99 – Tuesday, February 17

When Atwater sent the phone clattering to the floor, I jumped. I'd been thinking about Chloe.

"Penn, can you take the headset a minute?" he asked as he picked it up. "I need to go in the phone room."

The cord didn't reach all the way into the phone room, which was right behind the Service Desk. It was the workaday domain of Tekla, the Service Desk supervisor, and Brook, the

Delivery Coordinator; when they weren't there—which, given the number of hours we were open in a week and the fact that they usually got to leave at five, was much more often than not—it was vacant.

I came over and took the headset, sat down at the computer, and pretended I was doing something.

A man came to the desk. "Excuse me," he said. "I had a hundred-dollar gift card, but I lost it. Can I get another one?"

"No," I said, unapologetically but not impolitely.

The guy said "Hm" and walked off.

I had no respect for people who didn't put any effort into their scams.

I glanced through the window of the phone room. Atwater was leaning against the wall, eating M&M's. Tekla was at lunch.

A lady was now standing at my register. "Is anybody working Returns?" she asked me.

"I'll be with you in a second." I tapped on the window and Atwater reluctantly returned his candy to his apron and emerged.

"Hi," I said to the lady as I returned to my counter.

"Hi. I need to return this bottle of Febreeze. The spray thing doesn't work. I just want to get another one. I have the receipt if you need it."

I picked up the bottle and looked it over, then turned the nozzle from *OFF* to *ON* and pulled the trigger. A fine scented mist filled the air.

"Oh! I feel so stupid," the woman said, blushing. "I'm so sorry!"

I handed her the bottle. "I wish they were all that easy."

When Tekla returned from lunch, she beckoned me over. She was a woman who was passing gracefully through middle age, bringing her good figure along with her.

"I'm going to post this by the phone," she said, waving a piece of paper, "but I'm telling you now because Rex wants this started immediately. When you answer the phone, this is what you have to say: 'Thank you for calling the House Station and Rental Center at Garber and State, would you like to hear about our specials today?'"

"I don't think they're going to want to," Atwater said.

Tekla shrugged. "If they do, you just read off this card. It'll be posted, too. If they're interested in any of the offers, you can handle it yourself or transfer it to the appropriate department. Rex thinks this'll help increase sales, and he'll be checking on you, so make sure you say it every time."

"That greeting keeps getting longer," said Atwater unhappily.

Day 102 – Friday, February 20

Brad Landfield, who made simple questions annoying, was camped out at Returns. "You good? You need anything? Change? What?"

"I'm good," I said.

"Are you thanking all the customers? Are you circling the returns on the receipts when you get them?"

"Of course," I said, which was a lie. Nobody bothered with that stuff.

"Be sure you take all the RTVs back to Receiving at the end of your shift."

"I know how to do my job."

Landfill leaned in, looking concerned. "Listen, this lady was giving me a hard time down at the other end. She wanted to know why we don't have any racecar carts. I didn't know what she was talking about."

"Home Depot and Lowe's have carts shaped like racecars," I said. "We don't sponsor a NASCAR driver."

Landfill shrugged. "Seems like a stupid idea."

"No, they're a good idea," I said. "They calm the kids down who get mad because we don't have toys."

Landfill's expression suggested that he was giving this thought all the mental power he could muster. Then he said, "Kids, man. What's the deal?"

"I'll tell you a story about kids," I said, feeling unusually sociable. "If you go back to the bath section, the display toilets are mounted five feet off the floor. They used to be at floor level. Do you know why?"

"Why?"

"Because one fine day about a year and a half ago, a kid at a store in Kansas City sat down on one and took a dump. Then it happened again at a store in Arkansas. The House Station decided enough was enough, so now there are no display toilets at floor level in any House Station in America."

"That's nasty! Anyway, do you need to send any money back to the vault?"

"No," I said.

Cashiers on the regular registers weren't allowed to have more than five hundred dollars in their drawers; they had to periodically send their surplus cash back through the tubes. Rex said it was for the safety of the cashiers, but since the customers didn't know we did it, I didn't see how it was safer for anybody but the money.

"How much money is in your drawer?"

"I don't know, eight hundred dollars?"

"In twenties and above?"

"Most assuredly."

"Then you need to send some back! You're going to get in trouble! You're going to get *me* in trouble!"

"Landfill, my till *starts* at five hundred dollars. I give money to customers for a living. Why do you think I call you for *increases*?"

Landfill threw up his hands. "Okay, I'm just trying to help. I don't know why everything has to be so complicated."

With two victories under my belt, I turned back to my register and wiped down the monitor.

Not surprisingly, Landfill didn't take the hint. "Hey, let me ask you another question. Do you like Paige?"

"*What?*"

He laughed his irritating laugh. "I don't mean like *that*. I mean as a head cashier."

"Why are you asking me this, man?"

Landfill shrugged. "I'm just asking."

"I like her just fine," I said. "As a head cashier."

Blessedly, his phone rang.

"Hello? You need quarters *again*? I'll be there in a minute." He clapped me on the shoulder. "I'll be back in a while."

"Never touch me," I said.

Why had he asked me that? Did he think Paige and I were a thing? Was I sending out some signal I was completely unaware of? Or was *he* interested in Paige?

He wasn't her type. The few times I'd seen them interacting, they argued. Paige wouldn't touch Landfill with a ten-foot pole.

It was a good thing Landfill was the newest of the head cashiers, because none of them had patience for him telling them what to do (which was often wrong), much like how I didn't have patience for him telling me what to do (which was either wrong or something so elementary that I was already doing it on a regular basis or something I had no intention of doing unless Rex was standing next to me).

God forbid they ever put people under him.

Day 106 – Tuesday, February 24

My off days were Tuesday and Wednesday—once again, nothing remotely involving the weekend, but at least I had two in a row.

My little brother Anders, who was sixteen and who lived in Saint Louis with my parents, sent me an e-mail announcing he was going to be a writer and had fifty thousand words of a novel already.

A wave of insecurity washed over me. I didn't even have *thirty* thousand words yet! Anders was going to finish a novel before me? I'd had an eight-year head start, and I didn't have a title or a name for my main character.

Now hang on, I said to myself. How good could his book actually be? At the rate he was producing, not very, right? I was a slow writer, but my first drafts were equivalent to other people's third drafts—that's what my college English professors said, anyway.

I suppose the correct response to my brother's e-mail would have been to say I was proud of him and use it as added drive for my own work. Well, I didn't feel that way. A week ago, I was worried about whether or not my book would ever get published; now I was worried that Anders would leapfrog me.

I wanted Anders to make it, honest. Just so I made it first.

Action had to be taken. My graduate essays were finished and in the mail, and nothing stood in the way of me working on my own projects.

I'd written three short stories. The one I thought was best, "The Last Song of Morning," was about a conflict between a girl and her parents that explored the child's struggle for identity and independence. I'd made it a fantasy to lighten the tone a little.

I'd submitted the other stories to fifteen print and online magazines and received thirteen rejections; the other two had evidently considered me unworthy of a reply. But I'd never sent out "The Last Song of Morning." I'd finished it a month ago, then put it aside to work on the novel. Well, it was time for that sucker to spread its tiny wings and fly. I spent my day off revising and proofing the bejeezus out of it. I was in the zone. I found five magazines that I wanted to submit to, printed copies of the story and query letters, and got it all ready to mail and e-mail.

When I was done, I felt a lot better about life in general.

Day 107 – Wednesday, February 25

I threw myself into my novel, and I made a lot of progress, not counting the times I found myself daydreaming about Chloe. I was really getting inside the character of my protagonist, even though I hadn't found a name for him that I was happy with.

Jeff came and found me that afternoon. "Promilla's coming over tonight. She's making dinner. You're welcome to join us."

"I don't want to be your third wheel," I said.

"You won't. Her cousin is coming too."

I leaned back and crossed my arms. "Is he, now? Just out of curiosity, why aren't you doing all this at Promilla's apartment? Since it's her family, I mean."

"One of her roommates is having a bunch of people over. You know Susan, right?"

I did. Susan called to mind in all relevant aspects a constipated hippopotamus.

"Well," said Jeff, "they're not getting along too well since Susan got cracker crumbs in Milla's bedsheets."

"Don't they have different rooms?" I waved a hand. "Never mind, I don't want to know. Who's this cousin?"

"His name's Joe Rushing. He lives at Mossy Oak apartments. Seems like a nice enough guy. The few times he's been around, Milla's been in a hurry to go somewhere. But I know he's very active in his church."

"What church?"

"I don't know. Some little nondenominational charismatic place across the street from his apartment."

I chose magnanimity. "Sure, I'll have dinner with you. What are you making?"

"Lasagna. Milla makes the best lasagna."

"I'll lock up Drimacus, but I'm not locking up Adele, okay? If I lock them up together, he'll just harass her all night long."

"Fair enough."

Promilla arrived at six with bags of groceries and began cooking. I resisted the urge to barricade myself in my room and made an effort to be friendly.

"Smells good," I said.

"Thanks," said Promilla.

Yes, we'd really hit it off.

Jeff was tidying up the living room. "What time is Joe getting here?"

"He's supposed to get here at seven," Promilla said.

By 7:15, dinner was ready and there was no sign of Joe.

"I just called his house," Promilla said. "He's not there."

"He doesn't have a cell phone?" Jeff asked.

I wandered into the kitchen. "This drawer is still broken. Did you call them today?"

"I called them yesterday," said Jeff.

Since our apartment complex was so terrible at maintenance, we decided to try to nag them into submission. But all Towne and Associates seemed to be concerned with was collecting their rent checks and only hiring office workers with large breasts. That was well and good, but it didn't get the drawer fixed.

At 7:35, there was a knock at the door, and Jeff leapt to answer it. "Hey, Joe, good to see you, bro. Come on in."

Joe, pulling off his hat and gloves, looked chilled to the bone.

"We were expecting you a little earlier," said Jeff in his friendly way. "Can I take your coat?"

"Thanks," said Joe, stamping his feet. "Sorry I'm late. I was planning to ride my bike, but it was too icy, so I walked. Hey, your cat is really pretty."

"Thanks," I said. "You walked from Mossy Oak? That's like four miles away!"

Joe nodded. "Four and a half. I'm surprised my pedometer didn't freeze."

"Let's eat," Promilla said. "That'll warm you up."

Jeff said grace and we filled plates and sat on the couch and ate lasagna and garlic bread.

"This is exceedingly excellent," I said. Credit where it was due.

"Good job, sweetie," said Jeff.

"Thanks," said Promilla, who looked like she was more on edge than usual.

I waved a piece of garlic toast in Joe's direction. "So, what do you do?"

"I'm in the evangelist program at Blood of Christ Bible Institute. It's a two-year degree."

I stuffed bread in my mouth. This was unexpected. KLU was about as evangelical as they came, and even they didn't have much to do with Blood of Christ, which was best described with words like "fringe" and "unorthodox" and "unaccredited."

"So, what do you want to do with that?" I asked.

"I want to do inner city ministry."

"Here? Leetown doesn't have much of an inner city."

Joe laughed. "No, somewhere bigger. Maybe Little Rock, or Saint Louis. I'll be done in May. Then, wherever the Lord wants me to go, I'll go."

"That's admirable," said Jeff.

Joe was a little flaky, but he was pleasant to be around, mostly. After dinner, we played a board game, finishing around 10:30.

"It's been fun," said Joe, getting bundled up to leave. "Jeff and Penn, thanks for having me in your home."

"No problem," I said.

"You're not walking back, are you?" Jeff asked. "It's so icy! I'll give you a ride."

Promilla was glaring daggers at him, but Jeff didn't notice.

"It's okay," said Joe. "Not necessary."

"It's freezing!" Jeff imposed himself between Joe and the door.

"I couldn't possibly."

I sidled up to Promilla, who was still giving us the evil eye. "What's the deal?"

"Have you accepted Jesus Christ as your Lord and Savior?" Joe asked Jeff.

Jeff looked as bewildered as I felt. "What, me? Yeah. What's that got to do with the ice?"

Joe looked at me. "You all have?"

"Yes," I said.

"Are you familiar with the rapture?" Joe asked.

I still couldn't figure out what that had to do with anything. I opened my mouth to say it was theologically questionable, but Promilla gave me such a withering look that I just shut up.

"Look, it's twenty degrees outside," said Jeff, like he was talking to a child. This was as assertive as I'd ever seen him. "You can tell me about the rapture all you want in the car."

Joe looked at Promilla, then back at Jeff. "You guys don't understand. She didn't tell you, I guess. I don't ride in cars when other Christians are driving."

I choked on my spit.

"Say what now?" Jeff asked.

"That's why I don't drive myself," Joe said. "A car can be a deadly weapon."

Jeff shook his head. "I . . . I don't understand."

"Do you know what the rapture is?" Joe said. "It's when Jesus Christ comes back and takes all the believers away in the blink of an eye. 'Ye know neither the day nor the hour wherein the Son of Man cometh.' Think about it: Christians driving their cars forty, fifty, sixty miles an hour, when instantly, all those cars are unmanned and out of control! Think of how many unbelievers would be killed!"

"I see," said Jeff, who looked suddenly afraid.

"Have you seen those bumper stickers that say, 'In case of rapture, this car will be unmanned'?" Joe shook his head. "People make light of a serious situation. 'Ha, ha, when the rapture happens, this ton of steel is going to crush you to death because you haven't given your life to Jesus Christ.' There's no love there. That's not what Christianity is all about."

"All right," said Jeff, because quite frankly, there was nothing else to say.

"So I won't be a part of any irresponsible Christian driving," said Joe. "But I'm not judgmental; don't think I'm condemning you because you all drive. 'Judge not, that ye be not judged.'"

It was just too absurd. I decided to go with it. "You don't drive or ride in cars with Christian drivers. You bike and walk. Do you fly?"

Joe smiled at me. "When I was little, I wanted to be a pilot, but then I read *Left Behind* and it really changed my life. I have no problem flying as a passenger, though. If I get raptured off a plane as a passenger, there's really no possibility for harm to come to others, is there? Just like if I got raptured off a bicycle."

His use of "rapture" as a verb made my brain slip a gear. "That's very true," I said.

"I've been giving it a lot of thought lately," said Joe. "Cab drivers, truck drivers, anything like that—those aren't good jobs for Christians to have. Any job where a sudden disappearance would cause disaster."

"So a Christian shouldn't be the safety monitor at a nuclear plant," I deadpanned.

Joe nodded. "Yes, that's it exactly! Anyway, I need to be going. I have class in the morning. Thanks again for having me and for giving me an opportunity to share." With that, he was gone.

Jeff closed the door, then whirled on Promilla. "What was *that*?"

"What was what?" asked Promilla defensively.

Jeff waved his arms. "That! That . . . I don't know what that was!"

Promilla looked exasperated. "So Joe's a little quirky."

"A *little* quirky?"

"They're going to find him frozen to death in a snowbank," I said.

Promilla sighed. "He's been like this for the last year and a half."

"Why couldn't you warn us?" asked Jeff.

"Why couldn't you just let him walk home in peace?" Promilla snapped.

"You know, it's been fun, and thanks for dinner," I said. "But I'm going to go in my room now and let you work this out. Feel free to leave me some leftovers."

Day 111 – Sunday, February 29

It was Leap Day, an extra day of the year to labor for The Man. I arrived to find two new part-time head cashiers, additions rather than substitutions. Apparently business was picking up.

The first was Brandy, a tiny woman with a huge eighties perm. She was about Paige's height—maybe five feet—but with half the mass. She was the "emergency" head cashier, and would be spending most of her time on a register, which was good because she liked to walk around and pick up customers' babies.

The second was a good-natured, extremely dark man named Thoth Prow. According to Pete, he was from "Africa, somewhere" and his name was pronounced "Tot, like tater tots."

* * * * *

"Pete!" I called. "Page me a Lot Attendant. This gentleman needs some help loading a bathtub."

Pete signaled acknowledgment and dialed. After a moment, he called back, "He'll meet you out in the parking lot!"

My customer pushed his tub out the door on a flatbed cart and I went over to the Service Desk.

"Who's the Lot Attendant?" I asked.

"Superman."

"Still haven't met him," I said.

"It was a disappointment, let me tell you," said Pete. "He doesn't have an accent. Not any accent at all."

"That ruined it for you?"

"He's from *here*! He's from Saint Louis!" Pete's high voice ascended further.

I shrugged. "So?"

"Look, if your name is Siva-suva-slamma-lamma-ding-dong, you have no business being born and raised in Missouri. What were his parents thinking? They *weren't* — they were too excited from having just gotten off the boat!"

"Where he's born doesn't have anything to do with his last name. Also, you're racist."

Pete waved all this away. "His first name isn't any better. I don't even know what the hell it is without looking on the phone list."

"What's he got written on his apron?"

"Superman." Pete said this with pride.

Thoth came to the Service Desk, pushing a shopping cart overflowing with light bulbs. He was wearing a black and yellow House Station cap to complement his apron.

"What's that about?" Pete asked.

"We are selling fifty cents bulbs," said Thoth. He, at least, had an accent.

I introduced myself.

Thoth smiled. His teeth were dazzling white. "Good to meet you. Are you here to close? I close tonight with Bradley. Bradford."

"Who?" Pete asked. "I don't know any Brads."

"Landfill," I said.

"Oh, right."

"What is this?" asked Thoth.

"Brad. He prefers to be called 'Landfill,'" Pete replied.

"That is good to know. Have a good day, gentlemen!" Thoth pushed his cart up the main aisle, crying, "Fifty cents bulbs!"

A customer came and looked at us like we were under glass. "Is that Korean guy here? I need some help in Electrical and he's the only one who knows what he's doing."

Pete stared back. "Korean? There's no Kor— You mean Osric? No, he's not here. I can get somebody else, though."

Several minutes later, another man asked for help at the other end of the store loading concrete.

"I'll get somebody down there," Pete assured him. "How many bags do you need?"

"Fifty."

"Pull your truck up and he'll meet you by the big doors."

"Thanks."

"Fifty bags of concrete!" Pete looked at me expectantly.

"What?" I said. "What's the matter?"

"This looks like a job for Superman!" Pete cried gleefully.

I shook my head. "You're a nerd."

Pete was deeply disappointed. "Why? Because I made a comic book reference? Or because I play *Dungeons & Dragons* twice a month? Or because I have all one hundred and twenty-four episodes of *Voltron* on tape plus *Fleet of Doom*? What? Don't judge me! Only God can judge me! Anyway, it doesn't matter because I'm always the one with the information."

"What information? That's not even a segue!"

"All the information!" He lowered his voice to a stage whisper. "Did you know Chastity sells drugs to pay her rent?"

"You told me that before. What kind of drugs?"

"I don't know. Weed, probably."

"I thought she was on probation."

Pete shrugged. "I'm not her probation officer."

"How do you know she still sells drugs? Did she sell some to you?"

He pounded the desk. "Do you think I got where I am today by using drugs?"

I gave that a second. "Does she sell them here?"

"She's not *that* stupid."

I shifted my weight and leaned on the counter. "Let me sit down a minute."

Pete eyed me suspiciously. "Why?"

"Because this last week, my feet have started to hurt the last hour or two of my shift."

Pete got up. "Okay, but you've got to take the headset."

"No problem."

"And you need to get some new shoes."

"Why?"

"What are those? Vans? No cushion. No arch support. Look around: what kind of shoes do two-thirds of the people who work in this store wear?"

"I have no idea."

"Same as mine." Pete stamped his foot.

"New Balance?"

"New Balance."

"When I was in school, New Balance were buddies," I said. "A step up from those plastic Payless shoes."

"The world turns, my friend," said Pete. "Things change. They're cool; you missed it."

"I guess so."

"This is serious business," Pete said. "If there were no retail stores, New Balance would go bankrupt. Try some. You'll like them. Only cost about a day in the Station. Maybe a little more. I think I paid fifty-five for mine."

"Do they pay you to give people this spiel?"

70

"They should."

"I'll think about it," I said.

"You do that. Now tell me something: what's going on with you and Chloe?"

I looked at him sharply. "What? Nothing. Just talking. Why?"

"*Nothing* is why! Have you taken her out? Have you even called her?" Pete threw up his hands. "What are you waiting for? Have you decided to hold out for someone with bigger boobs after all? Somebody skinnier?"

"No!"

I liked Chloe so much I thought I was developing psychological problems. When I thought about her, which was all the time, I lost my appetite. I told him none of this.

Pete was holding eye contact with me. "So why haven't you called her?"

"I don't have her number."

He threw the phone list at me. "Solved."

"I'll ask *her* for it," I said, tossing the list back. "The next time I see her."

"Whenever *that* is. If you miss the boat . . ."

I scowled at him. "Why are you so worried about the boat?"

"I just want to know why you're farting around!"

"I don't know!" I exclaimed. "I don't know."

"Penn! Penn, it's not that serious. You're agonizing over the first date? For what?"

I scowled. "Why are you giving me advice? You don't have a girlfriend."

"How do you know?" Pete asked. "Okay, I don't. But that doesn't mean I don't know what I'm talking about. Just ask her out. And if you don't have the stones to do that, then just forget about it."

I sighed. "You have a point."

Pete leaned against the counter and folded his arms. "Penn, the reason so many people never get anywhere in life is because when opportunity knocks, they're out in the backyard looking for four-leaf clovers."

"What are you talking about?"

He shrugged. "Hell if I know; it's the motivational quote for the week in the break room."

My headset beeped. "Thank you for calling the House Station at State and Garber. How can I— What the—"

"What?" said Pete.

"It's an automated message. Somebody's trying to sell me burial insurance."

"Let me transfer it to Rex," Pete said. "This crap makes his day." He hit the transfer button on the phone and nothing happened. He slapped the phone and tried again. This time it lit up, and Pete transferred the call to Rex's office.

"This phone . . . Atwater knocks it on the floor every damn day." Pete picked it up and shook it, and something rattled inside. "I think you have a customer."

She looked like a gopher sniffing for food. I didn't want to get up.

"Can I help you?" I called.

"Where are your books?" the woman asked. "The how-to kind, I mean?"

"Past this desk, down the main aisle on your right," I said, pointing.

"Fifteen feet away, in your line of sight, in plain view," said Pete in an undertone.

Superman strolled by the desk with a soda. He was a young guy, Indian, short and well muscled.

"Don't let Rex see you with that soda," Pete said.

"I just loaded fifty bags of concrete," Superman said. "Fifty bags at forty pounds each. That's one ton of concrete. I don't want to hear it from Rex or anybody else."

"We meet at last," I said, proffering my hand. "Penn Reynard."

"Bhagwandas Sivasupiramaniam. Good to meet you."

It rolled off his tongue, and I couldn't have repeated it for a million dollars.

"I've been meaning to ask you," said Pete. "What brings you to Jerkwater, Missouri?"

"My grandmother," Superman said. "My grandfather died, and I came out here to look after her until my uncle can move here this summer. Then I'll go back to Saint Louis at the end of the semester."

"You're from Saint Louis?" I asked. "That's where I'm from."

"Yeah?" Superman said. "What part? Where'd you go to high school?"

"University City. Same as Nelly. And Tennessee Williams."

"I went to CBC. Mike Shannon and Larry Hughes."

"You stole Larry Hughes from us!"

Superman shrugged. "We won state."

Pete waved his hand for attention. "What the hell are you guys talking about?"

I ignored him. "So you're taking classes here?"

"At LCC."

"Everybody but you and me goes to LCC," Pete said to me.

"What are you studying?" I asked.

Superman shrugged. "Haven't decided. I'm taking general ed classes that'll transfer."

The intercom shrieked. "Lot Attendant, please come to Register Two!"

Superman tucked his soda bottle into his apron. "I hate these people. Duty calls."

When he was gone, Pete punched me in the arm. "Ask her out. I'm not kidding."

I sighed. "I will. I'm working up to it."

"'Working up to it.' Are you running a marathon?" Pete shook his head. "Kids these days."

Day 137 – Friday, March 26

"We need to get Landfill fired," said Paige, resting her ample bosom on my counter. "There's got to be a way."

"Huh?" I said. I'd been thinking about Chloe. A month later, I still hadn't asked her out. But we'd been talking more frequently. I was getting close.

"I said we need to get Landfill fired."

I looked at Paige. "Sounds good to me. What'd he do this time?"

"He's trying to be a head cashier when he's scheduled on a register. He keeps leaving to help customers. I've only got two cashiers tonight."

Pete came over from the Service Desk. He gave me a look that clearly communicated his concern over his whole imaginary me-and-Paige thing and how deeply indebted I was to him for running interference.

"Party over here?" he said.

"Shouldn't you be on the phone?" Paige asked.

"Atwater's got it until the end of his shift," Pete replied. "He's trying to dump it on me, but I'm not having it. He'll just wander off. What's up?"

"Paige is trying to get Landfill fired," I said.

Pete raised an eyebrow. "Why? What's his crime?"

"He's an asshole," Paige said. "Have you not noticed?"

Pete snorted. "That's not a crime. If it were, sweet Jesus, there wouldn't be enough prisons. We'd have to send them all to the moon. I'd have a county all to myself."

"On the moon, you mean," I said.

"Wait," Paige interjected. "You don't want to get him fired? You hate him as much as anybody."

Pete nodded. "Both statements are true, but I don't see how they're mutually exclusive."

"If he were here, he would come up to us and say something like 'Gee willikers, there are a lot of people here whose names start with P!'" I said.

74

"He might," said Paige. "If he doesn't stay on that damn register . . ."

"Tell Kord," I said.

Her eyes lit up. "I've got a temporary solution. He and Lucresha are my cashiers. I'll send her up here and tell her to help you guys clean up the desk. Then Landfill will have to stay put." Paige rubbed her face with both hands. "I just want to get a chain and chain him to that register. God, I'm going to get so drunk tonight."

About twenty minutes after seven, Lucresha came to the Service Desk. She was in her thirties, rail-thin, and had intricately braided hair.

"This desk is a mess," she declared.

She produced a can of Goof Off and set to work on the desk's many strata of gummy tape residue. Lucresha and Pete made small talk while I handled a rare three customers in a row, all with legitimate returns. When they were gone, I went back over to the Service Desk.

"Looks gross," I said, examining the gooey mess of tape, glue, and industrial cleaner she'd created.

"It looks like KY Jelly," said Lucresha.

"I wouldn't know," I said.

She sighed. "I would. I have to give my kid enemas all the time. He can't hardly take a crap on his own."

"Okay," I said, and went back to my register.

Thirty minutes before close, Pete said, "Take the RTVs back. I'll take care of Returns."

"I'll get to it."

"I think you should take them back *now*."

"What are you, my mom?" I said.

"Do it because I said so. Because I've had enough. Because you've dicked around for months. Because there are no customers at the Paint Desk *now*."

"What? She's not—"

75

"She's covering a shift."

"How do you know she doesn't have any customers?"

"I called her."

"You called her."

"Yes, I called her! Now take your ass back there! Jesus, I'm like your fairy goddamn godmother. If you come back without a date, then one or both of you better be gay and I never want to hear about any of this ever again. You're damn lucky she hasn't found somebody a little more motivated by now."

"You seem awfully confident about all of this."

Alarmingly, Pete said nothing.

"What else did you talk about?" I demanded.

"Just go! Procrastination's not going to get you anything except my foot up your ass."

After remaining where I was long enough to appear defiant, I loaded up the RTVs and headed out. Anxiety hit me like a breaking wave. When I got to the desk, Chloe was down an aisle, pricing merchandise. She didn't see me and I kept going. I deposited the RTVs and stood in the back of the store for several minutes.

Why *hadn't* I asked her out yet? Pete was right. What was I waiting for? What was the worst that could happen?

She could say no, be weirded out, and never talk to me again.

I was doing a terrible job of motivating myself. I'd feel a lot better when it was over, I told myself. I kicked the cart into motion before I could overanalyze further.

Chloe and I made eye contact the instant I turned the corner. Panic gripped me, but I couldn't very well stop in the middle of the aisle.

What was I going to say to her?

"Hey, Penn," she said.

God, she looked so gorgeous to me at that moment: the way her short hair framed her face, the way her lavender shirt set off her paint-stained yellow apron, the way the corner of her mouth turned up in the barest hint of a smile because she genuinely enjoyed Paint.

I parked the cart off to the side. "How's it going?" I said, looking down at the counter.

"Good. Kind of slow tonight."

"It's always slow."

"Not in Paint. It gets pretty crazy sometimes."

"Yeah?"

"Yeah."

I made myself look up and suddenly developed a terrible itch on the back of my neck. Come *on*, Penn, I said to myself.

"Listen," I began lamely, "are you doing anything Saturday night? Tomorrow?"

Chloe tucked her hair behind her ears. It was adorable. "Let's see . . . I'm pretty sure I'm busy tomorrow night."

"Working?"

"No," she said, slamming my heart against the rocky shores of rejection. "I'm doing something with Bethany. My roommate."

"I see." I was numb. "Never mind, then." She'd hit me with the vague excuse. There was nothing to be done for it now.

She crossed her arms and studied me a moment. "But I *am* free Sunday evening."

I don't mean to overdramatize in the slightest, but it was like the gates of heaven had opened. A sudden swell of courage opened my mouth.

"Would you like to have dinner with me on Sunday?" I asked.

"Sure, Penn."

I tried to think of something more. "Um . . . do you like hockey?" was the best I could do.

"I've never been."

I didn't dare stop talking. "Leetown has a very minor league team. They're playing on Sunday. I've only been to a handful of games myself. We could go if you want." It all came out extremely fast.

"All right," she said, still smiling.

"Great," I said. "I'll give you a call. Wait, I don't have your number."

Chloe took paper from her apron, scribbled her number, and handed it to me.

"Thanks. Well, I guess I should get back up to Returns," I said, wanting to linger.

"Okay. See you, Penn."

I pushed the cart back to the front of the store, feeling dizzy. The butterflies in my stomach were doing some kind of dance. The paper in my hand was gold.

Pete pounced immediately. "Well? You guys are going out tomorrow, right?"

"Nope."

"What do you mean, no?" Pete was horrified.

"We're going out on Sunday."

He punched me in the arm. He meant it to be hard, but Pete wasn't very strong. "You bastard! Well, that wasn't so bad, was it?"

"Yes it was. I need some Gatorade and a nap."

He shook his head. "Down the road, when you guys are married, you'll look back on this and laugh; all your farting around will seem stupid to you."

"It seems stupid to me now," I said.

Day 138 – Saturday, March 27

I'd never been good at the go-out-and-get-a-date thing. It never came naturally and it usually gave me anxiety attacks. I didn't know what the problem was. My self-esteem was fine otherwise. My face wasn't hideous. I'd played baseball in high school and made those baseball pants look good—so good, in fact, that it should have counted as a public service for all the ladies . . . but that didn't mean I knew how to talk to a single one of them.

I went through most of Saturday in a state of single-minded daydream. I had the morning shift and Pete had the closing shift, so there was nobody to talk to but Atwater. They'd stopped scheduling two Returns cashiers simultaneously on weekends because business wasn't justifying it. This was fine with me; I was grateful for the personal space. Only the occasional customer and the clatter of the Service Desk phone on the concrete floor interrupted my reverie.

At eleven, Kord brought me a stack of huge yellow paper signs.

"You're probably going home early," she said. "You like Returns, don't you?"

My guard was up instantly. "Compared to what?"

"Compared to being on the other end on a register."

"I've never *been* on the other end on a register."

"Do you want to?" she asked.

I shrugged. "I think I'm good here."

"If you're sure. You ever want a change of scenery, let me know."

"Is there a problem?"

Kord shook her head. "You've got some of the best cashier ratings in the store. But we like to rotate people so nobody's stuck on Returns too long if they don't want to be. Returns is more high-stress. In this store, everybody we've put up here besides you has hated it."

"I think going down there would be boring," I said. "Leave me here."

"Fine," Kord said. "Some of the signs you made got torn up. I need you to make some more."

"My signs are like my children," I said. "I love them all, but there's always more where those came from."

Kord looked surprised. "You have kids?"

"Oh, heck no," I said. "That was a joke. I'm not the type."

"Not the kid-having type?"

"I'm not *married*."

"So?"

"So for me," I said awkwardly, "That makes it a biological impossibility."

"Hm," Kord said. She was finally picking up what I was putting down. "Wow. So I wonder how you feel about me, being gay and all."

This caught me completely off guard. I had no idea what to say. The smartass part of me recovered fastest.

"You're *gay*?" I said.

"I mean it, Penn. I had no idea. I never would have guessed based on the way you've treated me."

"What do you mean?"

"You act like you don't care," she said.

I was on perilous ground.

"It doesn't matter," I said. "As far as us being cool and everything, I mean. Yes . . . I believe that it's wrong, that it's a sin . . . But I'm not going to act like it's somehow worse than any of the many sins that straight people do." I winced and looked at her uncertainly.

She looked back at me thoughtfully but didn't say anything.

"I mean," I continued, still uncomfortable, "We're all sinners here—I can be friends with you without condemning you. I can, you know, love you as a person without accepting it as right; those are two different things. I'm not going to be a jackass about it."

Kord shook her head. "I've never met anybody like you, Penn."

I didn't quite know what to say to that, so I said, "What was I *supposed* to act like?"

"I was raised Catholic, you know," Kord said. "So was my girlfriend. You can imagine we didn't get a very good reaction. Not from my parents—when I came out to them, my dad said, 'Yeah, no kidding.' But from everybody else, there was a lot of judgment."

"I can see that," I said. "Do you still go to church?"

"No. Not in a long time." Her phone rang. "Yeah? I'll be right there. Bye. Penn, I'm glad we talked about this. I have a lot more respect for you now."

I treasured up all these things and pondered them in my heart.

Day 139 – Sunday, March 28

It was Sunday, so I was working. I was going to come home at five, shower, go pick Chloe up, and take her to dinner. Then we'd go to the hockey game at seven. That *was* the plan, but this was the House Station.

"Can you stay late?" Landfill asked at 4:45. "Edna hasn't shown up yet."

I sighed. "When was she supposed to get here?"

"4:30. She's scheduled 4:30 to 8:30. We close at eight on Sunday, remember?"

"I know when we close!" I snapped. "Look, it's quarter to five. I have to count down. I'll get overtime."

The work week ended on Sunday at the House Station, and overtime under any circumstances was verboten.

"No you won't," Landfill assured me. "I called Kord. Since you went home early yesterday, you're fine."

I resisted the urge to grab him by his smug face. "You called Kord at home?"

"She told us to call if we had questions."

"Have you called *Edna*?"

"I tried. Her right number's not on file. You dial it and somebody'll tell you she doesn't live there."

"I can't stay late today, *Brad*." In my great need, I condescended to use his proper name.

"But I need you to! Atwater would be the only one up here otherwise!"

"So? He has a till. He can do Returns."

"But he hasn't had his lunch yet. Somebody has to be here to cover his lunch."

I sighed. "You want me to cover his lunch?"

"Yes."

"Who's going to cover the phones?"

"You are."

"And my register?"

"Move your till over there."

"What if we get a Service Desk customer?" I said. "I don't know how to set up a special order or a will-call."

"Um . . . You can call Rovergial. He's the ASM tonight. He knows all about the Service Desk."

"I can't stay late today!"

"Why? What have you got going on?"

I slapped the counter. "I have commitments! I have to be somewhere at 5:30!"

"Where?"

"It doesn't matter where!"

Landfill sniffed. "Doesn't sound that important to me. Can't you reschedule? You can go at six when Atwater gets back."

God, he was whiny. God, I was soft.

"Six," I said. "No later than six. Send him to lunch *now*. I'm going to count down at 5:30 whether he's back or not." That was an empty threat and we both knew it.

"Okay, good." Landfill clapped me on the shoulder, which only vexed me further.

I almost shoved Atwater out the door. I went to sit down at the Service Desk and stew, but I didn't get the chance: I got slammed for thirty solid minutes. I had a long line and constant phone calls, but fortunately everything was returns or sales and I didn't have to handle anything I didn't know.

Suddenly, it was still, silent except for the overhead music. All the customers were gone like dew from the morning grass. I sat down and took a deep breath.

And jumped back up immediately. I hadn't had a chance to call Chloe to tell her I'd be late. I dug in my pockets for the number, but I didn't have it on me—it was at home, on top of my dresser. Panic gripped me for an instant, and then I lunged for the phone list. I found her number and dialed.

"Hello?"

"Hello, Chloe?"

"This is Bethany." Then there was silence.

Take some initiative, woman! "Can I *talk* to Chloe?"

"She's in the shower."

"It's kind of important. Could you just give her the phone?"

Bethany sighed like she had a million better things to do right at that moment. "Yeah, hang on."

An elderly customer spotted me over the top of the monitor. I willed him to go away. He didn't.

"Hey, sonny, where's the ceiling fans?" he asked.

"Turn around," I said. "Look up."

"Oh! How about that?"

I realized I was grinding my teeth.

Finally, on the phone: "Hello?"

"Chloe?"

"This is Chloe. Penn?"

"Yeah, it's me," I said. "Listen, I'm still at work. My relief never showed up. I'm here until six covering a lunch. I can be at your place by 6:30, assuming Atwater comes back on time. We can still go to the game if you want. We won't have time to eat beforehand, though, I'm sorry. Or we can forget the hockey and just have dinner. Look, I—"

She jumped in when I paused for breath. "Penn! Take it easy. We can go to the game and grab something there. Or we can eat afterward."

"Are you sure?"

"It's fine, okay?"

"Okay. I'll get there as soon as I can."

"Okay."

I sank into the chair and let out a deep breath. It wasn't Plan A, but it was hardly a disaster, either.

Atwater didn't come back until 6:15.

I knocked and Chloe opened the door. She was wearing dark jeans and a pastel green collared shirt. For a moment I just stood and admired her.

"You look great," was the best I could do. She also smelled great. And I'm a huge dork, great.

"You clean up pretty well yourself," she replied.

I was just wearing jeans and a black polo—rarely worn items that had never seen the inside of a House Station. I didn't really know what else to do to get snazzy for a date.

"You might want a jacket," I said. "It's kind of chilly."

I guess Jeff was rubbing off on me, because I remembered to open her car door for her.

They were singing the national anthem when we arrived at the arena.

"I think our seats are that way," I said, pointing. "I've only been here a couple of times. Or did you want to get something to eat? Did you eat before?"

"Not really," Chloe said. "I mean, I didn't really eat before. We can get something." She made a beeline for the nearest concession stand.

I caught up and overtook her by the time she reached the line. "I've got it," I said. "What do you want?"

"A hot dog and a Coke." She pulled out some money.

"No, no," I said. "I'll get it."

"But you got both tickets," Chloe said.

"It's fine. I've got it. Please?"

She gave me a look. "Just this once." She slipped her money back into her little black purse.

84

"Soda, nineteen minutes," I said as I scanned the menu. "Hot dog, twenty-eight minutes."

"What's that?"

"Hm? Oh, Pete was telling me the other day how he looks at things in terms of how much time at work it costs him. The exchange rate is about seven minutes to a dollar, before taxes."

Chloe laughed. The perfect laugh, like a choir of angels or some such.

We got our food and found our seats with five minutes gone in the first period. They were decent seats, ten rows up and directly behind one goal.

"Okay, what have we got going on here?" said Chloe.

"Do you know hockey?"

"I played field hockey for two years in high school. I assume it's about the same."

I shrugged. "Probably. Okay, the team in white and gold is the Leetown Bling."

"The what?"

"The Bling. You know, rappers, jewelry. Bling. I have no idea who owns the team or who thought that was a good idea."

"Interesting."

"And the team in green—" I looked at my ticket stub "—is the Tyler Habaneros. I don't have the slightest idea where Tyler is, but this is a podunk independent league—that might actually be the name of it, Podunk Independent League—but it wouldn't surprise me if all the teams are from jerkwater boondocks."

"Like Leetown, you mean?"

"Yeah. No offense."

Chloe raised an eyebrow. "Why would I take offense?"

"Because you're from here."

"So? You live here."

"No kidding." There was a stoppage and I squinted at the players. "Okay, let's see. The logo on their jerseys is a chili

85

pepper wearing a cowboy hat, so I'm going to guess it's somewhere in Texas."

"So is Leetown any good?"

"I don't know; I haven't been to a game all season. You have a hair on your sleeve," I said, reaching over and plucking it off. "Orange longhair tabby."

"Well done," said Chloe. "It's Bethany's cat."

"I'm a cat person. I have two."

"Yeah?"

"Adele—you'd like her; everybody likes her, she's the friendliest cat ever. Nobody likes the other one. Even I don't like him. He's the stupidest cat alive. He burned half his whiskers off when he—"

I realized I was starting to ramble on about cats like an old lady and decided to quit talking. A glance at Chloe's face told me I had stopped before any damage had been done.

She opened her mouth and a siren wailed. The crowd went berserk. Leetown had scored.

I leaned closer to be heard over the din. "I guess most of these people are pretty dedicated."

When play resumed, Tyler scored almost immediately, quieting the crowd.

"So, how do you like the House Station?" Chloe asked, then twisted in her seat to face me. "You know what? Forget it. I take it back."

"What? Why?"

"I don't want to talk about the House Station. I *know* we have work in common. For me to ask you that now would just be filler. Let's talk about something else."

"Suits me," I said. "What'd you do today?"

"I got up, went to church, and spent most of the afternoon doing homework."

"Where do you go to church?"

"Good Shepherd Episcopal. It's down the street from the Wal-Mart."

"You were raised Episcopal?"

86

Chloe nodded. "What about you?"

"Lutheran. Although these days I spend all my Sunday mornings at work, or I'd go."

"They won't change your schedule?"

"I haven't exactly asked. But if it keeps up like this, I will."

"You should."

After a while, I said, "So . . . you told me you wanted to be a teacher. Let me ask you this: if you could do anything in the whole world, what would it be? Within your abilities, I mean—like, you can't be the first woman quarterback in the NFL unless you have some amazing skill set you haven't told me about. Something where all you needed was an opportunity."

"Would I still want to be a teacher, you mean?" She smiled. "That's a good question. I'll have to think about that. You?"

"Write. Assuming I didn't pass my tryout with the Saint Louis Cardinals."

Chloe snapped her fingers. "That reminds me. I finished reading your story. I'm sorry I took so long with it."

"You didn't take any longer reading it than I did getting it to you," I said. "What'd you think?"

"I really enjoyed it. It held my interest. I thought the conversations were realistic."

She was using a tone of voice that made me say, "But . . .?"

"The confrontation at the end, between the girl and her mom. I thought it was good, but it could have been more forceful. That's the punch of the whole story."

"More forceful how?"

"Well, it's like the breakout moment of her life, the first time she's ever stood up to her parents. But when she talks to them, she seems too restrained."

"Because she's afraid of them?"

"No, that's not it—the point of the story is how she *isn't* afraid of them anymore. She's too *respectful*."

"Okay, I can see why you say that, but why is it a problem?"

The first period ended and half of the crowd surged toward the restrooms and concession stands.

"I don't know," Chloe said. "It's not how I would have talked to my parents in that situation."

"Who's different?" I asked. "You, or your parents?"

"Both. Maybe that's why I wasn't thrilled by the ending. But that doesn't mean it's a bad ending—and the more I think about it, the better I like it."

"I can handle the truth," I said. "I'm not trying to convert you."

"No, I mean it. It's fine. Don't readers root for the character to do what they would do in her place?"

"What the reader *thinks* he would do."

"If you make her go off on her parents," Chloe continued, as much to herself as to me, "you run the risk of making her the bad guy. So you threw in a little 'honor thy parents.' It's good. Also, I think you're pretty good at writing women. You don't always see that with male writers."

"Thanks," I said. "For example?"

She crossed her arms. "Tolkien leaps to mind—he didn't even bother. Yeah, *Lord of the Rings* was great and blah blah blah, but he was awful at women characters. Maybe you can get away with having no real female characters if you're writing a nerd epic, but not in most genres of literature."

I didn't feel qualified to take any shots at Tolkien. "Because nerds don't know any better?" I said. "You sound like Angry Pete."

She punched me in the arm for that, harder than Pete ever had. "I think it was because Tolkien didn't have any sisters. Do you have any sisters?"

"No. A younger brother."

"Hmph. Then I have no explanation for it."

I shrugged. "One of my professors once asked me if I was a mama's boy when I turned in a story centered on a woman. I think he finally decided I was gay. So there's no good explanation for why I may or may not be good at writing women characters. I'm not even a particularly sensitive person."

"No?"

"No."

"I don't think people are good judges of their own sensitivity," Chloe said.

I stood and stretched. "I'm going to go to the restroom before the second period starts. You want me to bring you anything?"

"From the restroom?" she asked, masking a smile.

"Cute," I said.

I stood on the concourse for a few minutes, reviewing. I thought I was doing pretty well. We hadn't run out of things to talk about yet. She seemed to be having a good time. And the most amazing thing was, I was actually starting to feel a little bit comfortable with her.

Day 140 – Monday, March 29

"There's a computer around the corner," Angry Pete told the emaciated blonde girl across the counter. "You can fill out an application on that. Wait. How old are you?"

"Why?"

"Why what?"

She put her hands on her bony hips. "Why do you want to know how old I am?"

Pete rubbed the bridge of his nose. "You have to be eighteen to work here."

"What? How come?"

"Tools. Machines. Forklifts. They don't want you kids getting hurt on that stuff."

"I'll be eighteen in two weeks," said the blonde.

"Then you've got two weeks to rethink your life choices," Pete replied. "Come back then. If you fill out an application now, they'll put it in the trash. They won't hang on to it and they won't call you."

"Can I drop off a résumé?"

"We don't take résumés."

"What, not at all?"

"Straight in the trash."

"Are you even hiring?"

Pete shrugged. "I have no idea."

The girl made an irritated sound in the back of her throat. "Thanks a lot," she said, then headed for the door.

"If I don't see you, happy birthday!" Pete called. He waved me over. "Skeletal bitch," he muttered. "If she weighs more than ninety-five pounds, I'm Harry Houdini. Not bad looking, though."

"They're going to hire her just to spite you," I said.

"Yeah, probably. Anyway, tell me how it went."

"How what went?"

Pete raised a finger. "Don't give me that. I want to hear about the continuing adventures of my two favorite virgins."

"Pete . . ."

"Don't make that face. You look constipated."

"I should punch you in the face."

Pete shook his head. "People have been saying that to me a lot lately."

"Pete."

He twisted the headset cord through his fingers. "Everyone seems so angry these days, you know that?"

"Pete!"

"*What?*"

"Tell me you didn't ask her that."

"Ask her what? Oh, *that*? Oh, *hell* no. You think I'm stupid? You think I want to get bitch-slap decapitated? No thanks."

"Then how do you —"

He jabbed a finger in my face. "How is she so different from your puritanical ass? Hm?"

"What does that even mean?" I said.

"What does *what* mean what now? Penn, what the hell are you saying? Are you freaking speaking English?"

"Pete—"

"Freaking speaking!" Pete cried. "Madness! Madness has descended on the conversation! I don't know what the hell you're saying. I don't even know what the hell *I'm* saying. Thank you for calling the House Station and Rental Center at Garber and State, would you like to hear about our specials today? Fantastic, no worries. I'll transfer you." He punched buttons on the phone.

This was my chance to seize control of the conversation. "Pete, tell me why you said she's a virgin."

He looked at me with a puzzled expression. "Why wouldn't she be?"

"Okay, well, people change. Just because they're one way now doesn't mean they weren't another way before."

He raised an eyebrow. "What? Did she tell you something?"

"No, nothing like that," I said.

He gave me a scrutinizing look. "This is a big deal for you, isn't it? You're not going to do it until you get married, right? And you want it to be the same for her."

"Just forget it," I said.

"Penn, I'm sure she is."

"I said forget it."

"I'll find out for you if you— Hey, look who's here."

Edna, yesterday's scheduled relief, had come through the door and was heading down the main aisle toward the break room.

"Hey, Edna," Pete called.

She stopped. "Hi," she said.

"Where were you?" Pete asked.

"What do you mean? I'm not supposed to be here until twelve."

"Except for yesterday," I said.

Pete began to laugh uncontrollably. He fell on the floor behind the desk and lay on the dusty rubber mat. Edna looked at me, then at where Pete had been standing, then shrugged and went on her way.

Pete sat up and dusted himself off. "That was great! 'Except for yesterday.' Tell me about the date already."

He listened with unusual restraint, although he obsessed about the extreme likelihood that Chloe had been naked when I talked to her on the phone, which I had not previously considered.

"So when's the next date?" he asked.

"I don't know."

"Are you a couple now? Official?"

"I don't know."

At this point, he threw up his hands. "Come on, Penn! I can't help you every step of the way. You're a grown-ass man! Show a little gumption!"

"I *will*."

"Good. Now, off you go." He flicked his fingers and shooed me back to my register.

Day 141 – Tuesday, March 30

At the end of my shift, I dropped by the Paint Desk. When I saw Chloe, I suffered another attack of the spastic butterflies. They weren't putting in their A-game, but they were still at it.

"Hey, Penn. Are you off?" Chloe was wearing a chocolate brown collared shirt that matched her eyes perfectly, but I didn't have the composure to articulate that at the moment.

"Just about. Are you closing?"

"Yeah." She looked at me expectantly. "What can I do for you?"

You've got to give the people what they want. I forced it out. "I was wondering if you were free any time this week."

"When are *you* free, mister full-timer?" Chloe asked.

To my complete frustration, our schedules for the rest of the week were utterly in conflict.

"What about a week from Saturday?" I said. "I've got Thursday and Saturday off next week. It's amazing, really."

"I work that Saturday, but I get off at five."

"Well," I said, clearing my throat, "do you want to go do something?"

"Sure. What do you have in mind?"

"Uh, I don't know. I hadn't gotten that far."

She smirked. "Think about it."

"I'll do that," I said.

Quick, and nearly painless. Now all I had to do was wait a week and a half.

Day 142 – Wednesday, March 31

Colonel Goodenough, my nemesis, came through my line again. He didn't have a receipt for his returns, so the transaction suspended, again. To my horror, while we waited for the head cashier, he started a conversation.

"Did you go to KLU?"

Sometimes, when people write, they say someone "groaned inwardly." I groaned, vomited, and punched him in the face inwardly.

"Yeah, I went there," I said through clenched teeth.

"What was it, four or five years ago?"

"One."

"Are you in school now? Where are you going?"

"Not at the moment."

93

"But you're going to? What was your major?"

"English."

He nodded sagely. "Well, when you go back, just remember, it's good to go somewhere else, get some variety."

"You have no idea," I muttered when he'd turned away.

Finally, Kord arrived. "What did he do?" she said to Goodenough. "Did he break it? Did he screw up again?"

Ordinarily, this kind of thing from Kord didn't bother me in the slightest. We kidded each other all the time, no big deal. But I was mortified. I tasted blood in my mouth and I realized I was biting my lip.

"If it happens again, we can just fire him," Kord joked.

I turned away from the register and glared at nothing while Kord cleared the return.

At last, Goodenough left.

"Kord," I said.

"Yeah?" She turned. "What's the matter?"

I'm sure I looked murderous. "Do you remember," I said, my voice carefully measured, "how I told you about the guy at school who screwed me over with my gym credit? That was him."

Kord went red. "Oh, my God. Oh, hell. Penn, I'm so sorry."

I nodded.

She put her hands on my shoulders and looked me in the eye. "I'll make it up to you. I promise."

"How?"

"I don't know. I'll think of something, okay?"

"You better," I said, slightly mollified.

She gave me a quick side hug. "I will."

After she'd gone, the Lot Attendant, Booker Shoeboot, lumbered in with a load of carts.

"How's it going, Booker?" I said.

"Hey, buddy." He talked the way little kids talk—sing-song, almost. "I think it's going to rain. It's getting kind of cloudy and cold out. I'll see you around."

94

"Okay, Booker." I was still irritated. "Atwater, I'm going to the restroom."

He was busy running his fingers through his mustache and I didn't know if he heard me. I went anyway.

On the way back, I stopped by the break room, just to be away from Returns for a few minutes and get the stink of the last several minutes out of my mouth. As I walked through the doorway, I heard Pete's shrill voice.

"What is that? Why do you have two big-ass cans of Slim Jims in your locker?"

He and Landfill were huddled around Landfill's locker.

"They're not," said Landfill. "One's full of Jolly Ranchers."

"You should consider replacing that with a can of sit-ups," Pete suggested. "Hey, Penn."

"I thought you weren't working today," I said.

"I'm not. It hurts my insides to be here when I'm not on the clock. I forgot my jacket yesterday, in which are all my pay stubs that I need to do my taxes because these clowns get too excited about withholding my money, so I had to come in and get them, life's a bitch and so on and so forth, hallelujah, amen."

"Landfill, do you have any peach Jolly Ranchers?" I said.

Landfill, who was rooting around in his locker, looked up. "No. They don't include them in the regular variety pack anymore. They substituted blue raspberry. And don't call me Landfill."

"When'd they do that?" I asked. "I only liked the peach ones and the watermelon ones. You're telling me they don't make the peach ones anymore?"

"No, they do," Landfill said, "but they package them with the Passion Fruits, which are really hard to find."

"Lord almighty," said Pete. "I award you the Nobel Prize for Candy. Please tell me you own stock in the Jolly Rancher company."

"Hershey's makes Jolly Ranchers," said Landfill.

Pete opened his mouth, then closed it, then turned and stalked past me through the doorway. Not wishing to get stuck talking to Landfill, I followed.

"They put tablecloths on the tables in the break room," Pete said without looking back. "Did you notice that?"

"Can't say as I did."

"Plastic, country-looking gingham things. Talk about putting lipstick on the pig. Little house on the damn prairie . . ."

Kord stopped us. "Penn, remember we've got a cashiers' meeting Sunday."

"I don't have to go to that, do I?" Pete asked.

She squinted at him. "Are you a cashier? Oh, and the store meeting is next Sunday."

"Crap!" I exclaimed.

"Son of a bitch!" Pete cried simultaneously. "Let me sleep!"

"Can I just get a tent and live in the store?" I said. "Is there some way we're supposed to be finding out about these kinds of things?"

Kord shrugged. "It's posted on the wall in the break room."

"I never see that stuff," I said. "I go home for lunch."

"I saw it," said Pete. "The announcement was hand-written. Seriously?"

"Take it up with Rex," said Kord. "I don't have time to play daycare with you kids, okay? Run along home or wherever you're supposed to be."

We reached the Service Desk, where Atwater was handing a woman about his age a gift card. "Don't spend it all in one place, ha, ha," he said.

Pete rolled his eyes. "Hey, did you ever get that story published? The one you were telling me you sent out?"

"I haven't heard back yet."

"Maybe they think you'll take the hint. That was months ago. How long do they take?"

"Most places say six months."

Pete shook his head as he pulled on his jacket. "There's no excuse for that, not in 2004. Now, if you'll excuse me, I'm going to get the hell out of here."

Jeff was flipping channels when I entered the apartment.

He looked up and shook the glaze from his eyes. "I feel like I haven't had a chance to talk to you in a couple days. Crazy work schedules, I guess. I ran into your friend Goodenough at the Athletics Center today."

"What a coincidence," I said. "What did he want from you?"

"He was on me to get somebody to sweep the basketball courts. But we only had a couple of people there, and it had already been swept once."

I kicked my shoes across the room. "This was during class time? Figures. He came through my line and started a conversation."

"I'm sorry, bro. Oh, hey, I was looking for you the other night."

"Yesterday?"

"No . . ." Jeff thought for a moment. "Sunday. A bunch of us went to a movie. You should get a cell phone."

"Don't need one," I said. "Anyway, I was out."

"I *know* you were out, because you weren't *here*. I figured you were at work."

"Don't get sassy with me. I was at the hockey game. On a date."

"Oh, bro, way to go!" Jeff exclaimed. "Who is she?"

"Her name's Chloe. She works at the House Station."

"Are there going to be any *more* dates?" he asked, so cheesy.

"That's the plan."

"Cool, congratulations. I want to meet her. Hey—" Jeff snapped his fingers at the TV. "Does that look like the guy from *Gone with the Wind* to you?"

"It's not him," I said.

"I know it's not him. But it looks like him."

"I guess."

"What's that guy's name, anyway?"

"Rhett Butler."

Jeff shook his head. "No, the actor."

"I can't remember."

"That's going to bother me until I can think of it," Jeff said.

"Hang on." I picked up the phone and dialed my friend Dwayne, who, in addition to owning *Gone with the Wind*, was a font of useless information.

"Hello?" said Dwayne.

"Hey."

"Penn? Hey, man."

"Quick question for you. What's the name of the actor in *Gone with the Wind*?"

"Clark Gable."

"Thanks." I hung up the phone and turned to Jeff. "Clark Gable."

"That's right." His attention was still on the TV. "Who'd you call?"

"The Knowledge Hotline."

Now Jeff looked at me with a marvelous expression of awe on his face. "Is that free to call?"

I tried not to laugh too long. Then I went in my room to write.

Day 144 – Friday, April 2

Pete flagged down an apronless Kord heading down the main aisle.

"What?" she asked. "I'm trying to take my narrow ass home."

"You're off the clock?"

"Yes!"

"It'll only take a second!"

Kord stopped at the Service Desk. "What? I don't need your mouth right now."

"Yes you do," Pete said. "I'm the highlight of your day. Hell, I'm the highlight of my own day."

She laughed. "Make it quick."

"I have concerns about this," Pete said, indicating a display of Natural Citrus Air Freshener. There was currently a display of it at every register in the store.

"What about it?"

"It's not safe. Check it out." Pete pulled a permanent marker out of his apron and started scribbling on the countertop.

"Pete, what the *hell* are you doing?" Kord shouted.

"Just wait! Sharpie, right?" Pete ran his finger over the marks he'd made; they didn't smudge. He took a can of the air freshener and sprayed his marks liberally. "Like magic!" He wiped the counter with a paper towel, leaving no trace of ink. Only the pungent odor of chemical orange remained.

Pete looked at Kord expectantly. "So you really think it's a good idea to breathe this stuff?"

Kord was having difficulty looking as mad as she wanted to. "Don't let Rex see you do that. You know what, just don't do it again, okay? Not ever. Sell it, don't breathe it. Buy some and play at home."

Pete radiated innocence. "All I'm saying is, this stuff should be recalled."

"Penn, keep an eye on him," Kord said, heading for the door.

"Disintegrate your damn lungs!" Pete called after her.

Day 146 – Sunday, April 4

Cashiers meetings were all the same. First, somebody brought a lame snack, like a big bag of plain store-brand chips or maybe pretzels. But if you ate it, there was nothing to drink when you got thirsty.

About ten minutes after the meeting was scheduled to start, Kord would get tired of waiting for stragglers and begin. The stragglers, meanwhile, continued straggling in for up to fifteen more minutes. And there were always a couple who didn't show up at all.

Kord would begin by telling us what we were collectively doing well and what we were collectively screwing up; usually there was a lot more of the latter. This time, it primarily had to do with the continual failure of cashiers to keep the logs updated when tagged items set off the Sensormatic alarms.

Apparently the people in Loss Prevention (who were only heard about and never seen, except for Fielding Vargas) were making quite a big stink about our store. That was the way of things: the district people dumped on the managers, the managers dumped on the department heads, and the department heads dumped on us.

At our first meeting, I'd pointed out that at Returns, the Sensormatic alarm was on the store side of the register, so everybody who wanted to check out there with tagged merchandise set it off (and then they panicked, turned around, and set it off again). Kord had mentioned it to Rex, but it didn't get changed. Nothing ever changed.

Then we would watch a video that ranged from utterly boring to unintentionally hilarious. These videos covered whatever we were doing wrong or whatever new policy the House Station powers had decided to implement. The video would typically demonstrate proper cashier procedure and give several examples of incorrect procedure. I had little doubt they made them in-house with actual associates; the dialogue was corny and the acting was atrocious—House Station associates couldn't even believably act like House Station associates. If Kord happened to step out of the room during one of these films, somebody would hit fast forward. This time the film was about properly deactivating sensor tags.

We were given procedure booklets to go along with the films. There was a page in the back with multiple-choice questions we had to answer as we watched. Ninety percent of the questions were either common-sense obvious or worded in such a way that any answer but the right one was ludicrous. Kord was more concerned with making sure everybody had all the right answers than with anybody actually learning anything, so we went through them together like second graders before she collected them.

We usually didn't learn anything at these meetings, and that was fine. The corporate people made us go, so we went. We got paid and we got an hour cut from our schedules to make up for it, so on the whole, I guess it worked out well for everyone.

Day 147 – Monday, April 5

The customer pounded his fists on my counter. "Jesus Christ! I wish just once I could come here when it's stocked! Or find somebody to help me! Where are all your people? It's like a goddamn volcano in here! You can hear yourself echo! I'm never coming here again!"

He was looking at me, so I said, "Uh . . . okay."

"You!" the man shouted, and his eyes got big. "You're going to grow up to be a failure, kid, because you're not much of a merchandiser!"

The man headed for the door, muttering profanities.

"A volcano?" I said.

"Penn!" Atwater called. "Come take the phone for a minute."

If the world ever ran out of M&M's, the man would become a quivering ball of anxiety.

I went and took the headset. "Be quick," I said. "I'll be the only one up here."

"If you get a return, you can do it on my register," Atwater said.

"Not if it's cash."

Ideally, you never did anything on anybody else's register, but touching another man's cash was a fireable offense.

"Okay, okay," said Atwater, pulling off his apron.

You took your apron off when you had to get somewhere quickly. If you kept it on, a customer would pull you aside to help in some department you knew nothing about. It happened every time.

A man leaned over the Service Desk counter and waved a key at me. "Can you make a key?"

"The key machine is halfway down the main aisle on the right," I said. "I'll get someone to meet you there." The key machine fell under the jurisdiction of Hardware.

"Here, just take it. I have to go to the restroom."

"I'll *get* someone for you," I repeated.

"What, don't you know how?" the man asked.

"I can't leave the desk."

The man grunted, skeptical, but departed with his key. I dialed Hardware.

Day 149 – Wednesday, April 7

Kord came by Returns to chat. "You applied to grad schools, right? How's that coming?"

"I'm still waiting to hear."

102

"You know the House Station offers tuition assistance? Have you looked into that?"

I snorted. "Yeah. I talked to Helen about it. It's not going to help me. They only offer it for programs that have something to do with my job. If I were getting my degree in electrical something-or-other, *then* they would give me money. Which seems like they're missing the point: I'm going to school so I don't have to work here for the rest of my life."

"You're going for creative writing, right?" said Kord. "Tell them you need it to make me happy with your sign-making."

I smirked. "Think they'll buy it? I already filled out the forms and sent them in, and I got turned down. I guess I could try again. Anyway, I think the program is targeted to people getting undergrad degrees. What does anybody at the House Station need a master's for?"

Kord clapped me on the back. "It was worth a shot."

Day 151 – Friday, April 9

"You know what makes me mad?" Pete asked, interrupting my daydream about the time I'd get to spend tomorrow with Chloe.

I adjusted the headset. "Everything?" It was another dead Friday night at the Station.

"Mats," said Pete.

"Mats?"

"Mats. Look at these crappy half-assed mats we have here." He kicked at the long slab of rubber that ran behind the Service Desk. "It's as hard as the floor. It's like a car tire."

"All the mats are like that."

"In *this* store. Did you ever see the mats at Wal-Mart? They're twice as thick. They have give to them. You feel *good* when you stand on them. Next time you go to Wal-Mart, go find a register nobody's using and stand on the mat. You'll see what I mean."

"Does it really make that big of a difference?"

"Penn, why did you come over here and sit down and take the phone?"

"Because it's dead and I'm bored and I don't have any customers."

"And?"

"What 'and?'"

"And because your feet hurt, right? Your feet always start to hurt at the end of your shift—that's what you said."

"Because I stand up for eight hours."

"If you stood up for eight hours on cushiony Wal-Mart mats they wouldn't hurt."

"What are you, a podiatrist?"

Pete shrugged. "Just trying to help. Oh, you know I got my first overage the other day?"

"Congratulations."

Store policy on the tills was thus: at the end of the day, the amount of money in the till and the amount of money that the computer thought was supposed to be in the till had to be within five dollars of each other, or you got written up. Two in a month and you were on your last strike: another before the statute of limitations expired on the first one and you got fired.

Kord came down the main aisle. "Penn, make me a sign for a display of light bulbs. Make it clever."

I shot a rubber band at her as she passed. "Bring me some signs!"

I turned to find Pete jabbing an accusatory finger at my feet. "You've still got those crappy shoes on, man! When are you going to take my advice and get some better ones? If you want to keep wearing that skateboarder crap, fine, but then don't bitch about how much your feet hurt."

"I never do that."

"Sure you do. You come over here, you sit down, you take off your shoes, you rub your feet—it's gross. You're a passive-

104

aggressive bitcher. Look, Rhonda is the only cashier in the store who gets to sit down at her register. Do you know why they let her sit down?"

"Because she weighs three hundred pounds."

Pete guffawed. "Yeah, but what I meant was, do you know *how she got permission* to sit down?"

"She asked Rex?"

"Wrong! *You* ask Rex to let you sit down and see what happens."

I shook my head. "It's bad enough when he catches me sitting here without the headset."

"What did he say when he saw you sitting down?" Pete asked. "Did you tell him your feet hurt?"

"No. He asked me if I needed something to do."

"You should have said, 'No, man, I'm cool just sitting here.'"

"So how come Rhonda gets to sit down?" I asked. "You were about to tell me when you distracted yourself."

"Rhonda's got a doctor's note. Penn, don't you see? This job discriminates against people without health problems! *Self-inflicted* health problems! Once I get the legal ramifications figured out, I'm going to sue this dump."

I sighed. "Pete . . ."

"I'm serious! *I* can't sit down."

"You're on Service Desk," I said. "You sit down half the day."

"Okay, forget that. *You* can't sit down. And you can't get a doctor's note, either. Why? Because *you're* not morbidly obese, that's why!" Pete had worked himself into a bright red frenzy. "Don't even get me started on fat people! A drain on our damn healthcare system! Having all that diabetes and all those damn heart attacks! It's a freaking national crisis!"

I waited for him to calm down.

Pete took a deep breath. "You ever shop at Aldi?"

"Yeah. So what?"

Pete shook his head. "Try to keep up, would you? What about their cashiers?"

I thought. "They all sit down."

"Exactly! Every last one of them in every store I've been in sits down. I feel your pain. Solidarity." Pete thumped his chest. "Clearly, the solution is for you to double your body weight as quickly as possible. You have a customer."

"Thank you for calling the House Station and Rental Center," I said into my headset.

"I can help you over here," Pete called to the lady who was standing at my counter, looking around like she expected me to materialize out of thin air.

I didn't really have a call, but I didn't feel like getting up.

I watched Pete handle the transaction. The lady was returning a hose that she claimed leaked the first time she used it. Pete looked at it suspiciously, then at the lady even more suspiciously, then shrugged and tossed the hose onto the floor behind the counter.

"This refunds to my credit card, then?" the lady asked. "I need to buy a different kind." She had a nervous tic.

"Yeah. Look, ma'am, I need you to fill out the return slip," Pete said.

She gave the slip a suspicious look. "I have to fill out all of it?"

"Name, phone number, signature," Pete said, an edge to his voice.

"Oh, but I don't want to put my name," the woman said. "Or my phone number."

Pete drew in a long, slow breath, then let it out just as slowly.

"Can I just give you my driver's license?" she asked.

Pete made a choking sound and looked at me, incredulous. I turned away to keep from laughing. The lady was now hunched over the slip like she was taking an exam. For a full minute she stayed like that, clutching the pen and not writing.

"Just make something up!" snapped Pete.

The lady gave a start, then hastily filled out the sheet. Pete snatched it and gave her the receipt.

"That'll refund to your credit card. Have a good evening," were the words that came out of Pete's mouth, but his tone was more along the lines of "I hope you get hit by a bus soon."

The woman left in the direction of Garden, muttering to herself.

"Take it easy," I said as Pete rounded on me, mouth open.

"Do you get people like that often?"

I shrugged. "How often is often?"

"Once is too much. You're bleeding again." Pete picked up the hose and went to tag it for RTV.

"What? Where?" I held my hands up and turned them over. There was a long scratch on the back of my left hand. The blood had beaded and dried.

Pete came back. "How is it you never notice these things?"

I handed him the headset so I could get the first-aid kit. "It didn't hurt. I have a very high pain threshold."

"That's a good thing? Like, you could get your leg chopped off and bleed to death and not even notice, and that's something to be proud of?"

"Don't be mad because you're soft," I said.

Day 152 – Saturday, April 10

There wasn't a whole lot to do in Leetown, and in ten days, I hadn't come up with any date idea I felt strongly enough to commit to. After wasting half an hour in deliberation, Chloe and I settled on miniature golf.

"It'll be fun!" Chloe said. "I haven't been miniature golfing in a long time."

"Are you sure?"

She nodded vigorously, making her short hair billow. "Yes! It's a great idea."

Well, when she said it like that, it *did* sound a lot more appealing.

There were two miniature golf courses in Leetown. The closer one was awful: somebody had paved a lot next door to a bar, covered it with artificial turf, and outlined each hole with bricks. Instead of obstacles like windmills and such, one hole had a broken wheelbarrow cemented in the middle and another had a rusty fifty-gallon drum with holes you had to hit the ball through. Except for the turf and possibly the tetanus, you could easily duplicate this course at any construction site. We went to the other one, which was actually fun to play on and had fewer drunks.

It was an unseasonably warm evening. Chloe was wearing flattering jeans (I had determined by this point that every pair of pants she owned was flattering) and a tight, thin marigold jacket (I thought it was yellow, but she corrected me). I had once again gotten snazzy for our date by showering, shaving, and wearing clean clothes.

On the way, I was so vividly conscious of her presence that it was hard to focus on what she was saying. I had an almost overwhelming urge to reach over and take her hand, to touch her, to hold on to her. But I didn't.

When we arrived, I didn't open Chloe's car door, but I did open the door to Stan's Golforama for her.

"Thanks," she said, heading for the counter and opening her purse.

"Wait a minute," I said. "I thought we discussed this."

Chloe stopped and turned. "What?"

"I'll pay."

She gave me a warning look. "You paid at the hockey game. *And* you got the snacks."

"It's okay. I'll get it."

Chloe made a face that clearly stated she was humoring me. "Look, Penn, you're a nice boy. When you get your book published, you can pay for everything, okay? But in the meantime, let me get it." Her tone brooked no argument.

But in some small swell of bravery I said, "Fine. But after this, we're going to go have dinner, and if you go digging in your purse for that, I'll take it away from you."

"I'd have to call the police then, wouldn't I?" she said with a disarming smile.

We paid the man at the register and he plunked two fat tokens on the counter. I handed one to Chloe and we headed to the bank of gumball machines filled with golf balls. She immediately put hers in a machine filled with yellow balls. "Matches my jacket," she said.

I began to put my token in one of the machines.

"Don't get green!" Chloe exclaimed.

"Why not?"

"It's hard to see. It doesn't show up well on the turf. And if you hit it off the course into the grass, you'll never find it."

"It's that serious?" I asked. "Fine, what do you recommend?"

"Pink gives you a good contrast. Orange is okay, too."

"Orange it is," I said. "I think you might be spending too much time in Paint."

"Is that a fact?"

"Yes." I selected a putter from the bin. "It's not good to bring your work home with you. You don't have a color wheel in your purse, do you?"

Chloe jabbed me with her putter.

I got a scorecard and a scrap of pencil. "Shall we?" We strolled out to the course, which was nearly deserted.

The first hole was one of those anthill/volcano ones.

"Can I have a practice stroke?" I asked. "It's been a while."

"Sure."

I lined up my shot, and as I putted, I hit the rubber mat first. The ball squirted about halfway down the green, then meandered weakly to the side.

"All warmed up now?" Chloe asked as I retrieved my ball.

"Ha, ha," I said. "You want a practice shot too?"

"Wouldn't do me any good. One stroke here or there isn't going to make me into— into— into some lady golf pro."

"Are you going to putt with that purse on your shoulder?" I asked.

"Why not? Otherwise I have to pick it up and put it down every time."

"Suit yourself."

Chloe hunched over the ball. Purse and all, her stroke was fluid and her shot was true. It rolled up the volcano and into the hole. She let out a squeal of delight and jumped up and down.

"Well done," I said. "Ringer."

She stuck her tongue out at me. "It was luck!"

Then something unexpectedly grand happened. I put my ball down and she went to get hers. She leaned over the hole, giving me the most spectacular view of her behind. Under normal circumstances, her butt was practically breathtaking, but like this . . .

"Wow," I said aloud before I could help myself.

"What?" Chloe asked, straightening sharply.

"Nothing."

"You said 'wow.'"

"Wow, it's a really nice night," I said lamely.

She gave me a cunning look. "Yes, it is."

I made a small production of clearing my throat.

"You look kind of red," Chloe said.

"So how was work?" I was going to drag us kicking and screaming to a new topic.

"Oh, no," she said. "We've had this conversation. We didn't come here to discuss work. Now are you going to hit the ball or are you going to stand there looking embarrassed?"

But she was smiling.

It occurred to me then that she had to pick up her ball either sixteen or seventeen more times, depending on whether the last hole kept the balls.

Suffice it to say, I did not play my best miniature golf.

On hole sixteen, Chloe hit her ball off the course and into the pond.

"I'll get it," I said.

"No, don't worry about it. I'll go inside and get another one."

"It's fine, I can get it," I said, climbing down the bank, which was covered in flat stones. "I can see it from here."

But I started a minor rockslide and couldn't recover sufficiently to keep myself from pitching forward into the pond. Chloe shrieked as I went in, as did I, because the water was *cold*. To my credit, I kept my feet and didn't fall down.

"I've got your ball," I said, thigh-deep in frigid water.

"Oh, God! Are you okay?"

I waded out. "I'm fine."

"Penn, you're shivering! Do you want to go home? We can just go home."

"No way. I'm almost dry."

"You're not cold?"

"I don't really get cold," I replied, which was my automatic response to that question.

"It was very sweet of you," Chloe said. "Stupid, but sweet. Next time, though, just listen to me, okay?"

"No argument here."

"That water looks cold. Is it cold?"

"Do you want to find out?"

Chloe picked up both putters. "We're going inside. Come on."

I followed dutifully, checking my pockets. My wallet was dry, at least.

"Why do they even have ponds at miniature golf courses?" I said. "They all have them. What's the point? How many balls get hit in there every day? A dozen at least!"

"Nobody told you to jump in."

"I didn't— Just a minute," I said, and went to the men's room.

111

I took off my shoes and socks and put them under the hand dryer, wringing out the socks as best I could. I couldn't do much about my jeans. After a few minutes, I gave up. My shoes still squished.

"Are you okay?" Chloe asked when I came out. "You want to go home?"

"I said I wanted to take you to dinner," I replied. "I still want to."

"Penn . . ."

"No, I mean it," I said.

She looked at me with the sort of fond look one bestows on puppies. "Okay. We can go to dinner. But we're going by your house first so you can change."

"I wish Jeff had been home," I said, pulling the restaurant door open for Chloe. "He wanted to meet you."

"Told him all about me, did you?" Chloe asked.

"Well . . . no," I said, embarrassed. "But he found out I went out when we went to that hockey game, and you know how it is."

"Your cat was quite charming. The big one, I mean."

"Adele? Yeah. You guys are best friends now. And as far as Drimacus is concerned, you're another toy in his magical world of playthings."

The hostess seated us immediately, but the waitress was a long time in coming.

"So tell me something I don't know," I said, flipping through the menu.

"About what?" Chloe asked.

"Anything. Your family, let's say. Do you have any siblings?"

"Two brothers. One older, one younger."

"Tell me something interesting about them."

"The older one is Matt. The younger is Jonathan."

"That's fine, but it's not *interesting*," I said. "What does Matt do?"

112

"He's a professional football player," Chloe said.

I slapped the menu on the table. "That's awesome. What position? Who does he play for?"

She reddened.

"What?"

"He's a backup defensive back," she said, clearly discomfited.

"So? He's living the dream, isn't he? Playing professional football? Come on, what team?"

"It's not the NFL."

"Come on!"

Chloe sighed. "Last year he played for the Bossier-Shreveport Battle Wings."

I paused. "I can't say I've heard of them."

"You or anybody else," she said. "It's an Arena League team. Most people play offense and defense there, and he's not very good at catching the ball. Anyway, he mostly sits on the bench."

"It's okay," I said. "It's what he wants to do, isn't it? I understand quite a few people watch arena football."

"Do you?"

"Well . . . no."

She chewed her lip. "Neither do I."

"You shouldn't feel embarrassed," I said. "It's not like he works at the House Station."

"Hmph. People get so excited when they find out Matt's a football player. But when they find out he plays arena football, they think it's stupid."

"Okay, it's not the NFL, but I'd trade jobs with him in a hot minute, even though I wouldn't know the Battle Wings if I fell over them."

The waitress finally came and took our order.

"Could we also get some water?" I asked.

She grunted something and left.

"It was nice of her to stop by," I said.

"So," said Chloe. "Do you like traveling?"

113

"Like internationally? I don't know. I've never done it. I'd like to, though, someday."

"I found out LCC has a study abroad program, surprisingly. It looks like a lot of fun."

"Where?" I asked. "When?"

"Belgium. The spring semester of next year."

"Are you going to apply for it?"

"Maybe," she said. "It's kind of expensive."

"You should," I said. "It's not the kind of thing that comes along every day."

The food was as long in coming as the waitress had been, but we didn't run out of things to talk about.

"Can I get a side of ranch dressing, please?" I asked the waitress when the food finally arrived. I'd also asked for it when we ordered.

The waitress never brought it. She never came back until she brought the check.

"Do you have any change?" I asked Chloe.

"Sure. What do you need it for?"

"The tip."

"I have some ones."

"So do I," I said. "Bear with me. Give me all your pennies."

I pulled out some ones for a fifteen percent tip. This I hid under my plate, which had not been cleared. Chloe handed me nine pennies, which I arranged prominently into the eyes and frown of a sad face.

Chloe burst out laughing. "That's great!"

"Isn't it?" I said. "Let's get the heck out of here."

I walked Chloe to her door.

"I'll see you tomorrow morning, right?" I said. "The stupid early store meeting."

"I don't mind it," Chloe replied. "I have to work afterward. You?"

"I'm going to go back home and sleep. I have to come back at 10:30."

"I had fun tonight," Chloe said. "You certainly make things interesting." She looked at me with an intent expression that turned the butterflies loose in my stomach.

"Maybe we can go somewhere without a pond next time," I replied. Our faces were maybe twelve inches apart.

"It was completely worth it just for the entertainment factor," she said.

Eight inches, max. The butterflies were suffocating.

"I wasn't really entertained by that," I said.

"*I* was," Chloe said. "Isn't that what counts?"

Six inches and closing. I was holding her hand now. "Oh, absolutely."

"I'm glad you agree," she said.

Inexplicably, I jerked upright. "Good night," I found myself saying. I was furious with myself.

Chloe let out a short breath. Disappointment? Relief?

"Good night, Penn," she said. Then she went inside and closed the door.

Day 153 – Sunday, April 11

Dark and early, I dragged myself out of bed and drove to the store meeting. Even in my groggy state, I was already thinking about Chloe.

More to the point, I was thinking about how I hadn't kissed her. Maybe I wasn't recollecting correctly, but it sure seemed like she was going to let me.

It was too soon. That was what the hesitant part of me said, of course, but most of the rest of me agreed. Or maybe I was just rationalizing.

"Whatever," I said aloud as I parked my car.

I didn't feel awake. I staggered through the front door and clocked in on my register, then headed down to where the chairs were set up in the wide Lumber aisles.

Kord and Greg the ASM were cooking breakfast on electric skillets. There was an abundance of greasy sausage, and ten or fifteen associates were lined up for eggs. I found a cup of water and looked for a seat.

Chloe flagged me down from the back corner. She pulled her jacket off the seat next to her so I could sit down.

"Morning, sunshine," she said.

I was acutely aware that I was not at my best. I was wearing sweats and my hair wasn't remotely combed. "Morning," I grunted, rubbing my face. I still had eye boogers.

Chloe had a small plate of fruit pieces, which she offered to me. I waved it away.

"Not a morning person?" she asked.

"If God wanted people up at this hour," I replied, "he would have made it light outside."

"Are you getting a merit badge?" Chloe asked.

I shrugged.

"You have no idea?" She was determined to get me awake and conversational.

I shook my head.

"You're cranky."

I made an effort. "Sorry. I don't know. For cashiers it's all computerized. Average transaction time. Number of voids. Accurate till counts. Those types of things. I can't imagine Paint would have many stats to track."

"No, the department heads pick," Chloe said. "Tom got it last month."

I shrugged. I didn't really know Tom, except that he was better than most at getting his Returns.

Chloe persisted. "So if it's all computerized, you should know whether you're getting one."

"I don't know all the details. For Returns, it's different. I'm pretty fast, but you get a lot more voids that aren't your fault just from customers who don't know what they're doing."

"Surely they take that into account."

"They don't."

There was the unpleasant clang of metal on concrete as Angry Pete tried to wedge a chair between me and a rack of plywood. Pete rattled the chair. "Scoot over!"

"Good morning, Pete," said Chloe.

"Is it?" Pete mused. "I wonder."

Rex came to the front, picked up the microphone, and waved for attention.

"I want each of you to remember that we're all part of the House Station family, and that as manager, it's my job to help your dreams come true. The House Station has done very well in the last year—currently we're opening one new store each week across the country. Profits are up. We're still the third-largest chain, and we're gaining ground on Lowe's and leaving Menards behind."

"What the hell is Menards?" said Pete.

"Now, you may be wondering what all this has to do with you," Rex continued. "Well, first of all, it lets all of us keep our jobs." He wasn't joking at all. "And now, the House Station is giving all of us the chance to have a greater share in that profit. The House Station is beginning a program where every associate will have the ability to buy House Station stock directly from the company. I want to encourage every one of you to take advantage of this opportunity, to reap the benefit of the hard work and Excellent Customer Service that each of you put in every day. We'll be posting information in the break room about it; you can also talk to Helen or go to the Station Network website for associates for more information."

"Yeah, I'll get right on that," Pete whispered. "I make eight dollars and fifty cents an hour. How am I supposed to buy all this stock? Although, the way they exploit us, I bet our stock does pretty well."

Rex had moved on. "I know there's been a lot of talk about whether this store will be getting self-checkout stands. The answer is no."

"Job security!" said Pete.

"Self-checkout stands are profitable for supermarkets, although they always lead to increased theft. In a supermarket, this isn't a big deal, because everything sold is low-value," Rex said.

Chloe leaned toward me. "If theft goes up, how is it profitable to have them?"

"If you have them, you can get rid of half your cashiers," Pete said.

"The House Station sells many small items with high prices," Rex continued. "The self-checkout stands were tested in several stores, and they proved to be problematic. In short, there are no plans for our store to get any, either now or in the future."

"'Problematic' means the customers didn't know what they were doing and kept messing them up," said Pete.

When Rex finished his agenda, which included requests for people to quit stealing other people's lunches out of the fridge in the break room and for people to quit leaving their trash from eating other people's lunches all over the tables in the break room, all the department heads took a turn. None of the departments had made their projected sales except Garden and Décor.

Then Helen, the HR manager and scheduler, read us the "motivational" quote for the week: "Persistence is often the defining quality between those who fail and those who succeed." While I agreed with it in principle, I couldn't for the life of me figure out how it applied to my job.

Then they gave out the merit badges. I got one, my second. Pete got one, his third. Chloe didn't get one and looked disappointed. Superman got Employee of the Month.

"Maybe next time," Pete said to Chloe when the meeting was over.

"Sorry," I said to her.

"It's not a big deal," she said, and seemed to mean it.

I turned to Pete. "How do you keep getting these?"

Pete fingered his merit badge. Identical to every other merit badge issued by the Station, it was an embroidered fabric disc, not quite three inches in diameter, with the House Station logo and the words *Merit Badge – Excellent Customer Service* on it.

"Because I'm great. And because Atwater and I are the only full-time people up there. Some of these part-time people . . . dear God, Penn, you've seen how it is. Like Kirsten, the one that's always eating snacks at the desk. Crackers, pretzels, fruit. She says it's 'for medicinal purposes only.'"

"Pete, she's diabetic," I said.

Pete blinked. "That may be."

"And she's got a merit badge. Which she got here, working part-time."

Pete waved a hand. "Okay, forget that. I'm talking about Atwater. Did you think he was going to get one? No chance in hell. Man, last week—you were off, I guess—Atwater knocks the phone off the desk, and when he bends over to pick it up, he spills his goddamn M&M's all over the floor, the big peanut kind. And Tekla comes out from the phone room and slips on them and almost busts her ass." Pete giggled. "It was hilarious. She was *this* close to slapping him. She took him in the phone room and bitched him out for ten minutes."

"I saw him eating M&M's at the desk yesterday," I said.

Pete shrugged. "I never said he was a genius."

"You get a hundred dollars when you get five, right?" said Chloe. "You're well on your way. You should take us to lunch."

"Maybe I'll get four and they'll fire my ass," Pete said. "Then I'll have nothing."

"What does being fired have to do with anything?" Chloe asked.

"It has everything to do with everything," said Pete. "This is the House Station. Everybody gets fired sooner or later. Fired, wrongfully fired . . . it's just a matter of time."

"When you get fired, can I have your merit badges?" I said.

"Yeah, why not? They won't do you any good, though—it doesn't matter how many little discs you have; the store keeps the records."

I yawned fiercely. It was 7:30 and I'd been up for two hours. "I'm going home," I said.

Superman passed by and Pete grabbed him. "You're taking us to lunch, right?"

"What?"

"You're Employee of the Month. I guess they don't know how much you hate them. They gave you a hundred bucks, right?"

"A hundred and fifty," Superman replied. "But since I *am* Employee of the Month, shouldn't you take *me* to lunch?"

Pete clapped his hands. "Sneaky bastard!"

"Anyway, I'll catch you guys later," Superman said. "I have to make it to church."

Watching him go, Pete said, "I thought he was Hindu."

"Why?" I asked. "He never said anything about being Hindu."

Pete shrugged. "He's Indian."

"So? That doesn't mean anything," I said. "According to tradition, the Apostle Thomas went to India and —"

"Forget it!" said Pete. "Did I ask you to recite the damn encyclopedia? Why aren't *you* going to church?"

"Because I have to come back and work before my church's service gets over."

Chloe squeezed my arm. "I have to go get ready for work."

"Sure," I said. "See you later."

"Did you kiss her?" Pete asked as soon as she was gone.

I sighed. "Pete, I'm going to go home and sleep."

"It's a simple yes-or-no question."

I didn't respond.

"So no, then."

"It's too soon."

"You're right," said Pete. "I forgot who I was talking to. I'll ask again in eight or ten months."

Day 156 – Wednesday, April 14

"I've been giving this a lot of thought, so hear me out," said Pete. "I think I figured out why we're behind Lowe's. It's the ads."

I adjusted the headset. "Home Depot, Lowe's, the Station—the ads are all the same. They all have unnaturally friendly employees helping abnormally well-behaved customers."

"Yes, but look beyond that," Pete said with an arcane wave of his hand. "Who's the voice of Lowe's? Who does their commercials?"

"Gene Hackman. So?"

"So what does Gene Hackman have to do with some tools? Not a blessed thing! But what does it matter? He's Gene Hackman, damn it, and if Gene Hackman tells you to buy some tools, you take your ass to the store and buy some tools!"

"If you say so."

"Compare and contrast. Who does the House Station have?"

I shrugged. "Some guy with a deep voice."

"That's exactly who it is!" Pete exclaimed. "Some guy with a deep voice. Nobody you've heard of."

"And that's why we're third?" I said. "It has nothing to do with the fact that we have fewer stores than they do?"

Pete groaned. "You missed it. Try to stay with me. When Gene Hackman makes everybody buy more tools, profits go up. The company expands. More stores open. That crap is *simple."*

"Assuming for a moment that there's a valid point in there somewhere screaming to get out, what about Home Depot?" I said.

"What about them?"

"Who does their ads?"

Pete thought about this for a moment. "Well, they had that guy from *Home Improvement.* Then he died and they got that guy from *Dukes of Hazzard."*

"And this doesn't affect your theory at all?"

"My theory is about *Lowe's.* Home Depot is Home Depot; nobody's catching them. They have more stores than Lowe's and the Station put together. They could have *me* doing their voiceovers and half the people in America would think I was a girl and it still wouldn't matter. Plus, they have that catchy tune. The Station doesn't have that, either."

"So are you just going to cry about it or are you going to write to the people in corporate and make a constructive suggestion?"

Pete tugged on his apron straps. "Equally productive options. They don't care what we think. And why should they, considering that monkeys can—"

"Don't start with the monkeys."

"You're the one who always brings them up! Frankly, though, a large percentage of the people who work here don't deserve to have their opinions heard. I honestly can't blame the people in Austin, the marketing people, for not wanting to sort my kernel of wheat from the mountains of chaff. You have a customer."

I handed Pete the headset and went to my register.

The man waved a fistful of receipts. "I need to get the tax refunded on some purchases I made earlier."

This was not uncommon. People made purchases all the time for churches and schools, and more often than not they didn't have their letter from the Missouri Tax Commission. If they did, they filled out a form, we took the tax off, and that was that. Otherwise they had to bring the letter and the receipt back. It was simple in theory but annoying in practice because every tax refund needed a head cashier's authorization.

I took the first receipt from the man's pile and entered the information. It prompted me for authorization before I could do the next one.

"Well dang," I said. There were sixteen receipts.

"What's the problem?" the man asked.

"The register is set up in such a way that this is going to take me a little while. I have to run each receipt separately. Do you have any shopping you need to do?"

"Yeah."

"Okay. Just fill out this form and hopefully I'll have this all done by the time you get back." I slid a tax refund form across the counter.

"I don't have to fill out sixteen of those, do I?" the man asked warily.

"I'll get it photocopied."

As he left, I looked down at the stack of receipts. Lowe's, I'd heard, had this process entirely computerized. Maybe that was why they were ahead of us. I dialed the head cashier.

"Hello?" It was Paige.

"You got twenty minutes?" I asked.

"I'm with a customer," she said, and I heard a toilet flush. "I'll be there when I can."

I waved to Pete. "I'm totally locked up until a head cashier gets here."

"That's great, man," said Pete. "Great news."

"I've got to go to the back and make some copies of this anyway," I said, switching my register light off.

I walked to the other end of the store, made copies, got a drink, and came back. There was still no sign of Paige. I busied myself filling out the amounts on each tax slip.

The Sensormatic went off as a customer came up and dropped a huge band saw on my hand.

"Ow!" I cried, much in the same way any other person on earth would have. I yanked my hand free and massaged it.

"Excuse *me*," snapped the man, like it was my fault.

"*He* will help you over there," I said through clenched teeth, indicating Pete.

Grumbling, the man hauled his saw over to the Service Desk.

Finally, Paige appeared. She clutched my arm. "I'm supposed to warn you to watch out for people taking pictures of other people's credit cards with their camera phones."

"Yeah, sure," I said, flexing my sore fingers. "Everything come out all right? With that customer, I mean."

"Smartass. What do you need?"

"I need you to authorize sixteen tax refunds."

"Are you serious? Why are you so mad about it?"

The skin under my thumbnail was purple. I was gritting my teeth. I tried to relax. "Customer. It's fine."

"Poor baby. Want me to kiss it and make it better?"

"No, I'm good," I said quickly. "Thanks, though."

Day 159 – Saturday, April 17

"What the *hell* are you *doing*?"

I jerked my head up at Angry Pete's shriek from the phone room.

"Son of a bitch! You think this is funny? I'm going to kick your ass eight ways from Sunday! *Nine* ways!"

I was concerned for Pete, not because I thought he might be in danger, but because Rex was somewhere in the building and Pete's voice was really carrying. I threw the headset down and went to the phone room, almost running into Landfill, who was coming out.

I forced Landfill back inside. "What's going on?"

Pete was peeling duct tape off his apron. He was red and doing a fair imitation of my murderous face.

I occupied the doorway. "Pete, what happened?"

"I was filing some special orders and this sack of ass tried to tape me to the chair." Pete shook with anger. "What the hell are you, five years old?"

I entered the room and got between them. "All right, calm down. Rex is here. Take it easy with the shouting and swearing."

"It was just a joke," said Landfill blithely. "Jeez. Can't you take a joke?" His phone rang. "Hello? Yeah, I'll be right there." He hung up, cheerfully said, "I'll see you guys later," and left.

Pete seethed. "I'm going to beat his fat rapist ass."

I put a restraining hand on his shoulder. "No, you're not."

Pete wadded the tape into a ball and threw it on the floor. "Why not?"

"First, he's got fifty pounds on you. Second, you'd get fired."

Pete, still glaring, was undeterred. "I'll follow him home, beat his ass there."

"They'd still fire you."

"You're right—he's a tattler." Pete banged his fists together. "If I'm going to get fired, I'd rather do it here in front of God and everybody."

"That's not how you want to go out," I said. "Let's just tell Kord."

"He doesn't even know he did anything wrong!"

"You don't think Kord'll make that pretty clear to him?"

"I'll throw him under the goddamn forklift," Pete muttered. He was starting to cheer up.

"Come on out," I said. "There's nobody on the phone."

Grumbling, Pete followed me to the desk and grabbed the headset.

Landfill was coming back up the main aisle, heading for Garden. "If you've got time to lean, you've got time to clean!" he called to us.

125

Pete saluted Landfill's back with the double bird.

A few minutes later, Landfill came back with a flat cart, which he parked on the other side of my register in the place usually reserved for large returns. On the cart were three torn bags of solidified concrete that had obviously been rained on.

I waved a hand at him. "What's this? You can't put this here."

"RTV it," Landfill said.

"I can't RTV concrete just because it got wet. Take it down to Building Materials. They need to mark it down and throw it away there."

"Why was the concrete out in Garden in the first place?" Pete demanded.

"Because some people in Garden don't do their jobs," Landfill replied.

"You don't do your job either," said Pete. "Get that crap out of here."

"Somebody from Building Materials can get it when they come for their returns," Landfill said, and left.

Pete's eyes narrowed and he chewed on his lip. "God, I hate that kid."

I made a sign and hung it on the cart. "Crush-it-yourself gravel!"

"That's clever," said Pete. "Funny stuff."

Rex wasn't as impressed. I had finished with a customer and was starting to lean against my counter when he came booking it down the main aisle, a man on a mission. I straightened up and found some work to do the instant I saw him, but he'd already spotted me. He cut through my aisle without looking at me, paused briefly when he saw my sign, then kept going out the front door.

About two minutes later, he came back in, ripped the sign off, wadded it up, and threw it away, all without breaking stride. "Penn, call the departments and get them to pick up this stuff," he said, heading whence he came, probably to his lair in the back.

126

After a moment, Pete called, "It's Landfill's fault."

"What?"

"If he'd taken that crap down to Building Materials when you told him to, Rex wouldn't be pissed at you."

"I didn't do anything," I said.

Pete shrugged. "Doesn't matter. You never want to have Rex's attention."

"Why was he running outside?" I asked.

"Will saw somebody putting flyers on people's windshields in the parking lot. He called me and told me to tell Rex." Will was the head of Garden.

"You didn't tell me."

"You had a customer. I'm sorry, okay? Like I said, Landfill's fault."

"You're just shifting blame."

"What better place to shift it?"

I shook my head and turned back to my register, a vague anxiety tugging at me.

Day 160 – Sunday, April 18

Chloe had a bemused expression on her face. "Interesting date idea."

"I didn't invite him!" I hissed. "He invited himself!"

"He's going to break our rule."

"What rule?"

"That we don't talk about work outside of work," said Chloe.

Technically, that was *her* rule, but I didn't want to get into it.

This wasn't supposed to be a *date* date, but I'd been looking forward to spending some time with Chloe. It served us right for going to IHOP.

Pete returned from the restroom and slid into our booth. "Did I miss anything? Did the waitress come? Of course she didn't."

"Hi, Pete," said Chloe graciously.

"How's it going?" He craned his neck, searching for the server.

"Do you have tomorrow off, too?" she asked.

"No, I come in at eight. Why? You both have off? Going on some all-day date?"

Chloe said, "We're both off. But I have class."

"You're not hanging out with Penn just because he's a classless individual? Ha! Sorry, that was stupid." The waitress came and Pete shifted his attention to her without missing a beat. "Let me have the chocolate chip pancakes with some sausage. And some hot chocolate."

After the waitress left, Chloe, who'd ordered a salad, said, "How do you stay so skinny eating like that? I can't even imagine how many calories that is."

"Can't gain weight if I try," said Pete.

"Must be nice," Chloe muttered.

Pete steepled his fingers. "Let me tell you about a phenomenon I saw today. More of an observation about life in general. Well, a proverb, really. Okay, here it is." Pete held up his hands dramatically. "Old people *always* have exact change."

We just looked at him. "That's all you've got?" I said.

"Have you never thought about it?" Pete asked. "They do, and they always take the longest time to dig it out. That never happens to you? You never had an old lady digging in her purse spreading pennies and nickels all over your counter?"

"I had two today," I admitted. "One had a little coin pouch."

Pete clapped his hands with glee. "You see? But *why* do they always have exact change?"

"Because they don't like to use credit cards," Chloe suggested.

Pete scoffed. "I think we're about past that, aren't we? I mean, we've had credit cards for forty years."

"Fifty," I said. "At least."

"Why, then?" asked Chloe.

"I don't know," Pete said, tapping his chin. "But I do know that old people are the easiest to mug."

"Then maybe they'd rather lose a few nickels than their credit cards!" I snapped. "What does it even matter?" I was still irritated that he'd crashed our IHOP party and was out of patience for his inane chatter.

"It doesn't; but what does *anything* really matter?" Pete mused. "Are there really life lessons to be learned from these mysteries? Here's another one: fat people wearing pink. In all the world, is there anything that looks quite as pathetic as—"

"Stop," I said. "Just stop. Did you talk to Kord about Landfill?"

"Hell yes. Boy, was she *pissed*! Ooh, she was pissed!" Pete gave a delighted shiver. "I'm sorry he was off today."

"So that made your day."

Pete shrugged. "Yeah. Except nothing's going to happen to him. She'll yell at him, but they aren't going to fire him for it."

"He'll get written up. It'll go in his file," I said.

"So? Most people get fired outright way before there's enough in their files. Not Landfill, though—he's their patsy. We'll come back in twenty years and he'll be the store manager. He and the Station deserve each other."

The food came and Pete ate like he hadn't seen food in a week. As the first one finished, he proceeded to take advantage of his captive audience.

"At the Service Desk, we handle special orders and installations, right? So from time to time we have to be in touch with the Station Specialty Installer. Anyway, this lady, she was maybe sixty, was getting a new water heater installed in her house, and they were going to take away the old one. So the guys go in the house, and it smells like absolute crap."

"Pete!" Chloe exclaimed. "We're eating here."

"Sorry. So like I was saying, it just reeks with the terrible stench of animal dump. Straight *feces*. There's cat litter all over the floor. There's a big pile of it in the closet. And this lady has like seventeen cats at least, and the ones that don't run away from the installers are hissing and growling at them. And you know what the lady says?" Pete paused for dramatic effect. "She says, 'Don't mind my pets; they've never seen another human being before.'"

I put down my fork. "That's the worst thing I've ever heard."

"That can't really have happened," Chloe said, a look of consternation on her face. "What's wrong with that lady?"

"She's crazy!" Pete exclaimed. "No ifs, ands, or buts about it. Crazy old ladies and their cats."

"I have cats," I objected.

"Not the same. This lady has like eight times the cats you have. And she cleans up after them at least eight times less often. But as a cat owner, tell me this: why is it always cats? Why don't these creepy old ladies that live by themselves ever have seventeen dogs? Or fifty-seven hamsters?"

"Why would you think I'm qualified to answer that question?" I asked.

"I just want a second opinion," Pete said. "Because I don't have the faintest idea."

The food had improved my mood somewhat, and I decided to take a crack at it. "Well, you can't really have hamsters for companionship—they don't do anything but bite you, and they die for no reason, like goldfish. Besides, you can't have hamsters running around loose; they'll chew through your wiring and burn down your house. It's got to be cats or dogs."

"So how about dogs?" said Pete.

"Cats use a cat box. Dogs have to be taken outside. Now, it's true that an unattended cat box can get pretty disgusting, but as long as that box is there, even if it's piled to the heavens, there's still that excuse that they're litter-trained."

"That's disgusting," said Chloe.

"Sorry."

"Okay, cats, fine," said Pete. "But why *seventeen* cats?"

Here Chloe chimed in. "Because generally speaking, the friendliness of one dog is equal to the friendliness of several cats—well, maybe not Penn's cat. You don't need seventeen dogs for companionship; you need two or three, tops."

Pete snapped his fingers. "I think you've got it there. I really do. Yes, the friendliness of your average dog does equal the friendliness of, say, six of your average cats. Give the lady a prize. You have solved the equation."

Pete stayed with us until the end. Even after we'd paid the bill and were standing outside, he seemed reluctant to get in his car.

"Didn't you say you had to go in early tomorrow?" I said.

"Yeah." Pete sat on his bumper.

"It's 12:30."

He glanced at his watch. "I have 12:35."

"Don't you need to sleep?" Chloe asked.

He shrugged. "How much mental energy and concentration does my job require? Half? Half of my attention. Four hours of sleep, then."

"*If* you can stay awake at work," said Chloe.

"The headset beeps when you get a call. Anyway, I guess I'll leave you guys to it."

Finally, he got in his car and drove away.

"He lives with his grandparents," I told Chloe. "I wouldn't be in such a great hurry to go home, either."

"He needs a girlfriend," Chloe said.

I smirked. "Where do you propose to find him one? Work? There aren't any good candidates there."

Chloe looked indignant. "What are you trying to say? No, wait, you're right. But there's a lot of turnover. Somebody might come by one of these days; you never know. There's somebody for everybody. Even Pete."

"That's what they say, anyway. Do you want to have dinner tomorrow?"

"Sure," she said. "I should be free by six."

"You want to come over? I can cook," I said.

"That sounds fun. Let's do that."

"Great," I said. "Jeff might be around, but he won't be underfoot. Like some people."

"Oh, that's no problem," said Chloe. "I'd like to meet him."

"If I tell him you're coming, he'll probably clear out."

"Tell him he's not intruding. It's his house, too."

"Well, here's the thing: in his last apartment, before he moved in with me, Jeff would come back from work and his roommate and his girlfriend—his roommate's girlfriend, I mean—would be hot and heavy all over the couch. He learned to rattle his keys in the lock before he came in. He's pretty sensitive about that kind of thing. Won't watch any movies with nudity. He walked out of *Booty Call* when it turned out not to be about pirates. Why are you laughing? I'm serious."

"He sounds like a sweetheart," said Chloe, grinning.

"That's about right," I said.

Day 161 – Monday, April 19

When I woke up, Jeff was asleep on the couch with the TV on and the remote clutched in his fist. Drimacus the Eviscerator was chewing his socks.

I prodded Jeff. "Hey. Are you off today or are you late for work?"

Disoriented, Jeff sat up. "Oh, hey, bro. No, they switched the schedules around. I'm working some nights now."

"You spent the night on the couch?"

"Yeah, I guess I did."

"You know you can lock Drimacus in the bathroom whenever he bothers you," I said.

Jeff sat up, dislodging the little Siamese, who began gnawing his shoe.

"No, he was okay," Jeff said.

I picked Drimacus up and gave him a gentle shake. "You're too soft with him. That's why he doesn't respect you."

Drimacus's legs were churning like a windup toy's, so I put him down and he dashed off.

After scrounging for breakfast, I went back to my room with every intention of working on my novel. But my little brother Anders had sent me the first quarter of his novel, about twenty-five thousand words.

At first glance, it was every bit as bad as I'd expected. Anders hadn't given me any kind of heads-up as to what kind of story it was. It turned out to be about a bunch of kids Anders' age who went to a private school much like his—these were gun-toting kids who belonged to cabals and syndicates and secret societies and were always raiding the school in the middle of the night for some reason.

It sounded like a terrible anime. But about halfway through, once my disbelief finally suspended, it grabbed me, and I actually began to enjoy it. It wasn't good, to be sure, but it had potential. I got on board with the "sinister forces at work" concept, and I've always been a sucker for the whole "which character is the secret evil mastermind" plot device. There was no way in the world it should have worked, but somehow, it almost kind of did.

As I fixed my lunch, it occurred to me that I had no idea what I was going to make for Chloe when she came. I'd forgotten to tell Jeff, too.

Jeff was watching cartoons on his computer. I explained the situation.

"Dude, I can disappear," he said.

"Unless you're going to Promilla's, don't even try it. Chloe wants to meet you."

"Milla's at choir practice. You guys are already at the 'meet the roommate' stage?"

"That's a stage?" I said. "I met her roommate on the first date. And Chloe would have met you before, too, if you'd been here when she was here."

"Sorry."

"Don't apologize!"

"Sorry. I mean—"

I shook my head. "Forget it. If you're going to be around, you can eat with us. If you're going to the Athletics Center to wash towels, then forget it, forget you, and forget your mom."

"Thanks," said Jeff.

"That's better. Now what am I going to fix?"

"Penn, this is really good," Chloe said, politely but not enthusiastically.

"No it's not," I said. "I made it up and then I burned it."

"But it tastes fine!"

"Woman, I don't believe you."

I'd had chicken in the freezer, vegetables in the fridge, and this and that in the cupboards. In desperation, I threw it all together and ended up with the bastard child of a casserole and a college potpie.

"The garlic bread's really good," said Jeff.

"Jeff, *you* made the garlic bread."

"Yes, I did!"

"You've got to give me another chance," I said to Chloe. "I really am a good cook. I just needed to prepare better."

"He *is* a good cook," Jeff said.

"You had all day to prepare," Chloe said.

I made an exasperated noise. "I surrender. I slacked off and the food sucks. Let Drimacus out and we'll feed it to him."

"Don't be silly," Chloe said. "It's not *that* bad."

"Hmph."

"So what'd you do today?" Chloe asked.

134

"I spent most of the day reading part of a novel my brother wrote."

"Was it any good?"

"Is he better than you?" Jeff asked.

"No!" I said, too defensively. "It was okay. He has potential. It's a completely different genre."

"Yeah, most kids that age aren't going to write romance novels," Jeff said.

I scowled at him. "It isn't a romance novel!"

"How's it coming, whatever it is?" Chloe asked.

"Not as great as I'd like. It's hard to focus. I come home and I'm tired and I forget what I was doing the day before. I spend half my time just getting back into the frame of mind to work on it."

"I don't know how you do it, bro," said Jeff. "I had a hard time even writing a short story for English."

"It's nothing but discipline," I said. "Not that that's any guarantee it'll be any good. But you just have to make yourself sit there and do it. I once wrote for twenty-seven straight hours."

"Wow. See? I never could do that," Jeff said. "I've never even been awake for twenty-seven straight hours."

Chloe scowled at me.

I sighed. "I never wrote for twenty-seven straight hours."

"Man!" exclaimed Jeff.

Jeff and Chloe had hit it off pretty well, I thought, in sharp contrast to Promilla and me. I don't know that the girlfriend–roommate relationship was any kind of indicator, but it was something I thought about as I walked Chloe to her car later.

"Jeff *is* a sweetheart," said Chloe. "But you're mean to him." She was smiling, though.

"I'm not," I said. "I'm helping him grow as a person. It's what I do."

Chloe raised an eyebrow. "Is that a fact?"

"I have references. Did I ever tell you about the guy I roomed with in college? Three years I roomed with this guy.

One day, we're sitting in the cafeteria, eating lunch, and I say, 'Hey, Ron, how's it going?' and he goes, 'Pretty good. I got a hysterectomy today.' And I said, 'You got a what now?' And he says, 'A hysterectomy.' I said, 'I don't think you're saying what you think you're saying.' He goes, 'Well, I was feeling congested, so I went to the nurse and she gave me a hysterectomy.' And I just sit there for a second and then I say, 'Ron, do you mean an antihistamine?' And Ron says, 'Yeah, that's what it was. What's a hysterectomy?'"

Once again, I had Chloe in stitches. She punched me in the arm and thrashed around a little bit as she laughed.

When she'd settled down, she said, "I'm really glad I got to know you. You're extremely entertaining."

"Well, I try to keep myself entertained," I said. "If anybody else is entertained, that's a bonus."

"Don't I feel special! Oh, by the way, I'm taking your advice."

"Which advice would that be?"

"I'm applying to study abroad! In Belgium!"

"Good for you!" I said, and instantly felt a pang of regret at the thought of her leaving. Stupid. I was legitimately happy for her, and next spring was a long way away, and a lot could happen in that time.

While I was thinking these thoughts, Chloe leaned up and kissed me on the cheek, then got into her car.

That in and of itself made the evening a great success.

Day 166 – Saturday, April 24

My rough day began when a customer inadvertently gashed me with a claw hammer. This cut I noticed right away.

The store was packed, and all the wrong people were there, customers and associates. It was just a bad draw. Atwater was on the Service Desk, and he kept sending customers over to me when I had a line and he had nothing to do. Thoth and Landfill were the head cashiers. Thoth and I got along fine, but Landfill kept pestering me at inopportune moments. And Rex was on the prowl, which kept me on edge.

My feet started hurting before lunch, which was delayed an hour because Atwater came back late from his, citing car trouble. Then *I* was late back from lunch because I lost track of time while taking a nap. Landfill noticed and gave me grief about it.

In the afternoon, it was calmer. I'd taken some ibuprofen, but my feet were still sore.

Then I learned that there are some things a cashier should never, ever say.

"How are you today?" the woman asked as she began piling potted plants on the counter, giving me no room to operate.

"Not so great," I said pleasantly. A grievous error.

The woman turned feral like I'd flashed Tolkien's One Ring. "At least you *have* a job! At least you're not on welfare and you can pay the bills! You're not on *food stamps*! People aren't grateful for what they have!"

I did *not* say, "In that case, you can have my job."

Some cashiers, usually girls, had been known to burst into tears after such encounters, and it got under everybody's skin eventually. After that episode, my response to customers asking me how I was doing was never anything more or less than "good." It didn't matter what tone I used; I never had a problem again.

Of course customers didn't care what kind of day I was having—it was just part of the small-talk politeness ritual upon which American retail is built.

Customers tended not to look at their experiences with me as person-to-person interaction. I was just another part of the shopping experience: parking lot, shopping cart, merchandise, cashier. Most customers didn't ever look me in the eye if the transaction went smoothly.

To the customer, it didn't matter who the cashier was. It could be me or Gandhi or Hitler or Jesus as long as the magic happened. They wanted to hear that the automaton's day was good and they didn't want any lip.

The thought was simultaneously liberating and depressing.

Day 169 – Tuesday, April 27

Angry Pete leaned on his counter, scowling. "I have a grievance."

"You always have a grievance," I said, leafing through the Station circular.

"Actually, I have two. Firstly, do you have any idea how much part-time gets over on full-time?"

"What do you mean?"

"How do you think it works? They just get part-time workers to fill in where the full-time people don't work?"

"Don't they?"

"Hell, no. It's an injustice! Part-time gets first dibs!"

I gave Pete my full attention now. "For real?"

"Why do you think they give us all these terrible shifts? Moving us all over the place? Because part-time employees call their own shots and make their own schedules! We get the scraps! I asked because they've been jacking around with my schedule more so than usual."

"Who told you that?" I asked with the faint hope of discrediting his source.

"Kord."

"Dang!"

Landfill appeared as if out of nowhere.

"You're one of those little demons," Pete said.

Landfill was instantly bewildered. "What?"

"Like one of those evil genies or whatever. You just pop up and cause problems for people. I'm going to join the club to get you fired after all."

"There's a club?"

Pete shook his head. "Forget it."

"You're really weird. Hey, did you just hear that ad?" Landfill was talking about the plugs for our store that played over the store's speakers along with the music. "It said, 'Would you like to show your bushes you mean business? Then buy all kinds of things from us,' or something like that. But it sounds like, 'Would you like to show your bitches you mean business?' That's what I thought the first time I heard it. Isn't that funny? If we had books on, like, pimp training?"

"Get out of here, man," said Pete. "You're messing up my airing of grievances." He turned to me as though Landfill were no longer there. "Anyway, the second one. Have you ever noticed that rich people fuss way more?"

"Yeah, I have noticed that."

"Damn ungrateful people," Pete muttered. "Take everything for granted."

"What about you?" Landfill said. "You were born in America. You have a job. You take those things for granted. Most people do."

I was reminded of the encounter I'd had the other day and decided to stay out of it. Pete could take care of himself.

Pete turned. "What? You're still here? What the hell does that United Nations crap you were saying have to do with me?"

Landfill waved his hands. "Look, people take their jobs for granted. There are other people who don't have jobs, and they—"

"No, *you* look," interrupted Pete. "The difference between me and those people is that I don't take *me* for granted, whereas they do. I, as a House Station employee, pardon me, a House Station *associate*, am taken for granted on a daily basis, as well as taken advantage *of*, by management and customers alike, up, down, left, and right, every day and twice on Sundays. And you are, too. The question is, are you man enough to wake up and see it?"

"Take it easy, maybe," I said.

"Take it easy? Are you kidding me?" Pete's voice had risen to an agitated shriek. "Look, Landfill, yeah, okay, I'm glad I'm not some starving orphan in China, all right? I wouldn't want to *be* a starving orphan in China. I wake up in the morning and thank God *every day* that I'm *not* a starving orphan in China. But the fact remains, I hate this place. This job sucks ass, and a boatload of starving orphans can't make me change my mind. You got that?"

"Yeah, okay, I—"

Pete shook his head. "You missed it. Let me give you an example, okay? We make about the same amount of no-money as other poor losers in similar jobs at Lowe's and Home Depot, wouldn't you say?"

"I don't know," Landfill said.

"They do, okay? I know a guy at Home Depot who does your exact job, so shut up. Do you know who Richard Warren is?"

"Yeah. He was on the Mayflower!"

Pete at me looked incredulously. I shrugged.

Pete sighed. "Richard Warren was the House Station CEO before whoever the current asshole is. They forced him out because he sucked at his job. They gave him a hundred and eighty-million-dollar severance package. For *six years of sucking*. Do the math. I *did* the math. That's almost six hundred thousand dollars a week. Meanwhile, you don't take home more than three hundred and fifty dollars a week. Do you know what kind of difference that is? That's like two thousand times as much! Eighty-five thousand dollars a day! For getting fired! That's almost double the yearly earnings of the average American family! Look it up! *I looked it up!*"

Pete was forced to come up for air.

"Okay . . ." Landfill said, overwhelmed and even more confused.

Pete dove right back in. "I promise you that our current CEO has a similar deal, and that he doesn't know you or any other monkey in an apron from Adam, and that he doesn't care if you live or die as long as this store makes money. Ask me how I know that. I know that because for 2004, the House Station has twenty-five million dollars allocated for associates that provide Excellent Customer Service. For a thousand stores and a hundred and fifty thousand associates in all the House Stations in all the world! Do the math! We get hosed! So don't you talk to me about any Chinese orphans!"

Brow furrowed, Landfill said, "But don't you remember how in orientation Rex said that you could make a career out of the House Station and become a millionaire? Didn't you hear that speech?"

Pete snorted. "Oh, yeah, it was freaking hilarious. Penn, you remember that?"

I remembered. Rex told us about a guy he knew who worked at the House Station his whole life. By investing in the company, the man had become a millionaire, and we could do the same.

We calculated that to get a million dollars out of the House Station, you'd have to either win the lottery or work here for at least fifty years while living with your parents and having them pay all your expenses.

"Landfill, it's all crap," Pete said. "Rex has only worked for the House Station a couple months longer than we have, and he tells us he knows this guy and he knows that guy. It's on page 53 of the *Manager's Motivational Handbook of BS and Total Lies*. You must be crazy. And anybody who thinks I'm going to work here for ten, twenty, thirty, forty, fifty years is crazy, too."

"That's not a real book!"

Somebody called Landfill on his walkie-talkie and he immediately yanked it from his apron and said, "I'll be there right away. Over." To us, he said, "Sorry, guys, I have to go."

Pete glared at him. "Get the hell out of here."

Day 172 – Friday, April 30

I got lectured by Landfill for coming back late from lunch again—this time because the lady that rooted through our apartment's dumpsters tried to sell me some pork steaks so she could pay her cable bill. The day went downhill after that.

Sore from the knees down, I came home at quarter to ten and found Jeff sprawled on the couch. Adele was curled up next to him.

"You look exhausted," I said.

"Joe was here."

I stiffened. "Freeze-in-a-snowbank Joe? Don't-ride-in-the-car Joe? He's gone, right? Why was he here?"

"Milla came over for dinner. She invited him."

"How'd that go?" I kicked my shoes off and Drimacus, who had been lurking behind the couch, pounced on one.

"We just ate and played Monopoly," Jeff said.

I rubbed my sore insteps. "That sounds pretty safe."

"Joe had never played Monopoly before in his entire life."

"How is that possible?"

Jeff shrugged. "I never want to play another game with that guy again. Any game, I don't care."

"What happened?"

Jeff sat up. "It took us a while to get him squared away on the rules, first of all."

"He wasn't trying to tithe on his Go money, was he?" I said.

Jeff looked almost grim. "No, he didn't do that. But you know the card you draw that says 'Bank error in your favor, collect two hundred dollars'? He wouldn't take it. We said, 'Joe, it's just a game, take the money.' But he insisted it was dishonest and since he wouldn't do it in real life, he wouldn't do it in the game."

"I'd hate to see him if he landed on *Go to Jail*," I said.

"Oh, that he had no problem with. He just paid his money and got out, like anybody would. He's just so— so—"

"Obliviously self-righteous?"

"Yeah, I guess that fits."

"I wouldn't overanalyze it," I said. "You can't make sense of things that don't make sense."

I went and took some ibuprofen so that it would kick in by the time I went to bed; I wouldn't be able to sleep otherwise.

Day 175 – Monday, May 3

"Fielding Vargas from Loss Prevention is here," Pete said. "Brandy told me to tell you that, so watch your freaking back."

"Right."

Pete got the broom and began to sweep his area. "I saw this new show the other day. *NCIS*. You ever see it?"

"My not-at-the-Station hours are too precious to waste on TV shows," I said.

"I respect that. Okay, it's this Navy cop show. They run around and yell, 'NCIS! Get down on the ground!' Now tell me this: if a guy yelled that at you, would you get down on the ground?"

"Does he have a gun?"

"That's beside the point. If somebody chased me and yelled 'NCIS,' I wouldn't stop, because I don't know what the hell NCIS is. I want to get a badge and a gun and chase people and say some letters. 'LMNOP, bitch, get down on the ground!' How does that sound?"

143

"I'll visit you in prison."

"You know what your problem is, Penn? You really need to—" He broke off and almost jumped on the counter. "Holy crap, who's that?"

"Who? Where?"

"There. With Brandy."

Brandy the head cashier was escorting a skinny girl with a money drawer out to the Garden register.

"My God," murmured Pete.

"What? Do you know her?"

"No! Dude, she's so fine!"

The girl was of average height, which meant she towered over Brandy (not including the perm). She was thin as a rail, her hair bleached blonde. You had to be eighteen to work at the Station, but she looked like she was two years away.

"What's her name?" Pete demanded.

I shrugged. "I'm always the last one to know anything around here."

"We go through cashiers like Landfill goes through Little Debbies. Where's the phone list?" Pete rummaged around on the desk, found it, then swore mightily. "It hasn't been updated this week! These damn slackers! What do they do all day?"

"You could just go talk to her," I said.

"I want to know her name first," Pete replied. "I like to have the upper hand with these kinds of things."

"We wear aprons with our names on them."

Pete stroked his chin. "Yes, you have a point there. Man, did you ever see a girl that hot?"

"I don't think she's hot. At all. Sorry."

"Are you *crazy*?" Pete's voice was in the stratosphere.

"She has no figure. She's a skeleton. If she weighs a hundred pounds I'll come to work tomorrow wearing my apron and nothing else."

Pete looked at me pointedly. "You sure know how to ruin the mood."

"I'm just saying."

"Fine. I don't care. You can have all the fat ones."

"What are you, five?" I said. "Look, just go out there on your lunch hour and ask her out."

"Ask her out? Today? What kind of whore do you take me for? I haven't even met her!" Pete slapped the counter. "Look at you with the advice! Where'd that come from? You're the glacier of dating!"

"Looks like the shoe's on the other foot now, wouldn't you say?"

"It's hardly the same," Pete said. "I'm just formulating my game plan, whereas you met the girl, decided you liked her and wanted to date her, then immediately ran headfirst into a brick wall on which was written 'Penn's inability to communicate socially.'"

He kind of had a point there.

Pete wagged a finger. "I don't need tips from somebody whose relationship speed is comparable to a crawling baby with bullets in his kneecaps."

"You are sick and disturbed and I'm not talking to you anymore today."

Pete snorted. "You couldn't get through your day without me."

I waved him off and went back to my register.

Day 179 – Friday, May 7

"Is that Japanese guy here?" asked James Earl Jones with a Perm. "You know, the manager?"

"Osric?" I said. "I'll check."

I knew he was in the building, but Osric could be notoriously difficult to track down.

I called, and at last we spotted him heading down the main aisle toward us.

145

"Five bucks says he keeps walking," Pete said. "Doesn't even slow down."

But Osric stopped. "What do you guys need? Is this the customer?"

"I want a torchiere that uses halogen bulbs," said James Earl Jones with a Perm. "Your electrical guy couldn't help me."

"You can't get those anymore. They're a fire hazard." Osric talked the way he walked: slow and leisurely.

"Nobody makes them?"

"No, man, they'll burn your house down," Osric replied. "You'll set your drapes on fire."

"Oh," said James Earl Jones with a Perm, crestfallen.

When he and Osric had dispersed, I said, "Let me sit." Pete got up and handed me the headset, and I sat down and began rubbing my shins. "I'm taking your advice, finally. I'm getting some new shoes. I've had it."

"So you admit I'm a genius."

"I admit these concrete floors are killing my feet."

Pete shrugged. "I'll take it."

"Have you talked to that skinny cashier yet?"

"Not yet," Pete replied. "But I found out her name. Christine Smith. I found out her birthday, too. You know they have all the birth dates of all the associates on a sheet in the phone room?"

"That's so they can make sure we're on the schedule. How old is she?"

"She just turned eighteen. But forget that; why didn't you tell anybody your birthday's tomorrow?"

"What's the point?" I said. "I'll be here either way. Nobody's going to come up here and give me cake and ice cream."

"You didn't even tell Chloe?"

"No. I don't want her to make a fuss about it. I'll tell her tomorrow. What? You'd be milking this, wouldn't you?"

146

Pete straightened up the binders on the shelf. "You know I would. In many respects, a man can do as he damn well pleases on his birthday."

"Except stay home from work."

"Work is an immutable force of evil," said Pete. "Nothing you can do about that, unless you thought to ask for it off two weeks ago. The Station is a necessary evil in our lives. We wait and wait for it to become an unnecessary evil, and then we get the hell out."

"If I came to your house, would there be anti-Station manifestos and propaganda all over the walls?"

Pete shook his head. "I swing to the other extreme. There's not a shred of evidence that I work here."

"That's probably healthier," I said.

Pete sighed. "Sometimes I hate this damn place."

"Why don't you look for something else?"

"I did! Before I started here! What kind of booming hub of commerce do you think we live in? Everything else I found in this cowtown either sucked way more somehow and/or paid significantly less."

"Go to college," I said.

"Oh, right. I'll get a four-year degree, amass thousands of dollars in loan debt, and then be, oh, right where *you* are."

That one stung. "That was uncalled for," I said.

"Maybe. But it's not your fault, Penn, that's what I've been trying to tell you." Pete waved his arms at the massive yellow shelves around us. "It's work. *This* work."

"That's why I'm going to grad school," I said.

Pete shrugged. "It's worth a shot. Just make sure you don't end up back here afterward."

Day 180 – Saturday, May 8

In the morning, I went and bought some extremely comfortable New Balance shoes for sixty dollars, and I asked myself a thousand times throughout the day why I hadn't done it sooner. I also got some gel insoles for ten dollars and a foot spa for thirty. All told, about twelve hours at the Station, before taxes. These were my birthday presents to myself.

Chloe and I had plans to go out after I got off work. I still hadn't told her it was my birthday.

I took a look at the day's draw. Pete was off. Kirsten, the part-timer with diabetes and snacks, was on the Service Desk. I'd take her over Atwater any day. The head cashiers were Thoth and Brandy — a Landfill-free environment.

Life was ridiculously better with the new shoes. Soreness I didn't know I'd had was gone. The sun shined more brightly, the birds sang more sweetly, et cetera.

I didn't even mind when an old man who smelled like Play-Doh took fifteen minutes to write a check for his thirty-nine-cent pipe fitting (he must have left his exact change at home) or when the three-year-old took his pants off because his mom had to take a screwdriver away from him so I could scan it.

Shortly after lunch, a woman rushed up to my counter. "Where's the rat poison?"

"Garden. Aisle forty-two."

"Thanks!" She took off at a run. Twenty seconds later, she was back, throwing money in my face. "My dog ate rat poison! My kid put it in the middle of the floor and I have to buy a sample for the vet."

Then she was gone.

I entered my apartment, thwarting Drimacus' escape attempt. Adele was sleeping on the couch. Angry Pete was lounging next to her.

"Hey," said Pete.

I struggled for articulacy and failed. "I— How— Why are you in my house?"

Pete spread his arms wide. "Surprise, man."

Then I saw Chloe and Jeff and Promilla over by the kitchen. There were balloons on the table and a *Happy Birthday* banner on the wall.

Chloe came over and punched me in the chest, hard. "Happy birthday," she said sweetly. Then she leaned up and whispered in my ear, "If you ever pull something like keeping your birthday from me again, I will give you the worst beating of your life. Okay?" When she pulled away, she was smiling, but her eyes burned into me.

I was overwhelmed. "I didn't see any of your cars in the parking lot."

"Because it's a conspiracy," Pete said. "We parked around the side."

"And who let Pete in the house?" I said.

"Hey!" Chloe thumped me again. "You have Pete to thank for all this. He told me it was your birthday. Then I called Jeff and we set this up at the last minute."

"Thanks, guys," I said.

Jeff clapped me on the shoulder. "Happy birthday, bro."

"Okay, let's get out of here," said Pete. "I'm hungry."

"What?" I said.

"We're taking your sorry ass to dinner. Bust a move." He hadn't budged from the couch.

"Can I change out of my work clothes first?" I asked.

"Go ahead," Chloe told me. "We've got something in the oven that won't be done for a few minutes."

She was wearing a white shirt and olive khakis that made her look absolutely spectacular, and I told her so.

I went into my room and closed the door. There was just something about a woman in olive pants . . . She got more attractive every time I saw her.

I showered quickly, then put on my good jeans and a fresh shirt. I got a little carried away with the cologne, then tried to wash some off.

They took me to a barbeque restaurant because Jeff told them I liked ribs. Promilla was friendly and Pete was more or less on his good behavior. I think Chloe had threatened him with beatings, too.

When we went back to my apartment, we had cake that Chloe and Promilla had baked together. Jeff gave me a DVD and some socks.

"Sorry, bro, I couldn't think of anything to get you. But I figured everybody needs socks."

"Thanks, Jeff," I said. "They're great."

Chloe gave me two collared shirts. "To increase your work rotation," she said.

"I don't want to wear them to the Station," I said. "They're too nice."

She gave me a look that said plainly what she thought of that idea.

Pete gave me a big box, but all that was in it was a House Station gift card buried under several trees' worth of wadded-up House Station circulars.

"Thanks?" I said.

"Don't thank me," said Pete. "There's nothing on it. It's the thought that counts."

Then Jeff brought out the board games, and that kept us entertained for several hours.

Pete was the first to leave. "I have to open tomorrow," he said.

"Thanks for coming," I said.

"You're welcome."

After he left, Jeff said, "I'm going to clean up in the kitchen. Milla, can you give me a hand?"

In they went, although there wasn't anything to clean up except cake plates.

"It's a nice night," I said to Chloe. "Want to go out on the balcony?"

She followed me out, and I shut the door in Drimacus's face.

"I had a really good time tonight," I said. "Thank you."

"Good." Chloe hooked her arm through mine.

"Pete was unusually well-behaved."

"I promised I'd find out about this new girl Christine for him."

I turned to face Chloe and the butterflies exploded inside me. The darkness somehow made it easier. "You look gorgeous tonight," I said. "Just beautiful."

"Thanks, Penn." She gave me the smile that made me weak in the knees.

A chill breeze blew and she shivered. I put my arm around her.

"Do you want to go inside?" I asked.

"No, I'm okay."

I felt an odd rush of blood to my head. The next thing I knew, she was in my arms and I was kissing her and she was kissing me back. The whole world faded away. I was vaguely aware that Jeff was closing the blinds.

I pulled away slightly and looked into Chloe's eyes. "You're amazing," I said.

"I know," she replied. Then she took my face in her hands and kissed me again.

It's amazing what a new pair of shoes will do for you.

Day 220 – Thursday, June 17

Summer came, driving nails into the coffin in which were interred my graduate school plans.

The whole thing had crashed and burned when I got a letter from Ball State saying I wasn't accepted. Then the same

151

from Iowa. And then, to my shock and dismay, I didn't get into the University of Missouri–Saint Louis either.

The first two I could understand. In-state applicants typically got preferential treatment and moved right to the front of the line. But I'd lived in Missouri my whole life.

I called UMSL to ask why I didn't get admitted. It took six calls over two weeks to get in touch with somebody who could give me an answer: there were only six spots available for over fifty applicants. I didn't bother asking how high I ranked on the list of rejects.

I was angry and dejected. I had to wait a year before I could try again. What was I supposed to do for a year? Stay at the Station?

It took some time before I could put the whole sorry state of affairs in perspective. Jeff and I renewed our lease. I resolved to finish my book, retake the GRE and get a better score, and get into grad school next year.

On the bright side, maintenance finally came and fixed our broken drawer. That was the one condition we'd insisted on when we renewed our lease.

Day 222 – Saturday, June 19

"Are you sure this is a good idea?" I asked for probably the tenth time that day.

"Penn, stop being an old lady and hand me that roller," Chloe ordered.

Chloe and Bethany had just moved into a new apartment, and Chloe was intent on painting her bedroom a bright springtime green.

"What if they say something?" I asked, passing the roller to her.

"'They'? What 'they'?"

"'They' your apartment people."

"Why would they know? Who's going to tell them?"

"Chloe, they come in your apartment. They come to replace the furnace filter. They come to check the smoke detector."

"Neither of those things is in here. If they fuss, I'll paint it back when I move out."

I balled up some painting tape and threw it at her. "You're never seeing your security deposit again."

"Oh, come on! They repaint the apartment every time somebody moves out! Besides, it looks better this way."

"Then why not paint the rest of the apartment while you're at it!" I cried, and immediately regretted it.

"That's a great idea," Chloe said. "Penn, you're a genius!"

"I was kidding!"

"It doesn't matter! It's totally happening now."

I sat down on the drop cloth. "I give up."

She smirked down at me. "You know things always go better for you when you do that. What color do you think would look good in the living room with our dark green sofa? I'm thinking some kind of yellow."

"This conversation is too much like work," I said.

"A gentle, pastel yellow," she continued. "Not that garish highlighter blinding yellow like at the Station. You know, it's too bad we don't get a discount—we work there, but they don't give us any reason to shop there."

"It's conveniently located," I said. "I know what aisle everything's on."

"If you work at a clothing store, you get a discount on their clothes, even if it's only ten or fifteen percent," Chloe said. "All we get are those ten-percent-off coupons every now and again. Can you grab the stepladder, please?"

I retrieved it from the hall. "Doesn't this conversation violate your rule?"

She positioned the stepladder near the wall. "We're not talking about work. We're talking about economics."

I snorted. "Is that what we're doing? Okay, if the House Station gave all their associates ten percent off all the time, think of the problems that would cause with contractors."

"What do you mean?"

"Let's say I wanted to remodel my whole house," I said. "How much would that cost?"

"I don't know. A lot."

I sat down again to take the weight off my feet. "Thousands of dollars. So what would I do? I'd get a part-time job at the House Station. I'd buy everything I needed, and then I'd quit. Think about that going on all the time in every store. The turnover would be ridiculous."

"I see your point." Chloe turned to look down at me and I ripped my gaze away from her rear end. "But they could give us the discount and maybe give a discount to contractors, too. Make a special contractor House Station credit card."

"There is one."

"Well, let people who use that card get discounts on high-dollar purchases. How about that?"

"Sounds good to me," I replied. "But the Station doesn't do anything like that."

"Doesn't anybody?"

I shrugged. "Lowe's might. I get most of my information from customers who complain about how we don't do things as well as whatever other store they're used to going to."

"It just doesn't seem fair to not give associates any kind of discount."

"That's why they give us those stupid coupons," I replied. "But even those are a scam because they're only good for a week. They'll give you as many as you want, you know that? And they'll tell you to give them to your family and friends. So even then they're trying to compensate for any discount we might get by using us to drum up sales. At least they're fair — *nobody* in the store gets a discount, not even Rex. Of course, the difference there is, he actually makes good money."

"Oh? How much?"

"I have no idea. Generally speaking, everybody gets paid squat until ASMs. They get a good salary—until you consider that they work a lot of eleven-hour shifts and rarely go home on time. Clearly, the key is to jump right in at the store manager level, which is what Rex did."

"Where was he before?"

"He was the director of a small plumbing and bath installer. In Ohio, I think. The Station just hired him last year when the store was getting ready to open."

"Nice work if you can get it," Chloe said. "Now are you going to get off your butt and help me paint or what?"

"Yes, dear," I said.

Day 225 – Tuesday, June 22

I finished my page requesting all departments to come and pick up their returns. It was a page I made several times a day, and one that was rarely heeded.

"You look like Captain Morgan," Pete said. "What are you doing?"

I had one foot up on one of the ubiquitous yellow House Station buckets we sold for five bucks. "It helps my feet not get as sore."

"Thank you for calling the House Station and Rental Center at Garber and State, would you like to hear about our specials today? No? Can't say as I blame you. Yeah, I'll transfer you."

"Be careful who you say that to," I said when he'd hung up.

"The specials? Please. 'Save ten percent on tile when you hire the Station installers.' 'Save twenty dollars when you spend a thousand dollars.'" Pete waved his hands in a pretend-excited way. "I'll rush out of my house and on down to the Station! Got any more of that firewood left? Summer

155

clearance sale! Save two dollars when you buy fifty pounds of firewood!"

"Calm down," I said. "It's ninety degrees. We haven't carried firewood in months."

"Because we pimped it all out of here!" Pete snapped his fingers. "Penn, we're just a link in the pimping chain."

"The pimping chain?"

Pete held up both hands. "We pimp the firewood, or whatever other stuff they stocked too much of, see? So the House Station associate is above firewood on the pimping chain. However, the House Station associate is constantly pimped by the customer — getting pimped by the customer is, in fact, our job description. So the pimping chain goes customer, associate, firewood."

"What's below firewood?"

"I haven't finished my diagram yet," Pete replied. "But firewood's pretty much at the bottom."

"This is what you do when you go home at night?"

Kord stopped by the desk. "What are you two screwing up in my store now?"

"Two things," I said. "On the same topic. First, when are they going to let us wear shorts? More importantly, when are you going to get me a fan?"

"We'll try and get one marked down for you sometime this week," she said.

"Sooner is better than later," I said.

"God, yes," said Pete. "Unless you want him crying about how the backs of his *knees* are sweaty and his *drawz* are sweaty and —"

"Pete, shut the hell up," Kord said. "You guys are disgusting. Fine, go get one. Get a *cheap* one."

"This is just like Christmas," I said, and flipped my register light off.

* * * * *

"So how's it going with Chloe?" Pete asked while I was writing *Returns Desk – Do Not Remove* on my spanking new white tabletop fan with a permanent marker.

"It's going really well," I said.

"You guys are getting out more now that she's out of class?"

"A little. She's doing summer school so she can finish her degree next year."

"So how many times a week would you say you see her outside of work?"

I was concentrating on good penmanship. "Um . . . two, maybe three."

"That's why you guys never fight."

"Say what now?"

"You don't fight because you don't spend enough time together to get on each other's nerves."

I looked up. "Who says we never fight?"

Pete looked me in the eye. "Penn, do you guys ever fight?"

"No, not really. Not seriously."

"See? You aren't around each other all the time – it prolongs the honeymoon stage of the relationship. Familiarity breeds contempt."

I capped my marker. "Yet I keep talking to *you*. Why are you so interested in this all of a sudden?"

"There's no 'all of a sudden' about it," Pete replied. "Your business is my business. I thought you knew that."

"What's this really about?" I asked.

"What do you mean? Can't your friend ask you about your life? Okay, it's about Christine. I found out why she doesn't like me. Apparently, I was mean to her when she applied. I have absolutely no memory of it."

"This is your excuse for not asking her out after six weeks?"

"It explains why she's always ice-cold to me," Pete said.

"As far as I've seen, she's ice-cold to everybody," I said. "She's got sharp edges – that's not just a weight joke. Plus she's a lazy cashier. She's the Paris Hilton of the working class."

Pete considered this. "I don't necessarily disagree with you. But I haven't given up."

A customer stopped to ask for help in Electrical.

"I'll have Robert meet you there," said Pete.

When the customer was gone, I asked, "Who's Robert?"

"He's new. You haven't met him yet? Creepy little guy. Wears the same clothes every day. Boots, tight jeans, creepy dark glasses, creepy long goatee."

"Creepy how?" I asked. "Like the other creepy people we've had?"

"No, the other creepy people were 'I'll sexually harass you' creepy. This guy's 'I might shoot five or six people' creepy. A word to the wise: call him Robert, not Rob or Bob."

"Good to know," I said.

"Say, do I have any Returns?" someone asked from behind me in a booming voice that reminded me of Foghorn Leghorn.

I turned and saw a huge, muscular guy leaning over my fence—your typical former high school quarterback type. His blond hair was slicked back and his yellow apron proclaimed him to be one Lance B. He'd drawn a lightning bolt next to the B.

"What department?" I asked.

"Hardware."

I handed him what there was. He said, "Thanks, little buddy," and left.

"'Little buddy'? I'm six feet tall," I said.

"And he's a large young man," Pete said. "Six-four, at least."

I leaned on the counter and groaned. "My feet hurt and all I want to do is go home and soak them."

"Like in a foot spa? Come on, my grandma has one of those."

I was suddenly irritated. "So?"

"So it's kind of lame."

158

"Maybe you don't appreciate the fact that this place is giving me chronic health problems," I said.

"Jeez, Penn, I was just kidding."

"Do I look like I'm kidding? Do I look like I'm in the mood for kidding?"

"You look like you're in the mood to kill somebody."

I put a hand to my forehead and took a deep breath. "Have you ever woken up in the morning feeling like every bone in your feet had been crushed into gravel?"

"Jesus, man."

"Look, that happens to me every day. I—"

There came a strange whistling sound, like a falling cartoon bomb. Something huge and metal rocketed into the floor of the main aisle right in front of the Service Desk, making both of us jump. I ducked behind the counter as the metal something bounced ten feet in the air and landed in the book area next to the desk, where it ricocheted around with three or four tremendous clangs.

"*Holy crap Jesus what the goddamn hell was that?*" Pete screamed from under the desk.

I didn't hear anything but people yelling, so I emerged cautiously, adrenaline rushing and pulse pounding. There was a small crater in the floor where the thing had hit, and there were little chunks of concrete everywhere. I peeked over into the book section and saw a giant, dented propane canister nestled in a pile of spilled magazines. It hissed sinisterly.

Rovergial the ASM and a guy from Building Materials named Ben who I didn't really know came sprinting up the aisle.

"Where'd it go?" Rovergial asked.

I pointed.

"Go get some barricades and block off this area," Rovergial ordered, and I dutifully went off to collect a couple of the rolling, collapsible yellow safety fences we used to close off an aisle when somebody was using a forklift or an order picker.

We later learned what had happened: We have two forklifts; the big one runs on liquid propane. Down in Building Materials, at the far end of the store, Ben (who was fired as soon as the necessary paperwork had been filled out) had been changing the propane tank. He couldn't get it connected right, and when he tried to force it, he somehow ruptured the tank, instantly turning it into a missile — like when you blow up a balloon and let it go, but times eight hundred million.

All the customers were evacuated from the store. We the associates were sent to the break room, as though a propane leak was less of a fire danger to us than to customers. Pete suggested that perhaps our aprons were made of asbestos.

The fire department came and they had the propane canister out of there an hour later. To our great dismay, the store reopened immediately afterward. They patched up the floor that night.

Day 230 – Sunday, June 27

"Kord," I said, when she came at the end of my shift, "I need you to talk to Helen for me."

She handed me a canister for the pneumatic tube. "What's the problem?"

"I never get any Sundays off. I've told her, 'Hey, it'd be nice to have a Sunday off once in a while,' but she doesn't take the hint. I've only had a couple of Sundays off in the last six months, and the last two I got because I filled out a time-off request form. It's ridiculous."

Kord brushed dust from her baggy jeans. "Yeah, I can talk to her."

"Thanks. I just want to go to church."

Kord unlocked my tube and I put the canister inside, then sent it speeding toward the vault.

"Hey, did you see the new guy back in Décor?" I asked.

160

"No, what guy?"

"Chris. He looks just like you," I said. "Short spiky hair, same build. I thought it *was* you the first time I saw him."

"Nice. Is he gay?"

"I'd be astounded if he isn't."

"Oh, I need you to make me some signs for those stained glass-looking window treatments. Think of something clever by tomorrow."

"'Brighten up your life with some window treatments.' 'Add a rainbow of color to your home.' I'll work on it," I said.

"You'd better," said Kord. "I said *clever*."

I "accidentally" bumped into her as I stepped out from behind my register.

"Easy!" Kord exclaimed. "What are you, my little brother?"

"Oh, God!" I cried dramatically.

"Come to think of it," Kord mused, "you'd have made an interesting little brother."

"Is that a compliment?"

She thought about that for a second. "Yeah, I guess it is."

"Thanks, Kord," I said.

Day 233 – Wednesday, June 30

The beefy man in the *I Love My Swiss Skin Care* shirt was returning a paint sprayer. He claimed it had clogged up on him the first time he used it and he wanted to get a different brand.

Fortunately, it wasn't up to me to decide whether or not he was telling the truth. Yeah, he might have painted his whole house already, but I'm a cashier, not a detective. Per procedure, I called Paint to have somebody take a look at it. Chloe came up, opened the box, saw the mess, and immediately told me to RTV it.

I processed the sprayer and handed the man the return slip. "Fill this out and that'll refund to your Visa," I said.

"You're not going to get drunk and call my number in the middle of the night, are you?" he asked.

"No promises."

"Hey!" Lance's voice boomed behind me as he dealt me a staggering clap on the back. "Was that Chloe van Caneghem I just saw? She works here?"

"She works in Paint," I said, rubbing my shoulder. "You know her?"

"Oh, yeah! We went to high school together. Dated for a while."

My eyebrows went up. "You did, did you?"

"Yeah, little man! Not exactly a model, but how could I forget that *ass*? So yeah, you can say I *know* her, if you get my meaning." He gave a prurient chuckle.

My mind exploded. A million terrible scenarios played in my head, several of which involved me beating Lance with a close-at-hand pipe bender.

"Say, can you hand me my Returns?" Lance was saying.

I cast glazed eyes into Hardware's bin. "You don't have anything."

"Glad to hear it!" Lance headed off in the direction of Paint, whistling.

I had to sit down. I had to get off my register. "Atwater, I'm going to go to the restroom," I said.

"Okay!" said Atwater, knocking the phone on the floor.

Landfill passed me on the way. "*Penn*sylvania!" he exclaimed.

"Don't talk to me," I said.

I washed my face in the restroom, then went and sat down in the break room. The current inspirational quote was "Pride puts your focus on appearance instead of potential."

Lance and Chloe? I massaged my temples. My head throbbed like I'd been hit by a Chloe headbutt. What could she

162

possibly have seen in that loud, obnoxious oaf with the stupid accent?

His insinuations . . . Was it possible? We'd never discussed *that*. Never had a reason to. I remembered Pete's theories on the matter, which I had eagerly bought into at the time because they were what I wanted to hear.

But Pete didn't know anything about women, and he didn't know Chloe.

Did *I* know Chloe? Anxiety gnawed at my insides. Stop it, I told myself. Why was this even a big deal? It was all in the past anyway. Who cared?

I cared. There was only one thing to do. I was going to be nonfunctional until I went and talked to her.

What if Lance was still over there? What if I walked over there and they were standing there talking?

"Come on, Penn," I said aloud.

Pete would undoubtedly say something like, "Who cares if he's standing there? Who the hell is he? She's your woman, isn't she? So maybe once upon a time she—"

I silenced my mental Pete. I was too flustered even to be upset at the realization that I *had* a mental Pete. I lurched out of the room.

Lance was leaning on the Paint counter, practically sprawled on it. Chloe was chatting with him while she mixed paint. I was going to turn and go back to my register, but Chloe looked up and made eye contact. Lance's phone rang and he answered it, then straightened and walked away.

"Hey!" Chloe said.

"Hey," I returned, less enthusiastically.

"That was Lance."

"We've met."

"We went to high school together," Chloe said. "He and my brother Matt were on the football team together."

"Yeah, that's actually what I wanted to—"

I broke off as a page came over the intercom. "Penn Reynard, please return to, uh, Returns. Penn Reynard, please come to Returns." It was Atwater.

I ground my teeth. "I need to talk to you tonight. Can we get together after work?"

"Sorry, I can't," Chloe replied. "I have to go over to LCC. Working on a special group project for my Social Criticism in American Education class."

"What time will you be back?"

"I don't know. Could be after eleven. My group's been slacking. I have to try and light a fire under them."

"Call me when you get home," I said.

"I always do, don't I? Penn, is something wrong?"

I shook my head.

"Hey, can I get some help with this paint?" a customer called from down one of the aisles.

"I'll see you later," said Chloe.

I didn't have a very good day after that. At three, Rex came and told me he wanted to talk, and we went into the deserted phone room.

Rex leaned on the desk. "Penn, you know I've talked to you about this before. Your expression, your body language, your attitude. I've had two customers complain to me today that you were rude to them."

I didn't say anything. I was mad and my feet hurt, and if the expression on my face was anywhere near what I thought it was, I wouldn't blame anyone for skipping my line altogether.

Rex put on his patronizing face. "Look, I know you're a good guy, but that's because I've gotten to know you a little bit. These customers don't know that. Being friendly isn't an optional part of this job. You have to provide Excellent Customer Service. Listen, I don't care if you like the customers or if you hate them. That doesn't matter to me. You still have

164

to be friendly. Just fake it! Say, 'I'm glad to see you, you son of a bitch!' Okay?"

"Okay," I said.

Rex nodded. "Good. Now, is there something wrong? If so, you can talk to me, or you can call the House Station Helpline to talk to a counselor."

"No, I'm fine."

He clapped me on the shoulder just like Landfill always did. "Then I'll let you get back to it."

At the end of my shift, I went home and waited in vain for Chloe to call me.

Day 234 – Thursday, July 1

She didn't call me on Thursday, either. I called her house, but nobody was there. I didn't want to call her at work.

I spent most of the morning of my day off moping around the house. I tried to work on my novel and couldn't concentrate. I was soaking my feet in the living room when Jeff got up at noon.

"Hey, bro," he said, bleary-eyed.

"Hey. Do you have any Epsom salts?"

"I think you used them all up. Sorry."

"Don't be sorry. I'll buy some." I switched off the foot spa and toweled my feet dry. "So where were you last night? Did you close the AC?"

"No. I was hanging out with Promilla. When I got in, you were in your room with the door shut, so I didn't bother you. We watched *Fantasia*."

"With Mickey Mouse and those mops? Yeah, I saw that when I was little."

"Dude, it's terrible! I had no idea how terrible it was. It's got racism, it's got nudity, it's got drunkenness, and it's got devil worship." Jeff ticked these off on his fingers. "Oh, and evolution."

"Really? I don't remember any of that," I said. "We should watch it with Rapture Joe sometime. That'd be good for a laugh."

"Oh, Milla would kill me." Jeff snapped his fingers. "Oh, bro, I forgot to tell you last night. Chloe called and left you a message."

I jerked upright, almost hurting myself. "When? I've been here the whole time. I didn't hear the phone ring."

"I thought you were asleep. It was pretty late. It didn't ring. I picked it up to call Milla and she was on the line. Weird, huh?"

I waved this away. "What'd she say?"

"She said she had to go out of town on short notice this morning because her grandmother was really sick."

Her grandmother, if I recalled correctly, was in Kansas City.

Adele, who had been asleep on the couch, hissed and woke herself up. She looked around, confused.

"She also said her cell phone wasn't working," said Jeff, when he'd returned his attention to me.

I leaned back and pinched the bridge of my nose.

"I'm sorry, bro, I should have told you last night. Is everything okay?"

"I don't know."

A sick grandma out of nowhere? Stranger things had happened. Give Chloe the benefit of the doubt, I told myself. Did I really think she called in sick to work and made up some story about her grandmother just because that oversized moron Lance had showed up out of her past? Was she trying that hard to avoid me? It all sounded pretty silly that way, but it didn't make me feel any better.

166

Day 235 – Friday, July 2

I pointed at Lance, who had just walked off with his armload of Returns. "You always have all the answers, Angry Pete! Well, what's your answer to that?"

Pete stroked his chin thoughtfully. "She didn't call you last night either?"

"No. No calls, no e-mails, no note, nothing. I'm going crazy."

"It's 2004. You need to get a cell phone."

"Man, what are you saying?" I grabbed the headset off his head and shook it. "I spend at least twenty-two hours of every day within ten yards of a phone."

"I never promised one hundred percent accurate virgin detection," Pete said, replacing the headset. "Except in your case. You must be screwed up if I'm your voice of reason."

"Just answer the question! Do you think—"

"I think lots of things," Pete interrupted. "That doesn't mean they're true. Calm down and let's review the evidence. What do we know? One: that jackass shows up and implies he's done the nasty with your girl once upon a time. Don't make that face, Penn, it's facts. Two: Chloe suddenly goes AWOL. Three: there is no three. That's all you've got. What do we make of this? As far as I can tell, this whole thing boils down to whether or not Colonel Sanders is telling the truth. Do we believe him or do we believe Chloe? Is that really such a difficult decision?"

I leaned against the Service Desk counter and crossed my arms. "It's not that easy. I can't ask Chloe because she's not here. And in the ten seconds I talked to her, she did say she knew this guy in high school."

"So you think Chloe made up this excuse to avoid you? Why? So she can get back with Lance? That's not really Chloe's style, is it?"

"No, it's not. But there's got to be some explanation."

167

Pete sighed. "Fine. Here's your explanation: it's the twenty-first century. People have sex. It's not a big deal for most of us. You're about a hundred years behind the times."

"That doesn't help!"

Pete held up his hands. "I know, I know. You're saving yourself for marriage, it's a big deal for you. And people who save themselves for marriage save themselves for people who save themselves for marriage. But don't you think you're overreacting?"

I rubbed my face with both hands. "Probably."

He thumped me on the arm. "Any chance of stopping any time soon? Didn't think so. Quit your gloom and doom disaster prognostication and envision a scenario in which Chloe is innocent. You have a customer. Oh, I know that guy. He has zippers in his socks. Keeps his money in there."

My train of thought had suffered a horrific derailment, so I headed to my register and took care of Mr. Zipper Socks.

My next customer was buying various potted plants, and she spilled dirt all over my counter. When I told her the total, she pulled some bills out of her purse, stuck them in her mouth, and dug through the purse for more.

There was now a man behind her. He looked around impatiently. "Is this the only Returns line?" he demanded.

"Yes," I told him, although I could have just as easily sent him over to Pete.

Finally, the woman handed me her saliva-soaked bills and left.

The impatient man was returning some unopened light switches.

I scanned his receipt. "This is going to refund to your Visa."

"What?" the man cried. "Even when I pay cash, you refund it to my Visa! I paid cash! I want cash back! They give cash at Wal-Mart!"

I pointed out on his receipt where it showed he'd paid with a Visa. But he wasn't happy about it.

The next instant, I had a line five deep and Pete was busy with a special order customer.

Pete had finished with his customer and I was on the third of the five when he called, "Penn, you have a phone call!"

"So send it to my phone!"

"It's Chloe!"

I wanted to scream. "I can't talk to her right now! Tell her to call back in ten minutes!"

There was a pause, then, "She says she can't."

I kicked a dent in my bucket. "You talk to her!" I called desperately.

It took forever to get rid of my line—the last man had a wallet full of maxed-out credit cards. Finally, I made it over to the Service Desk.

"She's in Kansas City," Pete said. "That's what she said. Her grandma had a stroke."

"What else?" I demanded. "Did you get a number?"

"No. Don't get mad at me! I asked her! She said she was calling from a payphone at the hospital. Her cell phone's not working."

"She couldn't give you the number of the house or hotel where she was staying?"

Pete held up his hands. "Take it easy! I only talked to her for a minute! I'm sure she'll call back!"

"What else did she say?"

"Well, I only asked her the most pertinent question. The one I thought you'd most want to know the answer to." Pete had a pained expression on his face.

I crossed my arms and made no effort to compose my face. "What question would that be?"

"You are a terrifying individual, you know that?"

"*What question?*"

"I asked her about Lance."

I almost choked on my spit. "You asked her if they —"

"I just asked if they *dated in high school*. They did."

The reins of my self-control were slipping. "Listen, I need to go back to the break room for a minute, okay?"

"Sure. It's cool. I understand." Pete fished in his pocket and handed me some change. "Bring me a Dr Pepper when you come back, huh? Thanks, man."

Day 237 – Sunday, July 4

When I rolled out of bed, I felt like somebody'd hit me in both heels with a hammer. My feet had still hurt when I'd gone to bed, and somehow they were worse now. I downed four ibuprofens—this had become habitual—and went to work.

"Feel any better?" Pete asked me.

"A little." I leaned on my counter and tried to take the weight off my feet. "Not much."

I still hadn't talked to Chloe. She'd called the Station once on Saturday and missed me. She'd called me at home a couple times when I wasn't there and left a message. She said she'd be back on Tuesday. She'd left a number, but when I called it, nobody answered.

"You'll be fine once you talk to her," said Pete. "Anyway, the stupidest people on earth come to this store. This lady buys this ceiling fan kit. She brings it up here and goes, 'Can you open it and make sure everything's there? Last time I bought one, I got it home and it was missing some pieces.' So I open it up and everything's there, and she's like, 'Great, thanks, I forgot something, I'll be right back.' Ten minutes later she comes back with some more stuff and says, 'Oh, I want a different fan; this one's open.' She goes and gets another one. Are you kidding me?"

"I believe it," I said. I was trying to make myself think about other things, and Pete's jabber was welcome in that regard.

"You know how they say, 'the customer is always right'?" Pete continued. "'The customer is always an idiot,' that's what they should say. That kind of refreshing honesty would be good for business."

This made me smile a little. "You know how a couple times a day, we go twenty minutes without a customer?" I said.

Pete nodded. "Those are good times."

"What are the odds that a customer's going to come in at any given time? What's the math of that? I've gone forty minutes without a customer. What would be the mathematics of *no* customers? You know, for me to stand here the entire day and not get a single customer?"

Pete looked wistful. "Man, this job wouldn't be so bad if it weren't for the customers. Why are you hunched over like that? Do you have a cramp? No, let me guess, your feet hurt again? Why don't you go to the doctor?"

"Because I don't have insurance. I missed the enrollment period last December. Now I can't enroll until this December."

"Well, that was stupid," said Pete.

James Earl Jones with a Perm came to the desk. "Where can I find car shades?"

"Wal-Mart," I said, and he fled.

"That reminds me," said Pete. "Did Rex ever tell you his tire story?"

"I don't believe so."

Superman walked past. Pete waved him over, and we converged at the Service Desk.

"What's up, guys?" Superman asked.

"Not much," Pete replied. "How's your grandma doing?"

"She's good," Superman replied. "My uncle's about to close on a house."

171

"So I suppose you'll be getting the hell out of Dodge pretty soon too, right?"

"Yeah. I hate this place."

"Then why do you stay?" Pete asked.

He shrugged. "It pays better than anything else in town."

"So what are your plans?" I asked.

"I'm going to Washington University in the fall."

"Is that in Washington state or Washington, D.C.?" Pete asked.

"It's in Saint Louis," Superman and I said simultaneously.

"That's dumb. And you're studying . . . either medicine or engineering?" Pete guessed.

"Why do you say that?" asked Superman.

Pete shrugged. "You're Indian."

"Oh, the racial stereotyping," I said. "You went there."

Pete snapped his fingers at Superman. "Look at his face! I'm right! Which one?"

"Engineering," Superman said.

As Pete cackled triumphantly, I asked, "Are you going to live with your family?"

Superman shook his head. "No way I'm living with my parents. And my uncle, my other uncle, has a weird family."

"Why?" Pete asked. "Is there a good story here?"

Superman shrugged. "My aunt is pretty fat, okay? And my grandmother and I went up there to visit about two weeks ago. My aunt's on this diet—it's like an Indian version of the Atkins Diet. She tells us she's not eating any rice, which is kind of a big thing, because in my family we eat rice almost every day. She says, 'Do you want some grapes? I can't eat grapes because they have too much sugar.' I wanted to say, 'Auntie, grapes are the least of your problems.'"

"Wow," I said. "Words can't express."

"Yes they can," said Pete.

"Anyway, in spite of that, I'm looking forward to going back to Saint Louis. I love the city," Superman said. "It'll be great to go to some Rams games. God, the day the Rams lost

172

the Super Bowl was the worst day of my life. Not counting all the days I've spent here."

"That's why I like this kid," Pete said to me. "His hate is wide open."

"Since the day I filled out the application," Superman replied. "The questions they asked! Like, 'Agree or disagree: it is maddening when the court lets guilty criminals go free.' What does that mean? What does it have to do with the job? Why are they asking me that?"

"There are right and wrong answers for all of those questions," Pete said. "You can find them on the internet. Does anybody really get crazy when the court lets guilty criminals go free? Besides white people with O.J.?"

I dislodged Pete from his chair and sat down. "The internet? Did you *study* for your job application?"

"Don't knock it," said Pete. "The internet is the greatest resource of our age. It's all the brains of all the nerds in all the basements in all the world right at your fingertips."

"Just tell your story," I said.

"What story? Oh, Rex and the tires. You know how he's always going on and on about how we're supposed to have Excellent Customer Service. He tells this story about how one time, somebody tried to return some tires. The House Station has never carried car tires. Rex told the guy this, but he insisted he got them at the Station. So Rex took them back."

"What'd he give the guy for them?" I asked.

"I don't know. He never said."

"Wait a minute," I said. "At *this* store?"

Pete thought for a minute. "No, I don't think so."

"But this is the first place he was a manager."

"It seems like there's a hole in your story," Superman said.

Pete shrugged. "It's not my story, it's Rex's story."

I slipped my heels out of my shoes. "I call shenanigans. There's no way he gave somebody store credit for some tires. How would you even ring that transaction?"

"Hell if I know," Pete said. "I'm the middleman here. Take it up with Rex."

"Maybe I will," Superman replied. "I've got to go. Take it easy, guys."

Pete leaned over the counter and called, "Let me know if you find out!"

Day 238 – Monday, July 5

It was dead, my feet were bad, and Pete was bored.

"Let's prank-call somebody in the store," he said.

I stuck a finger in my shoe and rubbed my instep. "What are you, twelve?"

"What else have you got to do?"

"Stand here and massage my feet. I wish I had some rubbing alcohol."

"There are alcohol pads in the first aid kit," Pete said. "You of all people should know that."

"I used them all up. They haven't refilled it."

"You should tell somebody."

"I told Kord. She's not in charge of it. I told Helen. That didn't work. Then I put a note in the suggestion box."

"We have a suggestion box?"

"The customers' suggestion box."

"Good luck with that. Nobody reads those but Rex." Pete toyed with his headset. "I'm going to call your Hardware buddy. Let's see. What kind of customer do I want to be?"

"A stupid one?"

"What other kind is there?" Pete dialed Hardware. "Hello?" he said in the voice of a cartoon hippopotamus. "Is this hammers? I need to talk to somebody in the hammers department. Yes, my good man, do you have any hammers? What kind? Are they quality hammers? I need hammers, man!

HAMMERS!" Pete hung up because he couldn't contain his laughter.

"That was poor," I said.

Pete glared at me. "You know what? You're right. Wait. I've got another one." He called again and used a more normal-sounding voice. "Yes, hello? Is this the House Station? I need to buy some wood. What do you mean you want to transfer me? Isn't this the House Station? What do you mean this isn't the wood department? I just need to ask a question about wood. What kind? Wood, man, for building things! No, don't transfer me! Don't you work there? What's your name? Fine, transfer me, but I'm going to tell your manager that Lance doesn't know a damn thing about wood!" Pete hung up and looked at me expectantly.

"Better."

A few minutes later Lance came to the desk, looking confused. "Hey, Pete, I think you routed a call through to me that should have gone to Lumber."

"Sorry," Pete said. "Did you transfer them? Do you know how to do it?"

"Yeah, but—" Lance scratched his head and I could visualize two rusty gears grinding within. "I've been getting some weird customers today."

Pete made a sympathetic face. "It happens."

"Sure. Hey, is making keys Hardware's job?"

"Yeah," Pete said.

"Oh, no! I've got to go! See you later, Pete, Little Buddy."

"Why does he call me Little Buddy?" I asked when he was gone. "I'm bigger than you."

"The same reason he told you he slept with Chloe," Pete said. "To make himself feel good. And why does he need to do that? Any number of reasons. Perhaps because he's a pathetic loser with low self-esteem. Perhaps because he works at the House Station. Perhaps because he's a poorly-endowed ass pirate with feelings of inadequacy. Take your pick, or all of the above."

"Seriously?" I said.

Pete shrugged. "I'm just trying to help."

"I'm going into the phone room for a minute."

"Why? Need to cry again?"

"I need to rub a cramp out of my foot. I don't think you'd want me doing that out here in front of everybody. Take care of my customers."

Pete stretched in his chair. "Turn your register light off. You know how confused they get."

Customers were like moths. They came to the light whether there was somebody there or not.

I went into the vacant phone room and pulled off my shoes and socks. My insteps were swollen and there were unsettling black veins visible perpendicular to my arches.

I had heel pain and arch pain. My attempts at internet diagnosis made me suspect plantar fasciitis, which I knew little about except that it had to do with a tendon on the bottom of the foot. Or it could have been heel spurs. Or any number of other things.

"What are you doing back here?" asked Kord from behind me, making me jump.

"My feet are in bad shape today. See?" I pointed at my bulging vein.

She recoiled. "Nasty!"

"It hurts worse than it looks," I assured her.

"Why don't you go to the doctor?"

"I don't have health insurance. I missed the enrollment period."

"That was a dumbass thing to do. When can you get it next?"

"December."

"Why don't you go to the free clinic?"

I looked up. "What free clinic?"

"That low-income clinic on the south side. Gordon Clinic."

"Never heard of it. I'll check it out, thanks. Anyway, what can you do for me today?"

Kord sighed. "Get a stool from Paint."

"Thank you."

"Be sure you put it back when you're done. Now get out there. You've got a customer."

I found a man standing at my register, which had neither light nor cashier, looking around like I was hiding.

"Can I help you?" I asked.

The man plunked a bag of pipe fittings on the counter. "It's the wrong stuff! That's what happens when you send your wife!"

Day 239 – Tuesday, July 6

I spent much of the day in anxious anticipation: Chloe was coming back. My emotions were puréed: I couldn't wait to talk to her, but at the same time, I was deathly afraid of what she might say, that everything would just fall apart and that would be it.

The Station did its best to distract me. My first customer had his sweatshirt tucked into his sweatpants. Another man was wearing a shirt that said *I Eat Glue*. But the fashion highlight of my day was a husky bronzed contractor in tennis shoes, short shorts, and nothing else.

"That's gross," Pete said. "Marathon-running Kenyans don't wear shorts that short. I'm going to jab pens through my eyes and stir them around in my brain. He could at least comb his chest hair once in a while."

"Maybe put some barrettes on there," I said. "The little pink ones that look like butterflies that you always find on the sidewalk."

"Shut the hell up!" Pete cried.

Ten minutes later Paige came up and leaned on my counter. "The nastiest guy I've ever seen was just in here."

"I thought he was here to see you," said Pete, and she hit him.

A customer came up, stood beside Paige, looked up at the Returns sign, and said, "Is this Returns?"

"Right here," I said.

He plunked a Bosch carrying bag on the counter and handed me a receipt. "I bought this yesterday. It's a RotoZip. Or at least, it was supposed to be. What's in the bag was there when I got it home."

I looked at the receipt. It was dated yesterday and showed that he had, in fact, bought a RotoZip spiral saw kit for a hundred and fifty dollars.

I hefted the bag; it was about the right weight for the saw. The customer didn't say anything else, and I unzipped the bag with some trepidation, expecting anything from rocks to dead puppies. There were two huge tin cans inside, containing V8 and cling peaches, respectively.

It was the easiest thing in the world to take out the saw, throw in five dollars' worth of groceries, and bring it back. But when a customer does that, his plan depends on the cashier not opening the bag. This guy *wanted* me to look, not that that made it legit. It could have been reverse psychology.

I held up the can of peaches and gave Paige a questioning look.

"I'll call Rex."

Paige talked to Rex for a while, then handed the phone to the customer, who talked to him for maybe thirty seconds, then handed the phone back.

When Paige hung up, she told the customer, "Go get another one and we'll switch it out." To me, she said, "Rex says don't RTV it. Leave it up here and he'll come deal with it later."

"Whatever you say."

While the customer was gone, Paige said, "Just exchange it. Don't give him a refund. That's what Rex said."

"That doesn't make any sense," I replied. "He's got a receipt."

"So?"

"So if we're going to do this at all, how are we going to tell him he can't have a refund if he wants one? Okay, he switches it out for a real one. Now he has a real one and a receipt one day old. Why can't he return that one?"

Paige shrugged. "You're right. But that's what Rex said."

"And even if Rex won't take it, the guy can take his brand new saw and his receipt and go to the Station across town."

Paige put a hand to her forehead. "Just do it, okay?"

Chastity, our on-probation, allegedly drug-dealing cashier, came in the front door.

Paige pounced on her. "Where have you been?"

"What?" asked Chastity, failing to look innocent.

"Why are you late coming back from lunch? You were supposed to be back forty-five minutes ago. Everybody else's lunch is late."

"Uh, well . . ." Whatever excuse was in the works, nobody was going to believe it. "There's a *reason*."

Paige waited, but nothing more was forthcoming. "When you think of it, I'd love to hear it. Kord, too. Go clock in and get on your register, and tell Merlin to go to lunch."

Chastity muttered something under her breath. Then she perked up and said, "Hey! Whose peaches are those?"

"Nobody's that I know of," I said.

"Can I have them?"

"You'll have to check with Rex," I said. "But I'll put your name on them."

Robert, the weird new Electrical guy, walked up to my cage and peered at me through his dark glasses. "Now where did I stash that shotgun? You know, instead of 'going postal,' it should be 'going House Station.' We should license that so people have to pay us when they go crazy. Do I have any Returns?"

I handed them to him and backed away slowly. He was tiny and looked unthreatening, but that only made him creepier. Pete called me over and I didn't hesitate.

"You looked like you needed an out," he said. "Hey, you remember how Rex said we were going to be able to buy House Station stock directly from the company? I looked into it. The whole thing is a scam — it's not any cheaper! When the program came out, they made a big deal about how we wouldn't have to pay brokerage fees or anything like that, that we could buy it right from the company, but there are these other transaction fees that make it pretty much the same price. And customers can do it too! It's not even special!"

"You were going to buy some?"

Pete shrugged. "I wanted to check it out. I've always said it's better to own stock here than work here. Thank you for calling the House Station and Rental Center at Garber and State, would you like to hear about our specials today? Yeah, they're all pretty much crap. Hang on, I've got to put you on hold for a minute."

"That better be somebody you know," I said.

Pete snapped his fingers in my face. "It's your woman! Where do you want it?"

My breath caught. "In the phone room. Take care of my customers."

Pete transferred the call. "Tell me everything she says."

Finally, a chance to talk to her. Did I want to ask her about Lance now or wait until I saw her? Now, I decided. The phone would be better if I got an answer I didn't like. My heart was pounding as I picked up the call.

"Penn! I haven't talked to you in like a week! I've been trying to get a hold of you for the longest time!" The sound of Chloe's voice got the butterflies churning within me. "You need to get a cell phone!"

"Pete said you couldn't get through to my house. Are you back in town?"

There was a pause, then, "Actually, that's why I called. I won't be back until Thursday."

My heart turned to lead. "How come?"

"I came to Kansas City because my grandma had a stroke," Chloe said, and now emotion flooded her voice.

"Yeah, Pete told me. I'm sorry."

"She died last night."

"Oh my God, I'm so sorry," I said, meaning it.

Chloe sniffled. "The funeral is Thursday. I'll be back Thursday night."

"Okay. Is there anything I can do for you?" I asked.

"No, nothing. Just pray for us, I guess. For me and my family. I'm not taking it as well as I thought I would. Even though we kind of knew it was coming. We were really close when I was little."

"Sure."

She was silent for a long time. "Well, I should go. I'll call you on Thursday when I get back."

"Okay."

"All right, well, I'll see you soon." She sounded like she was about to burst into tears. I'd never heard her like that, and it broke my heart.

"Take care," I said. "Bye."

I hung up and just stood there until Pete realized I was off the phone.

"Hey! What'd you find out?"

I came out to the Service Desk. "Nothing."

"Nothing? You were supposed to ask her . . . you know."

"What was I going to say?" I snapped. "'I'm sorry your grandma died, by the way, did you ever screw this jerk who's always bothering me over here?'"

Pete held up his hands defensively. "Whoa! Sorry! I didn't know!"

I went back to my counter. I felt so bad for Chloe, but I was still frustrated that I hadn't been able to talk to her about my

181

concerns, even though they were stupid compared to what she was dealing with right now.

I thought that was very selfish of me.

Day 240 – Wednesday, July 7

"Call Rex and tell him there's a guy out by the propane smoking a cigarette," Landfill said.

I wasn't in the mood. "Call him yourself. You have a phone."

"Somebody got up on the wrong side of bed today!" Landfill smiled that smile that made people want to hit him. "I don't even see what the big deal is. It's not like he's even smoking in the store."

There was a tremendous bang and everybody, customers and associates, put a finger in their ear at the same time.

"Oh my God! Holy crap!" Landfill looked like he'd just packed his Pampers. "He blew up the propane!"

I looked down at my shoes to keep from laughing. Something heavy and flat and metal had collided with the concrete floor. Maybe a shelf had fallen over or something had dropped from an overhead storage bay on one of the aisles.

Landfill was hopping like an over-caffeinated rabbit.

"Stop," I said. "It wasn't the propane."

"How do you know?" Landfill had missed our propane bombing.

"The store's not on fire, is it? The wall's still there."

"I guess not. So, are you going to call Rex for me or not?" His fear had given way, once again, to his heart-rending idiocy.

"What does the guy want? A propane exchange?"

"Yeah, I guess."

"So do it for him. You're a head cashier."

"I don't have a key."

182

I realized I was grinding my teeth. "Then I guess you'd better go find somebody."

Almost ten minutes later, an irate customer came to my register. This was the fourth time today he'd been there. The first time, he'd returned paint. The second, he'd paid to have his empty propane tank exchanged for a full one. The third, he'd come to tell me he was still waiting for somebody to come unlock the cage that held the full tanks.

"Give me a refund," he said. "Nobody showed. I'll just take my business elsewhere."

"Okay," I said. I didn't argue with the angry ones if I could help it. I took his receipt and ran it quickly. "That's refunded to your Discover," I said, handing him the slip.

He looked at it like I'd handed him a dead squirrel. "You could have just called someone!" he shouted, then stormed out of the store.

I straightened up my area. Did he just like to yell or had he been trying to bluff me? What was this, poker? Either way, I figured, that one was on Landfill.

Pete came in looking extremely pleased with himself.

"What are you so happy about?" I asked. "Aren't you off?"

He rattled my fence as he passed Returns. "I left my wallet in my locker last night. I'll be right back."

Five minutes later, he was back, looking like he was going to burst if he didn't tell me his story right away. To antagonize him, I picked up the phone and paged the departments to come get their returns.

I finally gave him my attention. "Yes?"

"I asked Christine out!" He was about as excited as I'd ever seen him.

"I assume she said yes."

He scoffed. "When I turn on the charm, no woman can resist. I overwhelmed her with my masculine wiles."

I raised an eyebrow. "Such as they are."

Pete threw up his hands. "Can't you be happy for me?"

"I *am* happy for you. If you're happy, I'm happy. What'd you do?"

"I asked her if she wanted to go to IHOP tomorrow, and she said yes."

"Romantic."

"I thought it was better to try to get her out in a group setting. Figured I had a better chance that way. I told her that you and Chloe were off tomorrow, and—"

I held up both index fingers. "Wait a minute. I *am* off tomorrow, but I can't double date with you. I haven't seen Chloe in over a week. I've got to have it out with her. We're not going to IHOP."

"Oh, no!" Pete cried melodramatically. "You mean it'll just be the two of us? Me and her? That's *terrible*! What was I *thinking*?"

I caught on. "You're using my misfortune for your own personal gain."

He wrung his hands. "Oh, I hope I don't forget to mention this to Christine!"

"You're pathetic," I said. "Have fun."

"You know if she and I hook it up, it'll be PC and PC."

"What?"

"Pete, Christine, Penn, Chloe."

"What are you, Landfill?"

My phone rang. It was Kord, and she wanted me to come back to the office.

"What'd you do?" Pete asked when I told him.

"Nothing." Nevertheless, I had that vague feeling of alarm that accompanies being summoned by authority no matter how clean the conscience.

"Sit down," said Kord once we'd wedged into the closet-sized office. "This is only going to take about ten minutes."

"What is it?"

"It's your quarterly review."

"Quarterly? I haven't had a review since I've been here."

Kord shrugged. "It's already been filled out. I just wanted to talk about the grades with you."

The review mostly consisted of a list of "competencies." They included such sentence fragments as *getting things done, customer-driven, self-development,* and *ground-engaged,* plus everyone's favorite, *provides Excellent Customer Service.* Each had a letter grade from A to D. I had a C in everything but *getting things done,* which was a B, and *enthusiasm,* which was a D.

"What's up with all the Cs?" I asked. The bottom of the sheet stated that *A = Outstanding, B = Achiever, C = Performer, D = Improvement Needed.* "What's the difference between 'achiever' and 'performer'? How do I only get a C on 'acts with integrity' even though you wrote 'trustworthy and honest'?"

"This isn't a bad review," Kord said. "Some of the things that people get Cs for are things that we really haven't observed. I think you have a lot of integrity. But if I give you an A or a B, Rex is going to ask me why and I'd have to give him something concrete. Don't worry about that."

There were other comments written next to some of the competencies. Next to *enthusiasm* was written *Need to smile more and appear to be happy at work.*

"Looking happy is the biggest thing," Kord said. "You're a good guy, but you can be pretty scary-looking sometimes."

"I know."

"You need to improve. You *have* to improve. Customers notice. I notice. Rex notices."

"Need to improve" and "Rex notices" merged and became a thinly veiled threat to my job security.

"Other things you can work on: try to push credit card sales and extended warranty plans, okay?"

I sighed. I couldn't in good conscience offer people our credit cards. The interest rates were ridiculous. Most of our customers had no business getting one. I'd pointed this out to Kord before.

"Don't give me all your credit card sass again," said Kord. "You're not their financial advisor. Just do it. We're going to introduce incentive programs to reward cashiers who sell the most. Try hard, okay?"

"Okay."

"Otherwise, just show some initiative. You're good about doing anything and everything I ask you to, but you could be a little proactive."

"Okay."

"You're good at making signs for other departments. That's good. I've told the department heads they should come to you to have signs made."

"Sure." I enjoyed making signs.

"Any other questions?"

"What does 'ground-engaged' mean?"

"That doesn't really apply to cashiers. It's for people in departments: how involved they are with customers, how available they are to help," said Kord. "On the whole, your review's pretty good. Just try to smile more and be friendly."

"I'd smile more if I could sit down more."

"I told you this morning you could get a stool."

"Yes, thank you, I got one. And then I stepped away from the register to help a customer with the electric cart and Rex had carried it off by the time I got back."

"What did he say to you?"

"Nothing. I didn't see him."

"Then how do you know it was Rex?"

"He walked past right before."

"Nobody saw him?"

"He's like a sasquatch," I said, exasperated.

Kord sighed. "I'll talk to him. But you still need to get a doctor's note."

"Okay. Thanks."

She clapped me on the knee. "Anything else, little whiner?"

"Does this have anything to do with my raise?"

"Your raise isn't until you've been here for twelve months. You still have time to improve. Sign at the bottom. I'll get you a copy."

I signed.

"Okay. Get your ass back to work. You're here until five?"

"Six," I said.

"Rex leaves at four if you find your stool."

Day 241 – Thursday, July 8

"You look madder than usual," said Angry Pete. "You didn't even cheer up when that old guy got rammed in the back with that shopping cart. What's the problem? Feeling anxious?"

"Chloe wants to meet me for lunch."

Pete wiped down his counter. "Okay, so what's the problem? Take her to Wendy's and work things out. Well, maybe not Wendy's. I hate that place. When their fry machine beeps it sounds just like my alarm clock."

"I don't think lunch is enough time to discuss everything we need to discuss."

"Did you tell her that?"

"Of course not. She doesn't even know this is coming. And I wanted to have it out somewhere a little more private."

"So why don't you just put it off? Talk to her about it tomorrow."

"I can't wait anymore!" I snapped. "I'm sick of waiting and I'm sick of tomorrow!"

Pete held up his hands. "Okay, fine. Good luck. But you and I both know you're making way too big a deal out of this. I'll be off by the time you get back, but I demand to hear about it. You have a customer."

The guy was a regular who always wore those free T-shirts you get when you give blood at the Red Cross. He wanted to return a saw for which he did not have a receipt, and he threw not one but two tantrums.

"Fifteen dollars on a store credit?" he exclaimed. "Are you serious? I paid twenty-five!"

"Without a receipt, I can only refund it at the price the computer lists," I recited. "It refunds at the lowest price the item has sold at in the last six months."

"Call someone."

"Even the manager can't override the system," I said. It was the gospel truth, but they never, ever believed me.

"Call someone!"

I dialed the head cashier, and after a while Landfill came up to take some abuse on my behalf. I didn't feel bad for him in the slightest. The higher you climbed the managerial tree, the more dealing with abusive customers became part of your responsibilities.

"What's the problem?" Landfill asked.

"Are you serious? He's not a manager!" the customer exclaimed.

"I'm the head cashier on duty," Landfill sniffed.

I explained the situation to Landfill, who told the customer everything I'd told him but in a more confusing way.

"I want to talk to a manager," said the customer.

Landfill tried to plead the case for his own importance. "Sir, I can do everything a manager can in this situation—"

The man looked at him incredulously. "A *manager*."

Landfill dialed and pretty soon Madeleine, the nicest of the ASMs, arrived.

"I paid twenty-five dollars for this and he wants to give me fifteen!" the customer said, brandishing the saw under Landfill's nose.

Madeleine looked at me. "No receipt. Lowest price in the system," I said.

"What are you going to do about it?" the customer demanded.

188

"Unfortunately, sir, there's nothing I *can* do about it," Madeleine said, sweetly and charmingly. "I'm sorry. We can't change the prices in the system. If you keep your receipt next time, we'll be able to refund your return at full price."

He looked the three of us: Madeleine, friendly; Landfill, dazed; and me, like I wished he *would* try to come across the counter with that saw. And he calmed down. Madeleine had soothed the savage customer.

"Okay," he said grudgingly.

"Okay," said Madeleine, patting me on the shoulder. She and Landfill left.

"Okay," I said, and ran the transaction. "Sir, I need to see your driver's license."

"*What?*" He was red in the face again.

"For every return without a receipt, the computer needs the driver's license number. I can't finish the return without it."

"I don't want to give it to you."

"I'm sorry, but I can't finish the transaction without it."

"No? Just give me one of those store credits right there! You've got a stack of them!"

"They have to be activated," I said.

The man slapped the counter. "You need my driver's license number? Fine. Put one two three four five six."

"The system won't take that."

"Just put it!"

I obligingly typed it in and the computer rejected it.

He dug in his wallet and handed me an ID that was in German and had no photo. "Use this."

"Sir, this isn't going to work either," I said. "I need a photo ID."

"You're not getting it! I'm not letting you put my driver's license number into your computer! Put that in!"

I put in the number from the German ID and it didn't take.

"There's nothing I can do with this," I said. "Do you want me to call the manager back up here?"

The man ground his teeth. He picked up his saw and banged it on the counter. "No! Why the hell does everything have to be so damn difficult for you people? Can't you even do your jobs? I'm done shopping here! You can tell your manager *that*! I'm going to Home Depot!" He took his saw and stormed out, waving it menacingly.

I'd gone too far into the transaction to clear it. I dialed Landfill again. "I need a void."

I met Chloe at a little deli down the street. When she saw me, she jumped up from the table and threw her arms around me.

"I'm so glad to see you!" she exclaimed into my chest. She gave me a kiss and said, "I didn't order yet. Are you feeling all right? What's the matter?"

"I'm fine. I'm sorry about your grandmother."

"Thank you. You look like something's bothering you. Do your feet hurt?"

They actually hurt quite a bit. "No, they're okay," I said.

"Let's eat, all right?" Chloe led me to the counter and ordered a turkey sandwich minus the cheese and mayo.

"Just give me a Coke," I told the clerk. The prospect of the imminent conversation had murdered my appetite and dumped it in a ditch.

After we sat down, Chloe leaned across the table and said, "Out with it. You don't fool me for one instant. What's bothering you? Is it something at work?"

"No," I said. "Yes. Not exactly. Look, I don't really feel comfortable bringing this up."

"Let's hear it. You can tell me."

I sighed and massaged my temples. "I've been wanting to discuss this with you for a week," I told her. "God, it feels like a year."

Chloe dropped her sandwich. It thudded on her tray.

"Oh, God," she said. "You're breaking up with me."

I blinked. That had come from so far out in left field that it didn't process right away. The sensible part of my mind raged at me that while I was sitting there looking stupid, the girl across the table had become a ticking time bomb of tears on a very short fuse. Chloe's nose was red and her lip quivered.

"No!" I cried. "It's not that at all! I'm not doing anything of the sort!"

Or was I? What if I had it out with her and got an answer I didn't like? What then? Would I dump her for it? Somehow, I'd never gotten that far. God, I hated direct confrontation.

"Look," I resumed awkwardly, "it's not that."

Chloe looked sheepish. "I feel really stupid."

I didn't respond; I was too busy trying to put together what I wanted to say. "Listen, Chloe, this may seem kind of dumb to you, and I'm sorry. It's about Lance."

Alarmingly, her eyebrow immediately shot up and a wary expression crossed her face. "What did he do?"

I fidgeted nervously and tugged on my ear.

"He said something to you, didn't he?" she said.

This was not going as I had hoped. I sucked it up and dropped the hammer. "He said he slept with you." I wanted to die.

"He told you that?" Chloe looked away and shook her head. "I should have known. God, he never had any sense of propriety."

My teeth were clenched. Blood rushed deafeningly in my head. I couldn't stand to look at her. I had to get out. I kicked my chair back and stood suddenly, shaking the table and spilling ice and soda across the floor.

"Penn, what are you *doing*?" said Chloe.

"I have to get back to work," I said in strangled tones, and rushed out the door.

She called something after me as I left, but I didn't catch it, and I didn't look back.

* * * * *

191

I sat in my car in the House Station parking lot for almost ten minutes. The engine was off and the windows were up and the heat was stifling. I didn't care. I didn't want to see anybody and I didn't want anybody to see me.

My face was burning. I flipped down the mirror and saw my eyes were bloodshot, my countenance unspeakable. If I went in the store now, I was bound to get another lecture from Rex, or worse.

I wanted to go home, forget the rest of my shift, forget my job, and forget the House Station entirely. Finish my book. Heal my feet. Sit with Adele, the only creature in the world that loved me unconditionally. I felt stupid for feeling that way.

The rational part of my mind told me to be serious—I would never walk out on a job like that. Even if I did, then what? Get another job, one that paid the same or less and was just as hard on my feet? And what about my grad school plans, half-assed as they might be?

There'd been enough scorched earth today. Finally, I went into the store, clocked in on my register, then walked as fast as I could toward the break room, head down.

When I got to the break room doorway, Lance came bounding out and we slammed into each other. I fell back a couple steps and glared, holding my bruised right side. Lance had taken the edge of the doorframe in the small of his back.

"Jesus!" Lance exclaimed. "Watch where the hell you're going!"

It wasn't anybody's fault; it was just one of those things. I couldn't think of anything to say that would help the situation, so I said nothing.

He loomed over me threateningly, filling the doorway. "Did you hear me? I'm talking to you! Doesn't anybody have any damn common courtesy anymore? You could at least apologize!"

I happened to think of a few things that would *not* help the situation, and I said one of them. "Get out of my way."

192

Lance's eyes widened in disbelief. "Do you need me to kick your ass? Is that what you're telling me?"

I shrugged. "Here I am."

I honestly didn't care. I wasn't going to fight him. I wasn't going to throw a punch. If he wanted to beat the crap out of me, fine, but I wasn't backing down.

For a good fifteen seconds, neither of us spoke or moved, with my murderous stare pitted against his hulking physique.

At last, he muttered, "Goddamn people are so rude," and shoved past me.

I went to fill my water bottle.

Day 243 – Saturday, July 10

"We used to make hydrogen gas and explode it," Robert said, his expression unreadable behind his dark glasses.

"Is that so?" Pete, clearly uncomfortable, peered down Electrical's aisles, hoping for a customer in need of Robert's services.

Robert stroked his unruly beard. "We would react hydrogen chloride with zinc and fill a balloon with the gas. You wax the string, you light it, and you let it go. It's too much science for kids these days."

"You're probably right about that," I said.

Robert turned abruptly on his heel and stalked down the fan aisle.

"I hope he wasn't left unsupervised as a child," Pete said.

"I was meaning to ask you about your date with Christine," I said. "How did that go?"

Pete was suddenly gleeful. "That's right, I didn't see you yesterday, did I? Because I had a Friday off, did I not? As did you, did you not? And did not Thursday at IHOP go so well that it turned into Friday at IHOP, *plus* a movie?"

"You took her to IHOP two days in a row?" I said. "Really?"

"Well, you know how—" Pete snapped his fingers. "Oh, no! We're not talking about me until we talk about you! You went out of here on Thursday looking like you were going to go drown a sack of puppies."

"Thursday was a bad day all around. I got into it with Lance after I came back. And thanks to Rex, I haven't had a stool in three days."

"Rex made you constipated?"

"A stool to *sit* on!"

Pete touched a finger to his lips. "I'd like to discuss that Lance thing. But first, I want to hear about you and Chloe."

"I'm not talking about it."

"Okay, obviously it went badly. You didn't hear what you wanted to hear. Yes?"

I said nothing.

"So what did you do? You didn't kiss and make up. Did you dump her? Look, I know it's none of my business, but just tell me, okay?"

"No."

"Chloe called while you were at lunch. Did you know that? I told her to call you at your house."

"She did. I let the machine get it."

"You did that yesterday, too. She told me that. She wanted me to give you a message. Sure you don't want to discuss it?"

"What did she say?" My calm tone belied my churning insides.

"That you don't understand and she wants you to call her as soon as you get off work. Also that you were being a stupid idiot."

"Mm."

"Penn, listen, it sounds like she wants to stay together. I know you're a Puritan, and I thought she was too, and she pretty much is, even if she wasn't in the past, unless there are some other things I don't know about, and I respect that.

Okay, that's not helping. Look, are you going to let this wreck your whole relationship?"

"The better I get to know people, the less I like them," I said.

"I'd slap you if I didn't think it'd make you drive your car through the side of my house." Pete pulled on his apron straps. "Is this worth it? You guys were happy together. It was so sweet it gave me diabetes. Either deal with her past indiscretions and kiss and make up or dump her and move on. Whatever gets us past this psychopath thing you're doing."

"I have a customer," I said, and returned to my register.

It was an older man. "Can you check me out here and save me a walk?"

I rang his merchandise, bagged it, and told him his total. He handed me a check.

"This is a rebate check," I said. "It's made out to you."

"But it's from the House Station!" He stabbed a finger at the large logo in the top left corner of the check.

"Yes. But it's payable to *you*." My tone was only marginally hostile.

"Just take the money off of it! Can't you do that?"

"It's not a gift card," I said. "It's a *check*. To *you*. You take it to your bank and deposit it or cash it."

"That's the damnedest thing I've ever heard!" the man exclaimed. "You give me money and I try to give it back to you and you won't take it! I've a mind to talk to the manager!"

"Do you want me to call him for you? I'll call him for you." I reached for the phone.

"Hmph! We'll see what the fellows at the bank have to say about this!" He stormed, muttering, out of the store, which took a full minute because of his cane and limp.

When I looked up, Pete was almost to my counter, the cord of his headset tether stretched taut. "Talk to me."

"No," I said, as frostily as I could. It was like an ice age at my register.

195

Pete sighed. "Look, your scary-man routine doesn't work on me. I know you too well. I know what this is doing to you."

I raised an eyebrow. "Do you?"

"Yeah, I think so."

"Then why don't you leave me alone?" I snapped. "I don't know what I'm going to do, okay? Jesus Christ."

Pete looked at me for a minute, then turned and walked away.

Day 244 – Sunday, July 11

I was off on a Sunday. Siccing Kord on Helen had worked.

I made a rare appearance at church. Chloe and I had, once upon a time, discussed going to church together. Not today.

When I got home, I switched the phone off and had an unexpectedly productive writing session. I was getting close to the end of the story, and the dramatic tension between my primary characters flowed from my fingertips with uncharacteristic ease.

That bit of irony did not go unappreciated.

I was engrossed to a new level. I channeled all my anger and frustration into my work. I was pretty happy about that.

In the course of time, I was disturbed by the sound of Drimacus the Eviscerator working over the balcony screen door with his razor-sharp talons. It was time for a break anyway. I went into the living room and admitted him to the porch, where he began to devour our sickly potted plant.

Adele arrived to roll around on her back, heedless of the dust. Drimacus pounced on her immediately. She hissed and batted him over the head, and he retreated. The balcony was her territory, and out here, she didn't have patience for his antics.

I looked down at Drimacus, who was now attempting to dig up the plant. "You're about due for a neutering," I said grimly.

I yawned and stretched. It was a beautiful, cool day. Two birds in the tree across the way were building a nest. One flew by at about our level, maybe fifteen feet above the ground, looking for choice twigs. Drimacus was enthralled. He crept to the edge of the balcony and peered between the slats, leaning out as far as he dared. The bird flew back to the tree and he went into his predatory crouch, tail twitching and butt waggling.

"Be serious," I said. "You're not *that* stupid."

I was wrong. The next time the bird flew down, low and temptingly close, Drimacus launched himself at it. It was almost majestic: he did not leap down but *out*, as though he and that bird would fly away together. I was transfixed as it happened. It was simultaneously the most hilarious and the most horrifying thing I'd ever seen.

I charged for the front door.

I found Drimacus on the grass below, stunned but miraculously unharmed. I carried him inside.

"You're lucky you didn't land on the sidewalk," I said. "You would have broken all your legs."

As soon as I put him down inside, he shook his head vigorously, as if to clear it, and made a beeline for the porch again. I barred his way with my leg and pulled the screen shut.

"Your balcony privileges are revoked," I said. "Forever."

Day 245 – Monday, July 12

I found coloring books and crayons on every table in the break room, accompanied by signs that read *For those who feel*

197

the need to draw on the tablecloths: further defacing of company
property will result in disciplinary action.

I filled my water bottle and headed up to Returns. The registers had been set to ask for customer zip codes for the marketing people — that meant longer transaction times due to bewildered customers.

Colonel Goodenough, KLU's finest gym teacher, entered the store, but I saw him coming and evacuated to the restroom. Atwater protested, but I bought him off with some M&M's.

Shortly after I returned, James Earl Jones with a Perm arrived at my register. He put a new ceiling fan, still in the box, on the counter along with the receipt. "I want to return this."

"Okay." I ran the transaction. "It's going to refund to your credit card." As he filled out the slip, I picked up the fan and put it in Electrical's bin.

"Hey, bring that back!" he exclaimed. "I want to buy it again!"

Usually when people did this, they wanted to spend store credit instead. I re-rang the fan. James Earl Jones with a Perm handed me a gift card for thirty dollars, then put the rest on the same credit card.

"And I want to buy a gift card for fifty dollars," he said.

He again paid with the same credit card. I had no idea what he was trying to accomplish; as far as I was concerned, we were just playing register games. From start to finish, there had been three transactions taking over five minutes.

"So all we actually did here was get you a fifty-dollar gift card instead of a thirty-dollar one," I said.

"Yeah. I needed a fifty-dollar gift card, and I'd already bought this other one."

I was flabbergasted. "You could have just bought the new gift card and used the old gift card to help pay for it. For your future reference."

"Oh," said James Earl Jones with a Perm, in a tone that suggested that I'd better not question too harshly his avant-garde approach to cashiering.

I was walking toward the big automatic doors to go to lunch when Chloe came marching through them, looking fierce. I almost turned and ran.

Chloe stopped right in front of me, glaring. "You are a stupid boy," she said, hands on hips. "Now I am going to talk, and you are going to listen. Let's go."

I half-expected her to grab me by the ear. My resolve was crushed. She spun on her heel and walked back through the doorway, and I followed. She went to my car and stood by the passenger door until I opened it for her.

"Where are we going?" I asked.

"Wherever you want."

"My house?"

"Your house."

Neither of us spoke again until we were inside the apartment.

"You've been avoiding me the entire weekend," Chloe declared, arms crossed. "Sit down."

I obeyed. Instantly, Drimacus was chewing on my shoelace. I reflexively shoved him away with my foot.

"I was upset," I said lamely.

She scowled down at me. "I know that. I didn't know why at first."

I raised an eyebrow but said nothing.

"Penn, do you want to break up?"

I was silent for a long time. "Honestly, no. No, I don't. I wish none of this had ever happened."

"None of what? No, wait, don't answer that." Chloe sat down across from me. "I talked to Pete last night. That was when I realized exactly how little you understand the situation. What is this about, Penn? What started all this?"

"Lance."

"What about Lance?"

"He said you dated in high school."

"That's right. For a grand total of three weeks."

"And he said he slept with you."

Chloe gave a little sigh. "Which is one of the numerous reasons why I dumped him!"

I blinked. "What?"

"He's a huge jerk! Did you not pick up on that? He says a lot of things!"

I tried to put it together. "So . . . you didn't . . . ."

"No, of course I didn't!"

Waves of relief washed over me in a boundless tide.

"You took his word over mine, Penn. That hurts. A lot."

"I didn't! I waited until you got back so I could talk to you! The other day, in the deli! You made it sound like you were mad that he told me!"

"I *am* mad that he told you! Because it's a *lie*, not because it's some big secret! And if I had, what would have been the big deal? That wouldn't change who I am now, does it?"

I shifted uncomfortably in my seat. "I don't know," I said. "I guess."

"But it would bother you."

"Yes."

"Why?"

"I don't know! I just thought, well, you . . . And I—"

"I didn't," Chloe said.

"I believe you."

"I never have." She looked at me intently.

"Well, neither have I!" I exclaimed, and immediately reddened. "Look, I'm sorry. I've been a tremendous ass the last few days. I'm sorry for walking out on you and I'm sorry for not giving you the benefit of the doubt. I've made way too big a deal out of this. I don't want to break up with you. I love being with you. I'm sorry. I fall on your mercy."

"You're a big, dumb moron." She got up and patted me on the hand. "But you're cute. I'll forgive you . . . eventually. Now make me some lunch."

Day 246 – Tuesday, July 13

"You look a lot happier," Angry Pete said.

I shrugged. "My stool's back. Rex isn't here."

"Right." Pete was skeptical. "I heard Chloe literally dragged you out of here yesterday."

"Who told you that?"

"Atwater. He came by because he left his ridiculous trenchcoat here. Why is he wearing it? It's ninety degrees outside. That damn denim coat and cheesy mustache . . . he always looks like he's about to go to the park and expose himself to some old ladies. Anyway, tell me about Chloe."

"Things with Chloe are okay. We didn't break up."

Pete scratched his nose. "You forgave her and took her back, eh? That was a fine and upstanding thing to do. Can't let past indiscretions stand in the way of future progress. You did the right thing."

"She didn't sleep with Lance."

Pete changed course effortlessly. "Of course she didn't. She's not a tramp. She's chaste and innocent, just like you. You'll probably get married and have eight or ten home-schooled babies. You did the right thing."

"Home-schooled babies?"

Pete waved a hand. "Hey, since you guys are back to the land of sunshine and bunnies, do you want to double date tonight?"

I hadn't yet had the opportunity to see Pete with Christine. I couldn't quite picture it. "If Chloe wants to. Maybe you should just plan things through her for a while."

"Confiscated your man card, did she? I'll call her. Where should we go? IHOP?"

"We need to get some restaurants in this town," I said.

"I saw in the paper yesterday that they're trying to get Leetown an arena football team. Maybe that'll spark the economic boom it'll take to rise above the grease pits."

"Some people really like arena football," I said, thinking of Chloe's brother.

"Well, those five people aren't here," said Pete. "Let's not kid ourselves. If Leetown has something, it sucks. You know how much Leetown sucks? We're probably not even going to get an arena football team. How's that for sucks?"

"Sucks," I agreed. "Why don't you move?"

"Are you kidding? We can't leave Leetown. Nobody can. It's a vortex of soul-crushing suburban mediocrity."

I sighed. "IHOP, then."

My register phone rang. It was Kord.

"There's a middle-aged woman coming your way with a cart full of merchandise she's trying to steal. None of it's bagged and she won't have a receipt. Don't let her out the front door."

"You want me to knock her down and break her legs?" I said.

"Just don't let the cart out of the store."

The front door of the store is to thieving customers as the American shore is to seafaring Cuban refugees—once they were out the door, they were safe and sound. We could follow them outside and say, "Excuse me, ma'am, could you stop?" We could follow them to their cars, but we couldn't touch them. If we did, they could sue us for assault. We didn't have any security people.

I spotted the lady on the main aisle, moving at a good clip. I intercepted her close to the door as she set off the Sensormatic alarm, stepping out from behind the wall in the vestibule that separated Returns from the main aisle.

"Excuse me," I said, putting my hand on the front of the cart. "Can I please see your receipt?"

The lady jumped when I spoke to her, then looked around nervously for an out. She tried to keep going, but I had a firm grip on the cart. When she realized there was nothing doing, she made a pretense of digging through her purse.

The best she could do was, "I must have left it at the Garden register when I checked out. I guess the cashier didn't give it to me."

This was, of course, a ridiculous proposition. She'd come from the other direction.

"I'll hold on to your cart while you go get it," I said, and off she went.

There were all kinds of things in the cart: plants, tile, paint, small but expensive electronic devices from Hardware. Nothing was bagged. Some people just didn't try very hard.

I didn't expect the lady to come back, but I lingered in the vestibule to see how quickly she would make her escape from Garden. After about three minutes, she walked briskly to her late-model Jaguar and drove off.

I went to distribute the cart's contents among my bins.

Sitting across from me in one of IHOP's torn and tattered booths, Christine looked more frail than usual. Her unnaturally tinted blond hair betrayed drab brown roots, although her pale and slightly pimply face was not without a certain charm. Yeah, maybe she *was* kind of cute in an "I'm still in high school" sort of way.

Christine was wearing a low-cut powder blue tank top that, when she leaned forward, alluringly revealed an unhealthy hint of sternum. She and Pete were squeezed together in a way that's cute when you do it and uncomfortable when someone else does it.

I was sitting next to Chloe, although not nearly as cozily. I was still working my way back into her good graces.

We were talking about work, but Chloe didn't seem to mind.

"Dear God in heaven," Pete said. "I had this ugly lady at my desk today. Man, she was *ugly!*"

"How ugly was she?" I asked dutifully.

"She looked like the Joker on Botox," said Pete. "Ugliness like that goes against the laws of nature! Have you ever seen somebody so ugly it made you physically sick? Have you? Short out the damn security tapes!"

"I have a story, too," Christine said, when Pete had stopped grumbling. She tended to speak in declarations.

She looked at Pete, who shrugged. "Go ahead."

"I was out on the Garden register today, and Rovergial the ASM was using the forklift to put pallets of potting soil up into the overhead bins. Except somebody had left their tape measure on one of the forks of the forklift, you know, so when he lifted it up it was tilted all crooked and everything almost fell off. And then they had to put it down and take it off and put it back on again."

There was silence at the table.

Pete smiled apologetically. "Guess you had to be there."

Chloe turned her attention to the menu. "Oh, those chocolate chip pancakes look really good to me. With the whipped cream on them..."

"I could never eat that," Christine announced. "It's way too fattening. It would go right to my hips."

Chloe's eyes narrowed. "I don't eat it every day."

Christine didn't look up from her menu. "I never would eat it even once."

"Clearly," Chloe muttered.

"So, Penn, how's that book coming along?" Pete interjected.

"It's coming, although at this point, it feels like it'll never end, and I can hardly remember a time when I wasn't working on it," I said.

"You're writing a book?" Christine asked, marshalling all her deductive reasoning skills. "Is it anything I'd like to read?"

I found the question exasperatingly inane, but I tried to be polite. "I don't know. What kind of books do you like to read?"

"Oh, I'm very well read. I read a book just last month. Plus I must have read five or six books this year, what with my senior English class."

I glanced at Chloe, then at Pete, then back to Christine. "What books were they?"

She scrunched up her face in thought. "I don't really remember."

"What was the *last* book you read?" There was desperation in my voice.

Pete leapt to her aid. "I'll tell you the last thing *I* read. One of literature's great authors. Bram Stoker. He wrote *Dracula*." He said this like a teacher lecturing his class.

"We know that," Chloe said. "Most everyone knows that."

"*I* didn't," Christine declared.

"Well, you should have," said Chloe.

Pete glared at her, and I quickly said, "So tell us about it. You read *Dracula*."

"I saw the movie," Christine said.

"Bela Lugosi is classic," I said, still trying to meet Christine on her level.

"Bela Lugosi? I don't know who she is," said Christine. "Was she Keanu Reeves' fiancé?"

Mystified, I looked to Pete, who pounded his fist on the table, rattling the silverware. "I didn't read *Dracula*! I read some short stories!"

I held up an open palm. "Okay, go."

Having successfully seized the conversation, Pete settled down a bit. "Anyway, a lot of Stoker's stories are dreamy, nancy-pantsy-type nonsense. But a few of them are seriously disturbing."

"Do really we want to hear this?" Chloe asked.

"Too late for that now," said Pete forebodingly. "The story was called 'The Dualitists.' Have you read it? No? Do you know what pencil-break is? The game kids play in grade school where they bash their pencils together until one snaps?"

"Bram Stoker wrote a story about it?" I said.

"In a manner of speaking. It's about these two rich kids, I guess they're brothers. Anyway, they go around playing pencil-break with everything in the house, candlesticks and silverware and whatnot, blaming the broken stuff on the servants. After a while, they get tired of that, so they go outside and play it with some animals. Cats and squirrels and stuff."

I raised an eyebrow. "They bashed some cats together?"

"Gross," said Chloe.

"I've only just begun," Pete warned. "Classic literature, man, you guys are sleeping on this stuff. So after they kill all the animals in the neighborhood, they go around looking for something else to do, and they find two babies. They take them up on the roof and— Ow!" He broke off, howling, as Chloe kicked him hard enough to make the table shake and the drinks slosh.

"Hey!" Christine exclaimed. "There's water on my shirt!"

"Everybody take it easy!" I snapped. "Just take it easy. Pete, I don't think that one's making it onto Oprah's book list anytime soon."

"It's called Oprah's Book *Club*," Christine corrected.

"Who the hell cares?" Pete snarled, rubbing his bruised shin.

The waitress came then and everybody's mood improved. Chloe ordered her chocolate chip pancakes with a defiant look at Christine, who got a dinner salad with no dressing.

When the waitress had gone, Christine excused herself and stalked to the restroom like the runway model she no doubt aspired to be.

I saw Chloe's lips form the words *I don't like her*.

206

Pete glared at her. "What's the matter with you?"

Chloe reached out and took Pete's hand. In her sweetest voice, she said, "I'm your friend, Pete, and I only have your best interests at heart. You know that, right?"

"If you say so," said Pete warily.

"So tell me, what do you see in her?"

Pete sighed. "Okay, maybe she's not the most literary person around. So what? She's hot. She likes me. She thinks I'm funny."

"She's obnoxious," Chloe said.

Pete scoffed. "Compared to who? Me?"

"He's got a point there," I said.

Pete threw himself back in in the booth. "Jeez! I thought you guys would be happy for me!"

"We are," I said. "But she could be a little nicer."

Pete snorted. "Said the pot to the kettle."

"I'm nice," I countered. "I just don't *look* nice."

"Or *act* nice." Pete accidentally knocked his fork off the end of the table. He and Chloe both bent down to pick it up, and their heads smacked together.

Pete cried out in a loud voice and fell out of the booth. Chloe was unfazed.

"Good God Almighty!" cried Pete from the floor. "Holy crap, you have a hard head! Woman, your head is a *stone*!" He hauled himself dramatically back into the booth.

"Are you okay?" Chloe asked, without her usual concern.

"How many fingers am I holding up?" I asked.

"How many am *I* holding up?" Pete countered. The answer was one. Pete held his water glass against his forehead. "Like a damn aluminum bat. In medieval times, they used your head to batter down the castle gates."

"He's fine," Chloe said.

"'Fine'? I have a concussion! Get me some aspirin."

Christine slid back into the booth, inadvertently kicking me squarely in the anklebone as she got settled. Pete glared at me for the face I made, but I said nothing.

"Was anybody at work today?" Christine asked.

Nobody answered, but that didn't matter, because she just kept talking.

"Today just flew by! It was so busy out in Garden. The time goes so fast when it's busy."

There was only so much I was willing to take, and this was a good opportunity to earn some Chloe points. With a curt smile at Pete, I said, "Actually, I find that most of the time, my shift feels interminable regardless of how busy it may or may not be."

"Hm," said Christine.

"That's true," Pete admitted. "When it's slow, it gives you more time to sit there to think about how much your job sucks."

"As a matter of fact," I continued cheerfully, "Most days, when I go home, regardless of how busy it was, my first thought is, 'I'm nine hours closer to death than when I came in.'"

"Oh," said Christine. "That's not very friendly."

"I'm friendly on the inside," I assured her.

"Like a Twinkie?" she asked.

"Most definitely not like a Twinkie," I said.

Pete once again commandeered the conversation with all the grace of a TV cop yanking an elderly lady out from behind the wheel of her car. "Do you remember Charlton Heston?" he said to me.

"Yeah. 'Let my people go,' 'From my cold, dead hands,' and so forth. What about him?"

Pete waved a hand. "Not the *real* Charlton Heston. The one that used to work at our store."

I put a hand to my head. "Man, what are you saying?"

"Before we opened, there was a guy who looked like Charlton Heston. Am I the only one who remembers this?"

"I've had a customer who looked like Frank Sinatra," I said. "Or Kenneth Copeland. Those guys look alike."

"Who the hell's Kenneth Copeland?"

"He's a televangelist. The one who looks like Frank Sinatra."

Pete rolled his eyes. "Look, you don't remember the Charlton Heston guy?"

"What was his name?" I asked.

"I don't know."

"What department was he in?"

"I don't know."

"Are you sure he exists?"

Pete banged the table. "I saw him today!"

"I thought you said he didn't work at the Station anymore," I said.

"He was in as a customer!"

"I have absolutely no idea what you're talking about."

"*Nobody* knows what I'm talking about!"

"And yet you keep talking," I said. "Crazy."

"Maybe I am," Pete mused. "I asked Madeleine. She had no idea either."

"Did you ask Helen?" Chloe asked. "She did all the interviews."

"Good idea," I said. "Ask Helen if you're crazy."

"Enough of your nonsense. Food's here," said Pete.

"Who's Charlton Heston?" asked Christine.

Day 248 – Thursday, July 15

Rex shanghaied me as I was heading to my locker at the end of the day.

"Penn, are you done with your shift? Can I talk to you for a minute?"

I couldn't think of any good reason why not, and it didn't really seem like a question anyway, so I followed him to the break room. As we turned the corner, I almost collided with

Lance. We glared at each other, but with Rex there, that was all.

The break room was empty, and I sat down.

"I'm concerned about you, Penn," Rex said.

A sense of dread came over me. It was vague, because I hadn't done anything specifically wrong that I could think of, but at the same time, it was acute, because here we were. You'd never think a pudgy, gray-haired, round-faced, flannel-clad man could be so terrifying.

Rex seated himself not across the table from me, as I expected, but next to me. "Is everything okay? Is there anything you want to talk about?"

"Uh, no," I said carefully. "Everything's pretty much good."

"I understand you've been seeing Chloe van Caneghem."

Who the heck told him that? What business of it was his? Why did he bring it up? The House Station had no rules prohibiting relationships between associates as low on the totem pole as we were.

"Is everything okay there?" Rex asked.

Two responses sprang immediately to mind: "Yes" and "None of your damn business." I didn't have an occupational death wish.

"Fine," I said.

"A lot of the time, you look upset," Rex said. "Even angry. If there's anything wrong, I want to help. But it's got to change."

At last: the threat concealed behind the velvety curtain of false concern.

"Look, I know customers can be a real pain in the ass sometimes. But smiling and putting up with it is part of your job. Remember what I told you: you just have to say, 'I love you, you bastard.'"

"I don't mind the customers so much," I said. "Really. It's my feet. They hurt all the time."

"Why don't you go to the doctor?"

"I don't have health insurance right now. I do a lot better on days where I have a stool," I said, taking what I felt was a reasonable and diplomatic stance.

"Penn, I don't question your honesty. I'm sure your feet are as bad as you say they are. But it's about fairness. If I let you sit down without a doctor's note, I'd have to let everyone sit down. Sitting is just not professional."

I, thinking of the cashiers at Aldi with their chairs and conveyor-belt counters, saw no problem with letting everyone sit. I said nothing.

Rex dropped the hammer. "I can't let you sit down anymore without a doctor's note."

Part of me wanted to quit right there. However, a larger part of me, one that liked to pay the bills, quickly subdued it.

Rex leaned back and crossed his arms. "Go see a doctor. And act friendly. I can't have unfriendly cashiers."

"Okay."

"Penn, I know this isn't what you want to do with your life. You don't want to be here for the next twenty years. I don't blame you. You're young and smart. You want to be a writer, right?"

"Yeah."

"So what are you doing here? Why don't you go to New York?"

That was a question not worth answering, and I didn't.

Rex kept going. "Why don't you use all your experiences here for a book? You could call it *The Customer Is Always Right . . . Yeah Right!*" He chuckled.

That was unequivocally the worst title I'd ever heard.

I thought we were about done, but Rex spent some time expounding the virtues of Excellent Customer Service.

Around ten p.m., Rex pushed back from the table. We'd been there for half an hour. "Well, let's go home. Do you work tomorrow?"

"At *eight*," I said through my teeth.

211

"See you tomorrow, then," Rex said cheerfully. "Penn, you're a good kid. I know you can do better."

I went to my locker. I had one consolation: I was still on the clock. If I had to be lectured and threatened, then by God, I was going to get paid for it.

Day 249 – Friday, July 16

Pete heard about my meeting with Rex from Chloe's roommate Bethany, who worked the night crew. At the Service Desk, I obligingly provided the details as Pete sneered.

"That's the dumbest thing I've ever heard. Unprofessional? How many customers ever say, 'Oh, I'm not shopping at the House Station; their cashiers sit down! How unprofessional!' People come here in their underwear for tools, practically. Screw Rex and his stupid-ass black-tie nonsense. What do we need, a damn *maitre d'* like those retirement-home greeters Wal-Mart has? You should have told Rex it was all crap."

"You think I'd be here today if I—"

Pete held up a finger. "Thank you for calling the House Station and Rental Center at Garber and State, would you like to hear about our specials today? Just a second, I'll transfer you. What? Maybe, what's your question? The difference between aluminum and fiberglass ladders?" Pete looked at me and shrugged. I shrugged back. "Well, my dad never fell off a *fiberglass* ladder. Hm? Look, let me transfer you. Yes, you, too. Stupid damn morons. Penn, what the hell are you doing?"

I was on one knee, scrubbing my shoe with a wet paper towel. "How, I ask you, can I be expected to provide Excellent Customer Service if I don't have clean shoes?"

"Damn right!" Pete exclaimed, too loudly. "And how in the holy blue hell can I provide Excellent Customer Service if they don't let me lie down behind the counter and take a three-hour nap? Injustice! Jesse Jackson!"

James, a new guy in Plumbing, walked up, checked his Returns, and sat down on the bench across from my register. He was a big jovial guy, Santa Claus as a country handyman. He let out a ferocious sigh.

"Rough day?" said Pete obligingly.

"We fight a constant battle against gravity," James said. "It keeps trying to suck you back into the earth."

Paige came through the front door with a disgusted look on her face.

"You were supposed to be back from lunch twenty minutes ago!" Pete called after her. "Landfill's been up my ass like a damn colonoscopy!"

"I know! Shut up! Don't yell at me, I have a headache!" Paige came to my register to clock in, rubbing her front against mine before I could take a step back. "I got pulled over. The cop was an ass."

"What happened?"

"I rolled a stop sign and he got me. He said, 'Did you see me?' and I said, 'No.' So he said, 'You probably thought we weren't doing our job.'"

"Ass," Pete agreed.

"You got a ticket, didn't you?" James asked rhetorically. "They don't cut anybody any breaks in that mood."

"Hell yes, I got a ticket," said Paige. "Penn, where's your stool? I need to sit down a minute."

Day 250 – Saturday, July 17

Chloe reclined next to me on my couch. "What's the matter?"

Things had been going a lot better between us. We'd both moved on, mostly, from what had ultimately been a case of me

213

acting like a huge idiot. I'd been more afraid of losing her than I'd ever realized and was so relieved I hadn't—maybe she felt the same way.

I rubbed my instep. "Work sucked. My feet hurt."

"Poor baby. What else?"

I pointed to two letters on the coffee table. "I sent out 'Last Song of Morning' a couple months back, right? Two rejections today."

She held my hand. "But you still have three other ones out there. That's good, isn't it? I mean, the longer they have it, the more chance it has of getting accepted, right?"

"How do you figure?" I asked.

"Because maybe they're seriously considering it."

I shrugged. "Or maybe they forgot about it entirely. Or maybe they threw it away. Or maybe they ran out of toilet paper in the office the day mine got there."

"Penn, it'll be okay! You'll get it published. It's a good story."

"Thanks. Look, my feet are really bad. I'm going to go get the foot spa, if you don't mind."

"You're going to do it in here? On the carpet?"

"Yeah, why not?"

"You can't help but spill it, can you? That can't be good for the carpet."

"Neither is two cats giving themselves daily manicures on it," I said. "Never mind the other stuff they do. It'll get replaced when we move out anyway."

"Are you sure you didn't want to go to IHOP with Pete and Christine?" Chloe asked jokingly, trying to get my mind onto more pleasant things.

"I'm so sick of that place. They eat there three times a week."

She had a teasing smile on her face. "Is that the only reason?"

"You know what? I think it's hilarious that you don't like Christine."

"Why?"

"Because you like everybody."

Chloe shrugged. "She rubs me the wrong way."

"It's fine," I said. "I don't really like her either. Let me go get the foot spa real quick, and then I'll make dinner."

I pulled off my socks. That throbbing black vein on each foot was bigger than ever, and my insteps were swollen.

"That looks awful!" Chloe exclaimed.

"I spent half the day leaning against whatever could be leaned against," I said. "At the end of my shift, I couldn't stand up. Pete let me cover the phones for about twenty minutes, though, which was very timely."

"Penn! That's not okay! You can't keep going like this."

"What am I supposed to do?" I asked. "These days, my feet *never* stop hurting. I can't even remember a time when they didn't hurt. Maybe when I get two consecutive off days, if I can spend both of them off my feet, the pain subsides by the evening of the second day."

"Why don't you go to the doctor?"

I recited from my script. "Because I don't have insurance."

"Go anyway! You can't live like this!"

"I can't afford it."

"You can't afford *not* to go, pardon the cliché! This is *crippling* you. Penn, you can't wait until January."

I thought about this. "You're right, of course. God, I feel like I'm stuck in this terrible rut with the Station, the chronic foot pain, all of it. I don't know how to get out. I hate my life sometimes."

Chloe kissed me on the cheek. "You start by going to the doctor. Go to the Gordon Clinic." She opened her purse and handed me a sheet of paper with an address and directions on it. "I asked Kord about it for you. You've been stupid about it for too long. I will drag you if I have to."

I put my arms around her. "Thanks."

She smirked. "Don't you know that life goes a lot better for you when you just do as I say?"

215

"Yes, dear," I said.

Day 252 – Monday, July 19

I sucked it up and went to the Gordon Clinic, which was for low-income (and no-income) people. As such, it didn't have anything remotely resembling a podiatrist or an orthopedist. The doctor I saw quite clearly had no idea what was wrong with my feet, but I wasn't about to pay for X-rays.

I'd done my homework. I was certain I had plantar fasciitis—a tear in the tendon running from the heel under the foot. Pressure on the balls of the feet caused pain in the heels. The condition was associated with long periods of weight bearing. Contributing factors included obesity and weight gain, standing and walking on hard surfaces, and shoes with little or no arch support. It was an open-and-shut case: the House Station was all about standing on hard surfaces. *And* plantar fasciitis was typically a lifelong condition.

The doctor wasn't eager to accept my diagnosis. He thought I might have heel spurs. That was fine with me, since it was well documented that plantar fasciitis often caused them.

I left with a note that read *Limited standing due to calcaneal spur.* Those six words were magic in my hand. Everybody had been right—I should have done it months before. I didn't know what my problem was. I also had permission to take six Aleve a day, which was triple the maximum dosage on the bottle.

My golden ticket only cost me twenty-five dollars (or three hours at the Station), which, I discovered later, was less than the copay for the House Station health insurance.

Day 343 – Tuesday, October 19

With a stool Rex couldn't take away, I didn't hate my life near as much. Three months passed in relative tranquility. Several dozen House Station associates quit or got fired. None of them was Landfill.

Pete, somehow, was still with Christine, which meant that relationship had lasted about three months longer than I'd anticipated.

Chloe didn't get accepted into her study abroad program and would not be going to Belgium. She would not be going much of anywhere. She was completely disconsolate for three days, at which point she seemed to get over it completely overnight.

She was still the bright spot in my life—the thought of seeing her after work was what got me through the day.

In mid-September, the Station put out the Halloween stuff, including a garish display of light-up lawn fixtures in the shapes of skeletons and black cats and such in the vestibule. On my register was placed a display of environmentally, politically, and fire-departmentally correct battery-powered jack-o'-lantern "candles."

Relatively speaking, I was feeling pretty good. Things with Chloe were excellent, my book was almost done, and my feet didn't hurt every waking minute of the day. I even got my diploma from KLU, finally.

And then they moved me down to the registers.

You can't sit on a stool and scan a cart full of two-by-fours. This relocation changed my stool from the reason I was willing to come to work to decorative clutter behind my register.

I pitched a fit to Kord. She told me Rex wanted a greater rotation on Returns so more cashiers could get experience with it and so nobody got burned out there. I wasn't burned out at all, I countered, and I didn't want to leave. Kord said it was out of her hands.

217

I judged Rex's decision to be malicious. I felt like he was out to get me—he'd practically nullified the doctor's note for which I had long suffered.

Maybe he *didn't* order a department-wide reschedule just to get me, but who believed that? Not I, said the cat.

My weekly schedule was just as random as before, with my two off days (always weekdays) nearly always nonconsecutive. But now I was getting three, usually four shifts on a register and one, rarely two, on Returns.

Almost all my register shifts were 12:30 to close. Because our store was perpetually understaffed, I spent the last half of that shift as the only cashier. This shift was scheduled until 9:30, and while the store allegedly closed at nine, the Last Cashier Standing was lucky to get out of there before ten, because when customers came in at 8:55 to buy everything they needed to build a house from scratch, the House Station said, "Sure, take your time; none of our people have anything better to do, nor have they lives of any kind."

I was on Register One, which was theoretically next to Registers Two through Eight but was actually a lonely island walled on two sides by enough concrete to pave all of Leetown. It was the contractors' register.

The only other thing nearby was the Oops Paint. We had shelves of paint people brought back because it was the wrong color or the wrong sheen, and these were resold at a severe discount.

People tried to run scams with this stuff, too. The strategy was to pick out all the paint you wanted from the Paint Department, sparing no expense. You bought it, then returned it. Odds were, it would end up as-is on the Oops Paint shelf, where you could buy it again for twenty-five cents on the dollar.

Somewhere along the line, somebody caught on, and so it became unofficial policy to retint all the returned paint. Every Paint associate had his or her own style. Chloe liked to retint the paint just a little, and if there was a large batch returned (which was highly suspicious), she tinted each differently. Tom, in contrast, turned everything into either poop brown or ghastly turquoise. These two color families typically comprised eighty percent of the paint on the shelf. Like snowflakes, no two cans were alike. Nobody ever bought them, but that didn't stop him. Some colorblind person (or some Leetown type with no décor sense) was going to come along and get a sweet deal.

A gay couple was at my register, buying a handful of things. One of the men was wearing sneakers identical to mine.

"Nice shoes," I said.

"Oh, thanks!" he said.

I extended a leg out from behind the register. The man's partner tapped him on the arm and nodded at my foot. They both laughed.

I ran their transaction and helped them through a problem they had with their House Station credit card.

"He knows what he's doing," said one.

"That's unusual," said the other.

It seemed to me to be a well-documented fact that gay people were, by and large, a lot nicer than straight people, at least in our store. Give me gay customers every time.

Day 345 – Thursday, October 21

After closing on Wednesday, I opened on Thursday, which meant I was there at 6:30.

The money we started the day with on the regular registers was stupid. The cashier till was one hundred dollars sorted thusly: two rolls of pennies, two rolls of nickels, one roll of dimes, one roll of quarters, forty one-dollar bills, and eight five-dollar bills. As far as I could tell, this was entirely arbitrary. Just one roll of nickels was more than any man needed in a week, whereas three or four times a day I had to nag the head cashier for pennies and quarters. But because some anal-retentive guy in a vault somewhere needed us to start the day with exactly one hundred dollars, I had nickels out the wazoo and a dearth of everything else.

So, because being a regular cashier was astonishingly more boring than working Returns, because it did not in any way engage my higher brain functions, and because it helped me get my mind off the stinging pain in my feet, I did some calculations.

Assuming that each number of cents (from zero to ninety-nine) given to the customer as change in a cash transaction was no more or less probable than any other number, and assuming that the change was given to the customer using the largest (and thus fewest) coins, nickels will be involved 40% of the time, dimes 60%, quarters 75%, and pennies 80%. But while you often get two, three, or four pennies or two or three quarters in change, you never get more than one nickel.

Say you had a hundred cash transactions, each with a different amount of change given (the first transaction gives back zero cents, the second gives back one, the third gives back two, and so on and so forth up to ninety-nine cents). You would give out 40 nickels, 80 dimes, 150 quarters, and 200 pennies. In other words, one roll of nickels, not quite two rolls of dimes, three rolls of quarters, and four rolls of pennies.

Add in all the change that customers gave me, and I ended every day with five pounds of nickels in my drawer.

My first customer bought some hardware stuff that totaled twenty-two dollars and something. He gave me a hundred.

"I don't have enough cash to give you change," I said, not unkindly. "I'll have to call. It'll be just a minute."

I dialed the head cashier while the customer grew irritated.

Thoth appeared and asked me what I needed, even though I'd just told him on the phone, then stood and watched while I filled out the till increase form (a head cashier who was actively looking out for my best interests would have either filled it out himself or waited until after the transaction; unfortunately, that kind of head cashier didn't exist).

Finally, Thoth put into my hand fifty dollars in fives.

"I'm going to need more than this," I said.

"We will take care of that later," said Thoth.

I counted out seventy-seven dollars and change and handed it to the man.

He looked at the stack of cash in my hand, then at me, then back at his hand. "Are you really going to give me all those fives?" he asked, like I'd offered him Monopoly money.

"It's what I have," I said.

"That's ridiculous!" the man cried. "That's the stupidest thing I've ever heard!"

"I'm sorry," I said unapologetically. Thoth said nothing.

"I'll bring pennies the next time!" the man shouted, snatching up his bag. "How about that?"

"We'll take them," I said.

"No problems," said Thoth.

This made him even madder. "I will, then! We'll see how you like counting all those pennies!" The man stormed out of the store.

Thoth shook his head. "We will take the pennies. But he will have to stand there while we count them."

"That's true." I smirked. "And if one of us happened to lose count halfway through and had to start over, that'd be too bad, wouldn't it?"

When I got home, Chloe was there, talking to Rapture Joe.

"Oh, my," I said, temporarily forgetting my swollen feet.

Chloe got up from the couch and gave me a hug and a kiss. "Hey, babe. I just met your friend Joe."

Joe was sitting on the couch. Drimacus the Eviscerator was nibbling his pants.

"Hey, Penn, good to see you! Praise the Lord! How was work?"

"Not really good at all," I replied. "Thanks for asking. So, uh, what brings you over here?"

"I just dropped by to see Jeff."

"And where *is* Jeff?" I asked.

"He got a call from his dad. He's in his room, talking."

"How convenient for him," I muttered.

"Anyway, I was just telling Chloe how much I'd heard about her," said Joe.

"Not from me," I said without thinking.

"No, no, from Jeff," said Joe. "You guys have been dating for a few months, right?"

"Yeah," I said guardedly.

Joe cocked his head to the side, almost as though he were listening to something. Then he announced, "You two are going to get married."

Chloe had been taking a drink of water. She now expectorated this water all over the living room and began coughing horrendously.

I thumped Chloe on the back. "So, uh, Joe, why do you say that?"

He smiled. "Oh, sometimes you just know things, you know?"

I certainly did *not* know, and was about to tell him so, but he went right along without me.

"So, do you guys want to have kids?" he asked.

"We never discussed it," I said quickly. Chloe's coughing subsided, but she was still beet red.

My statement was semi-true. We hadn't discussed it seriously because we hadn't discussed marriage seriously or really at all. All we'd talked about was that number every person carried around in his or her head. I said three kids, she said four, and that was pretty much the end of that.

Chloe had control of herself now, and she directed Joe's line of questioning back at him. Her innate common courtesy triumphed over every man's instinctive response to Joe, which was to escape.

"What about you?" she asked. "How many kids do you want to have?"

"Good luck finding a wife to give them to you," is what I did *not* say. The idea of a bunch of little Rapture Babies running around made me queasy. What kind of woman would do that to the world?

"Well, that's something I've struggled with a lot lately," said Joe. "I've often wondered whether it wouldn't be better not to have any."

"How come?" asked Chloe.

Chloe was near and dear to my heart, but I really wished she would shut up and quit asking questions that did nothing but prolong our overexposure to Joe.

"Well," said Joe, "it's getting harder these days to bring kids up according to the Bible."

I marveled at Joe's ability to make an absolutely true statement sound corny and disagreeable.

"Anyway, I just think it might not be the best idea to bring kids up in this world," he said. "You're really taking a chance."

"The world's not such a bad place," Chloe said.

Joe shook his head. "It's not that. How do you know your kids will stay true to the faith? That they won't fall away and be lost forever?"

"Let me get this straight," I said. "You don't want to have kids because they might go to hell?"

"That's one way to put it, I guess," said Joe.

I was torn between speaking my mind and ending the conversation.

"No offense, but that doesn't say much for your faith, does it?" I asked.

223

"It's not *my* faith," Joe replied. "It's *theirs*. Each person has to have his own faith."

"Yes, but then it's not your responsibility if they don't have faith."

"Oh, I know that," said Joe. "But sometimes I think, why take the chance?"

"But how is that any different from anybody else in the world?" Chloe asked.

"It really isn't," Joe admitted. "But that's really not the point. I guess what I'm talking about here is a kind of population control for hell."

"Because the fewer people who are born, the fewer people who can go to hell?" I said.

"Exactly," said Joe. "We evangelize as much as we can, but we can't get them all."

"But the ones you're not getting to are in darkest Africa and Communist China and places like that," I said. "We're talking about your kids."

Joe shrugged. "There's only so much evangelism to go around. Evangelistic resources, I mean. Time, money, people."

I was done. The conversation had gotten too silly. For a minute there, I thought we might be on the verge of an intelligent theological discussion, but now it was time for a quick getaway.

"Interesting points," I said. "Anyway, Joe, it was great to see you. Chloe and I are going to run out and get dinner."

"Sure, man, good to see you, too. God bless your life together."

On the porch, Chloe said, "I thought you were going to make chicken."

"I'll cook for you tomorrow," I said. "God, woman, do you not know what's good for you?"

Day 347 – Friday, October 22

To our already cluttered counters were added stacks of flyers, each one a full page of House Station Halloween Safety Tips, which included such advice as "Don't carry a realistic-looking gun," "Don't enter someone's home," and "Parents, give children a cell phone or quarters so they can call home." Trick-or-treating had come a long way since I was a kid.

My favorite tip on the sheet was "Don't pet animals—especially ones you don't know," because it implied that you also shouldn't pet animals that you *do* know. Which was actually good advice where Drimacus was concerned.

The only other cashier scheduled for the morning was Lucresha, and she'd called in.

"She always calls in because her kid's sick," Paige said. "But then she bitches because she only has one shift a week and doesn't get enough hours."

While I appreciated the sentiment, it didn't put more cashiers on the line—the head cashier wouldn't get on a register unless I had a line eight deep. Which, as it turns out, I had for most of the morning.

A lady wearing the most ridiculous boots I'd ever seen bought three cartloads of building materials. These were black knee-high rubber boots, like a fisherman might wear, or Darth Vader. She asked for a Lot Associate. I paged one and told her I'd send him out to her car.

Two minutes later, she came back.

"The Lot Attendant hasn't shown up yet," she said, oblivious to the seven people lined up at my register.

"I'll page him again," I assured her.

I paged, and then I got through two more customers before she returned.

"Can you call the Service Desk and tell them that I need a Lot Associate and that I've been waiting out here and I have forty bags of concrete and some lumber that I need to have loaded?"

"Yes," I said, as soon as she stopped talking.

She came back five times over the next twenty minutes.

"Where's the Lot Associate? Can you call another one? Do you have change for a hundred-dollar bill?"

"In fives," I said. "And I'll call somebody."

I said "Excuse me" to my current customer, then called the Service Desk, the head cashier, the associate in Building Materials, and the MOD.

On the one hand, I don't doubt that it's very frustrating to stand outside and have nobody show up to help you. On the other hand, it's also frustrating to be hounded and nagged when (a) you're swamped in work and (b) you're not the best person to ask anyway because you're invisibly leashed to the register.

I was frayed. Right before lunch, I committed a gaffe. I broke my never-tell-the-customer-you're-having-a-bad-day rule. Not egregiously; a lady asked me how my day was going and I just said, "It's that kind of day, you know?"

The lady sighed. "I know. I'm having one right now. My sister died this morning."

Never again.

Day 349 – Sunday, October 24

"Hey, look at this dime!" Landfill exclaimed. "It's from 1909! Oh, and Fielding Vargas is here from Loss Prevention, so make sure your Sensormatic logs are updated."

"My Sensormatic logs are always updated. Let's see?" I took the coin from him and peered at it. "This isn't from 1909."

"Yes it is! Look at the date!"

It was hard to tell. The dime was worn and corroded.

"It says 1969," I said.

"It doesn't! It's old! It's got to be worth something!"

"It's worth ten cents," I said.

"You're wrong! Give it back! It's a hundred years old!"

"Landfill!" I exclaimed. "If it's from 1909, why is FDR on it?"

"What?"

"Roosevelt wasn't president until the thirties. Why would he be on a dime from 1909?"

Landfill wilted. "Oh."

"Sorry for crushing your hopes and dreams," I said, turning to an immensely fat customer who had just arrived, the sort who carried the weight of the world every time he stood up.

"Can you get somebody to carry these boards to my car?" the man asked. "They're kind of bundlesome."

Right after that came James Earl Jones with a Perm, buying trim for his house. When I rang it up, he refused to buy it, declaring that he thought it was forty-nine cents per piece rather than per foot. Each piece was sixteen feet long and cost about eight dollars. Customers got confused about prices all the time, but rarely so flagrantly unless they were deliberately trying to con me.

Then I got a family buying paint. The kid sitting in the cart had about thirty of the free wooden paint stirrers we give out. He was contentedly snapping them in half one by one.

"It's good to break them all," he told me.

I found this amusing. They weren't my paint sticks, and I couldn't very well take them away.

"Do you want us to go out of business?" I asked.

The kid appeared to consider my question carefully. Then he threw a broken paint stirrer on the floor.

The dad, a young guy, handed me a credit card that said "See ID, fool," on the back where the signature went.

"Can I see your ID?" I asked. "Fool?"

And I had a middle-aged, housewife-type lady try to pay with a two-hundred-dollar bill that had George W. Bush on it.

When I proved recalcitrant, she snatched it out of my hand, sniffed, and marched out of the store.

Somebody should have gotten her for counterfeiting. But again, we don't have any security. And I personally think that if you're going to counterfeit money, you should put in a better effort.

All in all, it was a pretty typical day at the Station.

Day 352 – Wednesday, October 27

I got a rare shift at Returns, and the retail gods were determined that I not enjoy it. Nuts to them; I had my stool and I was sitting on it.

Atwater was there; I hadn't seen Pete in over a week. I was so glad to be back at Returns I almost didn't mind.

I concluded that I live in a world in which no woman weighs more than 140 pounds, no matter how gigantic they might appear. Say some spherical lady comes through my line and writes a check. The register's going to prompt me to check her driver's license. This license will say this lady weighs 137, which was probably true twenty years, three kids, and God only knows how much chocolate ago. 137 kilograms, maybe. I understand why women aren't honest about their weight, but at least be believable.

I had three different customers come in to exchange miscut blinds. Blinds are another case where the customers really get over on the store. The official policy is that if the store miscuts the blinds, we'll replace them, but if the customer requests an incorrect cut, then we won't. For reasons that should be obvious, the store has never refused to replace a set of blinds.

But hey, they're not my blinds.

A man came through and dropped some merchandise on the counter. I started scanning and bagging it.

After a moment, he said, "Can I check out here? Save me a walk."

"I'm scanning your freaking crap," I muttered inaudibly.

He took about five minutes to write a check, then handed it to me.

"I'm sorry, sir," I said. "We can't take counter checks."

It's always amazing to me how quickly customers can go from barely aware of a cashier's existence to mad at the cashier, the store, the company, and the world.

He made a disgusted sound and slapped his hand on the counter. "Why didn't you tell me sooner?"

"Because I wasn't all in your business," I told him. "Sir."

"They take them at Wal-Mart!"

I doubted that was the case.

The man gave a melodramatic sigh. "I don't have anything else. I'll have to get some cash and come back." He said it like Sisyphus might have said, "I have to push this boulder up the hill again now." He said it like it made a difference, like I wasn't going to take the merchandise out of the bag and put it in my bins the minute he went out the door.

If Greek mythology were updated, Sisyphus wouldn't have had to push the stone forever; he would have had to work at the Station until he made a million dollars.

Kord stopped by on her rounds. "Look at all those people reading," she said, nodding at the book alcove at the far end of the Service Desk. "Sell them some books, Penn."

"It's like a reading library," I said. "Nobody ever buys books. We'd make more money if we put in a copy machine. Charge ten cents a page. They'd pay that."

She raised an eyebrow. "I don't think Rex would go for that."

I shrugged. "His loss. Hey, I had an idea. Since we have a bridal registry, we should also have a gift wrap."

Kord laughed out loud. "That's *your* idea?"

"No. I've had a few customers ask me why we don't have one. Look, I'm trying to help bail this store out of the sales gutter, that's all."

"That flows nicely into what I came here to tell you," said Kord. "Sell more ESPs."

The extended service plan—a longer, better warranty. The store had tried various techniques to get us to push them harder. The most recent campaign promised a cash reward to the cashier who sold the most. Everyone's favorite allegedly drug-dealing, on-probation cashier, Chastity, had somehow sold almost twice as many as anybody else.

"ESPs? Be serious," I said.

"What's the problem?"

"What's the point of selling ESPs?" I said. "In this store? We take everything back anyway. We even take *ESPs* back! People return them the day before they expire!"

Kord sighed. "You make everything so difficult."

Day 353 – Thursday, October 28

The new box of glowsticks at my register provided brief but wonderful entertainment. Whoever had designed the packaging either had a great sense of humor or was tripping on acid. Or maybe the rest of the world was completely missing out on just how fantastic these things were.

Glowsticks, according to the packaging, were "Good For Homeland Security!" I thought about this for a good while, but I couldn't come up with any reason why that should be, since they just made it easier for terrorists to see you.

Additionally, glowsticks were "A Safe Substitute For Fireworks!" This was true, but they were also a Fun-Free Substitute For Fireworks. I pictured a handful of little kids throwing their glowsticks into the air and pretending to have a good time—it was really sad.

Finally, the glowsticks were "Better Than A Flashlight With A Dead Battery!" This was indisputable, I figured. Except for Homeland Security purposes; I'd rather hit a terrorist with a nice heavy flashlight than throw a glowstick at him.

They sold like hotcakes.

A crazy Norwegian came through my line and regaled me with a confusing and boring story about how where he was from, everybody could either read or write, but not both. He was one of the readers, and thusly unable to write. I looked at him like he was stupid until he finally signed the credit pad.

A few minutes later, an ugly, wrinkled woman bought a few small bags of concrete.

"Do you need a Lot Attendant to help you with these?" I asked.

"Of course I do!" the lady exclaimed, like I should know better. "I had a bypass! Look, I had heart surgery! Look!" The woman yanked open her shirt to reveal a nasty scar bisecting her withered bosom.

I recoiled in horror, flinching back against my register before I could help myself or think any thoughts about Excellent Customer Service. My gorge rose and I tasted bile. I immediately turned my complete and total attention to dialing the Lot Associate.

While we were waiting, the Norwegian guy came back.

"Have you seen my twin brother?" he asked.

Day 354 – Friday, October 29

We did the usual IHOP thing. Chloe was working, so it was just me, Pete, and Christine. I don't know why I agreed to go, or why they wanted me to.

"Haven't seen you in a while," said Pete. "How's the register treating you?"

"I hate it," I said. "I'm always the only one there, we never close on time, and it's killing my feet. What's going on at the Service Desk?"

"You mean besides what happened to Rovergial? Nothing, really."

"Hold on," I said. "What happened to Rovergial?"

"You didn't hear about that? It happened last night. Were you at work?"

"I worked the early shift." I snapped my fingers at him. "What happened?"

"He got punched in the face by a customer."

"I heard about this," said Christine.

"I didn't!" I exclaimed. "Tell me!"

"Johnisha was on Returns and this guy brought in this belt sander. Your boy Lance comes up to check it out. He's been hitting on Johnisha like crazy, but anyway, there was some problem, so she called the head cashier, and then the ASM got called and it was Rovergial. Meanwhile, the guy with the return has just been standing there. No receipt. That was a red flag to me, him standing there calmly. You know if you think we owe you something you're going to be hella pissed sitting through all that song and dance."

"He stole it and was trying to return it."

"That's what I figured," said Pete. "And Rovergial, too, because he said no, he wouldn't take it. So the guy punched him in the face, absolutely decked him, grabbed the box, and ran out the door. You see what you miss when you're down at the other end?"

"Is Rovergial okay?" I asked.

"Yeah, he's fine. He had a big black eye, but that was about it. He didn't go to the hospital."

"That's good."

Perceiving a lull in the conversation, Christine exclaimed, "I'm getting a Hummer!"

"Okay," I said. "Are you rich? How are you buying a Hummer?"

"I'm not buying it," said Christine. "My uncle's giving it to me. And it's not a new one; it's an old H1."

"What happened to your Cavalier?" I asked.

"Nothing. But it's not an SUV! I've always wanted an SUV."

"A Hummer's not an SUV," I said. "It's a military assault vehicle."

"I've always wanted one!" she said petulantly.

I shrugged. "Fine. Those things get what, ten miles a gallon? On the highway?"

"What are you, Al Gore?" Pete said.

"Forget it," I said. "Enjoy your Hummer. It'll come in handy if you ever need to drive to Baghdad."

"I have to go to the restroom," Christine announced, and did so.

Pete glared at me.

"Rein her in," I said.

"How are you just going to say—"

I held up a hand. "Rein your woman in."

Pete leaned back, sighed, and nodded. "Drop it about the Hummer."

"Agreed."

After the food came, I asked Pete, "Do you ever miss Superman? He was entertaining."

"Can't say I've thought about him," Pete said. "But he was a funny guy."

"That's what I'm getting at," I said. "People leave and you never think about them again. They don't even have to leave; even if they're around, they're still out of sight, out of mind. Take the unfortunately named Merlin Van Gorp for example. I haven't seen that guy in a long time and he just popped into my head."

"Oh, he got fired a while ago," Pete said. "For lates. Lates and call-ins. I talked to him last week, actually. You know your job sucks when you're out of work for two months and it has no effect on your standard of living."

"Yet another cheerful perspective from which to view our lives," I said.

"There are so many," said Pete. "What about Edna? I haven't heard her shriek in a while. Did she die?"

I shrugged.

"Who's Merlin?" asked Christine. "Some kind of wizard?"

"He was a chubby college kid who worked on the registers," Pete told her.

"I saw that guy yesterday!"

"At work?" I asked.

"You're thinking of Landfill," Pete said.

"Oh." After a moment, she said, "Penn, are you doing anything for Halloween?"

"I'm standing at a register all night," I said.

Pete drummed his silverware on his plate. "Hey, you know those glowsticks we sell?"

I nodded. "Nontoxic. Twelve hours. Good For Homeland Security."

"Yeah, anyway, seeing as how they're nontoxic, do you think if you drank a bunch of them, your pee would glow?"

I considered this. "Only one way to find out."

"How many people are going to get drunk and try that?" Pete mused.

"You?" I said.

"Not me," said Christine. "I'm underage."

Day 355 – Saturday, October 30

When I came back from lunch, I was nearly stampeded by a herd of little kids.

"What in the world is going on?" I asked Paige.

"They're having a birthday party," she said.

"What, here?"

"Yeah."

"That's the saddest thing I've ever heard," I said. "Why would anybody do that?"

"Isn't it? The kid wanted to and his dad asked last week."

"So what does that involve? What is there to do?"

"They're going to do one of those craft projects," she said. "Then they're going to have pizza and cake in the break room."

On the first Saturday of each month, we offered a free project for kids. Typically it wasn't any more complicated than sticking two or three pieces of wood together to make something dumb like a box or a flowerpot holder, but it got the parents in the store and made people feel good about the Station.

I shook my head. "Man, it's just like Six Flags."

Shortly thereafter, Landfill dropped by Register One for a chat.

"Howdy, Pennsylvania. Have you ever noticed that it seems like the heavier an item is, the more likely the barcode is on the bottom? And invariably, the customer always turns the barcode side down?"

"'Invaritably' is not a word," I said.

"But isn't it true? Haven't you noticed?"

"Yes, I suppose it is true," I said, although the way he said it sounded lame enough to put up on the bulletin board in the break room, that selfsame break room which was, at present, packed with grubby urchins who wouldn't know a good birthday if it ran them over in the street.

"Do you get these customers where you can't understand what they're saying?" Landfill was asking.

"Every day."

"Like, they'll say, 'Are you doin' any harren,' and I'll say, 'What?' and they'll say, 'Harren!' and I'll say 'What was that?' and then they get mad. You know what he was trying to say? 'Hiring.' He wanted to know if we were doing any hiring. And then I had this other guy, he was pretty old, and he came up to me and said, 'I had one of these good hrmmahrmmahrm . . . I never did figure out what that guy was trying to say."

"That's great," I said, hoping he'd get paged.

Landfill turned his attention to the display of merchandise on my register's endcap.

"*Horno asador?*" he said. "That sounds funny. What does it mean?"

"'Roaster oven,'" I said.

"Oh. It looks like a crock pot."

"Whatever you say." Agreeing with Landfill sometimes made him go away sooner.

Landfill took a deep breath. "Well, I'd better go check on the other cashiers. Remember to thank all the customers."

"I'll remember," I said.

I'd remember; that was no problem. I just wouldn't do it.

Day 356 – Sunday, October 31

It was Halloween night, it was dead, and I was on Returns. All was right with the world, or as close to right as it was going to get.

The payphone in the vestibule rang.

"Let me get it," said Pete. He handed me the headset, knocked the phone on the floor, replaced it quickly, jogged over, and picked up the receiver. "Blockbuster Video. No, we don't have any Xboxes. Read a book!" He hung up.

"That's going to get you in trouble one day," I said.

Pete snorted. "How? That caller'll be over at Blockbuster complaining about how rude *they* were to him."

"Then you're going to get somebody at Blockbuster fired," I said. "How are you going to feel then?"

"Mighty good," said Pete. "You know, I had a dream last night. It was a vision of hell. You know how I could tell? Because it was exactly like being at this store. You have a customer."

I did not, exactly, have a customer, but there was a young couple struggling to open a lamp box near my register. I headed over.

"Can I help you?" I asked.

The man looked at me. "I'm just showing this lamp to my . . . um . . . my . . ."

"Wife," said the woman, jamming her left hand into her pocket.

"As opposed to sister," said the man. "Or girlfriend."

"Okay," I said. I had no idea what was going on, and that was fine. "Do you need some help with the lamp?"

He handed it to me and I began to work the tightly packed, foam-encased bundle out.

"How much does it cost?" asked the woman. She still had her hand in her pocket.

I went over to the shelf whence the lamp originated. "Twenty-nine dollars."

"Twenty-nine dollars?" the woman exclaimed. "It must be ugly!"

I did not point out that there was a picture of the lamp on the front of the box and that it was indeed quite ugly.

They bought it.

As I lounged on my stool, James the jolly Plumbing associate came by and collapsed on the bench.

"Rough night?" Pete asked. "It's been pretty quiet up here."

"It only takes one or two," James replied. "Make you drink an extra bottle of wine. Right out of the bottle. Put a big nipple on it."

A man walked in the front door and exclaimed, "Hey! Electric mowers! Wow!"

A moment later, an extremely attractive young woman — face, figure, the works — came in and headed over to us.

"Are you hiring?" she asked me.

To my credit, I looked her in the eye the whole time. "I really couldn't tell you. But you're more than welcome to fill out an application on the computer over there." I indicated the far side of the Service Desk.

She smiled sweetly. "Thanks very much."

Pete went and held the chair for her. "What are you applying for?"

"Cashier," said the girl, and sat down.

Pete returned. "I hope we hire her."

"Yes," I said.

Kord came to check on us.

"How much input do you have with hiring?" Pete asked her. "Of cashiers."

"A little," she said. "Mostly Rex and Helen handle it."

"You see that girl at the computer?" Pete asked.

"Yeah."

"She's hot."

"That's true," said Kord.

"She wants to be a cashier. Can you make it happen?"

"I'll see what I can do. What do you guys care for? You're both attached."

"Attached," Pete said. "Not blind. Come on, this place could do with a little sprucing up."

Day 358 – Tuesday, November 2

Drimacus the Eviscerator had begged for days to go back out on the balcony.

I had an idea. I picked him up, carried him outside and dangled him over the balcony, like Michael Jackson with a baby. The instant I held him over the edge, he began to cry desperately. I held him back over the balcony and he stopped.

"I guess you learned your lesson," I said, dropping him on the floor. "Moron. Fine. But if you die, I'm not going to cry about it."

I left the cats out there and went to collect the mail. It was a nice little stroll from our apartment to the mailboxes as long as nobody tried to sell you any foodstuffs.

In addition to the usual bills and ad circulars, I had a letter from *Lloyd's Beacon*, a short story magazine I'd submitted to. I let out a long sigh: another rejection letter. I tore it open; no sense keeping hope on life support any longer than necessary.

I hammered on Chloe's door until she opened it.

"Penn! What is it? What's the matter?" She raised her eyebrows at my dress shirt and slacks. "Why are you dressed up? Did somebody die?"

I jabbed the letter in her face. "I'm getting my story published!"

"That's great!" she shrieked, and *jumped in the air*. She was even more excited than I was, which I didn't think was possible. She threw her arms around me, crushing the letter between us. "I'm so proud of you!"

After a few moments, I detached from Chloe and we stepped into her living room, grinning like idiots.

"This is so great," Chloe said. "Are they paying you? How much?"

"Twenty-five dollars and five contributor's copies. As far as magazines and short stories go, it's a king's ransom. For the hours I spent on it, it's less than I make at the Station. But it's not about the money."

"I know!" She squeezed my hand. "Who cares about that? Great job!"

"Get changed. We're going out. And not to IHOP."

239

We went to a cozy little Chinese restaurant called The Rickshaw, a classy sit-down place that didn't do buffets.

Chloe was wearing a white turtleneck sweater and a pair of black pants that flattered her easily-flatterable hips.

"You look gorgeous," I said.

She smiled at me. "And you're very sweet."

"When I'm a big-shot writer and I sell some movie rights for a million dollars, you'll never have to go to IHOP again."

She laughed. "So when are they going to publish the story?"

"Sometime in May."

"But that's so far off! Why so long?"

I shrugged. "That's how they do these things. There has to be time for editing and proofreading and layout and getting it to and from the printer."

"Well, when they do finally get around to it, I want an autographed copy."

"You'll be the first."

Day 359 – Wednesday, November 3

The sign on the break room wall said, "I'm never down; I'm either up or getting up." I slapped it as I walked past.

Paige was pulling on her apron. "Rough night last night? Me too. Don't ask."

"Actually, I had a great night," I said. "But now I'm here, aren't I? And I'm on Register One, aren't I?"

"Yeah, sorry." She rubbed my back briefly in a way that was both sympathetic and made me a little uncomfortable.

I wondered if Chloe would have it out with Paige one day. I'd never discussed the way Paige acted around me with either of them; Paige was an unconscious flirt, she did it to everybody, and bringing it up wouldn't do any good if we were still going to be friends afterward. Anyway, Paige wasn't excessive and I didn't reciprocate.

As I walked out to my register, my feet informed me in no uncertain terms that I was in for a long shift. They were cramped and itching, and it was only eight.

From clear down at the other end of the store, I heard Atwater cry, like Ponce de León discovering the fountain of youth, "There's cake in the phone room!"

At least somebody was having a good day.

Rex had clearanced out all the Halloween leftovers and now the Christmas stuff was coming in. Today it was lights and tree stands. Tomorrow, who knew?

A chatty old man was seated on the bench near my register, talking to customers as they came through my line. At a point where I didn't have any customers and he'd been sitting there for almost half an hour, he turned his attention to me.

"Young man, you need to get your education," he said. "You have forty-five years to work. Hell, you may get sent off to war, or your kids."

"Right," I said agreeably.

I wondered if he was waiting for someone. Once in a while, we got a senile escapee from the nursing home down the block. In those cases, we called Rex or the ASM, who would come and chat with the person, then call the nursing home to retrieve their fugitive. The cashier's job in this situation was to keep an eye on the person and make sure he didn't wander off. Like into traffic, say.

Any further wisdom the man might have imparted was interrupted by a woman who wanted to discuss grout.

"I'm really not a grout expert," I said. "I can get somebody from Flooring if you want."

"I already spent fifteen minutes back there. Just take a look at these colors, will you?"

Thanks to time spent with Chloe, I now considered myself pretty good with colors.

The lady had five different packages of grout in her cart and a fistful of sample cards.

"Here's my tile," she said. "And here's what I'm looking at. What do you think?"

"Well, it depends what you're trying to do. A lighter grout lightens up the whole floor, and it'll give you a more traditional look. A darker grout will hide the dirt better and make your tile stand out a little bit." That sounded fancy but was the extent of my grout knowledge.

"I have three light ones and two dark ones here. You know what? The light's not very good here. Can we step over by the door?"

It was rapidly becoming apparent that she was afflicted with Grout Obsessive–Compulsive Disorder. We found a place where the sun shone intensely through the windows. The woman held the samples up to the light from every conceivable angle.

"What do you think now?" she asked.

"I like the lighter shade."

"Which one? There's Arctic Ice, Butter Cream, and Mexican White. Or maybe I should try the Snow White. The Bright White was so boring to me."

I could never work in Paint or Flooring. I didn't have the patience to deal with a hundred shades of white. "I like the Arctic Ice," I said. "Excuse me, I have a customer."

"Sure. Thanks for your help!"

I went back to my register and the mind-numbing, foot-killing tedium of ringing sales. It wasn't just that it was boring; lots of things were boring. The problem was, it was boring *and you had to pay attention*. You couldn't let your mind wander, because you'd ring something twice or hand back the wrong amount of change, which were things every cashier did from time to time in spite of due diligence and best efforts, but if you did it too many times, you'd be sitting at home with plenty of time to daydream.

I got a lull in my line, so I sat down for a moment and took a long drink of water.

Half an hour had passed. The lady was still over by the door, pondering the deeper mysteries of grout and its many-splendored glories.

It wasn't marriage, I thought; it was just grout.

Day 361 – Friday, November 5

My alarm went off.

"Damn it," I muttered into my pillow.

My feet still hurt and I was scheduled for Register One.

"Screw that," I said.

I rousted myself, went to the phone, called in, popped some Aleve, and went back to bed.

Calling in was a pretty simple process: you called, you got the Service Desk, you asked to talk to the MOD, hoped to God it wasn't Rex, and said, 'Oh, I don't feel well, I won't be in today,' and that was that. And it was *calling in*, not *calling in sick*; they typically didn't ask you what was wrong, and you didn't have to volunteer a reason. The job sucked, people got burned out sometimes, and most of the good people at the Station knew it, except for Helen, who would write you up the instant you surpassed your monthly truancy quota.

It was a privilege I was coming to abuse in recent weeks. Right now, I was averaging about one call-in per week. I didn't ever do it on Saturday or Sunday, because those typically weren't crowded days (and on most Saturdays there was a fair chance of going home early) and because weekend absences counted double.

It wasn't something I was proud of, but when you woke up feeling like your feet spent the night in a vise, your principles took a hit, too.

I got up again two hours later and found Jeff in the living room, watching an infomercial.

"I didn't hear you come in last night," I said.

"Yeah, I was out with Milla. Are you off today?"

"Yeah."

"Man, have I got a story to tell you! They've been doing the fat test this week, right?"

I got a glass of water and sat on the couch. "Sorry to miss that," I said.

Part of the complete waste of time and resources that was KLU's PE Department was that every student had to have a skinfold test each semester. This involved removing your shirt and your dignity and having your abdominal fat squeezed with ice-cold calipers. You were graded on how much fat there was to pinch, and this counted for ten percent of everyone's PE grade. Additionally, this service was only offered for two nights, so the line in the Athletics Center trainer's room was typically out the door, down the hall, and around the corner.

"I was the supervisor last evening," Jeff said. "I was covering a shift for a buddy. This guy came in, but he didn't have his ID."

You needed your student ID to get into the building.

"Janet at the front desk calls me and tells me that this guy says he left his ID in his locker. So I told her to send him back and I'd meet him in the locker room and make sure he got it. I go back there and wait for five minutes or so, and he never shows up. I come back to the desk and he's standing there in the fat test line."

"Slick."

"So I go up to him and say, 'Excuse me, sir, I need to see your ID.' He's talking to his friend and he says, 'Okay, just a minute.' I give him a few more minutes and still hasn't moved. So I go back and I say, 'Sir, I need you to step out of line right now.' And he says, 'Not now,' and he holds up a hand to shush me! And he pulls out a cell phone, and he's still talking to his friend, and he's completely ignoring me. Anyway, I'm starting to get a little bit mad."

Antagonizing Jeff, who was by nature gracious and merciful, slow to anger, and abounding in steadfast love, was no mean feat.

"So I go back to him and say, 'Sir, you need to step out of line right now and come with me, or I'm going to call Security.' And he says, 'Call Security. They won't do anything.' So I call Security and explain the situation and I tell them, 'The guy said you wouldn't do anything,' and they said, 'Oh really? We'll be right there.' And they were, like five minutes later. But in the meantime, this guy finally comes over to me, and he's talking to me like what he's saying is some huge secret. He says, 'Look, I teach a class for President Lee. I really have to get this taken care of, okay? People have been fired before for things like this, and I really don't want to see that happen, okay?' And I was pretty mad at this point, and I told him I didn't care and that Security was on its way. And he left."

"He expected you to believe that?"

Jeff shrugged. "Penn, I was so mad, even if he did work for President Lee, I didn't care."

"Did you get the guy's name? Are you going to be able to get him in trouble?"

"Yeah, let's see . . . It was Brad something. Brad . . . uh . . ."

I sat bolt upright and spilled my water on Drimacus the Eviscerator. "Was he chubby, about five-ten, light brown hair?" I asked eagerly. "Face that makes you want to slap him?"

"That sounds like the guy."

"Bradford Landfield! Amazing!" I cackled. "He works at the Station! Nobody likes him! This is brilliant!" I wiped tears from my eyes. "Thank you for this," I said. "Thank you so much."

Day 362 – Saturday, November 6

One half of one day was sufficient for the story to get around the entire Front End, and Landfill was obviously discomfited as he went about his business. The greatest thing was, he had no idea where the story had originated.

I was enjoying a brief sit-down at Register One when Landfill came and leaned on my counter, speaking into his walkie-talkie and invading my personal space.

"Are you there? What are you doing? Over."

I tried to scoot back, but I was up against the fence. "Is there something I can help you with?"

Landfill raised an eyebrow and stroked his chin in what passed for reflection. "You know, they call Pete 'Angry Pete.' But really, you're the angry one. It's ironic, isn't it?"

"Yeah, man," I said. "It's pretty ironic."

"See, that's what I'm talking about right there," said Landfill.

I nodded at a shopping cart at the end of my register with sheets of plywood stacked on top. "The customer that was going to buy those didn't have the money with him," I said. "Can you take that back to Lumber for me? Please? I can't leave the register."

"Sure, I'll take care of it," Landfill said. He brought his walkie-talkie up again. "Booker? How about now? Over."

"I'm out in the parking lot by Garden," crackled Booker's voice.

"I need you to come get some plywood from Register One and take it back to Lumber. Over."

"Okay, but it might be a few minutes. I'm loading some paving stone."

"Soon as you can. Over."

"Landfill!" I exclaimed. "Just take it to Lumber." Lumber was twenty yards away.

He smiled his infuriating smile. "Booker'll take care of it." Then he strolled off.

Twenty minutes later, the cart was still there. This was in no way Booker's fault, as he was undoubtedly busy, which was typically the case when there was only one Lot Attendant in the store. The cashiers resented the way Landfill micromanaged the Lot Attendants. So did the customers, although they didn't realize it, because they got mad when there was nobody to load their concrete.

I tried to tuck the cart into the corner as best I could, but it jutted out into my aisle.

Fifteen minutes later, a family with a little kid who was maybe three came through my line. He was jumping around, as little kids do, when he tripped, and a sheet of half-inch plywood on that cart split his head wide open.

The first thing I heard was the clang of the cart as it rocked. The first thing I saw was the blood matting the kid's hair.

I dialed the ASM, who was Madeleine, and told her to come quickly with the first aid kit. Then I dialed Landfill. My line was going to have to close while we cleaned up the blood.

"I need you to come to the registers immediately," I said.

"It'll be a few minutes, I'm back in the—"

"No, you get your ass over here *right now* or by God, I will personally get you fired by the end of the day," I said through clenched teeth, and hung up.

The kid's dad asked me for some paper towels, which I provided, and he pressed them against the boy's head as the kid sobbed quietly.

"Looks a lot worse than it is, I think," he said.

That was a pretty good first response, in my opinion, considering that I was expecting something more along the lines of "I'm going to sue this place for everything it's worth." Of course, the two statements weren't mutually exclusive.

Madeleine arrived in record time, and when the gash was cleaned, it didn't look too bad. An Incident Report was filled out. The family told Madeleine what happened, and they left without any threats of litigation.

When they'd gone, Madeleine turned to chew me out. "Why was that cart there?"

I related everything that had happened in the last hour. I didn't go out of my way to throw Landfill under the bus, but a fair and unbiased relation of the tale did a pretty good job of it anyway.

Landfill got written up and that was it.

Day 364 – Monday, November 8

I dreamed that I was at work doing the usual things: checking out customers, standing, just being there. Nothing crazy. It was the worst dream I'd ever had. I'd rather have had one of those dreams when you're getting chased by something that's trying to kill you and you can't run and you can't scream.

I woke up completely unrested. My feet throbbed. I felt cheated, like I'd just worked eight hours I wasn't getting paid for. The House Station was a parasite, and it was ruining my life. It had spread its tentacles beyond its doors and into my home. Almost all my non-sleeping time was spent at work, or counting the hours like a death sentence until I went back to work, or suffering the chronic pain the Station had so generously bestowed upon me.

I swung out of bed with grim resolve. I was going to get a new job.

Getting a new job was something that had been discussed *ad nauseam* by me, Pete, and most people our age at the Station. Apparently the only one in our demographic who was happy there was Chloe. Pete insisted that this was because she was part-time and wasn't on the Front End, and Chloe agreed that this was most likely so.

Why did we always talk about leaving but never do anything? My best answer was, we'd become so accustomed

248

to our crappy situation that we didn't really think we'd ever get out, just like how most people think they're not really ever actually going to die, only in reverse.

This fervor conveniently coincided with a chat I'd had the day before with Dwayne, my Knowledge Hotline friend. He'd recently been hired by Leetown Connect, which did contracted tech support for Nextel. I thought all those kinds of jobs had been outsourced to India for pennies on the dollar, but here Leetown Connect was, and they were hiring. And apparently, they were kind of desperate.

The job consisted of taking calls for eight hours, helping technological illiterates solve their problems, and upselling their policies when possible — in other words, sitting down for eight hours and not having to lay eyes on a single customer. It sounded like the dream job.

That thought was fairly depressing in and of itself. But I persevered. I went and applied. What skills did I have? I was good with computers and I worked in Customer Service; what else did you need? They told me they would call me back for an interview.

It was a start.

Day 365 – Tuesday, November 9

I was scheduled for Register One. I called in.

Day 366 – Wednesday, November 10

The Station started playing Christmas music. Mostly it was songs like "Frosty the Snowman" and "I'm Dreaming of a White Christmas." Occasionally you would get one of the old classic hymns, like "Hark the Herald Angels Sing," but it was

249

always instrumental. That was irritating. I liked the hymns, but I didn't care for the secular Christmas music—I didn't see the point to it.

I was on Returns, at least.

A man dropped an armload of merchandise on my counter, then stood there and looked at me.

"Are you checking out?" I asked.

He scowled. "What else would I be doing?"

"Returns, maybe," I said, nodding up at the sign. "Since this is Returns."

Then there was a rotund man who I dubbed "Mister Egg."

"Check me out here," said Mister Egg. "Save me from walking."

He was another angry one. You'd think somebody named Mister Egg would be jolly, but he stared me down the entire time he was at my counter. Once, I dared to look up and make eye contact. "Don't be staring me down," said Mister Egg.

Right before lunch, I got a lady returning a bag of bath safety rails and grab bars.

"I bought this for my mom, but she died," the lady said.

Good times.

I called Leetown Connect on my lunch hour to check on my application and they gave me the "reviewing your file, get back with you later" spiel. Not the most encouraging response, but it had only been two days.

Day 369 – Saturday, November 13

"Can I go home early?" I asked Kord.

"I don't know. Probably not today."

"Come on! You always send people home early on Saturday," I said. "I tell you what: let me go home, and I'll check out any customer that comes to my house."

"That's funny, smartass."

"What, you don't want to give me a hundred-dollar till to take home?"

Day 371 – Monday, November 15

I called in. My feet and my book were both more important than anything that was happening at Register One.

Day 373 – Wednesday, November 17

A week went by with no shifts on Returns, and I hadn't heard back from Leetown Connect. I checked in with Dwayne, who was just starting orientation. He said they were looking for a new batch of workers, so I called again.

They told me to come in for an interview, which I did on my lunch hour. It took so long I didn't have time to get anything to eat. There was no good reason why; I was there on time and I was the only one there, but I waited for twenty-five minutes.

I left with the distinct feeling that I'd bombed the interview, that my brain hadn't been working right, that I'd muttered and stumbled my way through it, that none of my good qualities had shone through. I was hungry, sore, and irritable when I got back to the Station. On my way from the break room to my register, I ran into Kord, and something snapped. Adrenaline surged. I was on the verge of a *Network* moment.

"Let's talk," I said.

We stepped into the break room.

"You've got to move me back to Returns," I said.

Kord clucked her tongue. "Penn, we've been over this. It's not up to me."

"This is the last time I ask you, one way or the other," I said. "Because I can't keep doing this. Not after everything I had to go through just to be able to sit down, and now I can't. So if I can't sit down, I'm going to have to find something else to do."

There it was: I'd just threatened to quit. *Now* my brain was working just fine, or at least my mouth was, dragging me along after it.

We just looked at each other for a moment. I didn't really know what to expect from Kord here.

She gave me an odd look. I saw resolve and, perhaps, anger on her face.

"I'll take care of it," she said.

I looked her in the eye and she held my gaze. She was going to take care of it.

"Thank you," I said. I felt myself getting emotional, and I bit my lip to quell it.

My shoulders slumped. The adrenaline was gone. Kord reached out to squeeze my shoulder and all of a sudden I was hugging her like she was my mom and I was getting choked up.

After a minute she pulled back and gave me a reassuring smile. "Now get your ass back to work, okay?"

"Okay."

"And no more call-ins."

"Right."

"No more."

"All right," I said. "No more."

Kord nodded. "Okay. I'll take care of it."

I got a big, full-color brochure in the mail from the House Station encouraging me to sign up for health insurance benefits. I was of two minds about that. I'd been chafing for insurance for months, but on the other hand, I could always go to the Gordon Clinic.

The mailing featured an impressive cast of models in House Station aprons. I was amazed that only eight people could represent every conceivable demographic — Captain Planet would have been proud. There was even an androgynous associate with short, spiky hair. If there was a House Station on the ground floor of the United Nations Headquarters, these people would work there.

Day 376 – Saturday, November 20

Drimacus hopped onto the coffee table and began chewing on Chloe's purse. I pegged him with a coaster.

"Penn, that pisses me off!" Chloe exclaimed. "How can you do this to me?"

I put up my hands. "Whoa! What did I do? I did nothing! It's not my fault!"

"What am I supposed to tell my parents when you don't show up?"

"The truth!" I said. "Tell them The Man is keeping me down!"

"Why didn't you ask for Thanksgiving off?"

"I did," I said. "But so did everybody else."

"You should have asked sooner."

She had a point there. Time off was first-come, first-served.

"Look, sweetheart, you're right," I said, in what I hoped was a soothing tone. Sometimes Thanksgiving just came at a bad time of the month. "I should have asked off sooner. I'm sorry. You know I'd rather be with you than at work."

"I know," Chloe said, more calmly.

"I get off at seven on Thanksgiving. I'll go home and change and then I'll come over, okay?"

"But it's forty-five minutes away."

I dusted off my charming smile. "I don't mind. I'll come. If I get off on time, I can be there by eight or 8:15. Maybe they'll let me go early."

Appeased, she hugged my arm. "Okay, good. It means a lot to me."

"I'm happy to." I really was. I'd met her parents; they were nice people.

"Why is the store even open on Thanksgiving?" Chloe asked. "Who goes shopping on Thanksgiving?"

"Nobody," I said. "It'll be dead. That's a plus."

"You could just call in," Chloe said. "Then you could come with me at two."

"I can't. Not on a holiday. Also, I'm kind of on attendance probation."

"You *have* been calling in a lot lately."

"I got written up. Hopefully Kord can get me moved back to Returns and it won't be a problem anymore."

Chloe tapped her chin. "What if everybody who was scheduled to work called in on Thanksgiving? What would happen?"

"You mean like a protest? A big walkout?"

"Yeah."

"That only works for people in unions. They'd just fire the lot of us and get new monkeys to train."

"That's ridiculous," she said. "I don't know why people put up with it."

"Because *we chose this as a career*," I said in a decent impression of Rex.

Chloe rested her head on my shoulder. "I hope you get that tech support job."

"Me too."

I sat up quickly. Drimacus was back on the coffee table, and he'd managed to chew through the strap of Chloe's purse.

All of a sudden, I was sick of the sight of him. I slapped him on his head and grabbed him roughly by the scruff, then forced him to hold eye contact. "I took you out of the snow and gave you a home, and all you have ever done in return is alienate and destroy. I should give you away."

"Don't be like that," said Chloe.

I shoved the cat down to the floor. "I'm sorry about your purse. I'll replace it."

"Thank you," said Chloe. "But you don't have to stress about it."

"If I'd known he was going to turn out like this, I never would have taken him in."

Chloe found this amusing. "You named him 'the Eviscerator.'"

"Everybody makes mistakes," I said.

"You wouldn't really give him away," said Chloe. "Deep down, you love him."

"No, honestly, deep down, I think I hate him," I said. "But you're right, I probably wouldn't. Because I'm too soft, or too responsible, or something." I shook my head. "I'm stuck with the little bastard."

Day 379 – Tuesday, November 23

Kord made good on her promise: the schedule for the second week of December had me on Returns four out of five shifts. In the meantime, I served my one shift of the week in the Promised Land.

Pete was off and Atwater was on, but you can't have everything. Tekla was there too, so there was a pretty strong chance Atwater would get yelled at before the day was out.

Things turned out to be interesting for very different reasons.

My jeans ripped. No, not down the butt. I wore the same jeans to work every day, and the fabric just wore out. They tore across my upper left thigh, from seam to shining seam.

My oversized apron covered the rip, but without it, casual passersby would be able to see what color briefs I was wearing.

Red.

Well, I said to myself, nothing a little duct tape won't fix. I fished the tape out of the drawer and peeled a nice long strip. It wouldn't tear. I pulled out my safety knife.

The safety knife was aptly named, as it required a herculean feat to cut anything with it. It was like a regular utility knife, except you had to hold the blade out with your thumb in a way that impeded your leverage and cutting angle.

I was one hand short for the operation: I needed two to hold the tape taut and one to wield the terrible blade. My creative solution was to wedge the end of the tape under my arm while holding the roll in my hand, but the knife stuck to the tape. I tried a little chopping motion—that seemed like it had potential. So I took a good swing at it, and the blade bounced off the tape and buried itself in the fleshy part of my palm, right at the base of my thumb.

I replaced the knife in my apron pocket and looked with detached fascination at the blood pooling quickly in my palm. I flexed my thumb, and the cut opened and closed like a mouth. My hand was tingling, but everything seemed to be in working order.

"Atwater! I need some paper towels!" I said.

He turned toward me at his usual oblivious pace, but when he saw the blood running down my forearm he leapt into action, tearing off paper towels like there were M&M's at stake.

While I attempted to stanch the bleeding, Atwater went and got Tekla, who knew what she was doing.

"Get your arm up. Press there, hard, and keep the pressure on it. Go back to the break room and wash it, I'll be there in a minute."

I went and stood at the break room sink, watching cold water run over the wound. It was nice and deep, one of my best, right up there with the time I'd cut off the tip of my finger with a razor-sharp as-seen-on-TV potato peeler while making soup for the homeless kitchen with my high school youth group.

Tekla arrived. She took my hand and gave my thumb a few tentative squeezes. "How does it feel?"

"Okay," I said. "A little weird. Like it's asleep, kind of."

"Do you want to go to the emergency room?"

"Heck no. I don't have insurance yet."

This was the deathblow to my uninsured lifestyle. Violence had succeeded where diversity and androgyny had failed.

"Does it hurt?"

"Now that you mention it, it does kind of hurt. Especially when you do that!" She was poking around the wound to see how deep it was.

"I think you'll be okay," Tekla said.

She bandaged me up, wrapping my hand with so much tape I couldn't move my thumb.

"Thank you," I said.

"Sure. I'm happy to bandage it for you tomorrow and so on. This place is dirty and you don't want to get it infected."

"I'd like to fill out an Incident Report," I said. "Just in case I have any problems with it."

Tekla nodded. "Let's go take care of that."

Running transactions one-handed took some getting used to. The customers, by and large, were not sympathetic. Of course, most of them didn't notice, because they didn't notice anything.

Around three, Christine came marching in from Garden and tossed her apron onto the Service Desk counter.

"You might want to tell someone there's nobody in Garden," she said to us, then continued down the aisle toward the break room.

"Uh, okay," Atwater said.

He and I looked at each other for a minute.

"Wasn't she on the register out there?" I asked.

Several minutes later, Christine came back with her purse. "You can tell Rex to go screw himself. Bye, Penn," she said, then went out the front door.

I dialed Kord. "Was Christine on the Garden register?"

"Yeah. What do you mean, 'was'?"

"She just quit," I said. "And left."

"Son of a bitch! Okay, let me get somebody out there right away."

Fifteen minutes later, Kord arrived from Garden and I told her what had happened.

"Any idea why she quit?" I asked.

"She got mad at me earlier today because she couldn't go to the bathroom right when she wanted to," Kord said.

In Garden, if you wanted a restroom break, you had to get a head cashier to wait until business slowed down so they could take another cashier off a register and bring them down, and it was a five-minute walk from one end of the store to the other. The whole process from initial thought to resumption of business as usual typically took about half an hour. One needed to plan ahead.

Kord was shaking her head. "Christine apparently called her mom, who called the store, fussed at Rex, and said she was going to come up here. What a baby."

"So is Christine fired?" I asked.

"She would be, yes," Kord said, "because she left her register logged on and unsupervised with money in it. And because she left that door unattended. Those are automatic fireable offenses."

"This is what we told you," I said. "Don't hire skinny girls. Hire some hot girls next time."

It wasn't like Christine and I were friends. And it wasn't like I wasn't going to keep seeing her with Pete at IHOP. But her walkout had livened up the day, and there would be further entertainment to come the next time I had a chance to talk to Pete.

Day 381 – Thursday, November 25

"Penn, I know it's Thanksgiving, but I need you to stay late," said Landfill. "Johnisha called in."

It figured. I'd just spent forty-five minutes matching one hundred pipe fittings to twelve receipts only to discover the man really wanted store credit after all, which would have allowed me to run everything in one transaction in about five minutes.

"What do you say?" Landfill asked.

I decided to try something new. What could it hurt?

"No," I said.

Landfill blinked. He wore that look he always got when somebody deviated from the script in his head. "What?"

"*No.* It's the first word little kids and pets learn. *No,* I can't stay, it's Thanksgiving, I have plans, for God's sake, there's nobody in the store, and I don't even know why we're open. *No.*"

"Um . . . I don't know if it's okay," Landfill said. "I'll have to check."

"If I have to stay late, I want to hear it from Rex."

"Rex isn't here today," Landfill protested.

"That's because it's *Thanksgiving.*"

"I'll go check," said Landfill.

"You do that." I waved him away with my bandaged hand.

It was ridiculous. The store had been dead all day. The Service Desk could handle Returns until nine. Even Home Depot was closed today, or so we'd heard. The most exciting thing that had happened all day was when nobody could figure out why the electric carts weren't charging. Then I went over and switched the power strip back on.

My phone rang. In a perfect world, it would be Landfill, telling me I was off the hook. In reality, it was Osric, the ASM on duty, telling me that yes, I had to stay until nine, for which I would be paid time-and-a-half. I was already getting time-and-a-half for working on Thanksgiving.

I squeezed my hands into fists. My right hand, at least; the tape job on my left prevented it.

Chloe was not going to be happy. And if Chloe wasn't happy, nobody was happy (at least, *I* wasn't, and who else's happiness was I worried about?). I hoped I could direct her raging torrent of wrath at its proper target: the Station.

At least I was off on Black Friday.

Day 385 – Monday, November 29

At 9:30 in the evening, Chloe, Pete, and I were the only ones at IHOP who weren't on the payroll.

"It's the day after Thanksgiving weekend," Pete said. "Everybody's feeling too guilty about the forty thousand calories they ate the last four days to go out."

"Where's Christine?" Chloe asked.

Pete looked at me, then at her. "What, Penn didn't tell you?"

"Tell me what?" Chloe asked.

"I dumped Christine."

"Why?" Chloe asked. "Because she quit?"

Pete rolled his eyes. "Please."

"Why, then? I thought you guys hit it off like . . . like . . ."

"Like hotcakes," I said.

"Please," Pete repeated. "Can you not discern the signs of the times?"

260

I unwrapped my silverware. "That sounds like something I'd say."

"Yeah, I heard you say it a few times. What do you want, royalties?"

"Tell your story!" said Chloe.

"Come on! It's Christine!" said Pete. "Do I really have to draw you a picture? She was kind of sketchy, yeah?"

That's why you dumped her?" Chloe asked. "Because she was 'kind of sketchy'? Did you have a fight?"

"No, no fight," Pete replied. "It was all quite amicable. On my part, anyway. You know how fussy she can be sometimes."

"What did you say to her? 'You're kind of sketchy, so it's over'?"

Pete sighed. "Look, it was just time. I had to cut her loose, that's all."

Chloe was indignant. "All of a sudden? How could you treat her like that? You just dropped her like— like—"

"Like hotcakes," I said.

"You just threw her aside when you were done with her!"

"Oh, yeah, she was my sugar mama," Pete shot back. "Is that what you think? I said, 'What, bitch? You lost your eight-fifty-an-hour job? It's over!' Be serious!"

"That's not what I meant!"

"No? What else would I be doing that I'd be 'done with her'? What are you insinuating?"

"I'm not insinuating anything!"

"Timeout," I said, but nobody paid any attention to me.

"She's crazy, okay?" Pete's shrill voice made my ears ring. "I dumped her because she's crazy!"

"She wasn't crazy! You get hung up on a few little eccentricities and—"

"What do you mean, 'wasn't crazy'? She is crazy! What are you going to do, anyway, headbutt me to death with your titanium head? You're talking about her like she's dead and—"

I slapped my good hand down on the table and kicked Pete in the shin. "Timeout!"

Pete blinked, took a deep breath, and glared at me. "What?"

"This is ridiculous," I said. "You guys are arguing like an old married couple."

"You're right," said Pete. "That's something I usually save for me and you."

"*Furthermore*, I'm confused. Chloe's defending someone she could never stand and meanwhile you're all of a sudden ripping into her like . . . like . . ."

"Like hotcakes," said Chloe acerbically.

"You always used to go to bat for her!" I said to Pete, who shrugged.

"She never did anything to make you treat her badly," said Chloe.

"Hey," Pete protested. "I never treated her badly."

"You talk about her badly!"

"Well, that's different, isn't it?"

"He talks about everybody badly," I said.

"How'd you break up with her, then?" Chloe demanded.

"That's none of your business."

"Did you tell her to her face?"

Now it was Pete's turn to look indignant. "Of course. What do you think? I just called and left her a message? Beep! 'It's over!' Please! What kind of man does that? I hate to break this to you, but I have *balls*. Oh, the food's here."

Day 387 – Wednesday, December 1

I didn't get the job with Leetown Connect. When I'd called them again to check on my application, they told me all the positions were filled. Leetown wasn't exactly the land of economic opportunity, but I was a smart guy with a college degree. I didn't get the job why, exactly? Because I maybe bombed an interview?

I drove to the Station, to the sinkhole forever sucking me in and down.

I thought all the Christmas stuff was out already; I was terribly, horribly wrong. In the front window of the store, directly in my line of sight, was an inflatable monstrosity that blotted all words from the mind except "big-ass snowman." The thing was fourteen feet tall at least, and it came with a huge inflatable sign that said "North Pole." Clearly, it was for rich people with no taste. We had smaller ones, too, for middle-class people with no taste. I wrote BIG-ASS SNOWMAN on a small yellow sign and tucked it into my apron. I thought it was funny.

One of my first customers returned a defective can of air freshener. I knew it was defective because when she banged it on the counter, it burst. I spent the rest of the day smelling like the chemical approximation of a rose.

Tekla invited me into the phone room to talk. Atwater hurriedly stuffed candy into his apron as we passed.

As we sat down, Tekla gave me an odd look. "You smell really nice, Penn. How's your hand?"

"Fine, I guess." I held it up. "I don't have to tape it so much."

"Penn, you're a really smart guy. You're wasted on Returns. I've talked to Kordelia, and we want to train you on the Service Desk. Are you okay with that? Is it something you want to do?"

Point of fact, it wasn't my first choice. Returns was easy. Service Desk was complicated. It wasn't more difficult, but it was more work. More work for the same pay was not something I was a big fan of. On the other hand, this wasn't the type of proposition to which you could just say, "Thanks, but no thanks."

"Uh, yeah, sure, I guess," I said.

The look on her face told me that this was not the enthusiastic response she'd been expecting.

"I, uh, just hadn't really thought about it that much," I said.

"Okay, so think about it. Service Desk isn't hard," said Tekla.

"I know. It's fine. I'll do it," I said.

"Great. Well, whenever you don't have any customers, come over to the Service Desk to observe, and we'll go from there."

Paige leaned across my counter. "It smells really good over here!"

"What's up?" I said.

"From now on, all the Returns cashiers are supposed to stand in the vestibule when they don't have customers. Okay?"

"Wait, what?" I said. "Stand in the vestibule?"

"Yeah. You can take your stool. They want the customers to be able to see you when they come in the door."

"They can't see me from here?"

"There's those shelves and things between you and the aisle," said Paige.

"What am I supposed to do, carry my stool back and forth every time I have a customer?"

"I'm sure you'll figure something out."

"But I'm supposed to be learning Service Desk."

Paige looked irritated. "I don't know anything about that."

"Tekla said Kord was okay with it!" I was becoming frustrated. Learning Service Desk wasn't great, but it was a million times better than standing in the vestibule, where there wasn't even a hard rubber mat.

"This is from Rex!" Paige said, which settled the matter.

I let out a long, slow breath. Rex taketh away yet again.

264

Kord came by at the end of my shift. "Make some signs for this stuff," she said, waving her hand at the smorgasbord of overindulgent Christmas bric-a-brac in the vestibule.

"What do you want me to put on that?" I asked, pointing at the gargantuan snowman.

"I don't know. Put 'big-ass snowman.'"

I pulled out my sign and slapped it on the counter.

Kord burst out laughing. "Oh, Penn, that's why you're my favorite," she said.

"So what's this about standing in the vestibule?" I asked. I hadn't been doing it. Paige came by once and reminded me, but I'd acted like I was doing something on the computer.

"I just got it today," Kord said.

"What about learning the Service Desk?" I asked. "What about my stool?"

She held up a hand. "I'll talk to Rex."

Day 389 – Friday, December 3

"This is a philosophical question, okay?" said Angry Pete. "Would you rather work at the House Station for the rest of your life or spend every meal for the rest of your life eating a bowl of scabs while sitting naked in a dumpster full of thumbtacks?"

I thought about it for a while. "Whose scabs are they?"

Day 390 – Saturday, December 4

"So I got this thing in my e-mail, and I thought it was pretty good," Landfill told us. "They're these four questions that test your thinking."

265

"I think you got kicked out of the KLU Athletics Center," said Pete.

Landfill scowled. "Let me tell it! Okay, how do you put a giraffe in the refrigerator?"

"Delete!" I said. "Unsubscribe! I get that freaking e-mail at least once a month."

"I've never heard it," said Pete. "What was the question?"

"How do you put a giraffe in the refrigerator?"

"Which refrigerator?"

"Any refrigerator. The one in your house."

Pete raised an eyebrow. "How big is the giraffe?"

"Regular size."

"Adult?"

"Adult."

Pete considered this. "I guess you'd have to chop him up."

"And then what?"

"What do you mean, 'And then what?'"

"And then you'd put it in, right?" said Landfill.

"Right."

"Wrong!" cried Landfill gleefully.

"How is it wrong?" Pete demanded. "Who are you to tell me what I can and can't chop up?"

"The correct answer is, you open the refrigerator, put in the giraffe, and close the fridge. See, it tests whether you tend to make simple things complicated."

"What?" Pete exclaimed. "Simple? You can't fit a giraffe in a refrigerator!"

"That's the answer," said Landfill.

"It doesn't make any sense! Let me see you put a giraffe in a refrigerator."

"Okay, never mind! Here's the second question: how do you put an elephant in the refrigerator?"

Pete sighed. "Open the fridge, put in the elephant, close the door."

Landfill clapped his hands. "Wrong!"

Pete looked like he was going to hit him.

Landfill smirked. "You have to open the fridge, *take out* the giraffe, then put in the elephant."

"Oh, *hell* no," said Pete. "Hell no! How are you going to tell me? First you say you can fit a giraffe in my fridge. That crap is ridiculous, but whatever. But you can't turn around and say I can't fit a giraffe *and* an elephant in there! I'll put the giraffe, the elephant, you, *and* your mom in my damn fridge! With room to spare, God damn it!"

"But that's the answer! It checks your ability to consider the implications of your previous actions!"

"My *ass*. That's *retarded*," said Pete.

"Retarded like a fox, you mean!" Landfill said.

Pete blinked. "That doesn't even make any damn sense either. Look, this fridge thing is single-handedly the stupidest thing I've ever heard. Either we're talking realistically or we're not, and obviously we're not, so your giraffe, your elephant, and your refrigerator can all go to hell."

"Come on, Penn!" said Landfill. "You've seen these questions! Help me out."

"It's a stupid e-mail," I said.

"Andersen Consulting said ninety percent of the managers they surveyed missed all the questions!" Landfill countered.

"Good!" said Pete. "Gives me some faith in humanity. Come on, what's the next question? This is almost as fun as a piñata full of cockroaches."

"Forget it," said Landfill. "Just never mind. Look, I have to go down and check on the cashiers."

"I agree," said Pete malevolently.

Day 392 – Monday, December 6

"That bastard Lance got fired, you'll be glad to know," Pete said as we worked on a special order together. "You should give me twenty dollars for telling you that."

"Awesome," I said. "What for?" I was sitting in the chair with the headset, which meant I was not standing in the vestibule.

"Rex caught him losing his temper with a customer. I don't think it was the first time."

"Good for him."

Booker Shoeboot came by with a little brown sack. "You guys have to pick a name," he said. We complied. No further explanation was forthcoming.

"Do I have to assassinate this person?" I asked.

"You didn't get your own name, did you?" Booker asked. "It's for the holiday gift exchange. You have to buy them a present for less than fifteen dollars. Bring it to the party. Okay, I have to go to the other registers now."

"I hate that stupid party," said Pete. "They had karaoke last year."

"Don't come, then. I like it. It's one of the few times they ever give us free crap. I got a fifty-dollar Target gift card last year."

Pete snorted. "I got a ten-dollar gift card for gas."

I looked down at my paper. "I drew Brandy. What the heck am I supposed to buy Brandy?"

"Well, what does she like?"

"Babies."

"What else?"

"Hairspray?" I said. "What do I know?"

"Women like things that stink. Body wash, lotion, soap. That kind of thing," Pete said.

"I'm supposed to buy her *lotion?* She's married."

Pete sighed. "I'm not talking about whatever pervert lotion you're thinking of. I'm talking about gift baskets and such. I don't know about you sometimes."

I endeavored to change the subject. "Did you see Landfill in the break room earlier?"

"No. Did he do something entertaining? Get a Slim Jim stuck up his nose?"

268

"He was eating this absolutely magnificent peanut butter and jelly sandwich," I said. "It was wrapped in a paper towel, in a big clear baggie. The peanut butter and jelly had oozed all over the bag. The sandwich was gigantic. Huge, thick slices of bread, with peanut butter and jelly all over them. And when he pulled the paper towel away, you could see the pattern of it in the peanut butter. It was like watching a train wreck. I couldn't take my eyes off it."

Pete shook his head. "That kid's a slob, man."

When I came home, Jeff was as giddy as a schoolboy. He was hopping up and down.

"Knock it off," I said. "You're creeping me out."

"Guess what happened!"

I couldn't imagine what could get Jeff this excited. If he were a dog, he would have peed on the carpet.

"Rapture Joe moved away?" I ventured.

"Even better! Hee hee!"

My eyebrows rose. Jeff had just said "hee hee."

"Milla and I got engaged!" Jeff shouted.

"What?" I cried, clapping him on the shoulder. "Congratulations!"

"Thanks!"

"Why didn't you tell me you were going to ask her?"

"I wanted it to be a surprise!"

"You're supposed to surprise her, not me," I said.

"I just picked up the ring on Saturday."

"You didn't even show it to me!" I said.

"Bro, I meant to, but I haven't seen you all weekend!"

"Well, congratulations," I said. "How'd you do it?"

I listened intently because Chloe was going to give me the third degree, and she'd crucify me if couldn't reproduce the conversation to her satisfaction (that is, verbatim).

"Last night I took her to dinner at *Le Fromage Mauvais-Sentant*, first of all."

That was the closest thing Leetown had to a snooty French restaurant. Founded by a non-Frenchman from Leetown, the restaurant *was* snooty and the food *was* French, but somehow the whole thing didn't quite work. But they got business—probably from the same people who would be lining up over the coming weeks to buy big-ass snowmen.

"Milla loved it. It's her favorite place, but it's so expensive. Then we went to the park." Jeff scratched his head. "That wasn't the greatest idea because it was kind of cold. But we sat on a bench and watched the moon rise over the pond and it was really nice. And I proposed. And she said yes."

"Well done," I said. "So when's the wedding?"

"I don't know yet. We're looking at April."

"I'll be there," I said.

Day 394 – Wednesday, December 8

"Did you see that lady that just came through my line?" Pete asked. "She looked like a movie star."

I craned my neck. "Where? Which movie star?"

"Clint Eastwood."

I shook my head.

"Why do people write 'Xmas'?" said Pete. "How is that short for Christmas?"

"Allow me to impart the Christmas knowledge," I said. I produced a pen and paper and wrote χρ.

"XP? Like Windows XP?"

"These are the Greek letters chi and rho. Chi looks like an X. It makes a K sound. Rho looks like a P. It makes an R sound." I drew the letters again with the tail of the rho vertically bisecting the chi. "You may have seen this symbol in traditional churches."

Pete shrugged. "It's been a while."

"Anyway, it's the first two letters in 'Χριστός,' which is 'Christ' in Greek." I wrote it out. "That's how it's short for Christmas. You're welcome."

"Wow," said Pete. "Ask a simple question, get a complicated answer."

"That's as simple as I can give it to you. What did you expect?"

"I don't know. Something more arbitrary, I guess. That actually has a point to it."

"Come with me to church sometime," I said. "You might learn something."

His eyes narrowed. "So you can rope me into some in-depth theological argument?"

"Yeah, Pete," I said. "That's exactly it."

Kord approached. "What are you kids doing? Loafing? Do some work. Pete, page all departments for Returns. I need to talk to Penn."

"I didn't do it," I said reflexively.

We went back over by my register.

"I've been talking with Tekla and Madeleine," said Kord. "Look, we all know how nice a guy you are, but that's not what most people see. Right?"

I tensed. "Right."

"Anyway, Tekla's been telling me how the Service Desk has been in disarray, which is one of the reasons she asked me if she could have you. What we'd like to do is create a new position. A phone room position. You would answer the phone and handle phone sales. Do all the paperwork. That kind of thing. You could sit most of the day. What do you say?"

I blinked. "Yes, thank you, please, sir, may I have another, would you like a hug?"

She accepted a hug.

"It's not official, though, okay? We have to make sure there's room in the budget and get it approved."

That meant Rex. Still, hope had dawned.

271

"That would be amazing," I said.

She clapped me on the shoulder. "I thought you'd be happy. Keep learning Service Desk. But in the meantime, if Rex is here, I need you to stand in the vestibule. Or sit. Take your stool."

"Okay."

Half a loaf, and so forth.

Day 395 – Thursday, December 9

"Hey, wake up!" said the customer, dropping a bag of merchandise on my counter. "I want to give this to you."

"Do you have a receipt?" I asked.

"I'm not returning it. I'm giving it to you."

I looked up. It was the guy who looked like Charlton Heston. He was real.

"I bought a shop vac here last night. I took it home and the damn thing wouldn't work. So I opened it up and all this stuff was inside. I don't want it."

I looked in the bag, which contained a bunch of little electrical pieces worth maybe thirty bucks total.

"Oh. Well, thanks, then," I said.

I called Kord and Hardware and pieced the story together.

Yesterday, a customer had put the vacuum in his cart. The ever-creepy Robert had noticed the guy spending a long time loitering in Electrical. Then he'd heard the unmistakable *zip* of packaging tape being pulled off the roll. As per House Station policy, he'd proceeded to follow the guy all around the store. The man noticed this, then finally left without buying anything. His cart was down one of the aisles and still had the vacuum in it. They'd opened it up, but nothing unusual had been inside. Somehow the man had switched boxes.

These kinds of things passed for entertainment at the House Station. The people we got weren't exactly criminal masterminds, but we enjoyed keeping ahead of them.

With shoplifting (as with fussing for returns), the direct approach typically worked better. Take, for example, the man in the huge puffy coat who walked in five minutes before we closed and asked us where the restroom was. When he left the store, he set off the alarm. Thoth followed him out the store, saying "Sir, come back, please," over and over like a mantra, while the man took off running and jumped the fence at the edge of the parking lot.

You'd think security would be better. You go into a place like the House Station and every aisle has a black globe hanging from the ceiling. You are meant to believe that these globes contain security cameras. This is not so. Cameras are expensive, and they don't bother putting them on every aisle. They were mostly just on the aisles with high-dollar items and above all the registers — at least, I hoped so. I knew there was one above Returns; after Rovergial got punched in the face, they'd given the film to the police. If something horrible ever happened to me at my register, at least it would be recorded for posterity.

Day 396 – Friday, December 10

Rex was in the building, so I was in the vestibule.

Landfill called my register. "What are you doing? I've had like three customers ask me if Returns was open."

"What? My light's on. I'm in the vestibule."

He made a disapproving sound. "Well, nobody can see you in the vestibule."

273

Day 397 – Saturday, December 11

It was unseasonably warm, and the Station was having a barbecue for us. The store did this occasionally. They took a grill and set it up around the side of the building, next to the break room's emergency exit. On our lunch breaks, we could look forward to burgers and hot dogs and all manner of Wal-Mart-brand potato chips. The only condition was we had to clock out to eat it.

On the one hand, I loved free food. On the other hand, if I stayed to eat it, I didn't have time to go home and take a nap.

A third option was to take a "bathroom break" on the clock, help myself, and eat so fast I choked.

Before I had a chance to head back there, a family came by with an exchange. They dropped off some defective merchandise and went to get replacements. A couple minutes later, the older of the two girls came back.

She was seventeen or eighteen, chubby and completely unattractive, wearing a rainbow camisole that was too small and no bra. What was mesmerizingly horrifying was her cleavage: there was a three-inch gap between her breasts, which looked like someone had taken a rolling pin to them until they extended past her navel. She almost could have tucked them into her pants.

"So," she said, in a voice that was supposed to be fetching, "how long have you been working here?"

I didn't feel like there was a good way to answer this question. I had no viable response. I turned to her and said, "Hi, can I help you?"

To my everlasting horror, she reached across the counter and started thumbing through the merit badges that hung from my apron strap. "Wow, you have a lot of badges! Are you the manager?"

I did *not* say about fifteen different things that popped into my head.

Something clattered on the ground. Pete had gotten up from his chair and was making his way toward Returns, farther than his headset tether would allow. He turned to collect the phone.

"No," I said, "I'm not the manager. Is there something I can help you with?"

The girl batted her eyelashes coquettishly, or tried to. She looked like she had something stuck in her eye. "Oh, if you were the manager, I was just wondering if you would hire me."

At that moment, blessedly, my phone rang.

"Excuse me," I said, and answered it.

It was Pete. "Hey, man, why don't you throw up on her?"

"I'm trying very hard not to," I said.

Pete hung up, but I kept the phone pressed to my ear, carrying on a conversation with no one. After a minute of this, I covered the mouthpiece and whispered to her, "Pete can help you over there if you need anything."

She turned and glanced at him, but didn't move. She just stood there looking at me.

Fortunately, her family returned, and I hung up the phone. Two minutes later, they were gone.

"I'm telling Chloe about this!" cackled Pete.

"You do that," I said. "Pretty hilarious, is it?"

"Hell, yeah, it is. She's going to want to know about her competition."

I rubbed my face with both hands. "Make your jokes. I've just been through a very traumatic experience."

A nervous man approached my register. "Um, I just wanted to let you know there are some people having a barbecue out back."

"Thanks," I said. "I'll take care of it."

"Oh, and I'm looking for something like this. I don't know if anyone makes it, but I drew a picture." He pulled out a crumpled sheet of notebook paper with an inscrutable

Goldbergian contraption sketched on it. It looked like a da Vinci schematic.

"Let me call someone," I said.

Day 399 – Monday, December 13

"Finished? Ma'am, that shelving is *pre*-finished! What? Yeah, I'll transfer you." When Pete was off the phone, he said, "Man, I miss the times before we opened. I remember this one time, when it was brand new, I went into the handicapped bathroom, lay down on the floor, and went to sleep. Remember, they had everybody coming in so early. What, you never went to sleep in this building? You don't doze off on that stool sometimes? At one time or another, everybody's gone into the bathroom, sat on the crapper, and taken a nap."

"I've only fallen asleep at store meetings," I said.

Pete shook his head. "Yeah, I would, too. I don't know why you go to those."

"What do you mean?"

"I quit going a long time ago. If you get an award, you can just pick it up next time you come in. Why do you go?"

"Because we're supposed to go."

"There is no 'supposed to go,'" Pete said. "You go if you want."

"Just a minute! Store meetings are *optional*?"

"You didn't know that?"

"*Optional?*"

Pete laughed at me for a long time. "Oh, hey, I was thinking, maybe there's something to the Bible after all."

I raised an eyebrow. "Is that so."

"Well, I was flipping through it the other day like you suggested. I found some profound truths about life."

"Oh?"

"It really spoke to me. I wrote it down." Pete pulled out a scrap of paper. "Here. Ecclesiastes 2:17: 'Therefore I hated life, because the work that is wrought under the sun is grievous unto me.' I didn't know they had the House Station in Bible times."

"Timeless truth," I said.

He nodded toward my register. "You have a customer."

It was a man with a handful of plumbing whatnot. The hundred-dollar bill he gave me was soaked in something reddish-brown and sticky. I gingerly took it by the corner and dropped it into my register.

The minute he was gone, I dialed Kord.

"I have a blood-soaked hundred-dollar bill," I said.

She sighed. "Is it your blood?"

"No."

"I'll be there in a minute."

We sealed it in a plastic bag.

"What the hell is this? What did the guy buy?" Kord asked.

"Pipe fittings."

Kord shook her head. "Help me understand. 'My sink leaks and I'm short on cash, let me shank somebody on the way to the Station'?"

We sent it back to the vault.

"What are they supposed to do with it back there?" Pete asked. "Throw it in the laundry? Test it for AIDS?"

"I need to go wash my hands immediately," I said.

Day 400 – Tuesday, December 14

"These freaking slobs in Tool Rental," said Pete. "Every day when we close, I have to call all the departments and see what their safety issue is. But Tool Rental never has one."

"Why is that a problem?" I asked.

277

"They *have* to have one. There has to be something on the sheet."

"So make something up."

"They do. Every day I call them, and every day they tell me there's water on the floor. So I put it, and that's fine, but it's weak sauce. That guy Walter over there is the worst."

"So what are you complaining about?"

Pete looked at me sharply. "What, I can't complain?"

"Far be it from me," I said. "Walter's the one with the greasy hair, right?"

"Oh, it's horrendous. We need to wash that crap with a pressure washer. Twenty-five hundred psi ought to do the trick."

"It'd explain the water on the floor," I said.

"You have a customer."

Goodenough was looking at a display in the vestibule.

"Oh, God. You take this one," I said.

"Why? Oh, that's your boy the Major, isn't it?"

"Colonel," I said. "You help him. I'm going to the bathroom."

"You really hate that guy, don't you?"

"Let me put it this way," I said. "If the Earth was going to explode and I had a spaceship that could hold the entire population of the world except for five people, he would be left behind."

Pete thought this was a marvelous idea. "Who else?"

I turned off my register light. "I don't know."

"Come on! Rex? Landfill?"

"No comment."

Jeff found me in my room and asked me if I was going to be at his wedding.

"Of course, I told you that already," I said. Something was afoot.

"Okay, bro, I just wanted to make sure. I would have loved to have you in my wedding party if it wasn't going to just be family."

"Don't even worry about it."

It was necessary for Jeff to have just his family in his wedding party—he had thirteen brothers and sisters. His parents used a foolproof form of natural birth control: it's impossible to get pregnant if you're already pregnant.

"Anyway, Milla and I are getting married in April, right?"

"Right."

Here it came. We had to talk about this sooner or later: he was either going to move out or kick me out.

"And we're both on the lease, right?"

"Right."

"And our lease goes until June, right?"

He was going to kick me out. I wondered whether I could "accidentally" leave Drimacus behind when I left.

"Well, if it's okay with you, Milla and I would like to stay here."

"I see."

"Well . . . but if you want to keep it, you can."

"No, no. You can have it. I'll get a one-bedroom," I said. "Or I'll find another roommate."

"Are you sure?"

"Yeah, man, I can't afford this rathole on my own. I'll get a smaller rathole. No problem."

"I really appreciate it, bro," Jeff said. "Um, I already asked at the office, and we'd like to put Milla on the lease, and they said they need all three of us to go over there."

"Any time I'm here," I said.

Day 402 – Thursday, December 16

At least twice a week I got a customer who threw a tantrum and said, "I hate the House Station! I'm never coming here again! I'm going to Home Depot!"

These customers were all liars. They were the same ones who went to Home Depot and said, "I hate Home Depot! I'm never coming here again! I'm going to the House Station!"

If all these terrible customers really did pack up and go to Home Depot, Home Depot would be the worst place to work in the entire world, and any fool knew the worst place to work in the entire world was the House Station.

When I got to Returns, my stool was nowhere to be seen. Pete was reclining in his chair, reading the job classifieds.

"You're going to get fired," I told him.

Pete looked over the top of the paper. "The hell you say!"

"I do say. When Rex sees you . . ."

Pete folded up the paper and stuck it in his apron. "Frankly, I don't give a damn. Rex can go to hell with Adolf Hitler and Landfill's damn giraffes."

"What happened?"

Pete leaned forward. "I want to tell you something I noticed." He said it in that tangential way where it was anybody's guess whether what he was about to say had anything to do with the question he'd just been asked. "You ever drive past this place in the daytime? When you're not working, just going somewhere else?"

"Sure."

"It's pretty inconspicuous, isn't it?"

"It takes up an entire block."

Pete waved a hand. "That's not what I mean. I'm talking about compared to driving past at night. At night this place is a shining beacon of despair. You can see the sickly yellow glow from a mile away. Can't you see the glow from your house?"

"No. It's blocked by the Wal-Mart glow. What did Rex do?"

"What do you mean, what did he do? He's Rex!"

"What did he do that you're openly looking for a new job while on the clock?"

Pete shook his head. "Same crap as always. I've just had enough. What did he do? He got on me for being late this morning. I was giving that bastard Atwater a ride, because his raggedy-ass Price Is Rightmobile broke down again, and it was his fault we were late because he wouldn't get in the car because he dropped his damn English muffin into the toilet somehow, and he had to make another one, and then he broke the jam jar all over the kitchen floor, and then he had to clean it like the freaking Queen of England was going to come over and eat breakfast off it. And who got written up? I did! Not Atwater. But where was Atwater while Rex had his foot up my ass? Do you have any idea?"

"At the snack machine?"

"Probably was. He sure as hell wasn't anywhere near to stick up for me. Stupid ungrateful bastard. You know what he said to me today? He told me we needed a mute button for the phone that deactivates when you talk."

"Why do you keep giving him rides?"

"Because he lives near me. Because I'm a good person. Because I enjoy the company of older men with mustaches. What does it matter? Here, try this." Pete handed me a polyurethane mallet from under his desk.

"What am I supposed to do with this?"

"It's a dead-blow hammer. Hit the floor. On the mat."

"Why?"

"Because it's cathartic. It's been getting me through the day."

I dropped to one knee and smacked the hammer down.

"No, not like that." Pete snatched the mallet back, raised it over his head like a crackhead blacksmith, and slammed it into the floor with all his might. There was no bounce or recoil.

He handed the mallet to me again, face flushed. "Do it like a man."

I did it like a man. It felt good.

"Not too shabby," I said. "Where'd you get this?"

"It was a return. I keep it under the desk for necessary occasions."

"Are you sure that's a good idea?" I said. "You might get excited and hit a customer. Or Rex."

Pete grunted. "That'd be a hell of a way to go out. 'Pete, your ass is fired.' 'Oh, yeah, bitch? Manifest the mallet madness!' Oh, I would be in jail after that rampage. Nobody would have any kneecaps. Penn, I hate everybody. I hate the company. I hate the customers. My damn spaceship would be empty."

"Take a deep breath," I said. "I'm just going to take this hammer and put it in the Hardware bin, okay?"

"Sure, man," said Pete calmly. "Whatever you want. Hey, I noticed Chloe came by and picked you up yesterday. Your car broken too?"

"No. Just in for service. She gave me a ride. We went apartment hunting yesterday evening."

Pete's eyebrows shot up like rockets. "Apartment hunting? You two? I don't believe it."

I quickly realized my error. "No, just for me. Jeff's getting married and he's kicking me out."

Pete jabbed me in the chest. "You need to say what you mean. Anyway, she was wearing those overalls; I thought maybe you guys were going on a hayride."

"I think Chloe looks good in overalls," I said.

"Do you like *farmers*?" said Pete. "Forget it. You think she looks good in anything. No, take it easy, it's cute. And I think it's time for your bathroom break."

"I just got here."

"And here comes your friend the Colonel."

"Twice in a week? Right. Excellent. Well done."

282

Day 403 – Friday, December 17

"Penn, I have some bad news for you," said Kord, a sympathetic, big-sisterly look on her face. She looked exhausted. "The phone room job isn't going to work out. Rex said there isn't enough money in the budget for it. I'm sorry."

I took a deep breath and let it out slowly. Who was surprised by this? Pretty much nobody, that's who.

"Thanks," I said. "Thanks for trying."

And thanks to you, Rex, for crushing my hopes and dreams, small and sad as they were.

"Yeah. I–" Her phone rang, and she answered it. She wandered a few steps away as she talked.

Pete came over and I told him what happened.

"That sucks," he said. "What are you going to do now? Move over to Service Desk?"

"I don't know," I muttered. "Probably, if Rex lets me. What's my alternative? Stand in the vestibule?"

"You need to get the hell out of here. Why are you still here? Get out!"

"I've tried."

"Try again!"

I scowled at him. "What are you, my guidance counselor? Why are *you* still here?"

"Why is *anybody* here?" said Pete existentially. "This isn't about me; I'll leave when I please. You're the genius with the college degree."

"Yeah, look how far that's gotten me."

"Penn, what you need to do is–" Pete broke off as Kord called his name.

"Come talk to me in the phone room right now," she said. "Give Penn the headset."

I raised an eyebrow at Pete, who shrugged.

Five minutes later, I glanced back through the window and saw Pete gesticulating wildly, which was nothing out of the ordinary. But Kord was just as animated, which was

283

unusual. Shortly thereafter, they came out, and Kord went back down to the registers.

I returned the headset to Pete. "What was that about?"

He shook his head. "Nothing. Just a misunderstanding."

"No way," I said. "You can't get off with 'just a misunderstanding.'"

"My mom got a hold of my cell phone yesterday. I left it in her car. She sent some text messages to Kord, pretending to be me. 'You should really give my mom another chance,' that type of thing."

"What?"

"They broke up last week. She moved out. My mom, I mean."

I held up a hand. "Wait, what? Stop. *Your mom* has been living with Kord for . . ."

"For like two years."

I massaged my temples. "Just a minute. Somehow . . . What . . . How did I go this long without knowing that?"

"Without knowing what?"

"That *that* was your mom! Jeez, I even met her a couple of times!"

Pete frowned. "You didn't know that? How did you not know that?"

"I'm mad I didn't know that!" I exclaimed.

"I don't know, Penn. You've really got your head up your ass sometimes."

I threw up my hands. "Nobody tells me anything!"

"I didn't know you didn't know."

"So isn't this all kind of weird for you?" I asked.

"Hell, yeah, it is. My mom takes my phone and does stupid crap like it's high school? Are you kidding me?"

That wasn't what I meant, and I wanted to discuss it further, but I became inundated with customers, most of whom were buying gifts, many of which would no doubt find their way back to my counter the week after Christmas.

284

Day 405 – Sunday, December 19

It was the Christmas party. Sorry, the holiday party. I didn't know which holiday in particular, because they wouldn't say (I asked, and Helen said "all of them").

Happy belated Ramadan, everybody.

Several folding tables covered with cheap plastic red and green tablecloths were heavy laden with Doritos, Wal-Mart cookies, and bottles of soda. Most everyone was standing around talking and eating. Osric was trying unsuccessfully to get people to come up and sing karaoke.

"Osric's too laid back to pull that off," Pete was saying. "Besides, there's no alcohol here. I don't think there's enough alcohol in Leetown to get me up there."

"Do you want to go, Penn?" Chloe asked.

"Wild horses," I said, and she made a face.

"Man, today was like senior day," Pete said, spilling chip crumbs down his front. "I've never seen so many old people. This one guy, he was like nine hundred years old, but he actually had a debit card. Anyway, he returned something, and I said, 'This is going to refund to your credit card,' and he was like, 'No, it's a debit card,' and he was ready to argue about it."

"See, here you go again," said Chloe. "All you ever want to talk about is work."

"We're *at* work." Pete crammed an entire cookie into his mouth.

"But we're not working."

It took Pete the better part of a minute to swallow. "Damn, that's a dry cookie. No, we're not working, but we're in this building, aren't we? We're here and we're not on the clock. It just doesn't feel right. I know Penn agrees with me."

I did, but I wasn't getting into it, and I told him so.

Pete was undeterred. "Yeah, so anyway, I had this guy with a no-receipt return, and he didn't have an ID. He got real pissed and told me to call this number. And I'm like, 'Look, buddy, it doesn't matter. That could be the phone number to the Oval Office, but when I hang up, I'm still going to need an ID.' And he starts yelling, 'Call the number! Call the number!' It was pretty funny to watch. Like all of his kind, he got nothing and liked it. Thus always to assholes."

At this point, Chastity became the first sheep to the karaoke slaughter. I don't know what got her up there (Pete speculated that she'd been drinking before she came), but she proceeded to hack her way through a cringe-inducing rendition of an inherently awful song—which, I suppose, is what karaoke was all about.

Pete didn't agree. "What the hell is this?" he demanded. "Staind? Sellout post-grunge nu metal karaoke favorites? It's almost 2005! Move on with your life!"

Chloe punched him in the arm. "At least she went up there and sang."

"'Sang' being a relative term, I suppose," said Pete, and got hit again. "Stop! Penn, get your woman!"

"Quiet," I said. "They're giving away free crap."

Free crap was the key to the whole affair. Free food was insufficient to lure disgruntled associates from their homes (except for Atwater, for obvious reasons, and all the managers, who had to be there), so they gave something to every single associate who attended.

When we came in, they handed us each a little ticket with a number. When they called your number, you went up and pulled a gift card out of a bag. Every so often, they'd hand out something good.

Pete got a ten-dollar gift card to a gas station.

"Son of a bitch!" he exclaimed. "This is the same crap I got last year! Half a tank of gas! Just what I always wanted!"

"Better than nothing," I said, and Pete muttered something I didn't catch.

Chloe and I pulled Wal-Mart gift cards.

"I got fifty!" I said. "That's what I'm talking about. Keep me in groceries for weeks!"

Chloe was jumping in the air again—she'd gotten a hundred.

Pete tried to crumple his gift card in his hand, but the plastic was too thick.

Then Landfill won an Xbox.

"I freaking hate that kid," said Pete.

Then came the gift exchange. I'd taken Pete's advice and gotten Brandy a gift basket from a bath and body shop. She liked it. It wasn't too weird. Mission accomplished.

Landfill had drawn my name, and he gave me a pair of Chinese meditation balls. They were each the size of a golf ball, and you rolled them around in your hand to purportedly improve circulation and mental health by stimulating acupuncture points.

From Pete, Chloe got a vintage but never worn *Beverly Hills 90210* T-shirt. She was ecstatic.

But it's not a real holiday party unless somebody shows up drunk and does something stupid enough to get fired—it happened last year and it happened again this year.

To everyone's surprise, it was Chris, the Kord lookalike from Décor. He wasn't even a dark horse candidate, mostly because he was quiet and we didn't know anything about him.

Chris had been having a heated discussion in the corner with Brook, the Delivery Coordinator. All of a sudden, the slightly built Chris kicked over a table, scattering cookies across the floor. Then he tripped and fell down.

Osric tried to help him up, but Chris shoved him away. When Chris finally got to his feet, Rex was there to steady him. Rex said something only Chris could hear; Chris swayed, then punched Rex in the face.

Rex fell back, clutching his bleeding nose, while Chris lurched out the door.

We were shocked, amazed, and enraptured.

"That's what I'm talking about," said Pete in an awed whisper. "That's how I want to go out. Sticking it to The Man himself. That was the highlight of the year. That dude is an

American hero." Pete threw his gas card in the air. "Merry freaking Christmas to all!"

Day 407 – Tuesday, December 21

The man in the suit and I did the usual dance. I said no, we couldn't take his paint sprayer back, the man yelled at me, I called Landfill, Landfill said no, the man yelled at Landfill, I called Kord, he yelled at Kord.

"Store policy is not law! It's store policy! I know that! I'm from New York!" shouted the man.

It played out as it usually did: Kord said no, we couldn't take it back, he fussed some more, Kord said yes.

"It's messed up," I said when he'd gone. "The system favors assholes. You can just fuss until you get what you want."

Kord shrugged. "It's true. But what can you do about it? Store policy. Better than losing a customer as far as they're concerned. Don't take it personally." She patted me on the back and left, at which point Landfill tried to make small talk.

"I was in the Home Depot the other day," he said. "Man, they have a lot of trashy-looking girls working there. They should call it the Ho Depot. Heh heh."

I wasn't in the mood. "Don't you know you're not supposed to go there?"

Landfill blinked. "What?"

"Don't let Rex find out you shopped at Home Depot. You don't want to get fired, do you?"

He went delightfully ashen. "Fired? Really?"

"Yeah, man. How do you think it looks? House Station people shopping over there?"

"I wasn't shopping! I was just there with a friend!"

"You can't be too careful," I said.

Landfill gave me a look that would have been sly on a cleverer man's face. "Seriously?"

I shrugged. "Ask Kord if you don't believe me."

After lunch, Kord called me to the back for my belated one-year review — my first chance at a raise. This review went more or less like the last one: Penn is really good at his job, but he's not friendly.

Every year, there was a certain amount of money allocated for raises based on how the store had done. Management divided it up as they thought best. Ultimately, my raise wasn't Kord's decision; it was Rex's.

I got a fifteen-cent raise.

"Thanks for nothing," is what I did *not* say. I tried to look on the bright side. Fifteen cents an hour would *almost* offset the money they were about to start taking out of my paycheck for my much-ballyhooed health insurance.

"Don't discuss your raise with any other associates," Kord said. "Some people didn't get raises."

"Fifteen freaking cents!" I exclaimed to Pete.

"I got sixty cents."

"Rex doesn't hate you," I said. "And you have Atwater to make you look good by comparison."

"Are you mad?"

I shook my head. "No. Screw Rex. What's fifteen cents one way or the other?"

Pete did some quick calculations on the Service Desk calculator. "That's a dollar and twenty cents a day. Twenty-four dollars a month. Not quite three hundred dollars a year. Before taxes. But it's not about the money, it's about the respect, right?"

"Something like that," I said.

"Sucks, man. Hey, have you heard anything about what happened the other night? With Brook and Chris? I heard he said some things to her."

I raised an eyebrow. "No, what kind of things?"

"Like racial things. Asian slurs. Then she said some things to him. Like gay slurs."

"That's it?" I said. "That's weak. There needs to be a better reason than that."

"Maybe it was all staged," said Pete conspiratorially. "Maybe he just wanted an excuse to punch Rex in the face."

I snorted. "Who doesn't have an excuse?"

A man came to the counter. "Is that Mexican guy here?"

"What Mexican guy?" I asked.

"In Electrical."

"He means Osric," Pete said. "I'll call him."

Day 408 – Wednesday, December 22

Pete arrived at the Service Desk, apron in hand. "Look at the delightful crap we're clearancing out just in time for Christmas! Buy one! Nay, buy several!"

The side of my little Returns cage that was typically reserved for merchandise the store was desperately trying to draw attention to was piled high with frog- and turtle-shaped solar-powered lights.

"Seriously, who buys these?" said Pete. "I'm sure Osric will. He buys everything that goes on clearance whether he needs it or not."

"Are you just now getting here?" I asked. "Where have you been all day?"

"Back safety training class. Everybody has to do it."

"I'll do anything that gets me off the register. Does it take a long time?"

"Not long enough. It was actually pretty interesting," Pete said with an unusual lack of sarcasm. "For example, most people think that they get back injuries from one bad lift instead of from a bunch of lifts over time. And a load at arm's length is like seven to ten times heavier than a load close to the body."

"You were into this," I said.

He settled into his chair. "It's legit. So you're leaving tomorrow? When are you coming back?"

"I'm leaving tonight as soon as I get off. I can't wait to get out of here. I'll be back on the third. I put in for this early – no way am I trying to be on Returns the day after Christmas."

"Man, they've got me here that day. That was good thinking," said Pete. "Are you using your paid vacation?"

"No. I thought about it, but I'd rather save it."

Pete shrugged. "I'd use it now. Money is money, and you can always get time off."

"Yeah, but when you want unpaid time off, you need a reason, and 'I'm sick of this freaking place and I need to go away before I too punch Rex in the face' doesn't look good on the request form."

James the friendly Plumbing associate came for his returns. A customer waylaid him and asked him about lumber. He directed the man to Pete, who dialed a Lumber associate.

"See, that's the mistake these customers make," said James. "Never assume the first person you ask knows anything." James sat on the bench and, over the next ten minutes, expounded several other crotchety but good-natured and unfunny maxims like "I'm having an allergic reaction to life" and the old "I'm not bald, I'm taller than my hair" chestnut.

Kord summoned me back to the office. I had that anxious feeling in the pit of my stomach even though I knew I didn't do anything.

As it turned out, I *had* done something.

"You had an overage last Friday," she said.

"Crap!" I said. "Sorry."

She smirked. "It's better than a shortage; you're making us money. I have to write you up, though. Tell me how you're going to avoid overages in the future."

"I'm going to count the money more carefully, and if I'm over at the end of my shift, I'll steal enough to balance it."

"Want to try again, smartass?" she said. "I have to write down what you tell me. It goes in your file."

"Oh. Um . . . always count out the money to the customer."

"That's better. Now get out of here and don't do it again."

Day 420 – Monday, January 3

I had a delightful Christmas with my family in Saint Louis, eleven days full of not standing and not going anywhere near a House Station. It was longer than I'd originally intended to be gone, but I couldn't resist the opportunity to take two full weekends off. I'd hoped that Chloe would have been able to come with me, but she'd had an immense amount of family come in from out of town and couldn't in good conscience leave.

While I was there, my brother Anders gave me a fairly polished draft of his novel. He'd taken a lot of my advice: the book had been significantly pared down, most of the boring parts were gone, and the beginning was much improved – this time, it sucked me in.

In short, his novel was better than mine.

I wasn't sure how I felt about that. Not jealous. As a writer, I got jealous all the time – not because other people's books were better, but because other people got the breaks with inferior products.

But if Anders got published before I did . . . well, then I'd be fairly jealous.

I was proud of him, honest. Even so, it was demoralizing. Maybe I wasn't even the best writer in my own family. Maybe I wasn't ever going to get my novel published. Then what? The House Station forever? That was more than I could bear.

However, when I got home, my spirits received a considerable boost from the unexpected presence of five complimentary copies of *Lloyd's Beacon*, containing my story, in my mailbox. They were accompanied by a note indicating that they'd moved my story up because of a sudden opening in their Winter issue.

After that, Anders swore I was the better writer, and I didn't argue too strenuously. After all, what did I know about anything?

Day 422 – Wednesday, January 5

"So Robert got fired," said Pete. "Probably for being too creepy; what else would it be with—" Pete broke off. "Holy freaking *scheisse*! Look who it is! It's a bird! It's a plane!"

"It's time for your medication," I said.

"What's up, guys?" said Bhagwandas Sivasupiramaniam, leaning on the Service Desk.

"Superman! What the hell are you doing here?" Pete clapped him on the shoulder. "Don't tell me you're coming back. You hate this freaking place."

"I'm in town until tomorrow to visit my aunt and uncle for a couple days before school starts again. My uncle's toilet broke so I'm here to pick some stuff up for it. And to see if you guys were still here."

"You should come hang out with us tonight," Pete said.

"I wish I could, but my family's got plans."

"How's school?" I asked.

"Oh, it's good. 4.0."

"That goes without saying, doesn't it?" Pete said. "Since you're Indian."

"That's racist," I said. "Model minority stereotype."

Superman shook his head. "I'm defying stereotypes: I'm on the soccer team. A couple of us were joking a while back about how Indians are unathletic as a race. At least, we don't really distinguish ourselves much in international competition."

"Why is that?" Pete asked. "God knows there's a big enough pool of people; you'd think you'd be bound to get a couple. Or is it because by the time you all get your PhDs, you're too old for sports?" That got a laugh from Superman. "Penn, don't look at me like that! It's technically not *racist* unless I say it's genetic!"

Superman said, "I think it's because most Indian parents are all like, 'Worry about school! Leave college early to be the number one draft pick in the NFL? Ah! What would uncle and auntie say?'" He said this in a thick accent. "But hey, at least we have Brandon Chillar going for us."

"He plays for the Rams," I said in response to Pete's blank look.

"Are his parents doctors or engineers?" Pete asked.

"So racist," I said.

"It's not racist if the stereotype is positive," Pete countered.

"You're not a stereotypical racist."

Pete hit me. I hit him back.

Superman cleared his throat. "Actually, I read his dad runs a 7-Eleven."

Pete hit me again. "Your mom! Your mom *and* your dad!"

Superman slapped the counter. "I'd love to stay and talk about dumb stuff all night, but I've got to get going. You guys take care."

Day 424 – Thursday, January 6

Chloe was so excited she was jumping up and down.

"Let me get this straight," I said. "You're going to Belgium *next week?*"

She clapped her hands together. "Yes! Isn't it exciting?"

"Exciting" wasn't the word I was thinking of.

Chloe's original application to study abroad through LCC had been rejected, but now, a girl had dropped out of the program and there was an opening. I didn't know how Chloe was getting everything arranged on such short notice, but she'd seized the opportunity with her typical single-minded determination.

"I'm happy for you," I said. "I'm not happy that you're leaving, but I'm happy for you."

"I know! I'm going to miss you so much!"

I had other concerns, which I did not voice. All of a sudden, we were going to have a Long Distance Relationship. I wasn't worried about some French-speaking Lothario sweeping her away. Not *per se*. But things happened. Things like, "Oh, Penn, it's not you, I'm just a different person now," or, "I need to reevaluate my life." It was always the people who left, never the people who stayed. People came back and things weren't the same anymore; you couldn't do anything about it. "Promise me you won't dump me when you get back" didn't work.

Chloe took my face in her hands and made me look her in the eye. "Penn, I want you to promise me something."

"Sure. What?"

"Get out of the House Station! It's wrecking your life and I don't even know if you can see that anymore!"

"Of course I can! Are you kidding? I hate that place!"

"You always say that, but you're still there!"

"I've tried to leave!"

"Then try again!"

I shook my head. "There's *nothing* in this town."

"Then leave!"

I blinked. "What?"

"Leave! Move! Go back to school!"

An icy fist squeezed my heart. "What are you saying? Do you want to—" I couldn't finish the sentence.

"Oh, God. You're getting insecure again, aren't you? Look, I love you, Penn. I do. Let me put it in words you can understand: I am not under any circumstances trying to break up with you, okay? But Penn needs to do what's best for Penn, no matter what that means. I love you enough to tell you that honestly."

"Said the girl who's moving to Belgium," I said.

"Yes! Finish your book! Get it published!"

"All right, all right. It's just . . . I'm worried that when you come back, things won't be the same."

Chloe chewed on her lip. "I don't know what to say to that. I don't think things will be the same. They could be worse: we'll grow apart and come back and it won't work anymore. That's what you're worried about."

"Yeah."

"I don't know how to stop that from happening."

I sighed. "I don't think there's anything you *can* do."

"But things could be *better*. I'll come back, you'll have a job that doesn't make you hate your life, you never know. Someday, down the road, maybe get married, have two, four, six, eight kids." Chloe said this last part very quickly.

My eyebrows shot up.

Chloe had a tiny smile on her face. "*Maybe. Someday.* You never know. But you have to do what's best for you."

I put my arms around her. "I don't know what I'm going to do without you."

Day 427 – Monday, January 10

"This is considerably less half-assed than I expected," said Pete, for perhaps the third time.

We were in Chloe's apartment complex's clubhouse for the going-away party for Chloe and some other girl who was also in the study abroad program — Chloe's roommate Bethany had rented it out in conjunction with her LCC friends.

Somebody had decided to make the going-away soirée a Belgium-themed costume party. The problem with this, of course, was that "famous Belgian" was something of an oxymoron.

So Pete and I were amazed by the effort turned out by Chloe's college friends.

"Wow," Pete said. "Everybody went on Wikipedia!"

"I think it's more likely that one person went on Wikipedia and passed the information around," I said.

Some costumes were considerably better than others, and you had to ask half the people who they were supposed to be, but the main thing was that most people had tried.

There were a couple of Hercule Poirots (including me: a suit, a bowtie, and a fake waxy mustache had taken care of that nicely), a Kim Clijsters and a Justine Henin-Hardenne, a Tony Parker, two Jean Claude Van Dammes, at least three Dr. Evils, innumerable Smurfs, various assorted Leopolds, and one guy dressed like a waffle.

Dreadful rap music was blasting at an extremely high volume. A King Leopold told me it was Belgian hip-hop.

Chloe, wearing an extravagant dress borrowed from LCC's drama department, made her way over to us. It was her party, so she was the Queen. Since nobody knew anything about any Belgian queens, she was just Chloe, Queen of the Belgians.

"Hey, babe!" Chloe said to me. "How's it going?"

"Fine!" I called over the din. "You look great!"

"Thanks!" She looked at Pete, who was just wearing a suit. "Who are you supposed to be?"

"I'm the prime minister of Belgium."

"Very nice. And who *is* the prime minister of Belgium?"

Pete blinked. "What? Me. I am."

There was a sudden press of people and somebody slammed into me.

"Hey, watch it! Oh, it's you, Penn. You have a mustache. That's funny!"

It was Paige, who was one of the Smurfs. She was slathered in blue makeup and wearing a tiny strapless blue-smudged white dress that she was constantly threatening to spill out of. It didn't take David Suchet to deduce that she was, specifically, Drunk Smurfette: she could barely stand up straight, she squinted when she looked at me, and she reeked of alcohol. She must have gotten started early; they'd just broken out the drinks here.

"Paige," said Pete, taking her arm to steady her, "you didn't drive here, did you?"

"Yeah, why? I have a friend who knows Chloe from LCC. Violet. You know Violet, don't you, Chloe?"

"We had some classes together."

Paige peered at her. "God, you look really nice. Anyway, Violet was supposed to drive, but we went to a bar earlier, and she just got too damn drunk. She can't drink for anything, I tell you what."

I took Pete aside as he wiped blue makeup off his hands. "I'm going to be here late helping with cleanup," I said. "Maybe you can take Paige home."

Pete's voice was low and grim and grave, and he looked at me like I was insane. "Oh, *hell* no. You don't take somebody of the opposite sex home when one or both of you is drunk. That's how disgusting, unspeakable, brain-scarring, life-destroying sexual encounters happen. Don't you know *anything*?"

"You're not going to be drunk," I said.

"I'd have to be to agree to that!" His voice ascended back toward its usual heights. "She's drunk enough for both of us! She weighs the same as I do! She'll drag me off! No way!"

I shook my head. "Fine. We'll find somebody else. But you're in charge of making sure she doesn't try to drive home. Maybe get her car keys."

Pete was mollified. "Okay. But you obviously don't know what you're dealing with here."

After a while, they switched off the music and called for everyone's attention. The now-tipsy waffle, who was at least four feet wide, pushed his way through the crowd, dragging Chloe to the front, and she pulled me along with her.

The waffle forged back into the crowd to find the other girl who was leaving. She, in comparison with Paige, was Modestly Dressed And Had Only Had Two Drinks, Maybe Three Smurfette. She joined us at the front with her boyfriend in tow.

The waffle gave a rambling and obviously impromptu goodbye speech, as though he'd flipped for the privilege not to and lost. The speech covered and re-covered various topics like how the two of them were going to represent LCC in Europe and how they were going to get all this culture and how all the LCC people were all going to miss them—this last was crap, of course—half the people were here because it was an opportunity to dress up, act a fool, and get drunk on a school night.

When the waffle concluded, he gave each of the girls an awkward hug. The hugs weren't awkward because they were inappropriate or because he was an uneasy hugger; they were awkward because he was a waffle.

Then Chloe, to great cheers from the throng, threw her arms around me and gave me a lingering kiss. The other girl saw and tried it with her man, and the group got louder.

Through this din came the crash of breaking glass, and everyone went quiet and turned in unison. Paige lurched forward, clutching her throat and spilling a plate of food. People pulled away from her like a receding tide.

I, Pete, and a guy dressed like Jean Claude Van Damme leapt forward as one (at least I thought he was dressed like Van Damme; there was no other satisfactory reason why he would be wearing a greasy mullet wig—I *hoped* it was a wig).

Pete got there first. "Choking? Are you choking? You're choking! She's choking!"

I caught Paige from behind as she staggered, and we both went to our knees. Pete's concerned face was only inches from Paige's. Jean Claude Van Damme, with nothing to do, hovered nervously behind him.

I began to administer the Heimlich maneuver. I'd learned it in high school health class, but I'd never had to use it. I thrust with my fists, and nothing happened. I heaved again. Nothing.

"Oh, God, please," I said.

Pete, panicking, leaned closer as Paige began to thrash like a fish out of water. "What are you doing?" he shrieked. "What should I do?"

Higher, I remembered. I had to press higher. I raised my fists under her bosom and thrust a third time.

Some kind of nut shot out of Paige's mouth and struck Pete in the forehead. At the same time, Paige exploded out of her dress, right in Pete's face.

Pete fell back with a cry as Paige gasped for air. She collapsed against me, heaving, her abundant assets on full display.

Chloe and another girl came forward to try to pull Paige together. I was relieved to get out of the way, and I went and helped Pete to his feet. His face was smeared with blue.

"Are you all right?" I asked.

His face was ashen. "That was the most horrible thing that's ever happened."

I put a hand on his shoulder. "It's all right. Paige is going to be fine."

Pete shoved my hand away. "I know *that*. I'm talking about *me*."

"What?"

He turned to me, his face hard. "Did you miss it? Were you out in the parking lot? No, you were right here! You *caused* the damn eruption! Mount Vesuvius! I about got smothered by her damn titties! Scar me for life!"

I understood. The last two minutes had been traumatic for all of us, and Pete was more sensitive than he let on.

"Sorry," I said. "Why don't you step outside for a minute and get some fresh air?"

Pete nodded. "Yeah. Good idea."

Chloe touched me on the shoulder. "Hey. Are you okay?"

"I'm fine. How's Paige?"

"Besides falling-down drunk? She's all right—passed out on the couch in the back the minute we got her there. You saved her life."

I grunted. "Anybody else could have done the same thing."

"Most people just stood there. *You* sprang into action. I'm proud of you!"

"Pete sprang into action. So did that other guy."

"Well, I'm proud of them, too." She pressed into me and I held her tightly.

We just stood there like that for a while. After a few minutes, the music came back on and the party continued.

I kissed Chloe's forehead. "Do you have to go?"

She smiled up at me. "I'll come back."

I smiled too. "Promise?"

"I promise."

That was all I could ask for.

Day 430 – Wednesday, January 12

"Who's the head cashier today?" I called to Pete. "Nobody's answering the phone."

"Let me check . . . Brandy's on right now. Paige comes in later."

"Did she make it in on Tuesday? I wasn't here."

301

Pete nodded. "She did. And all day, she was like, 'Oh, I'm so damn hungover,' and she was pissy the whole time. She didn't even remember what happened."

"That's probably for the best."

"*I* remember, though," he said solemnly. "I had an awful dream last night about it. There were these blue bowling balls flying around, and —"

"Stop immediately," I said.

We leaned on the Service Desk counter together in silence for several minutes.

"So Chloe's gone, huh?" said Pete.

"Yeah. Her flight left this morning."

"You miss her?"

"Not yet," I replied. "But when I do, it's going to be bad."

"She'll be back," he said. "She's like your wife. Seriously, it's like you guys are married. Marriage with all of the bad parts and none of the good parts."

"Thanks," I said.

A woman came to the Service Desk and asked, "Is that Vietnamese guy here?"

We looked at her blankly.

"He works in Electrical, I think."

"Oh, *Osric*," said Pete. "No, he's not here. I'll call somebody for you."

When she'd gone, Pete said, "That reminds me. I finally found out what ethnicity Osric is. He's half Polish and half Hawaiian. Many Bothans died to bring us this information."

"Nobody's ever guessed that one," I said. "How'd you find out?"

"I asked him."

"Hm."

After a moment, Pete turned and looked at me. "Chloe wants you out of here, huh? So what are you prepared to do? Are you man enough to up and quit?"

"My bank account's not man enough," I replied. "Ugh, and Jeff's getting married — I've got to find a roommate. That's not a subtle hint, don't get the wrong impression."

"No worries," said Pete. "With your crazy cat that jumped on my damn head that one time, there's not a chance in the world. Did you start looking for a new job yet? I've got some classifieds around here somewhere." He rummaged under the counter.

While he was looking, Landfill arrived.

Pete glanced up. "Oh, this freaking guy? Just what I need today."

"Hey, what are you guys doing?" Landfill wedged in between us, trampling our personal space underfoot.

"Trying to get the hell out of here, man, what do you think?" said Pete.

"Are those classifieds? You guys are going to get in trouble!"

"Why?" Pete fixed him with a sinister glare. "Are you going to tattle?"

Landfill scoffed. "No, man. I'm cool."

Pete was clearly skeptical. "We're not even looking at it. Having a newspaper's not a crime." He handed me the paper, which I folded and put into my apron pocket.

"Why do you have to be like that?" said Landfill. "We're all in the same boat here."

Pete sneered. "No, we're not, and don't you even. You know what the difference between us is? I do my job right and I don't go out of my way to make trouble for you. Also, I don't make that stupid face you're making right there."

Landfill shook his head. "You're such a dick."

"Yes, I am."

Landfill took a step back and tripped over the phone cord. The headset flew off Pete's ears, Landfill went sprawling, and the phone smashed on the concrete in a spray of buttons.

"Jeez, be more careful, you guys," said Landfill, picking himself up.

"Are you hurt?" I said.

"Nope."

"That's a damn shame," said Pete. Face stony, he looked down at the shattered carcass of the phone. "How the hell am I supposed to do my job now? The calls, man. Rex is going to be all over me."

"Just get another one," said Landfill. "There's more phones in the phone room, right?"

"'More phones in the—'" Pete shook his head. "You are the worst. You are absolutely the most useless person I know."

"Don't be like that," said Landfill. "It was an accident. We're all friends here."

Pete rounded on him. "Look, man, I may treat my published writer friend Penn here like the brother I never wanted, but you and I are *not* friends. We never have been. You are God's judgment on all the bad things I've ever done in my life. Every time you come in my circle, you make my life worse somehow. *Every time.* So why don't you take your ass back down to the registers before you get your feelings hurt?"

His malice was alarmingly genuine. I prepared to intervene.

Landfill's phone rang. "Yeah, I'm coming. Over."

"Get off my Service Desk," said Pete.

Landfill patted him on the chest. "I understand. You guys like to stand around up here and act like jerks. I get it. It's cool." Then he left.

"*I'm* the jerk?" Pete ground his teeth. "That guy's freaking clueless. I was ready to fight him. Go out in a blaze of glory. You know I was, Penn, you saw me."

"It wouldn't be worth it," I said.

"I don't know. It might be. There's always next time." Pete shrugged. "In the meanwhile, the never-ending struggle between good and evil continues."

Day 431 – Friday, January 14

I was more tired than usual—I hadn't slept well since Chloe left—and the store was dead. I sat on my stool and zoned out and thought about Chloe and our now-e-mail-based relationship. Nothing remotely interesting happened except for a brief encounter with a customer who had gold caps on each and every one of his teeth.

In the afternoon, Paige called me. "The propane truck is here, so you can sell tanks now."

"Okay." We'd been out of propane for two days. A few customers had been pretty upset about that, which meant that Rex was pretty upset, too.

"Also, Fielding Vargas is in the store, doing the Loss Prevention report. Make sure your Sensormatic logs are caught up and you're doing everything you're supposed to be doing."

"Right."

An hour later, I sat and watched Atwater ring up a customer. It had to be the first time Atwater had ever checked out a customer himself when I was free, I thought as I watched the customer walk past me and out the front door. Amazing.

"Did you check his receipt?" a man asked from behind me.

"Yeah," I said automatically, not really listening.

"Are you sure?"

I turned around. It was Fielding Vargas.

"What?" I said.

"Are you sure you checked it?"

"Yeah."

The word was out of my mouth before I had a chance to stop myself.

Fielding Vargas now looked concerned. My face got hot and my body went numb as he spoke.

"I watched the whole time," Fielding Vargas said. "You didn't check his receipt. That's one thing. It's not the end of the world. But then I asked you, and you lied to me."

I bit down on my lip.

"So I asked you again. I couldn't believe it the first time, so I asked you twice."

I opened my mouth to say something about how I'd had my eyes on the man the whole time from when he'd checked out until he'd left the store and how he couldn't possibly have stolen anything, but I changed my mind and said nothing. It wouldn't make a difference.

"I'm going to go talk with Rex," Fielding Vargas said. "We'll talk later."

So this was how it ended: not with a bang, but a whimper. I was fired, there was no doubt of that. My promise to Chloe was about to be fulfilled in a way I'd never anticipated. I felt tingly all over. I was utterly and completely ashamed of myself. This was not how I wanted to go out, in ignominy. This was even worse than the money-chucking rampage Pete fantasized about.

I expected them to call me back to the office at any moment and let me have it, but they let me finish my shift. God forbid that my firing caused Rex or the House Station any inconvenience. Beyond training my replacement, of course.

Half an hour before the end of my shift, Kord walked past quickly, heading for the exit.

"Kord!" I called.

She stopped, looking agitated. "What is it, Penn? I'm running late."

"Look, I—" All of a sudden, I felt like I was going to cry. I fought it down. "I'm sorry," I said. "I—"

Kord looked at me intently, an indecipherable amalgam of emotions on her face. She nodded. "I'll see you later."

"Okay," I said weakly.

I'd let her down. That realization made me feel worse.

After my shift, I got called to the back. I had to wait for twenty minutes for Fielding Vargas to show up from whatever he was doing. Then it was just me, Rex, and Fielding Vargas in that tiny office.

"Let me say something first," I said, still hot and almost teary. "I'm ashamed about what I did. That's not me. That's not the kind of person I am."

Rex knew this — good and well *knew* it — whether he liked me or not, but Fielding Vargas didn't know me from a hundred other guys in yellow aprons. This was a big deal to me. I was concerned that my brief speech might be misconstrued as an attempt to beg for my job, but I was asking only not to be remembered by this one moment, as a liar.

"Everyone makes mistakes," said Fielding Vargas slowly. "I understand that. Anyone can have a bad moment. But we are terminating your employment immediately."

I signed the paperwork without comment.

Rex came with me to my locker. "Whatever you don't need, you can leave," he said, not unkindly. "We'll clean it out. I have to escort you out of the building. It's store policy."

I took everything but my apron: my water bottle, my old paperwork, my merit badges, anything that happened to be in there.

It occurred to me that I was one merit badge away from the hundred-dollar bonus. Then I remembered I still had a week of paid vacation I'd never get.

Rex walked me to the front door like I was going to the electric chair.

"You're a smart guy, Penn," he said, not looking at me. "This place isn't for you. You're a writer. You should go to New York, get connected with the writers there."

We stopped at the door.

"I know you'll be successful. Good luck." Rex extended his hand to me. Out of politeness, I shook it. It was hard to tell if he was sincere. Probably, considering he'd never have to deal with me again.

I took a deep breath and stepped outside. There was a man leaning against the propane truck, smoking a cigarette.

A thought flitted through my head: if, someday, I wrote a book about my experiences at the House Station, at this point in the story, the propane really ought to catch and blow up the store.

Nothing happened.

"Bye, Rex," I said, and walked to my car.

Guilt remained, but despair had begun to lift. I began to think about all the things I could do now, things that other people took for granted, things I hadn't been able to do since I started working at the Station, like attend church, or plan an activity more than a week in advance, or go one whole day without debilitating pain. For the first time in a long time, there seemed to be *possibilities*.

To use the glorious cliché, it was the first day of the rest of my life.

ACKNOWLEDGMENTS

I am particularly thankful for my longsuffering wife, Divya, and for her constant support and diligent input.

The Reverend Doctor Kerry D. Lee, Jr. has been a faithful source of profound analysis for many years and has always insisted on treating my work as literature even when it by no means deserved it.

Jami Fullerton was an enthusiastic champion for this book's publication, and her encouragement is valued and appreciated.

I am indebted to Mary Anna Simon for her fine work and for her patience with me.

Others who provided feedback at various stages of this novel's development include Sue Boettcher, Sean Danker-Smith, Buz Hannon, David Lange, and Todd Murray. I am grateful to each of them.

ABOUT THE AUTHOR

Joshua Danker-Dake lives in Tulsa, Oklahoma with his wife and two children. A writer and editor by trade, he also serves as the Strategy and Tactics Editor for *Diplomacy World*, the flagship publication of the Diplomacy hobby. Other things he gets rather excited about include *He-Man and the Masters of the Universe*, bombastic European power metal, and St. Louis Cardinals baseball. Visit him at joshuadankerdake.com.

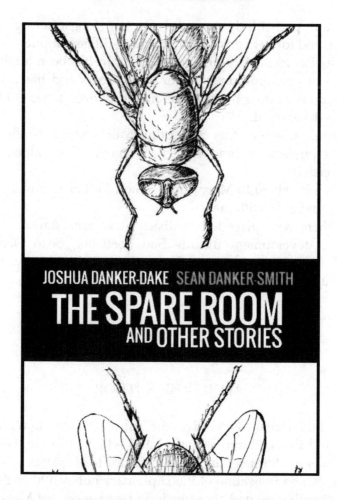

JOSHUA DANKER-DAKE SEAN DANKER-SMITH

THE SPARE ROOM
AND OTHER STORIES

THE SPARE ROOM AND OTHER STORIES

Spanning a variety of genres from fantasy to horror, this joint anthology from brothers Joshua Danker-Dake and Sean Danker-Smith brings you 26 original short stories ranging from the comedic to the downright grim, including "The Trash Gun," "The Devil's Amusement," "The Gibbins Tree," and "The Jerk and the Gypsy."

CPSIA information can be obtained at www.ICGtesting.com
Printed in the USA
LVOW04s1433120215

426796LV00015B/1037/P